Cheating to Survive

The Fix It or Get Out Series

Christine Ardigo

Published by the author as a member of the
Alexandria Publishing Group

Cheating to Survive

First Edition, May 2014

Cover Design by Kellie Dennis at Book Cover by Design
Interior Book Design by RikHall.com
Editing by Nick Soave and Keith Marder

ISBN-13: 978-1499521689
ISBN-10: 1499521685

Acknowledgements

I have a few special people I would like to thank.

My incredible cover designer, Kellie Dennis. I knew as soon as I saw a few of her covers that she was the only one for me.

Rik Hall, my wonderful formatter, who guided me through the process and answered all my questions with a great sense of humor.

Colleen Jackson, Adrian Iorizzo and Jennifer Ammoscato, for all their insights. Without their intuition, the book would have begun very differently.

My editors Nick Soave and Keith Marder, for all the time they spent making this book even better than I could imagine.

I would like to give a tremendous thank you to my co-worker Colleen Jackson. Not only did she listen to me talk about my writing journey every day for almost two years, but not once did she complain or grumble. Instead, she encouraged me further, supported me every step of the way and seemed as excited as I was for every new milestone I achieved. There aren't many friends like that in the world.

Dedicated to my silly daughters, Ashley and Autumn.
Never say the word "Can't."

Chapter 1

Heather

He was way too hot to be a dad. His leather jacket caught her eye, the biker boots, the black wavy hair. He pushed a young boy on the park swing. His nephew? A younger brother perhaps? No, no. Did it matter, though? She still wanted to grab him by the collar and toss him onto the slide. Climb on top and smash her lips into his. Ease her hand up his ribbed T-shirt, straddle him and then–

"Mommy, look how high I am!"

Heather Milanesi snapped out of her daydream and turned her attention to Rori, her four-year-old daughter. Rori stood at the top entrance of the crawl tunnel, just after the wobbly bridge. "Wow, so high." She strolled towards Rori but her peripheral vision remained on sexy-dad, who hopped on the swing next to the small boy.

Laurel and Gia, her pre-teens, chased one other and dumped woodchips down the fronts of each other's sweatshirts. If they ran a bit further away, Heather could join them and get a better look at him. Nothing like a little 'wood chip down the shirt' fun to end the rousing day.

Heather inched toward the wild and hysterical girls, grabbed a handful of chips and then–

"Mommy, where you going? You're not watching me."

Heather smiled at Rori and waved her hand. "I am. Just keeping an eye on your sisters, too." The wood chips left her palm and trickled onto the weedy dirt.

Hot-dad swung high. His boots reached the clouds and the boy giggled, attempting to kick his feet just as high.

The man let go, landed almost eight feet away, and tumbled

onto his hands and knees. God he *was* hot. Visions of her mounting him on the swing, legs wrapped around his rugged jeans, their lips inches apart…no, their clothes needed to be off.

It was something she had dreamed of doing when she was twenty-four. With *him*. Maybe sexy-dad reminded Heather of *him*.

What was she thinking? She had turned forty this year. Much too old for hot-dad. Was she? She could be a cougar. Maybe he'd like that. Maybe he wasn't even the pocket-sized boy's dad.

Wait, wait, wait, she was married! What the hell was she plotting, especially with her three daughters only yards away?

"Mommy! Lookit, I can run across the wobbly bridge now, I couldn't do it last year." Rori tiptoed across the bridge holding the chain link railing as she tottered along.

Heather should be paying attention to her daughter, not him. She strolled back to the playground and ran up the tall metal slide only grabbing the sides once. "I'm going to get you," Heather hollered. She crouched under the red roof and hopped down a step. Rori screamed and bolted to the curvy slide. Before Heather could reach her, she slid down, plopped onto the ground and took off. Toward her sisters. Toward sexy-dad.

"I'm coming after you!" Heather rounded the corner, ducked under the bridge and kept her eye on her dream.

Leather jacket guy picked the boy up and tossed him high into the air. Laurel, the older of the two, wrestled Gia to the ground and sat on her. Gia struggled to free herself. Rori scuttled to her big sisters while Heather gained speed. Rori leaped onto the pile and Gia let out a whoosh of breath.

"Ow, get off, get off. Both of you!" Gia kicked her feet and wriggled to her side.

Heather slowed her sprint and tried hard not to look at the hot man before her. He held the boy close to his chest but examined the tight *Josie and the Pussycats* T-shirt she wore.

She should scold them, act like a responsible mother in front of the little boy, but Heather was far from law-abiding herself. She smirked, bent over, and grabbed two handfuls of wood chips.

Gia's eyes widened. "Get off me. Get off me now!"

Heather took one hand, stuffed it down Gia's shirt, and then with the other, reached for Laurel's, missed and then managed to shove a few down the front of her pants. Rori clutched a mere four or five pieces in her tiny hand and chucked it, but the wind grabbed them, whisking the chips over her head.

Heather laughed and kneeled down in front of her three incredible daughters. They were hers. Forever. How lucky could one mom be?

Laurel released Gia and although their different personalities clashed at times, their need for retaliation combined perfectly now. The two of them pounced on Heather before she had a chance to retreat. With their mom pinned beneath, they reached for some chips, but secured the dirty sand as well, and shoved it down their mother's shirt.

She rolled over and lurched up, the gritty dirt clung to her hands, dust spewed from Heather's mouth. She wiped it with her hand and pretended to look for Rori, but caught the guy's inviting gaze instead.

The small child clasped his hands before him, a huge grin covered the entire lower half of his face. Sexy-dad tilted his head, smiled and winked.

An electrical jolt trickled across her chest. She plucked at her shirt and removed the final pieces of wood chips, hiding her trembling fingers. Rori picked up two chips and attempted to continue the game that was officially over. They flew four inches and hit Laurel's sneaker.

"Looks like fun," he said.

"Well, we love to come here on the weekends and–"

"Our mom's not normal," Gia interrupted. She twirled her finger around her ear explaining her mother's behavior.

"Normal's no fun," he said.

"No fun indeed," she agreed. God, she'd like to show him what she thought fun was. How about ditching the kids and having sex on the wobbly bridge? "Bridge," she blurted out.

"What?" he squinted, confused.

Heather flinched. "I...I like the...bridge. It's one of our favorites." What an idiot. She was having problems talking to someone half her age.

Laurel observed her mom's lack of verbal skills around the boy. She meant man! Yes, a man. He was of age, right? Yes, definitely over the required age of eighteen.

Laurel shook her head. What was Heather teaching her soon to be thirteen year old about engaging with the opposite sex? Hot-dad had more composure than she.

"The bridge is cool," he said. "Max loves it too, although he's a little s-c-a-r-e-d."

Heather pictured hot-dad and herself on the bridge, in the dark, naked. A branch cracking under a passersby's footstep. That would be scary.

"Your son will love it by the end of the summer."

"Oh, he's not my son, he's my sister's kid. Geez Louise, I'm only in my first year of college."

Uck. Was he even eighteen? Heather's intestines joined together and began kicking her abdomen. Five years without sex was really playing games with her head.

"Mom, can we go?" Laurel whined.

"Yes, we should be going. Nice meeting you...and you too Max." Heather snatched Rori, cradled her in her arms and made a beeline for her Jeep.

Laurel hopped in the front, Gia in the back and Heather helped Rori with her car seat's buckle. Heather's phone buzzed from the floor mat beneath. Ugh. She hated her phone. She only used it to keep track of the girls and they were all here with her now. Who could it be? Who else? Her mother-in-law and another one of her harassing texts.

No wonder Lance always complains about your cooking. You're too busy playing at the park instead of preparing a wholesome dinner for him.

Heather clicked delete and tossed it on the floor by Laurel's feet. An awesome weekend ruined by her again, and only another horrible day at work to look forward to tomorrow. Maybe she could pitch a tent in the park and live there with her daughters. Hide from all the crap.

Or maybe she should have flirted with college boy. Lied and said she was divorced. They could have met up later tonight at the park and talked about...term papers? Fake ID's? How wasted he got last night at a dorm party? Pitiful.

If she didn't have sex soon, she'd be hitting on Laurel's boyfriend's next.

****

Heather chose a card for her aunt's birthday amongst the slim pickings in her hospital's gift shop. The five-dollar bill in her lab coat crinkled in her palm. She tossed it onto the counter and grabbed a pack of Dentyne peppermint gum and two chocolate covered cherries.

The volunteer behind the counter wrinkled her face. "Bad for your teeth, you should know that."

"I'm a dietitian, not a dentist." Heather leaned over and grabbed two more chocolate covered cherries.

The woman scowled. She reminded Heather of her mother-in-law.

"I knew I'd find you here." Victoria Elling, her co-worker for over five years entered the gift shop. "Morning chocolate fix?"

"Of course. You know I like it rich and sweet. Melting in my mouth, the cherry liquid oozing between my teeth, as I lick the chocolate from my lips."

The volunteer tossed yet another glare. Too sensual for her? Heather smirked.

"Um, okay," Victoria squinted. "Having a bad day? Bored? Patient annoying you?"

"All of the above." Heather unwrapped one of the cherries and tossed it in her mouth. The crunch of the chocolate fracturing between her teeth and the syrupy liquor drenching her insatiable mouth eased her misery. At least for a few minutes.

"Don't eat them all, I was thinking of trying out a new restaurant for lunch today. I saw it on the way in to work last week. Sara said she went there last night with her friends."

"Is your daughter ever home anymore?"

"Once she bought herself that car, no. She calls it her vehicle-of-freedom."

"I need one of those." Heather tossed the change into her lab coat. "I'm in. Anything to get out of this place and away from the tyrant..." Heather glanced out the window at the incoming nuisance. "Great, another one."

Victoria peered over her shoulder. "Stop, be nice. Breathe."

"Good morning, good morning, good morning, the sun is shining, it's a bright new day!" Catherine Bordeau, Heather's other co-worker, skipped into the gift shop. All she needed was a basketful of goodies and her nursery rhyme look would be complete. "How is everyone today?"

Heather ignored her and unwrapped another chocolate.

"Oh, you're not eating chocolate so early in the morning are you? Tsk, tsk." Catherine bounced over to the balloons and selected a giant sun with the words *Get Well Soon* scrawled across its face. Her floor length skirt and brown turtleneck did not reflect the beautiful spring weather, or her age of thirty-five.

Heather scrunched the wrapper in her palm and winged it at Catherine's head. It missed and tumbled to the floor. Catherine hopped back to the cashier and removed a twenty from her Fendi wallet.

"Who's the balloon for?" Victoria asked.

"This poor sweet patient of mine. He's just so cute."

"You're buying a balloon for a patient?" Heather twanged the blue string. "Is he hot?"

"No, no, no. Not that kind of cute. He's this little ninety-six-year-old man. I could just squeeze his cheeks."

Heather opened her mouth to speak but Victoria stepped in between them.

"Catherine, I was thinking of trying this new restaurant for lunch today. Would you like to come with Heather and me?"

Heather tossed Victoria an incensed glare.

"Leave the building?" Catherine whispered. "Are we allowed?"

"No. We have to stay in the hospital chained to our nurse's station all day."

Catherine gazed out the door. Her eyebrows rose, as did her grin. "Okay, sure. It sounds just peachy!"

****

They crossed into the village of Brightmoor, a small town on the northern part of Long Island. Heather, alone in the back seat of Victoria's Toyota hybrid, slouched down until only her eyes reached over the window ledge. A young couple kissed passionately beneath a bus stop and the pounding in her head resumed. She repositioned herself until Victoria's *Advances in Nutrition and Cancer* textbook lying next to her on the seat came into view.

Heather sank deeper into her gloom. Her only joy came from her three daughters. The four of them exhaled silliness into the world and inhaled each other's love right back.

The expressions on the pedestrians they passed after leaving the park yesterday made her chuckle – Heather honking her horn, the girls waving wildly at complete strangers, their perplexed looks when they tried to figure out who the four of them were, some even waving back, all comical.

Laurel screaming, "How are you?" out the window.

Gia shaking her court jester hat with its bells.

Little Rori giggling until she ran out of breath.

Was it possible to love anyone as much as your own children? Thoughts of running away with them resurfaced. How much longer would the torment continue? She hadn't shed a tear in all this time though. Stuffed it down, held it in, and stayed strong for her girls. Don't let them see you cave. Fight.

Let nothing rattle you.

Victoria's front bumper smashed into a cement parking block. Heather propelled forward, the seatbelt held tight and choked her.

"Oopsie." Catherine giggled.

"Thanks. Next time you try to hang me, make sure I've had my last meal."

The three of them exited Victoria's car and strolled toward the rough textured stone façade building painted purple and green. Wooden benches reclined under a purple awning, green lamps dangled above them.

Heather read the storefront sign. "Peaz and Chaoz?"

"I think it means Peas and Carrots," Catherine said.

"Peas and carrots?" Heather grumbled. "You're such a dietitian. I thought it meant Peace and Chaos." She had enough chaos in her life, some peace would be just fine.

"Whatever it means, I hope the food's delicious. I'm famished." Victoria grasped the giant wooden handle on the purple and green striped door and they stepped in.

The hostess emerged behind an array of balloons similar to the violet crocus sprouting in Heather's yard. They followed the waitress towards the back of the restaurant to a leather booth. The sizzling fajitas and grilled shrimp tempted her ravenous desires.

Heather skimmed the menu knowing she would order a salad with grilled chicken, then turned her attention back to her co-workers. "Laurel's a runner up in the creative writing contest, I'm so excited for her."

"Oh, another award?" Catherine said sarcastically. "How positively wonderful, where will you find room to hang them all?" Catherine covered her face with the menu.

Heather smashed her glass of water on the wooden table top.

"So..." Victoria leaned forward, "not only is Sara receiving letters of acceptance from colleges already, but Andrew just informed me that when he graduates college next year he wants to rent his own apartment. It'll just be Ed and me in that big house."

"Why don't you think of selling it?" Catherine placed the menu down and grasped her water with both hands like a toddler.

"I could never leave my home, too many memories. Andrew and Sara were born there, not to mention all the work Ed and I put into it over the years. I couldn't imagine someone else living in it. It would kill me."

"You're lucky you married a construction worker," Heather said. "Lawyers aren't very handy."

"Neither are stockbrokers," Catherine interjected. "And they're never home."

Catherine's husband was never home because he thought he was still a bachelor. Late night dinners in the city, cocktail parties, happy hours.

"Yes, but you've both done a tremendous amount of work on your homes. Heather, your landscaping alone is so inviting. I wish I had a green thumb like you."

"It's my passion." She browsed out the window at a passing black Jeep. "An outlet."

"An outlet," Catherine snickered. "From what? You have the perfect life."

"No, I don't." Heather took a deep breath and held it. She pressed her fist against her mouth careful to control her voice and tone.

Catherine took another sip of water then placed the glass back exactly on the wet circle left on the tablecloth. "What exactly do you have to complain about, Heather?"

Heather ignored her condescending tone, suddenly wanting something stronger to drink. She waved the waitress over. "Can I have a Blue Moon? Bottle please."

"You can't drink alcohol, we're working." Catherine's shocked expression wavered only inches from Heather's face.

"I don't follow rules."

The server arrived with her grilled chicken and strawberry spinach salad but the smell of Victoria's charbroiled beef and crisp onion rings overflowing on the plate shifted Heather's taste buds to the variety of flavors and seasonings. No longer interested in her lifeless salad, she gulped half the beer before touching her food.

After lunch, Catherine excused herself and sauntered to the ladies room. Victoria bent over her plate and stared at Heather.

"What?" Heather said.

"What's going on with you today?"

"The past twenty-four hours were horrible."

"Lance?"

"This morning, Lance. Another fight. Then yesterday his mother."

"Again?"

"She's relentless. I can't...I just can't anymore. Then this morning I couldn't even eat a piece of chocolate without everyone questioning me."

"Sorry."

"No, not you, it's just—"

"Catherine putting you over the edge?"

"No one could be that bubbly all the time. And let's not mention how she stares at me during our meetings and don't tell me you didn't notice."

Victoria leaned back in the booth, her eyes focused on the ceiling.

"See, you do. If you notice it then how do you think I feel? And what about her little remark about my perfect life?"

"Maybe she thinks you have a wonderful life. Maybe she wants to be you."

"Uck." Heather wrenched her tongue out of her mouth. "Give me one of your onion rings." She reached over and chose the largest of the remaining ones. "They go good with beer. My one beer that'll get me so wrecked I'll return to work completely drunk, unable to do my job and they'll have to call security on me for being unruly."

"You're not giving her a chance."

"She's been there over six months now, my patience has run out."

"You must have something in common, you're close in age and so are your children."

"All she talks about is new brands of furniture polish and PTA meetings. When she does attempt to fit in, she brings up her sorority parties. Who talks about sorority parties when you're in your thirties? It's like they froze her in a time capsule and just defrosted her last year."

"She's been out of the work force for years, maybe she's caught in that mommy syndrome. You used to be like that."

Heather flicked an ice cube from her water glass into her mouth. "Sorry, I must be such a drag to be around."

"No, I can understand. But…sometimes I do miss the old Heather."

Heather pierced the remaining strawberry with her fork. "There's just no escape. Every day I feel like crying. Home is hell, work is hell."

"What if you—"

Catherine returned and detected the awkward silence. Heather glided back into the corner of the booth and finished the last of her beer.

"Hey, look at that table over there with those three adorable guys." Victoria's lame tactic to keep the peace. "If only I was younger."

"You're not old," Heather said, refusing to let the three ogling men catch her eye. Normally it would be fun, but today she was in no mood.

"Ed and I are celebrating our 30th wedding anniversary next year."

"That doesn't mean you're old. You married when you were six, right?"

Catherine giggled. "You know, they are cute, all of them. Hey, three of them, three of us." Her attempt at a seductive wink almost made Heather vomit her salad.

What did Catherine know about hot guys? Peter, with his slicked back hair looked like a chiseled parasite in a stiff white shirt. Then again, all she had was the picture on Catherine's desk to go by. What Peter saw in a nerd like her was more mysterious. Heather liked her men big and muscular, biceps popping, huge delts, washboard stomach. Yum.

Heather shook her head in disgust, then reached into her jacket pocket for a twenty and tossed a crumbled bill onto the table.

"One of them is coming over here!" Catherine put her hand over her chest.

"I'm sure he's just going to the bathroom." Heather stared out the window again.

"No, the bathroom's in the other direction. He's coming right to us."

Heather peered up to see a six-foot tall man with a Mets cap scrunched low on his forehead. Muscles stretched the confines of his raspberry colored T-shirt, his hands plunged into the front pockets of his dark blue jeans. Mmm. How good did his ass look in them?

He stopped in front of Heather, mouth remained shut, but lips climbed to a huge grin. Heather searched under his baseball cap for an answer. He tilted his head up and the fluorescent light hit the unmistakable features instantly.

"Hi." His timid smile unchanged after all these years.

Her eyes widened, mouth opened, unable to formulate words. The salad in her stomach twisted in knots and her breathing became restricted. "Hi, sorry, I didn't, I'm so sorry, I..." She nudged Catherine, then shoved her hard, and struggled out of the booth wrestling herself to a standing position.

It was *him*. She stood only inches away, his familiar Ralph Lauren cologne pulsed through her. How long had it been? She knew exactly how long it had been. Down to the month.

Chapter 2

Catherine

Catherine slid back into the booth angered at the abrasive way Heather shoved her, but more upset that the man in the Mets cap approached Heather and not her. The pain in her clenched jaw intensified. She turned back to Victoria, whose wrinkled brow deepened and hardened.

"What are you looking at?" Victoria asked.

"Nothing, how much is the bill?" She reached into her Coach bag. Darn it. She should have purchased the smaller Michael Kors one instead. She shuffled the contents around, searching for her wallet. "What are they doing over there anyway?"

"Talking."

"Well, who is that?"

"I don't know." Victoria snapped.

The whole thing was ridiculous. Why did she care? Catherine handed Victoria her portion of the bill and put her wallet away. She scooted to the end of the booth and her eyes glided to their corners to peek at Heather.

They sat face to face at the bar, the leather and brass nailhead-trim on their stools touched. Their legs interlocked on the bottom wood rungs, her muscular calves sandwiched by his. Heather placed her hand on his knee and he arched in never taking his eyes off her. Their grins mirrored one another.

Peter used to gaze at her like that. Now he barely caught her eye as he flew from room to room and then out the door again. The last time they made love was two years ago, when their daughter Emily turned five.

Heather suddenly looked different. Not the Heather Catherine worked with for the past six months, always angry and moody. Even from across the room she noticed the difference.

A roar expelled from Heather's mouth that spewed a laugh across the entire restaurant. The bartender looked up at her and smiled. The two men from his table perked their heads up too. They pointed and nodded with sheepish grins. Why hadn't any of them approached Catherine? She was attractive too.

Heather massaged her cheeks as if to release the ache from smiling for too long. That's what it was. Heather was smiling. Cheerful, jubilant, and laughing. She was even more gorgeous when she smiled, her true beauty revealed, she absolutely glowed.

"We should interrupt them," Catherine said. "It's getting late." Catherine rose, flung her large bag over her shoulder with the expectation of Heather noticing, but nothing interrupted her lock on him.

He lifted his hand and repositioned the long brown strands of Heather's flowing hair away from her face. His right hand slid down her cheek. Heather closed her eyes and placed her hand over his.

Victoria grabbed Catherine's arm, guided her to the front entrance and then nodded to Heather. Heather's smile plummeted. She looked at them puzzled, as if she forgot where she was and that they were here with her.

They pushed open the doors to exit the restaurant and once outside, Catherine strained to see through the tinted double doors. The man wrote something on a napkin. Was he giving her his number? Catherine's body tensed, her teeth grinded. Who did Heather think she was taking his number? She was married. She drew in slow steady breaths as heat flushed through her body. This had gone on long enough.

"Are you listening to me?" Victoria barked.

She jerked back. "Sorry, I didn't hear you."

"I said, let's go." Victoria plodded to her car and glared back at Catherine. "And not a word about this when she comes."

"What are you saying?"

"It's none of our business. If she wants to tell us she will."

"That's silly, she'll tell us."

****

Catherine and Emily entered the dance studio and headed to Room C for her five-thirty ballet class. Odessa Steenburgen and her enormous purple patent-leather handbag secured the space in front of the three-by-three window. Her purple leopard-print jacket needed the matching boots and then she could have passed for *Barney*'s mother.

Emily leaped into class like the pied piper, happy and enthusiastic. She changed into her ballet shoes while Catherine squeezed her head into the four-inch space left for her to peek in. Odessa waved at her daughter Madison as if attempting to flag a celebrity down for their autograph. Her hand came down hard on Catherine's head.

"Oh, sorry Catherine, I didn't see you. Is Emily here?"

"Yes, she's standing right next to Madison." Obviously. Why else would she be here.

"Yes, I see her now. No time to put her hair in a bun?"

"It is in a bun."

"I guess she did it herself."

"No, I did it. Her hair's just very thin."

Odessa's lips pursed. "Perhaps a hairnet or hairspray next time?" She pivoted back to the window and her handbag's buckle struck Catherine's shoulder. Catherine tumbled to the right, no longer able to watch her daughter.

Class began and Odessa pulled herself away from the spotlight and plowed her bag into Catherine's chest. "Madison will be doing competition next year. She'll have dance class five days a week."

Madison's mouth opened wide, her eyes drooped.

"Don't you think that's a little too much? They're only seven."

"Oh no, not at all, it's good for her. I'll drop her off at three-thirty, she'll do her homework for a half hour by herself and then the back-to-back classes begin. When we arrive home, she'll eat dinner and be visibly exhausted. Then right to bed, it's perfect."

Perfect for her. How could this possibly be good for Madison? "That doesn't leave much time for you to interact with her. When do you play with Madison?"

"Play with her?" She chuckled. "That's what her friends are for. We pay big money to tire them out so they crash as soon as you get them home."

Catherine shook her head. "Emily is just taking one ballet class next year. I feel it relaxes her after a long week in school."

"Just one class? Is that all you can afford?"

Catherine raced home pushing the speed limit, driving close to 43 in the 40 mph zone. That woman infuriated her, who did she think she was? She clutched the steering wheel tighter.

A woman with long brown hair climbed out of a Jeep Cherokee. Heather popped into her head.

She's another one. Heather's secretive visit with that man enraged her. Was she jealous? Ha! Silliness. Was it that Heather looked ecstatic? Such a rarity for Heather. She should be thrilled for her but the vision of Heather in the back seat of Victoria's car gazing out the window like some cartoon character shot with Cupid's arrow stirred her blood.

Emily scrambled into the house. Catherine wrenched her handbag from the passenger seat but then sprang back banging her head on the door frame. The handle had caught on the gear shifter. She tugged fast to release it but its contents dropped between the seat cracks. "Darn, Darn, Darn!"

She struggled to reach for her ChapStick, a small tube of toothpaste and a Tide to Go pen. After cramming everything back in, she slammed her car door, stormed into her house and found Peter lounging on the couch smoking a cigar. "Did the boys do their homework?" She snapped, hurling her bag onto the floor.

Peter's face contorted. He threw the TV remote control across the room knocking over the picture of their three children, then followed his cigar out and into the garage.

"Bentley! Colton!" Catherine screamed. Where were they?

"They're in the basement watching TV." Emily popped up around the corner, her ballet outfit still on.

"Why are you still wearing that? Get in the shower, you're filthy."

Emily leaped away and Catherine followed. Loud sprays of water shot out from the showerhead.

Bentley, the older of her two boys, sauntered by.

Catherine charged out of the bathroom and stopped him before he entered his room. "Did you do all your homework?"

He glared back at her, not answering.

"I asked you a question, Bentley, and where's Colton?"

Bentley retreated down the hallway and Catherine chased after him. She stopped at his doorway. A huge Shaun White poster hung over his bed.

He didn't.

"Please tell me you did not shove push pins into your wall. Or worse, tape!" But before Catherine could enter the room, he slammed the door shut. It shook the walls.

Colton appeared from behind her and attempted to sneak into his room before Catherine noticed.

"Colton. Colton! Get back here. Why is your backpack thrown all over the floor? Your lunchbox isn't still in there, is it?"

She reached down to unzip his Iron Man backpack.

"Hey don't touch that. It's mine. Why are you always touching our stuff?" Colton ripped the bag out of her hand. "It's mine. Get out! Get out of my room! I hate you."

She recoiled from his words. Not the first time he uttered them but still heart breaking. "Okey dokey." She tried to win him back. "How about some nice kiwi slices to sweeten you up?"

"What?" His mocking tone cut through her. He shook his head. "Go away. Leave me alone." Colton grabbed his new *Diary of a Wimpy Kid* book and slumped into the corner of his room.

Catherine left, placed her hand on the wall outside his door and crumpled. Think positive, be happy, smile, keep it all together. You can do this. Look upbeat at all times.

****

Catherine slicked her butterscotch hair back into a tight ponytail like tense piano strings. She sprayed the sides with an extra coat of hairspray incase the gel failed. She reached for her beige dress, but stopped to stare at herself in the mirror. Her pale skin matched the color of her bra and underwear. Hard to tell where one stopped and one started.

A naked mannequin tossed in the back of a store. A discarded Barbie doll, nude and forgotten.

Pathetic. No wonder Peter didn't initiate sex anymore. She did lose all the baby weight after each child, though, and kept her weight at exactly one hundred and twenty-five pounds. Her clothes ironed with a little added starch, hair perfectly groomed, no globs of slutty makeup, just some concealer and a dab of lip-gloss.

Catherine glimpsed at her breasts. Just for a second. Disgusting. They had grown so large with each pregnancy and with each breast feeding responsibility. She had hoped they would return to her peppy B cup but they loomed at the current DD size. She attempted to wear sports bras, bulky sweaters, loose fitting turtlenecks, and even buttoned her lab coat to the top. Anything to conceal them.

Embarrassed by them.

She pulled the front of the bra down and gazed at her two breasts. The nipples were dark and large too.

Gross.

Catherine swept her crème colored dress over her head and then tugged it down. It cleared her breasts and then hung on her like a Barbie doll wrapped in beige toilet paper. Even expensive clothes from Talbot's could not transform her. She had hoped the other moms would be impressed by all her name-brand clothing and accessories, but they avoided her at the school functions.

"Are you almost ready?" Peter hollered from the kitchen.

"Yes, one second." Catherine looked away.

No one wanted her. She tossed smiles at the doctors on her floor but they only tossed pitying grins back. The witty riddles and jokes Colton shared with her had failed with the doctors as well. *If an apple a day keeps the doctor away, what does garlic do? It keeps everyone away.* She thought they were funny.

Maybe she needed a little sparkle. A drop of jewelry to brighten up her ashen color. Catherine slipped on her mother's pearl earrings.

Chapter 3

Victoria

"**V**ictoria, have you completed the particulars for the Tough-Love 10K race?" Noreen Emberton, the Chairman of the Long Island Cancer Prevention Foundation, leaned back in her chair directing her attention to Victoria.

"Yes, it's to be held on Saturday, September 22nd, beginning at nine in the morning at North Meadow Ridge Park in Overton Hills. Six hundred participants registered last year and we're expecting a larger turnout this year."

"Have we procured any sponsors?" Noreen's emerald green suit out-colored the rest of the black suited board of directors.

"Gym Addiction, Cloveridge Water Company and Robust Protein Bars are all currently on board." Victoria flipped the page on her yellow lined notepad. "I'm currently working on Jameson Popcorn and," she paused, "The Amorous Baroness Inn." Victoria tensed as she spoke the name, seeming unprofessional in the current setting. Noreen's intimidating manner was overwhelming tonight.

"Very good. Promotional material? Press release? Local media coverage?"

"I'm coordinating with Sylvia and plan to work on that piece this week." The yellow notepad shook in her hand as she filed it inside the folder and eight pairs of eyes focused on her. Her euphoria hid beneath blankets of self-doubt, fueled by lack of support. It didn't matter how much she accomplished in her lifetime, each new ambition met with uncertainty.

Today though, her bliss stirred under the cloak, peeked out, then danced around the room. She knew she did well and attempted to hide her smirk. Victoria heaved a sigh louder than she planned and her childish act caught the attention of two elderly board members. They weren't actually elderly, probably only a few years older than her, but it appeared that every man her age had let themselves go. The one on her right had more ear hair than the other one had on his head.

The board meeting adjourned. Victoria collected plates of leftover food and empty cups to toss into the garbage. Not her job as the Director of Special Events and Fundraising Coordinator, but the thought of leaving it for someone else pained her. The bitter scent of coffee lingered in the room, half eaten plates of sandwiches and cookies appeared abandoned.

She valued her position as the oncology dietitian at Norlyn Plains Hospital. Fifteen years of employment brought a great sense of achievement to her life. Her desire to do more for the cancer community prompted her to join the Cancer Foundation.

She also needed an escape from her monotonous life.

Victoria scooped up Noreen's plate. One cookie, with a tiny nibble missing from the corner. A dry Royal Dansk butter cookie, no less. Why bother? As much as she admired her, the woman obviously needed to have sex.

Who was she kidding? *She* needed to have sex. When was the last time she and Ed did it? Too many years to remember.

Victoria deposited the empty pitchers of water back on the tri-level serving carts and their clinking echoed in the deserted boardroom. The hasty departure of the members crushed her spirit. She stroked her arms, but her posture wilted anyway.

Victoria trudged up the walkway and entered her home after 9 p.m. Her hunched posture continued, head drooped. The thump of her pocketbook onto the foyer table competed with fierce snoring emanating from the living room. Ed sprawled out on the sofa, pillow clenched under his arms like a teddy bear, his beer can standing guard beside him.

Victoria retrieved a blanket from inside the storage ottoman and the soft, plush material floated over him. Calm, unburdened, safe. He looked a good deal like her father – before her father grew ill and emaciated. She tucked the blanket around his back and then slipped out of the room.

She removed her black pin-striped suit and white button-down blouse, unfastened her pearl necklace, and the wood floor creaked beside her.

Ed entered. His hair spiked upward like a punk rock icon of the eighties. Curls of hair resisted Victoria's touch and sprung back in sheer defiance. "Is everything alright?"

"Yeah. Why you home so late?" Ed teetered then lurched over to their bed and collapsed on the edge.

"I had the board meeting tonight. I told you this morning before I left for work."

"I can't remember what you're doing."

"We discussed the 10K fundraiser I'm coordinating this fall. We raised over $40,000 at last year's race. It's a great deal of responsibility but I love the challenge and intensity of it. I feel important and—"

"What kind of food did they serve?"

Victoria's resilient posture crumbled again. "We just had wraps and salads."

"Did you bring any home?"

"There really wasn't anything left."

"Cookies, anything?" Ed scratched his belly. His stained white T-shirt, worn for the past three days, clung to it. The splotch of barbecue sauce had congealed.

"I have to schedule a meeting with *Long Island Perspective Magazine* and I'm anxious about it. I also need to work on our print materials, the flyers need our Logo and I was thinking we could display a video on our website to show—"

"I don't know what you're babbling about, but I'm beat. Gonna hit the sack." Ed crawled to the top of the mattress and managed to square his head in the middle of the pillow but only one leg made it under the covers. Victoria guided his other leg underneath and pulled the covers tight above his shoulders.

She returned to the kitchen, washed the dish and glass Ed left in the sink and then cleaned the counter tops. With the living room tidied, she retreated to her desk and computer in the basement to scratch out ideas for fundraiser prizes.

She leaned back in the chair and surveyed her desk for some incentive. Her Word of the Day calendar remained on March 11th, three days ago. *Confluence* n. The act of merging. A flowing together of two or more streams. "A favorable confluence of factors led to his success."

Victoria needed some confluence.

Her Aspiration & Achievement board that Sara bought for her birthday last year, empty, except for two pictures – one of Andrew and one of Sara. How disappointing. For years her creativity flowed. Unafraid to take on new challenges, she always sought out ways to enhance her knowledge. Her take-charge attitude never ceased.

She gazed at her framed photo of James Blake and the tennis ball he autographed for her at the US Open in 2005. What a smile. What would it feel like to be young again? Thirty years with the same guy. The same boring tighty-whities.

The second hand hustled on the wall clock. What had Victoria completed? Nothing. Was reorganizing the desk drawers necessary?

The front door clicked open, then creaked. She snapped up, flew out of her chair and ran up the stairs. Sara had returned from her date and Victoria loved hearing her stories, although lately she revealed less and less.

Victoria entered the kitchen just as Sara dumped her pocketbook next to Ed's tool bag. "Hi honey. How was your dinner, date thingy?" She sounded like Catherine now.

"It was amazing!" She removed her coat and chucked it on the kitchen chair.

Victoria's eyes shot open. "Is that what you wore?"

Sara had a tight red spandex skirt on. It barely covered her rear-end. Her cropped top showed off at least two inches of stomach. How she strutted around in those heels all night was unbelievable.

"Yup, just bought it today. How do I look? Do you think it made the right statement?"

What statement was Sara trying to make? Tramp for hire? I'm desperate and need a date for the prom? All right, maybe Victoria was being too old-fashioned. Was this what they wore nowadays? On first dates? Didn't she teach her better?

What had she taught her? Ed and her never cuddled on the couch, said I love you, kissed each other hello or good-bye. What role model did she have to go by? Andrew's girlfriends didn't dress much better.

"Yes, it's lovely."

"Oh my God, he was such a good kisser! I can't wait to tell everyone."

"Everyone? Wait—"

Sara took off towards her bedroom. The door snapped closed behind her.

They kissed on the first date? In that outfit? What else had they done? Had she had sex yet? Victoria forgot what sex felt like. The only person that touched her anymore was her OB/GYN, and she was a woman.

Victoria eyed her white pajamas with the tiny blue flowers. They were as boring and dry as Noreen's cookie.

Chapter 4

Heather

Heather, Victoria and Catherine sat in silence waiting for her to enter. The tyrant. Four-hundred plus pounds of uncouth, insolence, vulgarity and terror. Feared by the entire food service department and responsible for the resignation of at least ten employees including her own management staff, she kept her dietitians waiting while she finished her morning egg-white sandwich.

They avoided conversation, expecting the conference room door to open any moment with the usual wallop and smash into the grey wall, expanding the hole in the sheetrock. Their weekly meeting triggered anxiety and dread.

Catherine and Victoria crossed and uncrossed their legs nine times between the two of them. Victoria rubbed her palms down her hydrangea blue pants and Catherine cleared her throat in an annoying repetitive manner.

Heather only thought about avoiding her stench. She sprang out of her chair and propped the window an inch before retaking her seat. Outside, a profusion of sunshine burst from the forsythia bushes, and callery pear trees provided a white canopy along the hospital's parking lot, but Heather focused instead on the housekeeping employee dumping trash into the dumpster. What she wouldn't give to see a body or two tossed in there.

The door shot open fracturing the already damaged surface. A chip of sheetrock hung, teetered, then crashed to the floor. Jean Vollbracht, the food service director, took one step in and jarred to a halt, her ridged posture disturbed only by rapid gulping of air and nostrils that flared.

Catherine and Victoria flinched. Heather stretched, arms high above her head, and then returned to her seat, easing into it. Her pen whipped up and down between her fingers mimicking her co-workers' heartbeats.

Jean tramped into the room and slammed her papers onto the far end of the rectangular table directly across from Heather. The air quality was far better on this side of the room.

"Well?" Jean shouted.

Catherine and Victoria glanced at each other and then to Heather who shrugged her shoulders and tossed them a vacant look.

"No one has any ideas for National Nutrition Month?" Her fist pounded the table three times. "Why the hell are you working here if you're so incompetent?" She opened her mouth wide and swayed her head back and forth mocking their obvious stupidity. Bits of egg lingered on her hefty tongue. Heather's life could be worse. She could be an egg remnant.

As usual, Jean failed to mention what this week's meeting entailed. Catherine and Victoria shuffled through blank papers, stared at the ceiling and glanced at the clock. Heather cracked a bubble in her gum and flicked off her high heels.

"Well," Catherine's hesitant voice began, "we could discuss the importance of eating five to nine servings of fruits and vegetables a day. It's so important." She circled a random word on her paper, avoiding Jean's blazing eyeballs.

"Fruits. And vegetables? That's the most insipid, lackluster thing I've heard. Done to death." Jean shoved her chair away with her massive thigh, not because of anger, but because she couldn't fit in it. She always stood in their meetings.

Heather leaned back, arms folded in her chest and fixed her gaze directly on Jean. "We could talk about the myths of fat. How whole eggs are one of the most nutritious foods. How butter is high in lauric acid and how lard is loaded with Vitamin D, which we're all now highly deficient in. We can explain how people that order egg-white sandwiches but pile it on a deadly white roll, with fake margarine, sausage, bacon and cheese, are really not helping their cholesterol levels."

Jean arched over the table and dug her nails into the faux wood grain top, her veins tensed against her skin.

"What if we discuss how patients with diabetes no longer require a snack before bedtime?" Victoria interrupted Jean's impending outburst. "Educate the staff on how medications have transformed over the years no longer causing that drop in blood glucose levels over night."

Jean snatched a piece of paper, crushed it into a tight ball, and heaved it at Victoria. "If it'll save me money and decrease budget costs for my department, do it." A piece of egg remnant flung from her mouth and whizzed past them landing on the table several inches in front of Heather. "This year our topic will cover all new research on diabetes. We're doing it this Friday. Get to work."

"No, I only meant to educate the—"

Jean whacked her folder shut and then stormed towards the door. The meeting adjourned in less than five minutes without her contributing anything.

Before leaving, she twisted her neck back. "Oh, and Heather, in case the hospital policies have eluded you, there's no chewing gum anywhere in the building." She clutched the knob with her meaty fist and the door thundered behind her, shaking the walls.

"Too bad I don't follow rules."

"Why do you have to enrage her like that?" Catherine whispered.

"I don't, she's always enraged."

"You know darn well she eats that for breakfast every morning."

"Well then maybe I just educated her on something for a change. Must she always be right? Belittle us and when we do have a good idea, steal it?" She lurched up from the chair not wanting to discuss it further. A dead topic.

"I can't stand her." Catherine clenched her right fist as if she might actually do something for a change.

"Let's not argue," Victoria broke up their bickering again. "We have a lot of work to do before Friday. Let's get started."

****

Heather tried to breathe as three girls tackled her to the ground attempting to keep her restrained. Then the tickling began. Heather lifted Rori up on the soles of her feet but before she could steady her in the air, Laurel and Gia leaped in between the tower and flipped their mom to her side.

Giggles flooded the room while the heat from the fireplace crackled and sputtered. Heather's strength overpowered the three of them and she freed herself from the assault. She backed into the wall near the couch, arms raised and ready to attack. Heather tried to let out a low growl but it sounded more like a dying chipmunk.

The girls bent forward in fits of laughter, unable to catch their breath. Rori climbed the couch and used the cushion as a trampoline. Gia exploded into a cartwheel then grabbed one of the pillows and hurled it at Heather. She missed and hit Laurel instead.

Laurel's eyebrows raised several times, then she gave her mom a wink. She lunged at Heather and grabbed her by the shoulders but Heather whisked her around and flung her onto the couch like a two-pound dumbbell.

Rori leaped onto her mom's leg and plopped her hiney on her foot. Heather pretended she wasn't attached and stomped around the den with Rori's tiny body clinging to her calf muscle. Gia clutched two pillows and pounded them in the air like pom-poms, performing a cheer "Mommy! Mommy! Mommy!"

"What's going on here?" Lance charged into the room and silence overtook the four of them. Rori let go of her mom's leg and Gia placed the pillows down on the rug. Laurel stiffened. Heather's brow frowned creating deep cavernous folds. He would ruin yet another night.

"We're playing. You know, having fun."

"The room is trashed."

Heather spotted the two pillows on the floor. Messy indeed. She strolled over to them and arranged them into their proper positions on the couch, but not before punching them numerous times. She plowed her fists deep within them. The pillows needed re-fluffing before taking their place on the couch. Nothing should be out of place.

A snarl grew in the corner of his mouth.

"There. All done." Heather folded her arms.

Lance edged closer until he stood over her. His mouth parted and he inhaled a deep long breath. "If I brought someone from the law firm home with me, this would be an utter embarrassment, do you understand? I never want to witness this again."

"Witness what?" Heather released her arms. "Your children playing? Do they even know you have children?"

"What the hell is that supposed to mean?" His volume resounding.

The girls cowered together. Laurel lifted Rori into her arms and caressed her hair. A mother's responsibility not a twelve-year-olds. The three of them bolted out of the den and toward their rooms.

"It means I don't think you know you have children, let alone the people you work with."

"How dare you. Of course I know I have children, their picture's on my desk."

"A picture?" Heather shook her head. A photograph to prove his worth. "What picture?"

"The one you gave me. The one from Jamaica."

"Jamaica?" All emotion drained from Heather's body. "We went there before Rori was born." She traipsed into the kitchen unable to look at him further.

"That's your fault, you never gave me an updated picture. Your attempt to make me look like a fool at the firm." His hand slammed hard into the kitchen wall. "You've never supported me. You want to see me fail."

"I've never supported you? All I do is support you."

"You lie, right there before me. I've struggled at this firm for nine years to make partner and all I hear from your mouth is worthless crap about the kids."

"Worthless? They're your children."

"Don't you understand? I am working day and night. I don't have time for this."

"Time for your daughters?"

"Look, I've taken them on vacations."

"Vacations of your choice, all they've ever wanted was to go to Disney."

"Disney, are you serious? I can't walk around Disney." His face curled up into a head of cauliflower.

"Why not?"

"A high profile lawyer does not prance around Disneyland with Mickey Mouse and Adana."

"It's Aurora."

"You think you're funny, don't you?" He leaned over, pressing his hand on the sheetrock above her head. "I'll have you know, if it wasn't for my hard work the girls wouldn't have experienced the things they have so far."

"You? You've never done anything with them. Ever." Heather took a step to the right and then turned way. Pointless to continue. His ignorance amazed her. How someone could be so intelligent, yet so blind. He acted as if his girls were strangers, tenants living in separate parts of the house. He would never realize, it was clear now. Three children and still nothing.

It was his mother's fault of course, she contributed to the madness. Showering him with presents and not bringing any for the girls. Throwing him a party when the law firm hired him, the same year Gia turned one. His party eclipsed hers. Completely intentional.

Were they invisible? They were such wonderful girls, hilarious and full of life. It would never improve. How could she compete against such lunacy?

****

"This is ridiculous." The new nurse slammed the phone down in the receiver. "Three calls to Dr. Mangle's service and still no return phone call. How are we supposed to care for the patients if they don't return important phone calls?"

"He does it all the time," an older nurse said. "Get used to it."

"How is that okay?"

"It's not, but he always has an excuse. Never a good one but– "

The chatter terminated. Dr. Mangle sauntered into the nurse's station. His receding hairline revealed a perfectly combed brown coif. His pale grey suit made him look like a retired Florida doctor. Heather's eyes narrowed and she bit the inside of her lip waiting for the performance to unfold.

"Dr. Mangle, I left three messages with your service."

"You did?" His tone soft and comforting. "I'm so sorry, I never received those messages. What is your name?" He leaned over to read her badge. "Ashley? I'm so sorry Ashley." He reached out for her hand, lifted it to his mouth, and kissed it. "I've been having problems with my service lately. I'll have to look into it. This is inexcusable. Now, how can I help you my dear?"

The nurse's face turned red like a sun kissed pepper, and then as if on cue, the anger dissipated, all forgotten. Heather shook her head in disbelief. She watched him for years execute the same routine, everyone believing his bullshit. He pulled a chart from the rack, looked at Heather and leered. His capped teeth were too big for his thin, shriveled lips.

Heather looked away and refused to acknowledge him. She glanced at the clock instead, then stood and put her patient's chart away. Show time.

Heather plopped her one stack of photocopied handouts on the table in front of the tri-fold board in the cafeteria. "There I'm done, can I go home now?"

"Stop," Catherine said. "This'll be abso-positive-olutey fun."

Heather turned away before she jammed the plastic chicken drumstick down Catherine's throat.

"Just have to unpack all of mine now and organize them to be accurate and in order." Catherine unloaded her six handouts, each a different color of the rainbow, embellished with photographs of fruit baskets, sweet potatoes, beans and a farm stand overflowing with vegetables. On the far end, she laid out recipes for salmon with mango salsa, and quinoa with black beans and cherry tomatoes.

"Good thing I put my handout down first otherwise there'd be no room for it." Heather rolled her eyes, took a deep breath and held it.

Catherine wet her pale lips. "What handout did you prepare?"

"The myths of fats."

"She told you not to do that."

"No she didn't. Actually, she never answered me, so I just threw a new title on it." Heather held up the top copy, *Nutrition Tips for People with Diabetes*. "It's not like she's going to read it, she never makes it over here to see what we prepared."

"What do you mean?"

"She hides us in the back on purpose so as not to distract everyone from her presentation. All she cares about is that her salad bar is glistening and the berries are carefully placed on the angel food cake and her special decorations are positioned precisely where the CEO of the hospital will see them."

"Where did she get the decorations from?" Catherine picked up a vase that resembled a cluster of goiters.

"Her house. You have to see her salad bowl. It looks like one of those bowls you made in kindergarten art class out of clay, only bigger."

Catherine laughed. "Seriously? Where is it?"

"No idea but I'm not looking for it. If I hide back here all afternoon I'll be safe."

Victoria approached, carrying a dozen red and yellow balloons. The expression on her face was capable of popping them all. "I've had it. I don't get paid to play with helium."

"You had to blow up the balloons yourself?" Heather broke into hysterics.

Victoria shoved the twelve balloons in Heather's face. "Only after the beast cursed at me for not knowing how. But rest assured, she taught me a whole lesson in balloon filling and ribbon tying. I'm a professional now, can't wait to tell my family. My father would've been proud"

"So sorry," Catherine started, "not sure how the two of you put up with her for so long."

"Two years of Hell." Heather's body stiffened.

Jean sashayed into the cafeteria, her theater. All traces of evil vanished when in the presence of her audience. She twirled in her handmade yellow smock dress that resembled the yellow balloon Heather just tied to the table leg. Heather fantasized merciless punishments and then pierced the yellow balloon with her thumbnail.

The *boom* and *whoosh* caused several patrons in front of them to jolt. "Oops," Heather said.

"You just broke one of the balloons," Catherine said.

"No, really? You're so observant."

"Now we don't have an even amount."

"Who the hell cares?"

Victoria shot Heather a glare, shutting her up. Catherine's need for perfection tensed Heather's body into a fevered state, her rigid forearm muscles quivered as she fought off violent urges. Catherine personified the new-dietitian nerd mindset.

Only a job, that's all, life began once you left work. Did any of this matter? Not to Jean at least. Jean finished shaking hands with various members of administration, accepting their compliments on the fine presentation. The presentation the three of them worked on all week.

Half way through the four-hour ordeal, Jean charged over to their nutrition table. Her grin contorted into a wrinkled puddle of flesh, snarling. Her bloated feet clobbered the floor beneath them.

"Shit." Heather hid her gum behind her back teeth.

"Why the hell are the fruit salad platters half empty? You never let them get to less than two thirds full." Jean's chest heaved, loud breaths expelled. Seeing the food service director have a heart attack right in the middle of their National Nutrition Month presentation would be classic.

"We've been operating the booth like you told us," Catherine whimpered. She twisted the balloon string around her finger until the tip turned red.

"I never want to see a plate half empty. Fix it."

Of course she didn't want to see a plate half empty. When you weigh four-hundred pounds, that must be a scary site.

Jean grasped her front bra strap with both hands and tugged. "I can't wait to take this damn bra off and let my tits hang out."

With that, she stomped off. Catherine followed her like a baby duckling, then grabbed a bowl and piled layers of cantaloupe and strawberries onto the platter.

"I'm taking the girls to the children's museum this weekend," Heather said.

"Laurel and Gia are alright with that?" Victoria asked.

"Rori's never been there and they're actually excited to see her reaction."

"That's wonderful. The four of you are like the Brady Bunch, well without the boys."

"Without Lance." Heather folded her arms across her chest and ticked her tongue.

"He's not going again?"

"Does he ever? He's too important to prance around a children's museum, what would everyone think?"

"That he's a father enjoying a day in a museum with his daughters."

"Victoria, you're being unreasonable, surely you can't expect a lawyer trying to make partner to spend his free time with his children? What would they say? They could never take him seriously." Heather huffed, wafting a red balloon aside.

"He'll regret it one day."

"No he won't. First born son, only child in an Italian family, the world revolves around him, his mother assured it. No one else exists." Heather followed the circling pattern in the cafeteria carpet with her eyes. "I'm glad I had girls, you know. If I had boys, they'd grow up ignored by their father, bitter and resentful. They need someone loving and attentive, someone that will be there for them, support them."

Victoria put her hand on Heather's shoulder. "You're thinking about him, aren't you?"

"All the time, I can't sleep."

"I wish I knew what to say. I'm glad I finally saw him though, put a face to all the stories you've told me over the years."

"He looked good, right?" Heather's cheeks ignited.

"If you like them young."

"He's my age." Heather laughed.

"I like older, distinguished gentleman. Salt and pepper hair, wrinkled brow from all the pensive thoughts."

"I want it like the movies," Heather began. "Sitting in front of the fireplace, eating lo mein out of the carton with chopsticks."

"Him feeding you a few noodles, one slipping off the chopstick and landing in your lap."

"Then he nudges me in the shoulder."

"And you both break out into childish laughter."

"Exactly!"

The two of them stared off into a place they would never visit. A location often visualized but never traveled. One filled with romance and seduction. Something nonexistent. They didn't notice Jean hollering at poor Catherine.

****

After taking apart the nutrition booth, Heather returned to her floor and sat in the nurse's station looking through one of the seventeen charts she had to write notes in before leaving work. An impossibility.

An unfamiliar doctor in green scrubs pulled out a chair and sat at the far end. Heather perused through the endless illegible handwritings but could swear the new doctor was checking her out. She wanted to twist her head an inch, just enough to know for sure. She kept her head stationary but let her eyes slowly drift to their corners.

He was.

A tremor ran through her body making her jerk. She froze and swallowed hard hoping he hadn't noticed.

"Cold?" He rotated his body towards her.

Heather spun her head, unable to move. Holy crap. Mammoth shoulders, chest pressed against his green scrub top stretching it, reaching for her. A chocolate-colored leather cord gripped his neck tightly, alloy rings hung from the center.

"I said are you cold?"

"What?" She sputtered like a frog shooting its tongue at a fly.

"You trembled, I asked if you were cold." He rolled his chair a few feet closer.

Most of the doctors in this small community hospital were nothing to look at. Old, short, fat, bald. He was definitely none of those. His eyes pierced hers, gluing her in position. He moved closer, his large muscular thighs thrusting himself across the floor.

She still had not spoken.

"No, I'm not cold." Her heart fluttered when she spoke. What was wrong with her?

He slid his chair adjacent to hers, settling only inches away. "I'm Dr. Silvatri, new gastroenterologist. Just teamed up with Dr. Bettman's practice."

"Hello, nice to meet you. I'm Heather, one of the–"

"I know."

She squirmed in her chair, legs folded into a knot.

He leaned forward and lifted her binder. She had plastered the red book with pictures of Laurel, Gia and Rori, camouflaging the boring nutrition forms organized between the pages underneath. He placed it back on the counter, his pinky finger slipped alongside hers. It lingered, and his warmth fused their fingers together like a magnet to steel. Electrifying. She continued to look at her photos, afraid to behold his perfect chiseled jaw.

"Are these your daughters, how old are they?"

Her eyes remained focused on the photographs. "Yes, they're twelve, ten and four."

He nudged her finger forcing her to look at him, his eyebrows flicked. The floating globes within, transfixed her. She never saw blue that riveting before.

"Your eyes look like my birthstone, sapphire." Heathers' words spilled out now. "I mean..." Shit.

"Libra, my wife's a Libra." He stretched, extended his leg and pretended to shift his weight. His foot now bonded with hers.

"The best sign there is."

"Really?" he chuckled. "I beg to differ."

"It is. It's the sign of balance."

"So, on one side you're a devoted wife, mother and nutrition person..."

"Registered dietitian," she corrected. A smirk trickled across her face.

"Sorry, registered dietitian." His fingers patted her shoulder. Each touch like a spark plug, charged her skin. "And on the other side is what?" He grabbed his sultry chin, tweaked it repeatedly waiting for an answer.

"I like to garden." What a dork. What was wrong with her today? Where was the fiery Heather hiding?

"Nope, that stays on the side with the mommy things." He leaned back in the chair and rested his arms behind his head. His scrubs pulled tight across his crotch. Heather scanned his pants and envisioned the masterpiece beneath the cloth. He relocated his right hand and planted it in between his legs interrupting her examination. His smile enlarged.

"I lift weights," she blurted.

He arched forward and squeezed her bicep through the tight lavender fabric. "I can see that." He stood and towered over her as if to heighten his experience. "I could show you a thing or two, Heather. Let me know when you're interested."

The wad of gum slid down her throat.

"At the gym I mean."

"Of course." Heather froze. An inferno radiated across her body, burning through her clothes. Dr. Silvatri exited and his overly confident, but delicious ass, strutted down the hall. Before sweat erupted, she removed her lab coat and dumped it on the chair.

Chapter 5

Catherine

Catherine snatched the second row in church with Emily, Colton and Bentley. Peter mounted in the back, muttering to his friends, tossing tales about their week. Emily brushed her doll's long blonde locks with her pink brush. Her two sons pinched each other, abrupt jolts and lurches ejected from their pews.

"Stop it, you two," Catherine whispered. They both glared at her, Bentley made a quick disgusted snort, Colton snickered and flapped his hand at her in dismissal.

The waterfall above the holy water basin trickled and splattered, relaxing the members, the choir song eased and trailed off, the priest launched his sermon despite her family's apparent disrespect. She strained to see Peter to get his attention and some help with the boys. His back provided Catherine with her answer.

"As we look at our family, God is looking for a man who builds his wife's self-esteem, and builds the confidence in his children. A man who will teach his sons to respect their mother and in turn respect their wives..."

Bentley and Colton took turns kicking each other's sneakers, each thrust delivered harder than the last. Catherine's cheeks burned, her ribs squeezed together.

"...God understands we have things we need to do—work, play, hobbies, they all need our attention. We say we'll get around to our family some other time. Husbands, love your wives, nourish and cherish them just as Christ loved His church..."

Bentley knocked Colton's sneaker off after smashing the heel numerous times. The sneaker, now free, rolled under the pew in front. Catherine clutched Bentley's arm to stop him, but he whipped it away in one quick snap. Her knees locked together, hands gripped her elbows, as she gazed down. Peter's voice intensified, his tone loud, piercing, penetrating.

"...being profoundly loved by someone gives you strength, but we mistakenly assume that if our partners love us they will act in certain ways..."

Colton reached for his sneaker but Bentley took his foot and shoved it into Colton's backside propelling him forward. Peter's conversation amplified, impaling Catherine's ears, loud, louder, his laughter sharp and stabbing, painful. Her chest pounded, feeling naked and exposed.

"...focused attention is needed. Marriage is a real thing, to be valued, appreciated ..."

Colton's head slammed into Emily's knee twirling her small body. She rotated on her silky dress and fell off the pew. Peter's voice rose higher and sharper. The shrill, the obvious laughter— she knew others were now laughing at her, judging.

"...then the Lord God said, It is not good that the man should be alone, I will make him a helper, his partner..."

Emily and her doll dropped to the floor, the pink hair comb launched into an elderly woman's shoe. Thunderous hilarity echoed from Peter and his friends as they snickered and mocked her, stabbing her repeatedly. The stone slab walls echoed his hysterics and elevated them to the stained glass ceiling. Sweat mounted under her dress, her heart raced.

"...for this reason a man shall leave his parents and be bound to his wife, and the two shall become one..."

Catherine's' hands drifted from her elbows, to her chest and up her neck. She clutched her throat; tears suffocated her lids and distorted her vision. Emily's wails parroted Peter's blistering howls. Catherine thrust her hands over her ears, no longer able to take it.

She rotated her head to the back of the room to find Peter all alone, his hands by his side, a puzzled expression on his face.

"What's wrong?" he mouthed.

She was losing it.

Chapter 6

Victoria

Victoria's wet boots flicked the rain onto their welcome mat. Her side of the garage was clogged with Ed's ladders and assorted tools, forcing her to park in the driveway. Ed's side sheltered his prehistoric truck.

The doorknob slid under her wet grasp but the only thing waiting for her was Ed, on the couch watching reruns of *The A-Team*. She removed her raincoat and waited for him to explain his early arrival and the relocation of his tools. Nothing.

She strolled into the living room. Two cans of Budweiser stood like soldiers next to the TV guide. The ashtray held three cigarette butts but the odor was evident before she entered the room.

"What's for dinner?" Ed asked.

"Why are you home?"

"I got laid off." He fidgeted on the couch but kept his eyes fixed to the screen. She bent forward and blocked his view of Mr. T. He tossed the remote onto the coffee table and grumbled. "What!"

"What do you mean you were laid off?"

"Exactly that, do you need an Encyclopedia?"

She hated when he used that phrase. Little did he know they invented computers for the home and the Internet. Google much? Victoria marched into the kitchen. "I bought you new underwear, I'll put it on the table."

His silence ripped through her.

"I picked up a colorful pack of briefs this time. Red, blue, black."

Ed's concentration left the TV screen long enough to view the plastic package in her hand. "I don't want that, white is fine. Why are you trying to change me? I am who I am."

She tossed the underwear back in the K-Mart bag and then retreated to her bedroom, tripping over the overflowing laundry basket. Victoria lifted it to start a load but Andrew's clothes weighed it down. Was he home from college? Did he get a ride?

She opened Andrew's door to find him asleep, comforter wound around him like a 'pigs in a blanket,' his shades drawn to block the bright spring day. Did she smell Cheese Doodles? The door clicked behind her.

Sara's room remained empty, abandoned. Between high school and work, not to mention all the senior parties, Sara spent an insignificant amount of time at home. Even with them both home, their rooms remained lifeless.

Once the washing machine hummed and rocked, Victoria removed her charcoal pantsuit and then retreated to her office to work on the information for the *Long Island Perspective Magazine*. The screen provided no insight, no support.

She returned to the living room and sat next to Ed on the still springy cushion on the other end of the sofa. "Ed, I need to advertise for the fundraiser and thought I could brainstorm with you."

"What fundraiser?"

"The Long Island Cancer Prevention 10k Race," she shouted.

"Why are you yelling? Look, I don't need this, I lost my job and it's always about you." He lurched out of his hollowed cushion and wandered into the kitchen. "I guess cooking me dinner is out of the question."

"It's only four-thirty."

"All these late night parties and I'm stuck with leftovers."

"Parties? I'm on the Board of Directors. I coordinate events in addition to my regular full time job."

"Sorry I lost my job. Throw it in my face why don't you? Don't you even care about me?" He threw his head into his hands.

Victoria's heart oozed. The sorrow in his eyes sparked memories of her father. "I'm sorry, I'm being inconsiderate. Let me start dinner and then we can talk while we eat."

"I don't wanna talk to you, I just want food."

After dinner, Victoria cleaned the dishes while Ed snored away in their bedroom. Seven o'clock and he was already down for the night. She clicked off the kitchen light and retreated to the living room.

The room, although well lit, filled with darkness as the still air thickened and suffocated her. Warm beer and cigarette odors lingered, choking her thoughts. Ideas drained and left her body, and replaced themselves with worry and fear.

A game of Candy Land, Sara and Andrew playing in the middle of the brown rug fighting over the blue gingerbread man, resurfaced. Although Andrew leaving for college proved difficult, Sara venturing out every night with her friends broke her heart. Every mother wished their children success and happiness, but their concurrent departure caused muscle aches and migraines.

The anguish inside her needed to go.

Her head pounded as she searched for ideas to bring life to the cancer fundraiser, but surrounded by this emotionless fog, inspiration concealed itself. Victoria shoved her yellow notepad aside. It remained empty and laid fallow like her. She tilted into the sofa and wound into a cocoon.

Heartache submerged deeper into her core and took over every cell. Hidden, locked away, she refused to reveal her collapse to anyone. She kept her sobs low in the event Sara returned without warning, refusing to let her see her in this state.

She promised her father she wouldn't settle for less than the best. Excellence in all achievements, but Victoria's enthusiasm and motivation washed away with each passing year. Tears saturated the pillow, visions of her father's cachectic body and frail hands surfaced while her creativity sank further into the hollow gorge within her.

No inspiration left.

Chapter 7

Heather

Heather stomped out of Jean's office after another exhilarating ass whipping. Did Jean twirl a spinner with Heather's name on it this morning? Let's attack Heather for no apparent reason, I'm bored and need to feel important.

Another argument with Lance yesterday and now Jean reminded her of some ridiculous thing Heather did three months ago. *"Those that forget the past are condemned to repeat it."* Did she really think Heather would forget how she reamed her out after the Pharmacy and Therapeutics meeting in January, simply because she answered a question Jean didn't know the answer to? Sure, Jean looked like an idiot, but she *was* one. How was that her fault?

Heather took a short cut through the kitchen, ignoring the hairnet box on the wall to her right.

"Hey, hey, Heather, don't look so sad." Tyrell, one of the cook's sang to her. He rubbed his eyes like a small child.

"Stop, I'm not crying." She hid the smile growing on her face.

"Yes you are, boo hoo hoo."

Heather took a towel from the counter and whipped it at him.

"Ooh, rough, I like it."

"Knock it off, silly." She shook her head and grinned.

Tyrell was extremely intelligent and it upset Heather that he worked here. She encouraged him to go to college and find another job, but he worked with his classmates, neighbors and relatives. None of them went to college; he only knew this life, a wasted talent.

Heather charged up the six flights of stairs to her floor. They had their weekly nutrition meeting in fifteen minutes but she needed time to cool down after the bout with Jean. She reached the stairwell door and shook her thighs to release the inferno, then rubbed them, discharging the lactic acid.

She pulled out a chair on Six-North but a nurse immediately approached her.

"Heather, don't kill me but that lady in 614a wants to see you."

"Why?"

"I don't know, she just said she wanted to see a dietitian."

Heather groaned. Did it ever end? She shoved her chair back under the counter and then entered the patient's room.

Unbrushed mat of hair, crusty feet with long yellowed toenails, the room reeked of body odor. She pretended to scratch her nose as she inhaled into her hand. "Hello, I'm Heather, the dietitian for the floor. You wanted to see me?"

"Yeah, the food here sucks, can't I get something real?" Her low scratchy voice let Heather know a carton of cigarettes was her best friend.

Of course it was about her meal. God forbid they wanted nutrition literature and education. Perhaps enhance their health so they wouldn't be a frequent-flyer in the hospital? Some guidance on what they should do to improve their disease process? You know, diet counseling that her friends charged a hundred dollars an hour for in their private practices?

"What's wrong with the food?" She had perfected her fake smile after sixteen years of abuse. Heather's lips curled back to reveal her welcoming, kindhearted, sympathetic teeth.

"It's disgusting, I can't eat this stuff." The bag of potato chips by her beside sprayed its contents across the tray table. Half eaten chocolate muffin. Two-liter bottle of diet Pepsi on the far end.

"What do you want to eat?" She folded her arms across her chest, knowing this was a sign of distancing yourself, but as the odor whiffed toward her distance was all she thought about.

"Normal food."

"Like what? Give me some examples of what you eat at home." She knew the answer already. McDonalds, Burger King, Kentucky Fried Chicken, Taco Bell.

"Just normal food, this stuff's crap."

"We serve four hot choices a day, seven days a week. That's twenty-eight wholesome nutritious hot meals. Grilled salmon, chicken parmesan, pepper steak, lasagna, beef stew, all of this is foreign to you?"

"Yeah, I'm not eating that garbage."

"If you'll just tell me what you eat at home I can see if the cooks can prepare something to your liking."

"Just send me something I can eat."

Anger and frustration punched each other under Heather's skin. "If you can't tell me what you normally eat I can't help you. Name something, anything, just one dinner item you normally eat."

She assessed Heather from head to toe, then shifted her eyes to the TV. "Just forget it, I'll have my family bring me in food."

Heather fled the room and then inhaled deep gulps of fresh air. Fresh floor wax replaced the gagging odor of crotch and some rotting infection. She leaned against the wall in the corridor and banged her head into the cold hard surface several times. This day could not get any worse.

"Problems breathing?" Dr. Silvatri asked.

Heather's eyelids flicked open.

"You're supposed to use your mouth, not your head. Here." He placed his fingers under her chin. "Now inhale, exhale, inhale, exhale."

His fingertips, like anesthesia, paralyzed her. Was his tongue circling inside his parted lips or had she imagined it? She looked at her shoes avoiding his steady eye contact.

Every day he looked more gorgeous. Was she imagining it? Could someone grow hotter with each interaction? He was the only thing that enticed her to come to work anymore. She hadn't seen him the past two days and left work disappointed. What was she thinking? This wasn't happening.

He had brought her a brownie from the doctor's lounge the other day and watched her as she ate it. Any man that brought her chocolate was worth entertaining.

"Dr. Silvatri," Maddie, a cantankerous old nurse interrupted, "the patient in 609b wants to know when you're doing her colonoscopy.

Heather giggled at the word.

He studied her expression. "You're next." He tapped her exposed collar bone with his finger.

"Never, are you kidding?"

"Why not, don't trust me?"

"It's not a question of trust, I'm...just...not having you look up there."

He sent out a roar of laughter. "What do you mean? I do this all day long."

"Not to me, you won't."

"You don't want me getting all invasive like that?" His eyebrows climbed and descended, and he lifted his palm waiting for an answer. With his enormous bicep in her face, its blood vessel pulsing at her, she convulsed. He reeled back. "What was that?"

Heather wanted to crawl into the lounge and cry. "You did not just see that."

"Uh, yeah, I did. The thought of me performing an invasive procedure on you gives you the chills? Hmmpf, interesting."

"Dr. Silvatri, the patient is waiting to speak to you." Maddie threw Heather a contemptuous glare.

He slanted in again. "I could be as gentle or as rough as you like my little Libra." Silvatri strutted away never glancing back, his mystique left her pinned to the wall.

Maddie slithered by and gobbled her up.

Heather unlocked her feet, shuffled down the hall, then once she reached the far end of the corridor, dashed up the stairs to the top landing in a chemically altered state. Looks like she'd be late for their meeting.

Chapter 8

Catherine

Catherine squirmed in her chair and picked at her cuticles. At 9:59a.m., she sucked in her bottom lip and bit down until certain it would slice off. Victoria scribbled on a yellow, lined notepad but crossed off more words then she kept. Heather absent, and it was unlike her to be late since she usually secured the chair directly across from Jean, probably to intimidate her. It made Catherine more nervous.

The door flung open but this time it wedged securely into the sheetrock. Jean attempted to pry it loose but the image of an obese woman in a strawberry-milkshake colored smock grasping and pulling on a door handle was comical. Catherine's breathing slowed and eased, her tension loosened.

Heather entered, not realizing Jean was to her left. She sauntered to the right to her usual seat, with an enormous grin on her face. "Where's the ogre?" Heather began. "Eating herself to death?"

Catherine and Victoria cringed, neither spoke. Catherine's heartbeat soared, thumping faster than previously. She pinched her eyes shut and clasped the middle of her yellow flowered skirt.

Heather pulled out her chair, still unaware. She flopped securely into her seat and met Jean's gaze as well as the acid that poured from her eyes. A smirk appeared on one side of Heather's face. It was slight, but Catherine picked it up immediately.

Jean let go of the door handle and stepped toward her podium, a new addition to the conference room after Jean snapped off an arm on the chair she tried to sit in. She positioned her loose papers on the podium. The now unresponsive room echoed the volume of Catherine's heartbeat.

"Heather," Jean shuffled her papers, "I have been asked by the hospital's administrative staff to host a catering event for its board members to promote our new patient-centered care initiative." She scowled at Heather, her enormous chest rose and fell like an accordion. "You," Jean paused, "will be at my side for the entire event."

Any remaining upturn of Heather's mouth dove along with her forehead. Heather's leg flinched under the table.

"Victoria, would you like to explain to them what patient-centered care is?"

Catherine knew as much as the rest of them what it was. Jean's ignorance became more evident as Catherine grew to know her. This was Jean's way of learning something without admitting she was oblivious.

Victoria tilted her head toward Heather and rolled her eyes. "It's when a patient's culture, personal preferences and family situations are taken into account when making clinical decisions. Instead of the traditional 'I know what's best for you' approach, we take patient's lifestyles into consideration; abide by what patients are willing to do."

Jean stared at Victoria. For a good fifteen seconds. The information processing and formulating inside her brain. "Yes, that is correct, Victoria." Jean rolled her neckless head back to Heather. "We'll meet in my office every Wednesday at eleven o'clock to discuss the particulars. We have a lot of work to do."

Bile built up under Catherine's tongue. She swallowed it, preventing herself from vomiting. Glad it wasn't her. Heather deserved it.

****

Tuesday, on Catherine's day off after working the weekend, Peter woke and took his shower. The sound of the water spray lulled her deeper into sleep. She felt his presence float in and out of the room, into the closet, back into the bathroom. She vaguely heard Peter mumble something but could not be sure. The pillow, soft and cuddly, she pulled the blanket closer to her ears and squished herself into a tight ball. "Catherine, can you pick up coleslaw and potato salad today? Catherine? Catherine!"

"What?" she mumbled. The words tried to form in her dry,

45

sleepy mouth.

"I said can you please pick up coleslaw and potato salad today?"

"Mmm." The other side of the pillow, cold and soothing, she coasted back into her dream. Birds chirped merrily outside the window and reminded her of weekend mornings when she was a child. Comforted, she fell back to sleep.

The last of her children hopped onto their school bus and her day off began. No husband, no children. Her standard plan for the day: cleaning. The house had to be spotless, she left nothing undone. She had a routine, and if accomplished, she would not have to clean like this again until the next time she worked the weekend, three weeks from now.

Catherine secured a handful of Q-tips and maneuvered them into the crevices of every piece of furniture, including the moldings and paneling on the walls and doors.

She vacuumed the entire house, lifting heavy furniture away from their familiar surroundings to find any hidden dust balls. There never was any, but today, a stray Cheerio hid behind the blue couch's leg.

Catherine selected crisp sheets for their four beds, but had to flip the mattresses first to prevent an unnecessary sagging. She opened her spiral notebook to determine which direction she last turned them. This time she would only have to twist them around one hundred and eighty degrees.

With multiple loads of laundry churning, she cleaned windows, glass doors, mirrors and appliances. Had she dusted the chandeliers last month? She forgot to log it in her notebook. Once she folded the laundry, Catherine tossed the bathroom rugs into the washing machine and switched her attention to the three bathrooms.

She organized Emily's clothes in her closet in the sequence of when she last wore them and lined them up to reflect the days she had gym. Pants and skirts followed blouses in a prefigured pattern. The boys refused to let her touch their clothes anymore. She snuck in anyway and repositioned them so that the hangers all faced the same direction.

Cushions overturned on couches, wood floors polished, the rest of the floors mopped. Blinds and curtains vacuumed. How could dust accumulate on blinds so quickly? With the dining room table polished, she saved the kitchen for last and climbed Peter's metal ladder to scrub the white cabinets, the surrounding walls and the soffit. She untied the burgundy cushions from the kitchen chairs and decontaminated them in the washing machine as well.

The house smelled like a muddled air freshener infused with lemon, bleach and floor wax. Seven hours after her children left for school, they returned home and homework began.

Two hours later, Peter drove into the garage as the last of them took their showers. The door flung open and Emily ran to Peter's arms. "Daddy!" she squealed.

He picked her up and swung her in a large circle. "Did you pick up the food?" Peter asked, putting Emily down on the carpeting.

"What?"

"The coleslaw and potato salad, did you get it?"

"What are you talking about?"

"You're joking right?" He slammed his hand down on the counter. "I asked you to pick it up this morning before I left."

"When? I don't remember even speaking to you this morning."

"I asked you and you answered. Now I have to run out and get it."

"What's wrong, mommy?"

"Nothing Emily, why don't you pick out a board game and I'll play with you." Emily scampered into the den and chose Mouse Trap of all games. Catherine scraped off the remains of her nail polish and examined the spotless floor.

"The one thing I ask you to do and you can't even do it. I work all day and now I have to go back out. Sorry to ruin your day off."

"My day off? I spent the last seven hours cleaning what you demolished over the weekend."

"So this is my fault? Don't blame this on me, you messed up."

"I scrubbed the entire house, didn't you even notice?"

"How can I? All you do is clean. What's the difference between one piece of dust and three?" He plucked a Heineken out of the fridge and cracked it open with his bottle opener. "Don't worry about it, I'll go back out and drive to the deli and buy it myself. I wouldn't want you to spend your money on anything but another fuckin' pocket book." Peter slammed the door behind him.

Catherine shuddered, then trudged over to Emily who tried to attach the Mouse Trap slide to the stairs but it refused to connect.

Emily ripped it apart and chucked it across the room. The slide slammed into the back door. Her crooked smile let Catherine know she heard the entire argument. Again.

Chapter 9

Victoria

Victoria slumped in her chair and listened to Jean drone on about how the Director of Communications complimented her on the Family Practice Physicians luncheon on Saturday. Jean obviously chose Monday morning for meetings to personify the "I hate Mondays" mantra.

"I'm quite brilliant, you know. It must be hard for the three of you to work under me. I can't help it if I'm an A+ employee while you linger around the C mark. If you stopped coming up with your useless, lame ideas and paid attention more, maybe you'd be successful like me."

Victoria hid her yellow note pad, the blank one that only contained five more pages. The rest disposed in various garbage pails. The pages ran out along with her ideas.

The conversation redirected to Catherine and Victoria cringed.

"Can you explain yourself? This entire report is incorrect." Jean threw the mass of stapled papers at Catherine hitting her in the mouth. Catherine wiped her lip and then glanced at her fingers.

Heather snapped up and glared first at Jean but longer at Catherine. Victoria knew why. Say something, will you?

Nothing.

Catherine leafed through the papers, her puzzled mien surfaced. "I've never seen these before."

"Of course you haven't. Lydia typed them up." Saliva sprayed from her lips with each breath.

"Then how could I—"

"You gave me this information."

"On refrigerator temperatures?" Baffled and trembling, the words barely materialized.

"I looked like a fool in the Infectious Disease meeting! How dare you!" Jean held up a fist and crushed her chunky fingers into a tight ball. Her face furrowed until she looked like she sucked a dozen sour lemons.

Heather straightened and clasped her hands in front of her. "When have the dietitians ever recorded fridge temps?" Her strong nature worked against the group at times. Better to take Jean's abuse than add more momentum to an already doomed situation.

Jean's Grand Canyon forehead relaxed, but only for a second. She wheezed, as if asthma consumed her, then smiled in a chilling manner. "On another note, I submitted the proposal for the cardiac rehab center to hire its own dietitian. They loved my ideas and appreciated my honesty."

Victoria's head jerked back, but unable to speak she clutched her throat. Her oatmeal curdled in her stomach. Jean's snub melted what little self-worth she retained.

"I proposed that idea," Victoria mumbled.

"They're looking into it and if they hire their own, well then you'll have me to thank for it." Jean propped her chest out like a proud rooster and grinned.

"I recommended that and you said it was ridiculous, that they'd never hire another dietitian. You said– "

"Of course, your work load will be lessened which means you will have to take on more responsibilities."

Heather shook her head and scoffed at her delusion. "The whole point was that we had too much work to do because we were constantly helping them."

Victoria abandoned her dispute, pointless. Jean was a performer in an empty theater, only needing her own accolades.

Why did Victoria subject herself to this discourtesy? She built her name up within the hospital after fifteen years of service. Over the years, she initiated Weight Loss Management sessions for employees and taught Cardiac Rehab's nutrition classes. She instituted the monthly oncology meetings and assembled a great team to support it.

Her responsibilities on the Board of Directors for the cancer center taught her more than she imagined. Her master's degree in Public Health, obtained while working full time, proved she could juggle several undertakings at once. Then why did she allow Jean to steal her ideas and present them as her own? She should inform someone, but whom?

"On to the next agenda," Jean announced. "I need some ideas for the Memorial Day cafeteria menu. I want it to be absolutely awe-inspiring."

****

Victoria helped Sara carry her shimmering gold prom dress into the house. "It really is stunning, Sara."

"I know! I'm so excited." I can't wait to show everyone, I'm calling the gang now. Do you mind if they stop over before dinner?"

"No, not at all, I'd love the company." Victoria removed the hanging philodendron from the hook in the ceiling and placed it on the dining room table. She climbed back on the chair and hung Sara's dress there instead.

"There, that looks more festive than some silly plant."

She remembered her own prom with Ed, the most riveting night of her life. Not many things topped it, possibly more exciting than their wedding. The magic took a nosedive after the honeymoon.

Victoria's fingers ran down the full length of the charmeuse halter dress. What would she wear to her 30th wedding anniversary next year? She'd kill to wear something as sexy as this, but who would care? Who would notice?

Chapter 10

Heather

Heather strained to reposition her arm a mere inch or two to contact her mark. Her slow creep and crawl, as she stretched her fingers and edged forward in a calculating manner had purpose, she could not fail. Her right toe swooshed up and over her hip to touch the red target. She would do it. She gave them a side-glance and nodded.

"Left foot on green," Rori said.

Impossible! Heather struggled to move her left leg but the weight on her back from Gia and Laurel caused her to crash to the floor. "No!" Heather cried, "I will not be defeated." Rori leaped into the pile and the four of them burst into a roar of cackling and snorting. The room sounded like a gathering of witches around their poisonous brew. Toxic ingredients concocted for their nemesis.

Heather stood and seized the three of them drawing them in to her chest. "I love you guys so much. You know that, right?"

"No, actually we don't, we've no idea. You hate us, it's obvious." Gia pretended to look at the ceiling.

"Oh, yeah?" Heather said, "I guess it's time for...the kissing monster." She snatched Gia by the back of her head and smothered her with eight kisses before Gia pulled away. Laurel stood before her, wide eyed. Heather lunged for her, planting her lips all over her forehead and nose.

She broke away long enough to observe little Rori perched on the side of the Twister mat, hands clasped in a knot in front of her Tigger shirt. Heather's eyebrows rose and fell as she snaked over to her. Rori shook her head but Heather pounced and hugged her tight, smooshing her tiny face with oodles of kisses. "Kissing monster never fails to reach her mark."

"No, no," Rori tried to sputter in between giggles.

The front door swung open, Lance charged in plopping his briefcase on the hallway rug. "Great news, everyone!"

"What is it, daddy?" Gia entered the kitchen and extended her arms for him to lift her.

Instead of picking Gia up, he stepped around her, lifted his arms like a preacher at a sermon, chin held high, shoulders back, a gleam in his eye, and waited for all of them to respond. Would barfing on his shoes be an appropriate response?

Cue the chirping crickets.

"I did it, I made partner. Finally. They made me partner today!"

Heather pulled Rori into her lap and straddled her reedy legs around her. Heather's shield. Unable to respond, she contemplated her word choice. Instead of enthusiasm, her heart twisted into a lump. Empty.

Laurel sensed the pause and threw herself into her dad's arms. Gia and Rori, unclear of the meaning to his news, followed. Three beautiful girls hugging their father, but his eyes remained on the ceiling.

Heather wrestled herself to a standing position and managed a weak smile.

Lance pushed the girls aside like they were a pack of mischievous puppies and sauntered into the center of the living room. "Yes, I did it. Partner. I knew they'd come around. They couldn't resist me, knew I'd be an asset to their team. Only a matter of time."

Nine years. Yep, only a matter of a decade. They probably realized he'd never go away and asked him out of sheer aggravation.

"Bet they discussed it all week. How they would tell me. Catch me at just the right time, spring the surprise on me knowing others would scoop me up if they didn't."

She'd like to scoop him up. Like dog shit. And toss him in a bag and dump him in the bottom of their garbage can. Watch the garbage men come, heave the can up and smash it on its side, emptying the contents, the bag perhaps breaking and spilling his remains on top of toddler barf, spoiled chicken parts and maggots.

Lance thrust his hands on his hips flipping his suit jacket tails back. "We have to celebrate of course…a party or something. This is an enormous accomplishment."

"So was my graduation from college, passing my RD exam, landing my first job, the birth of your three daughters, their birthdays, graduations, dance recitals…"

"Yes, a party, a grand one. I'm sure my mother will have no problem throwing one for me."

And Heather would have no problem throwing his ass out, and she was sure mommy would have no problem taking him back. His bed still had his Jets pillow on it and let's not forget Shooba his stuffed puppy.

"In fact, we should go on vacation. The whole family." He threw his arms into the air waiting for the audience's applause.

Rori spun the spinner on the Twister game, unaware his babbling continued.

"Ooh," Gia shouted. "Disney, you promised."

"I did no such thing. Disney? That's for kids."

The cleft between Heather's eyebrows collapsed from the flames thrust from her pupils. "They *are* kids. Yours. Laurel will be thirteen and none of us have ever been to Disney."

"That's not true, I've been to Disney countless times."

"*We* have not," she exploded. "We agreed the next vacation would be in Disney."

Lance scanned each of them, then paused on Rori, pointing a finger at her. "She's too little, we can't take *her* to Disney."

Rori's chin trembled. Before Heather reached her, Rori chucked the spinner across the room smashing it into the wall. Tears gushed down her face, her mouth opened and quivered but no noise materialized. Silent yelps spewed, crushing Heather's heart.

"And now she's going to cry, ruining my moment. This is supposed to be about me."

When wasn't it about you?

Laurel gritted her teeth, but unsure what to do, she bolted to her room. Gia stepped back, stumbled over a sneaker and fell on her butt.

"Well that's gratitude. I'm going out. My own family can't even be happy for my success." He stormed toward the kitchen but glanced back at Heather before he reached the front door. "I blame you for this. You've turned my girls against me."

Chapter 11

Catherine

Catherine trudged out of Meadow Lakes Elementary school following a long drawn out PTA meeting and after working all day alongside Jean who needed help for a catering event when her prize employee called out sick. Jean had no problem pulling her dietitians from their floors to prepare food in the kitchen when it involved schmoozing administration. Hairnets, gloves and plastic aprons reminded Catherine of her first job working the tray line in a nursing home. She loved her clinical role, and playing with hors d'oeuvres when her patients needed her tensed her body. Her jaw would certainly hurt in the morning.

She steered into her driveway, turned off the ignition and collapsed into the car seat. Catherine nudged her bag of half-eaten baby carrots yearning for something more satisfying. Her insides roared, craving stimulation.

Did Peter save leftovers for her? She opened the door and slogged into the den.

Peter paced the room, cell phone in hand, homework tossed in bunches, unmatched sneakers littered the floor, the smell of popcorn wafted through the air. Peter hollered into the phone and dug his nails into his black gelled hair. Catherine retreated into the kitchen eager to fling even a morsel of food into her mouth. Her arms dangled beside her but there appeared no reason to raise them. Only abandoned popcorn bowls with worthless kernels dotted the counter tops.

Emily skipped into the kitchen still in her school clothes. "Hi mommy." She reached up to give Catherine a tight hug.

"What are you doing up? You should've been in bed a half hour ago."

"Playing with Colton and Bentley. Daddy bought them a new video game, *Demon Brain Hunters.*"

"That sounds...horrible." Catherine marched into Bentley's room where the two of them sat collectively on his bed, game controllers in their hands.

"Why aren't you two in your pajamas and in bed?" They ignored her, fingers flying wildly, faces scrunched like dried fruit. "I want you in bed now. You have school tomorrow. Did you do your homework?" Nothing.

Catherine twisted back to Emily. "What did the three of you have for dinner?"

"Popcorn," Emily whispered.

She grabbed Emily's hand and led her to her room. "Pajamas, now." She returned to Bentley's room, extended her arm and ripped out a few wires, uncertain what they were. The screen went black.

"Hey, what'd you do that for?" Bentley screamed.

"It's time for bed."

"Dad bought it for us, it's none of your business." Colton chimed in.

"I'm your mother and it is my business. Colton, go in your room, Bentley, lights off."

Catherine stormed back in to Emily's room where she found her perched on the end of her bed buttoning her Cinderella pajama top. She sat down, wrapped her arm around her and pulled her in tight. Catherine's hunger vanished, no longer desiring anything. "What did your dad buy you?" she asked.

"Nothing." Emily played with the fuzz on her pajama pants. "He said I was too young for the video game."

Of course she was too young, but he could have bought her something else. "Don't worry, the two of us will go shopping this weekend, that'll fix everything."

"No it won't. It never does. All you do is shop, shop, shop."

Catherine's heart shriveled into a hollow lump. Clearly, Emily was tired. She knew Emily loved shopping as much as she did. What girl doesn't like pretty new things? It made Catherine happy, and the other mothers eyed her possessions at the meetings. She was finally fitting in.

She tucked Emily into bed and read *The Giving Tree.* Halfway through, she felt like the foolish tree. Cooking and cleaning, running to school functions, volunteering as Emily's class mom. There would be nothing left of her. What was she getting out of all of this?

She left Emily's room and searched the house for Peter. She found him in the garage smoking a cigarette. "Hey," he grinned.

Catherine wanted to yell. She wanted to tell him how she really felt, but knew the repercussions would be worse. The arguments they had over the past year, shriveled her self-confidence into a forgotten raisin. A pounding vibration throbbed in her ears; she stiffened and suddenly needed to run.

"Well? Are you going to speak or just stand there staring at me like a mime?" Peter lifted his hands and pretended to be locked in a glass cage, mouth wide-open and swaying, tongue hanging out. The image jolted her.

"I didn't understand why..." The words jarred to a halt within her mouth. She felt dizzy, her empty stomach now a rigid mass.

"What did I do wrong now?"

Catherine's nose filled, salty fluid slid down her throat. She would not show him tears tonight. She sucked air in through her nose and squeezed her hand until nails dug into her palm. She could do this. "I was wondering why the kids had popcorn for dinner, and why they were still awake."

"Look, you had to go to one of your stupid 'I need to be a part of the spring tulip extravaganza meetings.' I was extremely busy tonight, and I didn't have time to cook. They won't die."

"It wasn't a tulip meeting," Catherine whispered, barely audible. "It was—"

"Sitting around with a group of other woman cackling." Peter switched to a high pitch voice, "Now shall we pick the pink tulips or the pale yellow ones?"

"It wasn't...a tulip...meeting." Her chin trembled.

"Then maybe it was a meeting to discuss why we should go door to door selling jelly beans, or perhaps Rice Krispies Treats."

"We...don't...do that."

"I got it. Why not sell Coach bags door to door? Yeah, that's a great idea, think big. Forget the chump change, go right for their savings accounts."

"We don't do that! We discuss important matters that affect your children."

"How about important matters like your children needing dinner tonight, and their homework to be checked? They need you here, not at stupid meetings."

"I like the meetings."

But he didn't hear her. He jumped into his car and zoomed out of the garage.

"It makes me feel important," she hollered at the empty garbage pail. "I am important. I am, damn you." Catherine whipped her hands up to her face but not before tears fell from them and drenched her palms.

Chapter 12

Victoria

Victoria laughed out loud at the story the unit secretary reenacted. Two other nurses joined in and soon the entire nursing unit exploded into a giant laugh fest comparable to a comedian's opening night.

"I never laughed so hard," Victoria snorted. "I need that, the last few weeks have been—"

"Victoria, excuse me, can I speak to you a moment?" Dr. Pierce bent over Victoria's computer and the bags under his eyes shot at her. She recoiled and then inched her chair away from him. She hated close talkers.

"Yes, what can I help you with?"

"I happened to pop into one of my patient's rooms, a patient with *diabetes*," he emphasized, "and I was shocked to see a container of apple juice on his tray."

"And?"

"He's a diabetic."

"No, he *has* diabetes, he's not a disease."

Dr. Pierce squinted. "Regardless, they should not be receiving juice on their trays."

"Why not? A carb is a carb. It doesn't matter if it's juice, or bread, or a Snickers bar, they are all pre-portioned to provide one serving. Fifteen grams of carbohydrates equals one serving of– "

"You are not understanding me, I'm a doctor."

And what the hell was she? Did she not attend college specifically for a degree in nutrition? "Yes, and I'm a registered dietitian. Your point?"

"Then you should know that diabetics cannot get juice."

Victoria cringed at the word again. "Says who? We practice carb counting here. They're allowed three or four carbs at each meal. All our food is portion sized, they can choose the carbs they want and we ensure they receive the correct amounts with the correct portions. And also they– "

"They are not allowed sugar or sweets."

"They're not children. They can have whatever they choose as long as it fits into their carbohydrate allowance and have mixed nutrient meals that will safeguard against any– "

"Then how do you explain their high blood sugars?"

"Blood glucose," she corrected. "Are you going to let me complete any of my sentences?"

He folded his arms and rested his elbows atop his paunch. The bags under his eyes deepened and obtruded.

"Do you want to know what I see causing hyperglycemia in our patients? I see incorrect diets ordered by doctors, IVs with dextrose, medications that raise blood glucose levels, illness, stress, infection, all common causes of high blood *glucose.*" Victoria squared her shoulders and arched closer to him. "But mostly I see the inappropriate use of insulin. Not enough insulin, insulin not being titrated appropriately, no pre-meal insulin, stopping insulin inappropriately. That's not a dietitian's fault, that's a doctor's fault."

Dr. Pierce leaned away. The former cluster of chortling employees focused their attention on him now. "Well, I need proof of this information. I only abide by evidenced-based practices."

"Not a problem. I can have a copy of the *American Diabetes Association's Clinical Recommendations for Nutrition* and one on *Caring for Diabetes in the Hospital*, both from the 2008 Clinical Practice Recommendations Standards of Medical Care. I can have them for you by tomorrow. Will you be around?"

His eyes skipped around the room, surveying the health care professionals that pretended not to see his ass just get whipped. He squirmed, reached for his phone and stepped out of the nurse's station. "I'll be here tomorrow." He then retreated.

****

Victoria cut across the hallway during her meals rounds and jarred to a halt at the clamor from the TV in the patients' lounge. The beam on her face replaced the anger she still harbored from her argument with Ed this morning.

"The Wall Street Journal," she hollered at the screen. "Yes!" Applause tumbled from the room into the hallway.

"1929," she fired off. "Correct again." Victoria suddenly felt bigger, taller, stronger. Alex Trebek smiled and raised his palms to congratulate her.

"Benito Mussolini."

"You're not watching Jeopardy again, are you?" Heather snuck around the corner to find Victoria in her favorite spot. "Do you ever get a question wrong?"

A gentle tingling swept up the back of her neck and across her face. "Once, I did."

"What?" Heather gave her a side-glance. "The crazy thing is, you're probably dead serious."

"I need some fun in my life, don't I? Or am I doomed to live this monotonous life forever?"

"I hear you. Let's torch Jean's office and then take off on some wild adventure."

"Sure, just let me clear out my bank account and I'll meet you at JFK before dinner."

"You're on. Now, should we torch her office after she leaves or while she's still in it?"

"Hmm, hard decision." A sneer touched the corner of her lips. "So, what brings you to the fifth floor? You rarely come down to visit anymore. I'm not annoying you like Catherine, am I?"

"No, silly. I...of course not. Just...busy."

"Busy? Since when has that stopped our little chats?"

Heather's face took on a pondering air. Her eyes grew distant and she drifted off as if forgetting where she was. "No, nothing. Just busy. But I'm here today."

Heather was definitely hiding something, but she wouldn't pry. Not yet. Heather wasn't one to keep anything in, at least not since she told Victoria about her past. Since then she's been pretty much an open book. Victoria, on the other hand, refused to reveal her chronic depression to her. No need for two people to moan about their miserable lives. Then again, misery loved company.

How happy was Catherine? She portrayed the perfect wife and mother. Always so well put together, peppy, perfect, punctilious, PTA participant. Punctilious. Word of the day.

Were all her tales at lunch true? Successful stockbroker husband with two handsome, athletic sons and an attractive daughter. She had yet to meet any of them. All she knew came from pictures and stories. They must be doing well though – his BMW, her Lexus SUV. The way she spoke about name brand clothes and objects gave Victoria the impression she worked in Bloomingdales for years...or at least shopped there.

Maybe Victoria went about it all wrong. Maybe she should have kept the fire going with Ed. Sure, their children occupied many years of their lives but Catherine pulled it all together somehow. How could her hair and clothes, not to mention her eating habits, be so impeccable? Did she have a nineteen-inch waist?

She bet her sex life was ideal as well. One of those quiet ones that performed wild acts in the bedroom like hanging from the chandeliers with handcuffs while the children were off at religious instruction. Catherine's perfect hair slicked back in place and sheets changed before the children returned home.

Then again, maybe Catherine hid dark secrets like the two of them. Did we all have demons?

Chapter 13

Heather

For weeks, Heather watched Dr. Silvatri saunter past her nursing station pretending to talk on his phone in front of the glass partition that divided them. Multiple times he pretended to look for a chart in the rack when she knew he didn't have patients on her floor. A few times he'd strike up a conversation with a doctor near her, clown around and howl at ridiculous lame jokes.

She'd let herself catch his eye and act surprised to see him. "Good Morning," she would say. It was all he needed to sit down next to her. Then he used Heather's binder full of photographs to start a conversation. He had a six-year-old son himself, the love of his life. He spoke about him daily, only mentioning his wife once, the wife he was currently separated from.

He kept the conversations going, interested in getting inside her head, but she refused to indulge, revealing very little.

Nowadays, feeling more confident, he'd walk into the nurse's station, pull out the chair beside her and ease into it as if they were old pals. His visits came daily, all his downtime between cases spent with Heather.

Today he strolled into the nursing station with his partner, Dr. Richard Bettman. Had he mentioned anything to him about her?

"Hey," he said first, exhibiting self-assurance in front of his partner.

Dr. Bettman smiled, then took off to see his patient, leaving them alone.

He settled into the chair and leaned well into her space, brushing his massive shoulder against hers. He twirled her pen between his impressive fingers. Heather captured his blue eyes with hers and the two of them gazed acquisitively. His head tilted, eyes crinkled, attempting to read her mind. If only he could.

Silvatri winked.

A bolt ran through her. What did he see? How she wanted him to grab the back of her head and kiss her? Now, right here in the nurses station for all to see? Yes, it was true. She visualized his plumpy lips every night before bed. What did they taste like? The feel of them on her mouth, stuck together, lipstick gliding off.

She wanted to look away, but lingered to see what developed. Heather's mouth parted, her breathing too heavy for her nose. What was he thinking? Her heart clobbered her ribcage. Could he see it through her sheer white blouse, see her heart pounding for him? Could he read her mind now, as she imagined him unbuttoning her shirt?

After two months, he still sent waves of excitement through her. Heather's day revolved around his visits. Not wanting to miss any of them, she rushed upstairs to her floor and remained there until a minute before lunch. Victoria was right, she was neglecting her. Was it a crime to want some attention though?

Once Silvatri arrived, she didn't want him to leave. Their interactions were never tiresome. Their friendship, if it could be called that, sprouted into invigorating exchanges. But the clash between pleasant conversation and bottled up sexual tension was obvious.

He provided a small escape from her disregarding husband at home and her degrading boss at work. A small vacation into fantasyland.

Silvatri and Heather acted professional in front of other employees, but did he feel the same way she did? Did he dream of her at night? She pictured them lying naked in his bed countless times.

It was wrong. Certainly. God, it was wrong. So wrong.

But to know someone else liked her gave Heather hope. No one but her knew about these fantasies, and if she kept them to herself, what harm would there be?

She tried to reveal her feelings to Victoria last week but what if this damaged their friendship? What would she think of her? Victoria dedicated twice the amount of time to her marriage than Heather did, demonstrating her faithfulness and upholding her vow. Victoria would think Heather was only repeating her past mistake. But was that a mistake, and would this be too?

No, never again. She promised. The hurt she caused the last time...

"Are you ready?" His partner approached.

Silvatri stood, examined her from head to toe like a beautiful marble sculpture, not blinking once. The left side of his face curled into a grin. He handed her pen back, providing one last contact between them and held on when she attempted to remove it. His mouth opened, as if to speak but then closed again, eliciting a smile instead.

Dr. Bettman pushed him along like a father redirecting a child hypnotized by a toy store window. Stealing him.

She wanted more.

****

Heather climbed into bed Friday night irritated that she had to work this Memorial Day weekend. The weather promised to be gorgeous – cloudless skies, eighty-degree temps, barbecues and beach parties. The imprisonment of work only annoyed her further.

After only three hours of sleep, she heard wailing from Rori's room. The clock laughed at her and blazed 2:13 a.m. Bad dream? Maybe if she ignored it Rori would fall back to sleep.

Five minutes passed and it only intensified. She looked over at Lance. He heard, but never once clambered out of bed in the middle of the night for any of their children, to feed them, change a diaper or tend to them when they were sick.

The heaviness in her body weighed her down, pushed her deeper into the mattress, eyelids refused to open. She needed to wake at five o'clock for work and her muscles forbid her to move.

Heather yawned, dragged herself out of bed and shuffled her feet across the floor. She crept into her room without turning on the lights. Rori bolted up in bed and screamed. She attempted to rub her back, pacify her, but nothing worked. Heather flipped on the light switch and spotted the throw-up all over her sheets and pajamas.

Not tonight.

She replaced Rori's clothes but when she attempted to change her sheets, the frightened girl insisted on being held. Her sluggish one-armed bed-making skills irritated Rori causing her to cry out again. Rori's exhaustion trumped Heathers. She called out to Lance, asking him to hold her while she finished the sheets. He hobbled into the bedroom and banged his shoulder against the doorframe.

"What is it?" he grimaced. "I'm trying to sleep."

Heather's eyes protruded. She held her tongue and handed Rori to Lance. She jabbed the fitted sheet around the four corners smashing her knuckles into the wall. When she tucked the flat sheet under the mattress, Rori's cries returned. She spun to find Lance lying on the carpet, fast asleep. Rori, a few feet away, had rolled out of his arms.

"Are you serious?" she yelled. "Get up and bring her into our bed. How could you be so inconsiderate?" Heather tossed the comforter back on the bed, searing with fury. She put a clean blankie under the covers and Rori's stuffed koala bear next to her pillow.

The piercing howls returned.

Heather turned on the hall light and stomped into their bedroom. Rori had thrown up in their bed now. Lance curled himself into a ball, snoring away.

"Lance," she screeched. "You're not even taking care of her. She threw up in here."

"What? What do you want from me? I'm tired." He chucked the covers off himself and marched into the living room, leaving Heather to change their sheets as well. He was tired? She had to work in the morning, not him. He fell asleep at least two hours before she did, passed out and snoring loud enough to be heard while she cleaned the den on the other side of the house.

She carried Rori back into her room and tucked her in her bed. The ill child immediately fell asleep from the chaos and disorder. Heather changed their sheets, started a load of laundry and then slinked back into bed. The clock sneered. 3:04 a.m.

Wide awake.

Heather's feet dragged into work the following morning. Her desk chair creaked from her body collapsing into it. She yawned. Alone in the dietitian's office and glad no one else worked with her on weekends, she knew she could sleep there without anyone knowing. She placed her head on the desk and daydreamed of a life without throw-up, homework, temper tantrums and middle school drama. Her eyes glossed over and then drifted shut.

The only thing Heather dreamed about anymore was Silvatri. Him picking her up in the middle of the night, sneaking her out the bedroom window like high school kids and discovering what his lips tasted like. Was that so much to ask? Just one tiny kiss.

Of course it was. This was insane. Married with three kids and dreaming about some doctor sweeping her off her feet. Literally. Even if he liked her that way, God she wished he did, what would happen? They'd share lunch together in the hospital cafeteria? Plan a romantic dinner at a fancy restaurant on a Saturday night? Chat on the phone in the evenings while doing Gia's American Revolution homework? Perhaps meet up at a nearby park with their kids and push the youngest ones on the swings?

No. Heather was doomed to play out this charade of professional chitchat and casual pats on the shoulder and maybe an occasional wink here and there.

Wasn't she a good mom? A devoted wife despite Lance's clueless nature? Clean house, kids had no cavities, all did well in school. She kept herself in shape, had a great job. What was in it for her? There had to be more.

Just one tiny peck on the lips. No, it wouldn't be enough. She could almost taste his tongue inside her. Moist and warm. Would he hold her tight, squeeze her into his warm chest?

The hospital intercom hummed, paging Dr. Silvatri overhead. Her fatigue vanished.

Her hand, no longer under her control, dialed the operator. Before she had time to comprehend, the operator answered.

"Good morning, Norlyn Plans Hospital, Samantha speaking, how may I direct your call?"

"Can you page Dr. Silvatri to this number, please?" The phone crashed into the cradle and she sprang back in shock. As she scowled at her insubordinate hand, the phone chimed.

She stared at the phone. Her hand, now paralyzed.

Stupid hand.

What did she do? What would she even say? Maybe if she ignored the call he wouldn't find out it was her. No, the damn answering machine had Victoria's voice on it with their message. She snatched the phone. "Dietitians office, how may I help you?"

"Yes, this is Dr. Silvatri, did someone page me?"

"Yes, hi, it's Heather. I heard them page you overhead and I...didn't realize you worked weekends and I had a question about your patient...in the ICU and when I heard you get paged I thought to page you before...you left the hospital." The lies spilled out one after another.

He snickered into the phone, seeing through her sham. "Yes, I'm here, where are you?"

"I'm in my office. Alone." Did she just say that?

"Where's your office?"

"On the fourth floor, the old maternity wing, all the way at the very end, the last office on the right."

"I'll be right there."

What the hell did she do? He couldn't come in here. Plus she hadn't slept. What did she even look like? Her plain pink T-shirt and short khaki skirt screamed boring old mother. Why'd she call him? She was married, sleep deprived, bags under her eyes, probably still smelled like puke.

His mighty fist pounded the door causing her to jump. She threw a piece of gum in her mouth and then opened the door. This huge muscular thing took up the entire width of the door.

Heather invited him in and he grabbed the first chair by the door. He swung it around to lean his massive chest onto the backrest and straddled his legs underneath. She stepped back and selected a chair on the opposite side of the room.

Breathe.

All alone in a closed office.

"So," he began, "you're the only one here on the weekend?"

"Yes, only one of us covers the weekend."

"Is it a lot of work to cover the entire hospital by yourself?"

"It could be at times, but it's doable." How contrived would this conversation be? She felt like she was on a job interview with the president of the company.

"So why won't you let me do a colonoscopy on you?"

Her heart switched off. "What? I don't need one. I'm only forty years old."

"You never know, it's important to maintain good colon health."

Heather's face immersed in red flames, burning and melting before him. "Well, I'll keep that in mind."

"You still haven't answered my question." He rested his chin on top of the chair, the corners of his velvety lips inched up, the smirk that she secretly dreamed about at night, the lips that drove her crazy. His eyes refused to leave her gaze. He licked his lips like a lion waiting to dine.

Either fatigue or numbness, a sort of calmness overtook her. For the first time in fifteen years, her body relaxed and expelled destructive, toxic forces. She inhaled a long deep breath of renewed air, crisp and moist, injecting her with contentment, peace, and harmony. Resentment fled through her pores.

"It's a very personal procedure," she whispered.

He jerked his chair two inches closer. She looked down at the floor beneath his wheels and then back into his eyes. He raised his right eyebrow, tilted his head.

He whispered back, his seductive voice teasing the hairs on her arms. "You'd trust a total stranger rather than someone you knew?"

His chair moved another two inches closer.

"I trust you, it's just..." Heather exhaled. Tingling raced through her body. "If I knew you on a more personal level I wouldn't care if you looked up there, I mean I would care but, I wouldn't..."

His head sprang up and he leaned against the wall behind him, raising both his eyebrows this time. Stunned. "You mean if you and I were on a more personal level than it would be okay?"

"Of course, yes, I mean no, I think it would be something that if you and I were..." She squeezed her fist in between her thighs. "Well, we couldn't anyway."

"Why not?"

"We're both married."

"Is that a problem?"

Heather's heart pounded so furiously against her chest she felt dizzy. She stared at him for a good fifteen seconds. "Your call," she heaved out, her breathing rapid now.

He no longer inched toward her. Extensive thrusts propelled him across the room as if he had waited forever for her to say those words. Right before his chair knocked into hers, Silvatri leaped up, whipped it around in a half circle and crashed back into it, removing the obstructive backrest. He secured her cheekbones under his thumbs and drew her lips in to his.

His juicy mouth smashed onto hers, biting and sucking, like former lovers reunited. The feel of his powerful tongue against hers, was exactly as she imagined. She drove back wanting to climb inside. Silvatri's right hand clutched the back of her head and clamped down on her hair. They say it's in his kiss, and it was. Passionate and yearning, a deep desire concealed for months. There, in his kiss, she felt it.

Heather snagged it. A kiss. A tiny wish of hers, finally granted and her life took on new meaning. One kiss and hope restored.

But in one swooping motion, he removed his hands from her

face, grabbed her ass and lifted Heather onto his lap. Heather froze. Only a kiss. His mouth covered hers again, but with each motion, she unraveled and let go. His commanding precedent erased the past fifteen years of faithfulness she maintained with Lance. She wanted him, wanted this.

She wrapped her arms around his neck. His hands travelled from her ass, down her skirt and back up her legs. His thumbs probed the tiny folds between her thigh and pelvic bones, teasing.

He glided his hands to the underside of her skirt and cupped her bare ass. He pulled away and they looked into each other's eyes while their breaths poured out in quick successions. "Wasn't expecting that," he panted.

She smiled, hoping her face remained colorless. At least the thong she threw on this morning redeemed her lifeless mommy apparel.

He snapped up, hoisted her by her ass into the air like a small child, and took two large strides over to the wall, pushing her against it. Silvatri released her and then leaned in, rubbing his loose scrub pants against her body. She questioned if he wore underwear as his erection hung down across his thigh. The cucumber she cut for Rori's snack yesterday entered her mind.

No. Not now. No kids!

He pulled away and staggered into the wall behind him, breathing as heavy as she. "How private is this office?"

He wouldn't. Not here. Would he? Would she?

"No one knows I'm in here." He looked at the door. "It's locked," she continued, "I'm the only one with the key."

That's all he needed to hear. He seized her hand and then bent her over Catherine's desk. Of all desks, why hers? She tipped over Catherine's picture frame of her children with their grandparents and shoved it to the side. The image of the grandfather smoking a cigar with his vile toupee nauseated her. Then she thought of poor Rori throwing up last night. What was she doing?

He ripped the thong off her in one snatch, thrust his scrubs down next and the feel of him entering her, those initial seconds, incomparable.

Just his tip, touching the outside flesh, enticing, sent tendrils of vibrations throughout her as he rotated it around in slow circles. When the tip entered, ripples took off in numerous directions, alerting the rest of her body to the incoming delight. He penetrated inch-by-inch, paused, then moved slightly forward. Their low huffs escalated to moans, with the steady increase of him filling her.

She awaited his full length inside, unable to control her eagerness. He continued to torment Heather and her impatience heightened the anticipation. She squeezed her muscles around him and he let out a howl unable to contain himself any longer. When he delivered the last inch, driving it in, she roared, releasing her last trace of bitterness. Her body absorbed him, he felt her warmth. The complete insertion, instantaneous fulfillment.

"It's been so long," She whispered. She promised she wouldn't do this again.

He leaned over and kissed the back of her neck, then slammed her hard, harder, but there was no pain. Heather welcomed his savageness, remembering the sex she had before she married Lance. "Harder," she said. The desk slammed against the wall with rhythmic movements, loud and obvious.

The absence of any passion in her life, evident now. She seized her high point, convulsed from his sheer dominance and fell forward, vanquished by the gift of Silvatri.

After her family fell asleep, Heather reclined on her hammock and observed the cloudless sky fill with twinkling stars. Her smile persistent. She swirled her finger over her naked body remembering his touch. The featherlike breeze roused the hairs on her skin, her nipples reached toward the stars. Awakening her. She had awakened.

Chapter 14

Catherine

Alone, on the far right corner of the gym, Catherine waited for Emily's spring chorus concert to begin. Other couples, parents, and grandparents gathered to see their children perform. She waved at another mother, but she only dispensed a meager grin back.

She took pictures and video of Emily holding a bouquet of daisies in her hand, one of the few students chosen to do so. Why didn't she sing louder though? Emily, once a chatterbox, had backslid into a shy, withdrawn child this year. Catherine inquired whether a classmate harassed her, but her teacher insisted that all the children worked well together.

The concert ended. Catherine signed Emily out of school and they strolled toward their minivan. She buckled in Emily, who looked on with brooding eyes.

"Why didn't daddy come to see me?"

Her heart dropped, crushing pain followed. How dare he do this to her. She put up with it, but Emily? How was that fair? "I'm sorry Emily, I'm not sure why."

"Maybe I can ask him." She wriggled the toy bunny in her hand.

"No, I'll speak to him, honey. When we get home, start your homework and I'll get you a special snack."

"Hungry caterpillar fruit salad?"

"Sure." Catherine chuckled.

"Oh, yummy."

Emily finished her homework at their kitchen table when Peter rocketed through the door screaming into his cell phone. Catherine shuddered by reflex and Emily mirrored her.

"I don't give a shit what he says, this is my decision. He can go to hell for all I care."

Emily's hands flung over her ears. Catherine motioned to Peter, holding her pointer finger to her lips. He slapped her hand away.

Emily waited for her mother's reaction. Catherine reached for a yellow sponge instead and hurried to the kitchen table, wiping a stray raspberry into her hand.

He pitched his phone onto the kitchen counter and then rubbed his face with both hands multiple times. Emily and Catherine remained silent but watched for another explosion.

"What?" Peter said removing his tie and belt. "What is it?"

Catherine sent Emily to her room. The little girl took off as if chased by a zombie.

"Why didn't you come to Emily's concert? I reminded you this morning."

He shook his head and huffed as if she was clueless. Had she forgotten something again? Peter darted towards the garage door. She followed him and his wicked mood, knowing there'd be consequences. "You should've been there, she asked for you, wanted to know where you were..."

"Sorry but my job is taxing. I don't serve rice pudding to patients all day."

"I don't serve food. I don't have anything to do with their menus."

"I don't care. I have to keep the trades going, money flowing. That's my job. I have clients relying on me, why can't you understand the stress I have?"

"I have patients relying on me, but I still make time for her."

Peter grabbed a pack of cigarettes concealed behind a bottle of Armor All.

"You're smoking? Since when?"

A twitchy feeling spread through her body. Flashes ignited in front of her, her vision clouded. She grappled between the pain of defending her daughter and her new fear of him. Why couldn't she speak up?

She inhaled long and hard. "You had no problem showing up to your son's lacrosse game last weekend."

Peter stepped to his right but scorn grew on his face. She waited for his reply, an outburst, a bombardment of curses. She held strong, but he spun back and hurled a container of motor oil against the wall above her. Catherine buckled and collapsed onto her knees. Her sight dimmed, then blackened. The cold concrete beneath, froze her in place.

Chapter 15

Victoria

Victoria scooped the last mouthful of yogurt into her mouth and then watched as Heather chewed her Kashi Go Lean cereal. Passionately. Something Heather had done all week. Licking frozen yogurt off her spoon, sucking milk up the straw with intense drags and crunching on each grape as if it was a Godiva chocolate truffle.

"So where do you think Catherine is?" Heather asked. "It's not like her to call in sick. God forbid she missed one day of work, helping all these defenseless patients. What would they do without her?"

"Stop, she's new at this and excited. I'm sure you were like this when you first started."

"Oh, I was the ultimate dietitian geek. Stayed late every day, did daily meal rounds, ran down to the kitchen several times a day to get the patients whatever they wanted."

"See, Heather the nerd. Who would've thought? Now look at you." Victoria studied her reaction. Heather put down her spoon and examined Victoria's expression in return. "What's going on, Heather?"

Her eyes widened and then glanced at her Styrofoam bowl. She looked back at Victoria and her face changed.

"You met him, didn't you?"

"Who?"

"That guy. Nicolo."

Heather sank into her chair. "Nicolo?" She laughed. "No. I definitely did *not* see him."

"Then what is it? Something's up, you're too happy."

"I can't be happy?"

"Heather, Jean almost mauled you this morning with insults and you just blinked and agreed to whatever she suggested."

"I have to do that catering event with her Friday night, what do you want me to do?"

"Please. Now I know something's up. You never miss a beat when it comes to slinging it back at her. Spill it."

Heather peered over her shoulders and then bent in leaving only six inches between her and Victoria. She opened her mouth and then shut it. Victoria drew her eyebrows together and refused to let her evade the question.

"You can't tell anyone," she began.

"You've never kept anything from me in the five years we've worked together. And when have I ever repeated anything you've said?"

Heather flashed a smile. "Okay, but..." She lowered her voice further until barely a whisper crept out. "I slept with Dr. Silvatri over the weekend." Heather plopped back in her chair and winced.

Victoria's jaw plunged. The two of them studied each other. Victoria could not piece together the information. Sleeping with someone else? Cheating on Lance? Sure, she was miserable, sure he was an incredible ass, but she loved her daughters more than anything and to risk her marriage? For what? Some new doctor?

Heather grinned like a child admitting she pulled the fire alarm in the school hallway. Victoria continued her silence. Was she upset with Heather? Victoria assumed it was that, but disappointment was not what she felt. She was actually...intrigued. Curious.

"Are you going to give me the details or what?"

Heather filled Victoria in on Silvatri's flirtatious visits over the past two months, ending with this weekend's finale. Victoria's pulse quickened. She dragged her chair closer to Heather and heeded every word. Heather spared no details and Victoria's mouth moistened with the vision of fiery sex. Something that no longer existed in her life.

"How'd you feel during all of this?"

"You're expecting me to say guilty, right?"

Victoria scrunched the napkin until her hand ached. "No, actually. Not at all. I was hoping to hear it was amazing, that he made you walk into walls."

Red crept across Heather's cheeks. The glow colored her face into puffs of cotton candy. She blinked and jiggled her head. Victoria did not budge, she waited for her reply.

A smirk edged up on Heathers face. "It was amazing, mind blowing. Zigzagging all over the hospital the rest of the day. Skipping through my house all night."

"Really? Wow. What's going to happen now?"

"Happen? Nothing."

"I mean, are you going to see him again?"

"I saw him this morning. We snuck off into the patient's lounge and wow, his kiss just leaves me breathless.

"I'm confused."

"Me too. I'm not sure what to do. I'm not happy anymore though, that much I do know."

"You were never happy."

"True." Heather inhaled a few deep breaths and then shook her head. "You know, we're expected to make decisions on who we'll marry before we even know ourselves. All this pressure to find a man and have a family. It's a job, a responsibility on top of all the other responsibilities we have as women."

Victoria nodded. "My mother told me you were expected to please your husband and make everything perfect. If you divorced, it was always the woman's fault. She used to iron my father's boxer shorts, can you believe that?"

"Yup." Heather giggled. "No matter how much you did, it's still your fault."

"I'm sure pressed boxer shorts were on the top of his list." Victoria chuckled.

"I mean you chose to listen to punk rock music when you're eighteen, but when you get older you find yourself listening to jazz and that's okay. Your taste changed, they say.

And at eighteen you have to decide what you want to do with your life. At eighteen. So you decide, go off to college, get a job and then fifteen years later you realize this wasn't what you expected and you go back to school or get a new career and that's okay, too. You've grown and matured and you are commended for your bravery and for following your dreams.

But when you choose your spouse at eighteen, you're expected to stay with him until you die. Who made up this rule? At eighteen you make a decision and if you divorce you're going to hell?"

"Both of us went to our proms with our husbands," Victoria said.

"That's what I mean. We were so young, Victoria, what the hell did we know?"

"Did I ever tell you why I chose Ed? I mean, to be my husband?"

Heather leaned back again and brushed the hair out of her face with both hands. "No, do tell."

"We dated for three months and he asked me to the prom. I was thrilled. He was my first real boyfriend. I took my work money and bought this gorgeous pink fluffy gown. It was hot pink though. Other girls bought pastel colored gowns, but mine was extraordinary. Expensive, but I had to have it.

My three girlfriends arrived at my house for pictures and we waited for our dates. Ed was last to show and as each of their boyfriends entered, they gave my friends their corsages. Two were white carnations, plain, unimaginative. The third a pale pink carnation with these giant green balls and leaves, some weird fillers."

Heather laughed at Victoria's contorted facial expression.

"Ed finally arrives and he presents me with this beautiful white box with a gold lace design. Now he missed how the other three just shoved the corsages at their dates leaving them to open their own boxes and attempt to pin the corsage on themselves. Ed's clueless. So, just as my poor father wrestles himself up from the couch and makes his way into the foyer, Ed kneels down in front of me and opens the box."

"No, he didn't. Did you think he was proposing or something?"

"No, but my father did. Nearly had a heart attack on top of all his other medical problems. Anyway, he takes the corsage out and it's stunning. Giant hot pink Gerber daisies, two of them, surrounded by tiny pale pink roses and white stephanotis, my favorite flower. He gently pins it to my dress."

"Wow, I can't imagine that."

"Then he tells us how he insisted that the florist make this corsage and the florist argued with him that no one does this. They all get carnations. Ed had to call the manager and they finally agreed to make it. He said he wanted something special for the most beautiful woman in the world." Victoria closed her eyes and pressed them tight.

Heather grasped Victoria's hand, gave a light squeeze and refused to let go. Victoria's eyes welled up when she released her lids.

"A few months later, right before my father died, he asked if I was going to marry Ed one day. I said yes. He squeezed my hand like you just did and he said that made him very happy."

"Where'd we go wrong Victoria? I don't get it."

"I think we thought we knew what we wanted back then. Maybe we did, but things change. We change."

"So what's the answer?"

"I'm still trying to figure that one out for myself."

****

Victoria and Heather parted and Victoria headed back to the fifth floor. An oncologist stopped her before she made it to the nurse's station.

"Victoria, I want to pick your brain." He dropped his pen into his front pocket. "I have a patient, in 501a, not eating, planning to start tube feedings. He has diabetes but also in renal failure, may need dialysis and I wanted to know which tube feeding formula you'd recommend."

"Which is worse, the diabetes or his kidneys?"

"Well, at this time I would say his kidney function. Barely putting out any urine now."

"Then I would definitely suggest a renal formula. Let me check his height and weight and make a recommendation." Victoria walked to the other side of the nursing station and found her calculator. She wrote down her estimate but before she presented it to him, Jean stampeded down the hall barreling towards her. The clip clop of her cheap shoes overpowered the rest of the floors clatter.

"Oh, Victoria, just the person I wanted to speak with." Jean leaned over the desk partition but her large abdomen kept a two-foot wedge between them. "A scientist guy from Sand-something labs needs someone to give a lecture to his staff on nutrition and cancer and I suggested you. I told him next Friday would be good. Four p.m. I'll let you leave early to do the presentation. The information is on your desk. Don't disappoint me."

Don't disappoint me? You'll let me leave early? Victoria hardened every muscle in her body to prevent herself from pitching the calculator down the hallway and striking Jean in the back of the head. She had no time to prepare a lecture. Her magazine article was due in two weeks and she'd failed to type one word yet.

Motivation lacking, imagination absent, words lost. She needed something, something equivalent to what Heather experienced over the weekend, but that was out of the question. Maybe if she imagined the two of them having sex in the office that would do it. No, no, no. That was disgusting. What was she even thinking?

Victoria left work but stopped at the mall on her way home. She headed for the lingerie department in Macy's and lugged a dozen outfits into the dressing room. A sour taste filled her mouth with each slutty get-up she attempted to arrange onto her fifty-three-year-old body. She chucked them into a pile, refusing to hang them back up. She chose white-lace angelic pieces next, but they sickened her more.

She returned to the room one last time with a few plain negligees. Her last choice, a cranberry baby-doll in satin with a matching short robe, glistened on her. Lace embellished the top, which played up her less than perky breasts. She twirled around in the mirror and felt beautiful for the first time in years.

After dinner, when Sara left the house with her boyfriend, Victoria took a quick shower and slipped on the ensemble. She called Ed into the bedroom and then lounged across their bed.

"One second," he called out.

Three minutes passed. Then five. She watched each number change on the digital clock. "Ed!"

"What is it?"

"Can you please come in here?"

"For Christ's sake, woman." Ed's feet pounded the wood floors. Victoria repositioned herself on the mattress. Her chin pointed down, her eyelids fluttered. Ed entered the room and gawked at her, stone faced. "Well?" he said. "What is it?"

Victoria smiled, despite her heart hardening. She flung back the cranberry robe to allow him the full view of the outfit.

"Are you going to lay there like a mute or say something?" Ed raised both his hands, palms facing up. "Is this some kind of joke?"

It *was* a joke. Victoria reached back and clutched the edge of her robe. She trailed it back over her thigh and covered herself. What a fool. Sexy clothing could not enhance her aging body. Revolting. No wonder he didn't notice. Perhaps he did and didn't want to insult her.

Ed grumbled, finished the last of his Budweiser in one gulp and retreated to the couch. A cold shiver spread through her bones despite the warm temperatures outside.

Chapter 16

Heather

Heather dragged her ass into the hospital in her black pants with a white button-down shirt to look as waitressy as she could. She entered the kitchen and found Jean sashaying around in a blazing-red smock dress. This was going to suck.

She followed Jean to the conference room on the second floor and beheld the two-tiered circular tables arranged in precise locations throughout the room. She plopped the box of paper goods on the floor and pushed back against the wall with her foot. Jean strutted out.

"Hey, hey, we got Heather the waitress helping us out tonight!"

Heather rotated and found Tyrell towering over her. Her frown reversed. This would be an interesting night indeed. "Thank God you're here," she said. "We'll be tortured together."

"Tortured? I've been looking forward to working with Jean the Eating Machine for weeks."

Heather dropped her face and stared at him, hands on her hips.

"No really, this is cool. Catering with Jean after working all day in the kitchen with her and then coming back tomorrow to do it all again." His white teeth gleamed against his dark chestnut skin.

She shook her head, dumfounded, and drew her lips in to hide her smirk. She bent over and lifted the tablecloths out of the box. A flutter swept past her ear. "I picture having sex with her all the time," Tyrell whispered.

Heather jerked up, his face positioned only inches away from hers. "You, are gross." She poked him in his chest. Then she stepped back. "What the hell are you wearing?"

"What? What's wrong with this? You don't like?" He spun in his own rendition of James Brown, whirling and swaying back and forth on his toes.

"You're too much."

"Yeah, yeah, you like it. Admit it, I got style. Oh, yeah."

"You got something alright. Maybe you should go talk to one of the doctors upstairs. Preferably on the seventh floor."

"You saying I'm crazy or something? Okay, I see how it is. None of this for you."

"Me? You *are* nuts, go flash someone else."

"Come on baby, you want this. Six foot three, big biceps, stylish gear." He continued to strut around the room.

"Okay, enough weirdo, you're going to get us both fired. Get going before boss lady comes back."

The guests arrived in swirls of dresses and suits. The Board of Directors exited their meeting and entered the presentation. Jean traipsed around like one of the ballerina-hippopotamuses in Disney's *Fantasia* movie. Tyrell winked at Heather from across the room and she buried her head to hide the giggles.

Jean spent the night chatting and promoting herself. She boasted about the hot gourmet treats, never mentioning how the cooks in the kitchen prepared them all. She bragged about the cold hors d'oeuvres, failing to acknowledge the hard work from the salad room staff.

Jean accompanied the CEO to the table where Heather parked herself. Her eyes bulged at Heather, hinting that she'd better behave. Her fluorescent blue eye shadow and blood red lipstick reminded Heather of a fat lady in the circus.

"This is what I call...roasted...vegetable...cornucopia." Jean glided her bloated hand over the display.

"I thought Tyrell brought that recipe in from home. He made it for his family for Thanksgiving last year."

Jean seared Heather with torches of fire that cast from her eyes. Heather threw an exaggerated smile back toward the CEO.

"Here we have an arrangement of lovely spring rolls that I– "

"Yes, Anna from the kitchen prepared these. Delicious. Have you tried one?" Heather picked one up with her gloved hand and the CEO gladly accepted. "Fresh mangoes, grilled shrimp and this wonderful Thai sauce Anna created entirely by herself."

The CEO took a bite and closed his eyes as the flavors exploded on his tongue. "Oh yes, delicious indeed."

Jean hip-checked Heather and slid between the two of them. "Well these fried artichoke hearts were my idea." She scowled at Heather without the CEO noticing.

"I don't eat fried foods." He grimaced.

Jean clutched her dress and tugged it down. Her anger inflated like her ass. "Heather, I clearly told you that when the plates are only two thirds full they need replenishing. You're not following instructions." Jean lifted up a plate of blackberry and blue cheese stuffed mushrooms and handed them to her.

"Actually, this plate had thirty mushrooms on it and now it has twenty one. I'm watching it very closely." Heather's fake smile streaked across her face showing off her newly polished teeth.

"Very well, then. Shall we move onto another table?" Jean guided the CEO to an abandoned back table.

Heather caught Tyrell in the corner of her eye. He skipped up and down like he was peddling a bike, then flipped his hands out as if pointing two guns at her. She shrugged her shoulders not quite understanding.

He glanced at Jean whose back was to them. Jean lifted up a platter of eggplant salad toasts that Catherine had suggested. Tyrell glided over to Heather and tried to hide behind the food display. They both ducked down a few inches lower than the tallest pier.

"What are you doing? She'll kill you. Get back to your station."

"I'm on a break," he joked.

"Break? There are no breaks. Knock it off."

"I can handle myself. I'm the man."

"A dead man is more like it."

"Is there a problem, Tyrell?" Jean appeared from around the corner. "I expect more from Heather but you..." she examined him from top to bottom. "...you don't have a college degree, what could you possibly understand? You're lucky you passed high school, or did you?" She strutted away before anyone could speak.

Heather put her arm on his shoulder. "Tyrell, I'm so sorry. She's just evil, you know that."

Tyrell sucked in his lips and inhaled through his nose. "Yeah, yeah, I know."

"Why didn't you say anything? She can't talk to you like that."

"I need the job, ya know. It's alright, she ain't nothing."

****

Heather crawled back into her home after eight hours of work and an additional four hours of catering and clean-up. Some Friday night. If one more person shouted TGIF in front of her, she planned to deck them. Her pajamas called to her when she stepped onto the foyer rug.

Laurel, Gia and Rori tackled Heather with bear hugs. Lance stood behind them, dressed to pick up prostitutes. He donned a flaming red shirt that was unbuttoned almost to his belly button. A thick gold chain, ancient and shrieking "1990," circled his neck. His thick mass of greying chest hairs made her gag.

"What are you wearing?" she asked.

"I'm going out. Since none of you planned a party to celebrate my promotion, I'm meeting friends for dinner."

"Tonight? I just got home."

"Once again, it's all about you." He snatched his car keys and disappeared through the door.

At 3 a.m., the phone rang. Heather waited for Lance to answer it but as usual, he ignored any intrusion of his sleep. She scrambled over him to get the phone, only Lance was not there. His pillow cold and propped against the headboard.

"Hello," she choked out.

"Heather? It's Jenn Marconi, Doug's wife."

"Who?"

"Doug. He works with Lance at the law firm."

"Oh, okay, um, yeah?" Heather sat up in bed and rubbed the crunchiness out of her eyes.

"They were in an accident. Car accident. They're all at Beachmill Hospital near you."

"Oh my God, are they okay?"

"Doug and Steve are all right, they're releasing them. Stan is getting some x-rays but Lance, well, they said he's banged up pretty bad."

"Are you there now?" Heather leaped out of bed and then grabbed a pair of sweats.

"On my way. Should be there in five minutes."

"I'm leaving now too."

Heather tiptoed into Laurel's room, told her what she knew

and that she'd be back before the other two woke.

She sprinted into the hospital's ER and ran down the hallway knowing this was her fault. Punishment for sleeping with Salvatri. How could she be so foolish to think she would get away with it without any repercussions? Her children fatherless, all because she needed to get laid. She would pay for it now, but please, not her daughters.

A woman with sandy-blonde hair stepped into her path. "Heather? Heather Milanesi?"

"Yes, Jenn?"

"Sorry to meet this way. They need to keep Lance overnight. He was fine but then—"

"What happened? He said he was just going out to dinner. I was exhausted and fell asleep."

"Well it appears they were on their way home from the strip club when this young girl ran a red light and—"

"Strip club?"

"Yes, the one on North Harbor Turnpike. The Filthy Flamingo. The girl supposedly ran the light and slammed into the front end. The driver's side, and Lance was driving. He said his shoulder and neck were bothering him."

"His shoulder?" Heather's sarcastic tone could not be controlled. "And neck?"

Heather's fear turned to anger, her guilt turned to satisfaction. Glad she cheated on his filthy flamingo ass. And there she was feeling sorry for him. Sex had always revolved around him anyway, no kissing, no foreplay. Just a quickie from his morning hard on. It had been years since they had sex. She refused to indulge him after Rori was born.

Was this his first time there? Had he received a lap dance? Did he fuck any of them?

She whipped the curtain back that surrounded his bed and found him asleep, or hopefully dead. She peered over and heard him breathing. Damn. She asked the nurse for his belongings and then opened his wallet to find seventeen one-dollar bills and six five-dollar bills. Heather wondered how many he gave away.

The ER doctor approached and greeted Heather.

"We're waiting for test results but it appears he may have a tear in the cartilage of his shoulder. Better known as a SLAP tear."

She'd like to slap Lance, forget his tear. He'd probably whine about it for weeks now, lie on the couch with a blanket and ask for his meals to be brought to him. He'd better think again. This meant war.

Heather took Lance's wallet and clothes and then slipped out of the hospital. Let him sleep off his shoulder injury. His mother could drive him home tomorrow in his hospital gown.

Chapter 17

Catherine

Emily sailed and flounced across the room during her ballet recital's dress rehearsal. The light pink costume and fluffy tulle skirt carried a thin black striping along its edges, giving it depth when she leaped through the air.

The music strummed and rose until Catherine's heart sprang from its cage. The final note resounded and the beautiful swans held their pose. Catherine's hands reddened from their loud hammerings but she continued until Emily curtseyed for her.

Madison peered out the window searching for her mother, excused herself and then retreated to the hallway near Catherine. Madison scanned the crowded hallway but when her target could not be located, she approached Catherine. "Have you seen my mommy? Did she see me dance?"

Odessa had escaped out of the parking lot practically running Catherine over on the way in. She wanted to lie and tell her she did, but knew the truth would get back to Madison.

"I'm not sure, honey, I think she may have left."

Madison sniffled and then charged towards the bathroom. She hid there for the remainder of the class.

The stampede of butterflies marked the end of class and Catherine helped Emily remove her frosted-rose ensemble, swapping it with a white sweat suit.

Madison inched out of the bathroom in the midst of girls racing about. She collapsed near a closet that held abandoned coat hangers and sat on the dust and grime covered floor.

Hoards of mothers and daughters exited the dance studio but

Catherine stalled her departure despite Emily tugging on her shirt numerous times. She strolled over to Madison, a forgotten child that crumpled into a ball, her head buried in her knees as if in a cocoon. Catherine squatted and swept her hand over the child's hair-sprayed locks and down her back. Madison quivered as if hiding her sobs.

"What the hell do you think you're doing?" Odessa screeched. "How dare you." She pushed Catherine aside and then jerked Madison off the floor by her arm. Madison's confused expression volleyed back and forth off the two of them. Odessa inspected Madison. "Did she hit you? Did she push you to the ground?"

The three of them stood in silence, dazed. None of them knew what to say except Odessa. "If her costume is ruined you'll pay for this, you hear? How dare you touch my child. Come on Madison, stay away from her."

Odessa dragged her by the arm preventing Madison from removing her pristine slippers. The child struggled to keep up. Catherine blinked, for that was all she could do.

Emily clutched her mother's hand. "What happened, mommy?"

The familiar tongue-lashing fossilized Catherine.

"Why didn't you say anything?"

Because she never does.

****

"I received a complaint from this patient." Jean shoved a scrap of paper with a name and room number toward Catherine. "He said that since admission he hasn't received what he ordered on his menu." She bawled up her fist and slammed it on top of her desk. "Can you explain yourself?"

"I don't have anything to do with the menus. That's the diet clerk's job."

Jean rammed her finger less than two inches from Catherine's face. "Are you saying you have no idea what happens on your floor? Your floor is *your* responsibility."

"I do, but they handle the menus."

"You're fuckin' incompetent. I don't want to hear complaints from anyone, is that clear?" Jean plopped back in her chair and removed her Easy Spirit shoes, a gift from the entire Nutrition Department for her birthday. An obvious ploy to get her to ease up on them. It didn't work. She flung the shoes to the right of her desk, the odor immediate.

"Yes, but..."

"But what? What? Do you have anything to say for yourself? Anything at all?" Jean's nostrils expanded. "Patients should not be complaining about food. If they are, it's your fault."

Catherine's hands wrestled in her lap. She'd hyperventilate, but it's an impossibility when you stop breathing altogether. She spent every second of the day in her patients' rooms coddling them. She loved her job and treated the patient's as if they were her own family. It never seemed enough. How much more could she do for them?

"Are you listening to me? Answer me!"

Unable to speak, she receded until she could no longer hear Jean. Muffled rants disappeared altogether as Jean's chins bounced up and down upon one another. She needed to leave.

On the verge of losing it, Catherine slid herself out of the chair and exited the office. She never replied, unsure if words still propelled from Jean's vile mouth. Was she still yelling? Rising from her chair to come after her? It would take time for her to put her shoes on though. Shoes that stretched and flattened to fit her pizza-for-one looking feet.

She wandered down the hall and to the front lobby, ignored the stairwell and pushed the elevator button instead. She waited, and waited, not realizing it was under repair. A security guard pointed to the *Under Construction* sign. She plodded to the stairwell and grasped the door handle. Before she went through, her eyes caught sight of Heather and Victoria on the lobby sofas crouched behind a magazine display. Third time this week she caught them sneaking off to talk, excluding her.

Chapter 18

Victoria

Victoria emerged from her car and found Ed in the garage opening and closing the drawers to his giant tool chest. Each drawer banged louder than the next.

"Hello," Victoria said, "how was your day?"

Ed slammed the bottom drawer shut. He rose, accidentally smacked his head on the top of the tool chest, then wrenched himself toward Victoria. "How do ya think it's going? No work for two months. I'm bored out of my fucking mind."

He had a point, but Victoria ran out of things to talk to him about. Their conversations deteriorated over the years, but these past few months crippled them.

When they first dated, their daily phone conversations captivated her. Each time the kitchen phone chimed, she hoped to hear Ed's voice. With each new adventure in her life, he seemed to pull away, showed no interest in her endeavors and his lack of friends and hobbies left little for her to inquire about.

After decades of him careening from one job to another, she grew weary of paying all the bills, working multiple jobs and taking care of the house and children by herself. The years passed and she felt more alone while he blended in with the sofa. Just a handy man screwing in a light bulb here and there.

"What are you doing home so early, anyway?" Ed asked.

"I'm giving my lecture at SandCrest Laboratories this evening for the Cancer Research Depar—"

"Laboratory?" He reached up and continued to look in earnest for whatever it was. "When you cooking dinner?"

Her fists tightened. "The lecture's at four o'clock. About an hour. I'll be home in time to cook you dinner."

"Oh, sorry it's such an inconvenience."

"It's not an inconvenience." She lowered her voice not wanting to upset him further. Victoria plunked herself onto the garage step. His silence pained her more than anything. She attempted to shift the conversation. "The article I wrote for the magazine is due next week and it's a disaster. I wouldn't want to run the race after reading it."

"Magazine? You're writing for a magazine now? Here I have no work and you have a million jobs."

"It's not a job, it's for the 10K race."

"Why do you insist on talking about things that're over my head? You trying to make me feel stupid?"

"I'm talking about writing an article, for a magazine, to promote my fundraiser. Is that too difficult to understand?"

"I don't have time for this shit." Ed kicked the front of his tool chest.

"Time for what? Talking to me? When do you ever talk to me? You only talk to me when you want something."

His construction boot belted the side of the tool chest. Two screwdrivers rolled off the top and plunged onto the cement floor.

Victoria charged inside. She leaped onto her bed and released the tears she harbored. They fell onto the teal quilt leaving a deepened hue on the patch. Andrew had returned from college for the summer and although he closed his door, she refused to let him hear her cry. No one could see her in this weakened state. Failure intolerable.

But she had failed at her marriage, incapable of making her husband happy anymore. Her article a flop, incompetent at work, and now an important lecture loomed ahead of her. Her life corkscrewed out of control.

****

Victoria drifted through the glorious grounds of SandCrest Laboratories in awe of the kaleidoscopic landscaping and sculptures surrounding the buildings. The perfectly trimmed hedges, the quaint cobblestone walkway lined with perennials, and the Tudor style buildings comforted her.

They greeted Victoria in the front lobby and directed her to the Stephan Granderson auditorium. She carried her briefcase and laptop into the vast conference room and the rows of black-plush cushioned chairs startled her. At least 300 seats. The ten-foot long screen assembled on the stage enveloped her small podium.

She paused at the door, then journeyed to her podium unsure where to find the program leader. Masses of people crowded the room devouring the catered food, while more piled in. Vinegar whizzed past her nose making her already queasy stomach volatile.

Victoria climbed the four steps to the stage. A man in a tapered black suit mounted himself on the far end. The stage lighting made his suit sparkle with a glossy appearance, his salt and pepper hair glistened like a tree frosted with morning snow.

He rotated slowly and his lavender shirt played up on the black and silver checked tie knotted tightly around his neck. His green eyes hit her, encircled by lunging eyebrows and an upward curve of the right side of his mouth.

"Victoria Elling?" He extended his right hand while his other rested in his left pant pocket.

"Yes, hello."

"I'm Aiden McLoughlin, the program leader of the Cancer Research center. Nice to meet you."

"I'm excited to be here." Victoria examined the architecture on the ceiling but her view returned to Aiden. Like a magnet.

"We're delighted to have you here today and are excited for your presentation."

She beheld the large crowd and a rolling feeling overtook her stomach. "As am I."

"Don't be nervous. You're the expert and we're here to gain as much knowledge as we can." Aiden motioned to the food. "Would you like something to eat?"

Food. Was he serious? She couldn't stomach anything and failed to eat prior to the lecture as it was. The room spun and her head filled with helium. "Perhaps a drink. I mean juice or something?" Of course a glass of wine wouldn't hurt either.

"Certainly, and Joe over here will help you set up." He disappeared down the stairs and his rear-end bounced up and down under his jacket.

"Oh God, this is not happening."

"What?" Joe asked.

"Nothing, sorry. Here's my laptop."

In the first few minutes of her speech, her voice quavered, but then she caught sight of Aiden in the front row. He whisked back his frosted spiked hair and winked at her. Instead of escalating her angst, he transferred his soothing manner to her.

She would not disappoint him. She fired away the latest research in nutrition and cancer and her striking power point slides caused Aiden's eyes to widen numerous times. Her late night hours paid off. She felt self-satisfaction and fulfillment for the first time in years. A valuable asset instead of an incompetent dietitian.

Her knowledge shined and in the end, thundering applause erupted. Aiden bolted upright and clapped, triggering others to follow and stand as well.

Victoria attempted to pack her briefcase with her materials but instead, attendees stormed the stage with numerous inquiries. An hour-long lecture turned into two with questions and commendations. She managed to put the last of her supplies away when Aiden approached from behind.

"That was truly enlightening, Victoria." He shook her hand but held it a moment longer. "Have you eaten at all? You must be starving."

"I do feel hungry now."

"Please, let me treat you to something, you've been standing for almost two hours. There's a nice bistro located on the main level."

"Maybe I should just grab something from your buffet here."

"Nonsense. You will not stand a moment longer, I insist."

Victoria relished the succulent food Aiden ordered for her. Beef tenderloin, roasted fingerling potatoes, and Key West vegetables. She wolfed down every morsel while he spoke about his career.

"...and then they offered me the position of program leader for the Cancer Research Center. We're currently working on tumor development and progression. Also exploring the genomic changes in a variety of cancers."

Victoria did not know which stimulated her more, the delectable food or intelligent conversation. She clung to every word, devouring them.

"Genomics can have an extensive impact on various forms of medical care. It can identify the best strategy to fight certain cancers." He paused and watched her savor the meal.

Little did he realize she relished his conversation more. Or was it his eyes? Eyes that bounced off his hair like green streetlights shining through snow covered trees.

"I'm so sorry, I've been babbling, not giving you a chance to talk. Please, Victoria, tell me about yourself."

What could she tell him? That she was sad, depressed, lonely? That she felt abandoned and isolated.

Or, perhaps, for the first time in years, she wanted to run through the crashing waves on the seashore with the moon shining down on her. Naked. She felt alive. Hungry. Sexy. She licked her lips and wiped the gravy off her chin.

Chapter 19

Heather

Lance bounded into the kitchen and ignored Laurel and Gia, both sitting at the table. Textbooks, pencils and worksheets covered the wood surface.

For once, he flashed a grin upon his face. "Family, I have good news! Heather, come here."

Heather struggled off the den carpeting leaving Rori to finish the Madeline puzzle herself. She took three steps into the kitchen, folded her arms and leaned back on the kitchen counter.

"I have a surprise for all of us, something pretty exciting."

Please let it be the Disney vacation. Please. Hopefully a week of the silent treatment snapped Lance into reality. The girls cried until they discharged him from the hospital and even when he returned home, they clung to him. He sensed her disappointment in him as well.

"What is it daddy?" Rori asked, wanting to be included.

Instead of answering, he clutched one of the kitchen chairs, its legs scraped against the tile floor in an annoying, high-pitched screech. He climbed up and raised his good arm into the air. The Statue of Liberty would've be offended.

"Well, are you going to tell us?" Laurel bit the end of her pencil.

"Guess," he said, extending the melodrama.

"A toy?" Rori asked.

"Nope."

"A trampoline?" Gia asked.

"Wrong again."

Laurel examined her mother for the answer, but Heather

shrugged her shoulders. "Disney?" Laurel prayed.

Lance shot her a glare. "Nope, not even close."

"Please tell us. Please. Pleeeeease." Heather's sarcastic tone droned on.

"You won't believe it, I'll just have to show you." Lance led the pack into the garage and then towards the driveway. He twirled with arms out-stretched like one of the models on the Price is Right.

He didn't. He did.

A Corvette convertible. The girls ran to the car screaming with enthusiasm. Gia grasped the door handle and yanked the door open.

"No, no. You can't touch it."

"What do you mean? You said you had a surprise for *us*." Gia said.

"Well it is a surprise, but it's for me. A late promotion gift." He slid his hand over the roof of the car. "With my other car totaled, this fits the bill."

"It only has two seats," Heather said.

"Of course, it's a Corvette. Duh."

"We have three children, did you forget? Duh."

"Oh, no, no, no. The girls will not set foot in this car. There will be no Cheerios tossed around or fingerprints on this baby."

"And what do we do when we go on trips?"

"That's what your Jeep's for. You wanted that and you got it, this is my choice."

"And what happens when my car's in the repair shop?"

"No one is stepping inside this car but me." Lance ran both his hands through his hair and jerked on it. "Once again you have to ruin my happiness."

★★★★

Heather practically skipped out of the patient's room. Finally, someone interested in learning about their diet. The patient asked many questions and she enjoyed helping him and promised to return later with more literature.

Heather's fascination with nutrition and fitness began in high school and she hoped to share her enthusiasm with others. Unfortunately, people showed no interest in changing their lifestyles and she found her job more and more frustrating over the years. All this knowledge and no one wanted to listen.

She wrote in the chart about the patient's good understanding and his expected compliance, then smelled the familiar pungent scent of sour cologne. Dr. Mangle strolled into the unit, a bitter tang rose in Heather's mouth.

His bony fingers perused the rack for his charts and then he secured three under his armpit. He turned to find a seat but two steps in, a nurse blocked him.

"Dr. Mangle, I asked you yesterday to call Ericka Pesina's daughter. She's very angry that you haven't returned any of her calls."

"I did try to call, several times, but there was this peculiar busy signal. Is her phone operating correctly?"

Heather wanted to throw her chart at his head and smack some sense into the man. How naive could everyone be? Were they so gullible, so dense to believe him every freakin' time?

"I don't know," she said. "Maybe her phone wasn't working or perhaps she was on another line. I'm so sorry."

"No, not at all," Dr. Mangle slanted toward her. "Did you do something new with your hair Jessica?"

Jessica flushed and then ran her hand over her unwashed, greasy, up in a ponytail, mess. "Um, no, in fact I need to get it done."

"Nonsense, it is simply beautiful just as it is."

A choking, barfing noise burst from Heather's throat. Dr. Mangle twisted his neck, spied Heather and then grinned. The chair next to her wrenched out from under the counter.

"And Heather, how are you today?"

"I was well but suddenly I have this burning in my mouth and a need to spit."

"Maybe you're coming down with something and need an examination. Do you have your own doctor? You can always come in to see me." Dead twigs scraped across Heather's shoulder and then down toward her elbow. Heather flinched. He lowered his voice, "if I ever do anything that makes you feel uncomfortable, just let me know."

"Look," she bent in leaving only inches between their faces, "there's no way I would ever let you examine me or..." she removed his crusty hand from her arm, "...touch me. Consider this my letting-you-know, got it?"

He reclined in his chair and leered.

"You might fool these new nurses, but not me. You'd have to be pretty desperate and have some low self-esteem to fall for your crap."

She snapped up and exited the unit knowing if she stayed it

would only escalate. Her heels clicked down the hallway toward the patient lounge. She opened the door and then slammed it behind her.

"Heather?"

Her head spun. "Tyrell, what are you doing in here?"

His face withered but then a poor attempt at a smile lifted. "Nothing, just taking a break."

"In here, by yourself, during the lunch line?"

He tucked his white cook's shirt in his pants and straightened up.

"What's wrong?" she asked.

"What's always wrong. Jean. She gets under your skin, ya know?"

"Yeah, I know, we all know. What'd she do now?" Heather sat next to Tyrell.

He fixed his eyes on his hands and spoke slowly. "I was carrying the soup for the line. It was heavy, hot, and spilling on my hands. Burning them. Even with the gloves on it was getting underneath. I'm putting it into the hole when Jean storms out. She just went nuts yelling and cursing at me."

"For what? What'd she say?"

"Wanted to know if I checked the temperature, that patients complained the soup was cold so it's my fault. Wanted to know where my hair net was."

"Your head is shaven."

"She cursed, in front of everyone. Told me I was fuckin' incompetent."

"I don't understand how she gets away with this. It's ludicrous. Tyrell you have to go to human resources about her, she's harassing you. You're in a hostile work environment."

"Like they'll believe me over her. Please, you don't get it, I'm nobody. And besides, administration loves her."

Chapter 20

Catherine

Catherine cut through the cafeteria to find an ice bucket for Jean. She removed one from a shelf above the sink and caught site of Victoria and Heather at a small table behind the cash register. Their heads hung low, only inches apart, whispering. Again. She had enough.

Catherine left the ice bucket in Jean's office, glad the troll no longer sat in her massive throne. She marched back into the cafeteria to confront them, but found only Heather standing near a garbage can, sipping the last of the contents in her Styrofoam cup. She approached, heaving in deep breaths, the smell of breakfast sausage still lingered.

"It's bad enough you talk to me like trash but I will not tolerate you talking behind my back."

Heather whipped around. "What are you talking about? Who's talking behind your back?"

"You and Victoria, I saw you."

Heather glanced at the table and then back to Catherine. "What makes you think we're talking about you?"

"Come on, the two of you are always in the corner somewhere whispering. Whenever I approach, you instantly stop."

"And that means we're talking about you?" Heather chucked her cup into the garbage. The wrinkles between her eyes grew heavy.

"It's so obvious. Don't patronage me, I've had enough."

Heather's scowl dissolved and her eyebrows lifted. She bit down on her lower lip as if thinking, then a long, draining huff expelled. "Come with me." She grabbed Catherine's arm and guided her to the table she previously occupied with Victoria.

After a long pause, Heather threw her hair back into a ponytail and arched in. "Catherine, I'm truly sorry–"

"I knew it," she screeched. Heather obviously hated her and now the truth would come out." Her quivering increased and spread to every cell in her body.

"No, no, you don't. Stop! Will you just stop talking? This is very difficult for me. Either listen or I'll leave."

Catherine jerked her head back, her skin still tingling. "Fine, speak."

Heather squeezed her eyes shut and paused for almost a minute. Did she fall asleep?

"I've been sleeping with Dr. Silvatri."

Her words, unexpected and indistinguishable. Catherine sat in silence not knowing what to say. The words forming in her mouth were harsh but she held her tongue waiting for Heather to finish.

Heather's breathing shifted into labored gasps. "I don't know how to explain this to you, it's hard."

"Oh, but you have no problem telling Victoria, is that it?"

"Listen Catherine, I don't have to tell you anything. You going to listen or not?"

Catherine swung from enraged to curious and chose to shut up.

"Look, as much as you think I have this perfect life, I don't. I've been a good wife, no, a great wife for over fifteen years. I appear unhappy when you see me, because inside I'm dying. Every day I struggle, I deserve so much more."

"So cheating's the answer?"

"See, I'm not so perfect now, am I?"

"Is this a joke? This is why you did it, to prove to me that you're not perfect, that you're some badass that refuses to follow rules?"

"Yes Catherine, that's why I decided to cheat on my wonderful husband. To make a point to you."

Heather lurched up to leave but Catherine seized her hand and dragged her back down. "I'm sorry, I didn't mean it. I'm just confused, it makes no sense. You're Catholic, like me."

"What does that have to do with anything? Look, you'll obviously never understand and that's why I didn't tell you and now you'll probably run around the hospital telling everyone. Go ahead, I don't care anymore."

"I would never do that, is that what you think? I thought we were a team but you always make me feel left out." Catherine put her hand to her temple and rubbed. "Look Heather, my life's not perfect either, but cheating? How does that solve anything?"

"It doesn't, but it gives me an escape. An outlet, remember?"

"Gardening is an outlet, not cheating."

"In your pretentious world it is."

"How dare you. You have no idea what my life is like."

"You're right, I don't. I just see this façade of Aldo boots and Coach bags and the fake smile to go with it. Who is Catherine Bordeau, or does she even know?"

"Why do you hate me?"

"Hate you? I can't hate you. It's impossible to hate someone that's not real. You don't even know who you are. You try to impress everyone and make them like you. You appease everyone but yourself. What do *you* like, what do *you* want, what is *your* goal in life? How can I possibly hate someone that doesn't exist? When you figure out who the real Catherine Bordeau is then I'll let you know if I like her or not."

"I hate my life, alright." Tears filled and then plunged from Catherine's eyes. "I hate everything about it, from the time I wake up until the time I go to bed. My only hope is I won't have nightmares when I sleep and maybe those few hours will be wonderful. I have no friends, my kids hate me and I hate Peter. I wish him dead sometimes. Dead. Isn't that horrible?"

Heather stood and gathered a cluster of napkins from the dispenser behind them. "Catherine I'm sorry, I had no idea. You hide everything from us." She handed the napkins to Catherine and put her hand on her shoulder with hesitance. "I'm messed up and tormented as well, and no, this isn't the answer. But you know what? I'm happy. For the first time in a long time I have something to look forward to every day. I come to work, avoid Jean as much as possible, and look for him. I'm surviving."

Catherine wiped her tears and then raised her head up to Heather. For the first time they looked long and hard at each other. "What made it happen? Why'd you do it?"

"Well...it's not the first time."

"Heather, no."

"Listen, you might as well know everything. This is the hardest part for me." Heather took half the stack of napkins.

"Catherine, when I met Lance I was young, seventeen, and he had it all. Good looks, off to college to become a lawyer, drove a

Nissan 300zx, high profile friends and family. At seventeen, that's what it's all about, right? What the hell did I know? I watched my parents struggle financially for years, I didn't want them worrying about my future.

Then, halfway through my first year of college, I met this guy at work. Nicolo. He was only there a short time but the connection was immediate, we became friends instantly. Inseparable. I couldn't wait to go to work every day to see him. I never felt that way with Lance. Never.

I took off from work one Friday because Lance bought tickets for a show in the city. I returned to work Monday to find they fired Nicolo. That was it, he was gone, forever. I had no way of getting in touch with him." Heather paused again, gripping the napkins in her right hand.

"Five years later, I went to happy hour with my friend Brooke. It was March. I remember clearly, because I was finishing my master's degree and was numb from the coursework. And there he was. I didn't recognize him at first, neither of us recognized each other, but we connected. Again. Talked all night. The bond was still there. Well, I wasn't going to let him get away a second time. We exchanged numbers, talked for hours on the phone and well, eventually it just happened."

"What happened?" Catherine asked.

She broadened her eyelids and tilted her head. "It was inevitable I guess, the best year of my life. We proceeded into a torrid love affair that extended the course of the year. We fell in love, deeply. I knew I wanted him, it was always him. I planned to tell Lance that weekend.

Lance took me to dinner Sunday night and the plan was to break up with him then, but Lance had to be Lance and it wasn't a romantic dinner for two. He rented the back room in the restaurant and, as only Lance could do, proposed to me in a way that I could not refuse."

"Oh, Heather."

"We married a year later and– "

"Wait what happened to the guy?"

Heather's eyes flooded now and her hands began to shake. "A year later we married and then I became pregnant a year after that. It was good for Lance, good for his profile. A hotshot lawyer looking to make partner and having that wife and kid by his side. Well, two years after I had Laurel, I became pregnant with Gia. I'm walking through the mall one day in March to get my friend Brooke a baby shower gift and there he was. Five years since I last saw him but I recognized his walk immediately."

"What did he say?"

"I never spoke to him. What would I say? Plus, pregnant and all. I hid or something, I really don't remember. I was ashamed...mortified how I ended it."

"How did you end it?" Catherine's head continued to wave, her mouth wide open.

Heather ignored her question. "So, I had Gia and then five years later on the first day of spring, I decide to take the kids to the beach. Lance and I fought continuously at this point and I needed to get away. On the drive there, I decided I had to leave him, I couldn't fake it anymore. I wasn't in love with him, I never was. He just wanted me around to look good for the firm.

So, I'm entering the boardwalk, the girls run to the sand and Bam! He's right there in front of me with some woman with a big huge rock on her finger. This time he recognized me though. He looked different. Thin and almost sickly, like one of Victoria's terminal cancer patients on 5 North"

"Did you talk? Did you get his number?"

Heather glared at her once again. Catherine, unable to follow the story. "He was with a girl with an engagement ring on her finger. What did you want me to say? It was a horrible, awkward five-minute conversation. I never even looked at the woman. The sun just kept hitting the ring. I felt like she twisted her hand on purpose to blind me. She could have been four feet tall with purple hair and I wouldn't have noticed. I was dumbfounded, sick to my stomach. We couldn't talk at all.

If you can follow this part of the story, Rori is six years younger than Gia. Yes she was an oops, a big one. I dreamed about Nicolo all night after that day on the beach, it was so vivid, so real. He really was there with me. But I woke up realizing it was Lance that I just had sex with. Rori was indeed a surprise and so I couldn't leave Lance then." Heather's fingers circled the pen marks on the table, getting lost in her thoughts. "Five years later– "

"Come on now," Catherine said. This was too much. Every five years? Surely, she was making this up.

"Five years later," Heather shouted, "in March, my two co-workers and I are sitting in Peaz and Chaos and who walks in?"

Catherine gasped, finally following one part of the story. "It was him, that guy with the Mets cap. Oh God Heather, I don't know what to say." Goose bumps flooded her arms. She sat back in her chair and rubbed her hands up and down them. "You got his number though, I saw you, this time you got it."

"Sure I got it. I stared at it all week. Then one night I had another amazing dream about him. We were twenty-four again, he was holding my hand and turned to look at me like he always did. I woke in the middle of the sex part of the dream and found stupid Lance next to me snoring. I got up this time though, and crawled into Laurel's bed. The next morning I came to work and met Silvatri. He made the hair on my skin vibrate."

Catherine laughed but inside, jealousy brewed. She tried to brush it off. "Do you love him?'

"Who, Nicolo?"

"No, Silvatri."

"Silvatri?" Heather shook her head. "No. Just a distraction, I guess. He makes me feel. Feel something anyway, I've been numb for so long."

"Are you leaving Lance?"

"No, I can't. Rori is confused enough with both her siblings attending middle school and she hasn't even started kindergarten yet. She needs some stability. Plus, Lance just made partner, then the car accident...there's never a good time."

"But you're miserable—all the time, every day." Catherine grimaced at her remark. "Sorry."

"No, you're right, I was. But the last few weeks have been uplifting."

"You have been happier. You're even hassling Jean less."

Heather laughed. "I do like taking my anger out on her, though." She took Catherine's hand. "I'm sorry I took it out on you, and I'm sorry you feel your life is horrible too. I guess we have more in common than we thought."

Catherine gave Heather's hand a tight squeeze and a smile erupted. "More than you know."

Chapter 21

Victoria

The article for the *Long Island Perspective Magazine* shook in Victoria's hand. She had submitted it along with photos earlier in the week and now the editor asked to meet with her. Was it that bad?

Before leaving the house, Victoria applied lipstick to brighten her pallid face. All color had drained from it and ran down to her toes.

Ed increased the dent in the couch as reruns of *Cheers* blasted from the TV. He had not spoken to her since she failed to return home that Friday from her conference to cook him dinner. The mouthwatering meal and gorgeous company fogged her memory. More disturbing was that she didn't care.

"I'm meeting with *Long Island Perspective Magazine* now." Silence. "The editor wants to discuss the article with me." Nothing. She didn't bother telling him when she'd be home, tired of always having to update him on her schedule down to the minute. He would spend the weekend on the couch. The idea of friends and hobbies eluded him.

Victoria waited as Pearlie Zelman reviewed the article in front of her. More silence. Doubt soaked into her pores. Perhaps it was not as good as she thought. She found her inspiration though. She pretended Aiden sat beside her as she clicked away on her computer.

The woman read the text closely, evaluating the effectiveness of the piece. She finished, placed the paper down beside her and clasped her hands as if in prayer.

"Victoria," she began, "as an editor, I enjoy publishing things that will actually be read and appreciated. I receive hundreds of articles that simply bore me. It's unusual that I would reach out to someone who wrote an advertorial, but this caught my eye. Although you're just advertising for an event, your writing style is dazzling. Exciting. It made me feel as if I need to run this race. Yes, it's for a good cause, but lately my evening jogs around the neighborhood have been so dull I've been putting them off. After reading this, I think this may be what I need to get myself back into it. A focus, a goal."

Sweltering temperatures engulfed her body. Not a hot flash, not now. "Thank you. I did work hard on it."

"Victoria, do you write other pieces? You're a dietitian, correct?"

"Yes, I am."

"You should consider handing in some pieces on nutrition. We have many articles on general health, even fitness but no one is writing anything specifically on nutritional concerns. Would you be interested?"

Victoria jumped into her car, her fingers unable to turn the ignition. Writing? She never considered this. What exactly had she written? She pulled out a copy of the article and held it up to read. The glorious sunlight sparkled on the page and magnified its excellence. This represented a fine piece of work.

The phone hummed in her pocket book. She snatched it dreading Ed's voice on the other end. Obviously he wanted something. Food? Beer? More white underwear?

The number unfamiliar, she hit the green key. "Hello?"

"Victoria? It's Aiden McLoughlin, from the Cancer Research Center."

Of course she knew who he was. He was all she thought about lately. She dreamt of that salt and pepper hair, spiked and gelled into soft peaks. "Yes of course, how are you?"

"Quite well, and you?"

Victoria sank into the car seat and looped her finger around a clump of hair. His voice fluttered through the phone like the sweet lullabies she sang to Andrew and Sara as children. She managed to block her humble nature and disclosed her meeting with Pearlie Zelman to him. The excitement still pulsed through her core.

"Why, that's wonderful Victoria, you should feel very proud. I expressed to you how incredible you were. You must take her up on her offer, you have a lot to offer this world."

Victoria squirmed at his continued accolades. It has been so long since she received praise for her achievements. Her body tingled under the skirt, too bad he couldn't see for himself.

"Where are you now?" Aiden asked.

"Still sitting in the parking lot."

Aiden chuckled. "Please, join me for lunch, I'd love to celebrate your accomplishment."

Feeling as if she was on autopilot, she agreed.

Aiden sat across from her, twirling the ice in his glass of water with the straw. The cubes jiggled and clinked but his eyes never looked away from hers. The waitress arrived and coffee flowed as did their conversation. No loss of words, no silence. Aiden, a widow of three years, listened intently to Victoria while she shared tales of her thirty years of marriage.

Victoria glanced over her menu unable to decide what to order. Too nervous again to eat but the chicken salad with walnuts, grapes and avocado tempted her.

"So, what is your position at the hospital like, Victoria?"

"I've worked there for over fifteen years. I cover the cancer unit and CCU. I love my floors and the staff but Jean, my boss for the last two years, is condescending and demeaning."

"How is that any way to work? She should be encouraging and supportive, bring out the best in you, use your impressive resources to her benefit."

"She feels there's no one better than her. We're her puppets."

"Does she realize your background? Your achievements and potential? She's wasting talent. Why isn't Ed pushing you to your potential? Does he support your efforts?"

Victoria's neck and ears grew hot. She hid her face before the humiliation surfaced. He continued to inspire her when the waitress returned. Still unable to decide, she let Aiden order first.

"I'll have the chicken salad with walnuts, grapes and avocado, please," he said.

Victoria's pulse accelerated. Too embarrassed to order the

same thing, she chose something from the back corner of the menu.

The waitress returned with their sandwiches and Aiden thankfully turned the conversation away from her hollow job. "You're on the Board of Directors at the Cancer Foundation. How did you venture into that?"

"Almost a year ago, we hired a new dietitian at the hospital. Catherine. It was her first job working in a hospital. She had three children shortly after she married but hadn't worked in years. When she began she was so enthusiastic, passionate. I wanted to feel like that again. About my job, about my life." Her mouth crooked down, as did her head.

Aiden gently placed his hand under her chin and lifted her head to face him. "Why so sad, Victoria? I notice there's always a halting air about you, as if you're afraid to free yourself completely."

"No, not at all. I'm sorry."

"No, really. What's troubling you? I don't like to see you upset, you have so much going for you."

"Really, I'm fine. Just hungry I suppose." She took a large bite out of her roast beef sandwich and then continued her story about how she met Noreen Emberton, the Chair of the Cancer Foundation, at a nutrition networking conference.

"I'm impressed again," he said. "Tell me, when is this 10K race? I think I'd like to join."

"No, really, you don't have to."

"I would love to. You're running too?"

"Me? No, I can't run."

"Why not? We should train together, it would be fun. You never know what you're capable of until you try."

This was happening too fast. The lunch, the compliments, the encouragement. Now training for a race together? Suddenly she felt ill.

Victoria excused herself to the bathroom. Her watch informed her that she had left the magazine interview over an hour and a half ago. She pressed her hands against her stomach, the sandwich laid there like a boulder. What was she doing here? With him? Having lunch with a man she barely knew.

Just grabbing a bite and having a little chat. Yeah, right.

She rinsed her hands and returned to the table.

"I took the liberty of ordering us some dessert." Victoria peered down and saw a blueberry cobbler, her favorite. "I even asked for a small scoop of vanilla ice cream on the side. I hope that's not too much for a dietitian. I thought something with fruit would be appropriate."

"It's wonderful, truly. So thoughtful of you and yes, it's actually one of my favorites." Victoria's cheeks glowed. A silly grin appeared on her face while she focused on Aiden's strong features. She smiled at nothing, smiled at everything. His tongue licked a smidgen of sweet violet crumbles from the corner of his mouth. A morsel of blueberry stuck to his lip and Victoria found her finger wiping it away.

He flinched, as did she. Aiden touched the spot her finger just left. His chest rose and fell with each quickened breath. He leaned back as if to protect her from his thoughts.

"Thank you," he said. "How silly I must have looked with that on my face."

"No, actually you looked kind of cute." Victoria gasped. What was she saying? She was acting like a child, a schoolgirl in a playground. She looked down at the dessert.

Aiden slanted toward her. His mouth separated, as if to speak, then closed. He grasped his fork instead and pierced the cobbler. Victoria's fork clinked the bottom of the plate a moment later. Their utensils connected, intertwined, and Aiden immediately let go, dropping his fork on the plate. Victoria's head shot up and the two examined each other, considering, suggesting, exposing.

Aiden accompanied Victoria to her car and then held the door for her to step in. She wanted to speak, say something witty, something as incredible as the way he made her feel during the past two hours. But her car door slammed shut, the sound denoted the inevitable end of their meeting. Victoria opened her window to provide one last good-bye.

"You know Victoria, if you weren't married, I would have loved to take you out on a real date."

Chapter 22

Heather

At one o'clock on Saturday, Heather left work on her lunch hour and drove to Dr. Silvatri's office, a quick five-minute drive from the hospital. She eased open the main door, scanned the patient's waiting room along with the receptionist area, but found both vacant. The knob on the door leading into the examination rooms rotated in her grasp and she peeked in.

After waiting an additional minute, she slipped into the corridor and inched her way down the hall. Had she made a mistake? He told her one o'clock. Was it today? Or Sunday? Would someone see her sneaking in?

Heather hesitated calling his name in case any employees lingered behind. She tiptoed down the hallway and with each glance into the unoccupied exam rooms, the shakiness in her limbs increased. Disinfectant and alcohol prep pads filled her nose, eliminating the sweet smell of her banana-cream body lotion. The deserted office, both eerie and unsettling, urged her to turn back.

She reached the final door and paused, took a deep breath and then slid her right foot ahead one last step. Heather arched her body forward inch by inch, and peered into the doorway. There, sat Silvatri, behind his desk with his feet propped on top, hands folded behind his head, and a smile extending clear across his face.

She shook her head. "You think you're funny? You heard me come in, didn't you?"

Silvatri summoned Heather to him with the curving of his finger.

She sauntered over to him and then he unlocked his legs from his desk and entwined them around her instead. She teetered from his restraint but only until he bolted up, grasped her head and drew it into him, parting her mouth with more intensity than before.

His hands clutched her shirt and freed the top button, then another. It was off and thrown to the floor in a wink. He stepped back, viewed her black lace bra with pink embroidery and the metallic thread weaved through it. His hands traveled from her waist and then under the lace on one side, while his mouth joined in, finding the soft flesh on the other.

Silvatri stopped, examined his desk, and then launched an immediate removal of his papers, frames, and books while Heather removed her red skirt. He twisted back and jarred to a halt. She fidgeted with the elastic on the top of her thigh highs attempting to remove them.

He lunged at Heather, prevented her from removing them and then ran his fingers across her thong, brushing the scallop-laced fringe that hung over the band. Silvatri's breath heaved and his eyes shut tight, then unlocked to reveal cannons that sparked fire, thirst and his unquenchable appetite.

He grasped her shoulders, crushing them and smashed his lips onto hers, pushing Heather back with his mouth until she lay across his desk. His door remained wide-open. The hallway one left ajar as well. Her heart thundered knowing anyone could enter and hear them, see them, naked upon his desk.

Her bra and thong ripped from her, only the thigh highs remained. He unzipped his pants and lowered them to his knees. She had yet to see him completely naked, only his upper thighs revealed themselves to her each time. Heather wanted to see his perfect chest, his muscular stomach, his broad shoulders. His ass.

Silvatri stood on one side of the desk and tugged her body close to the edge so he could enter. She closed her eyes as he slid himself in. He hammered away and she lifted her legs up and rested them on his shoulders.

Thoughts waved in and out of her mind. The vision of her black blouse tossed to the ground on a stack of files. His eager eyes as he ripped off the thong with such yearning. The warmth of his mouth. The wide-open door and the thought of a misguided patient wandering in. The obvious bruises on her back she would acquire from the hard desk.

He pumped harder and moved his hands to her shoulders pushing her into him. She glided with him in sync – the perfect fit.

Heather enjoyed her escape. Although only sporadic moments like this existed, it became her diversion, lasting with her until their next encounter. Arguments with Lance and Jean became mere annoyances and she knew in the end she'd won. Let them yell, let them harass her. She discovered an amazing reward that the two of them could never take away from her.

He finished, bounced himself inside several more times, and let out the usual howl. Heather adored his sounds and roars. Lance's silent romps made Heather feel like she was alone in the room, having sex with the mattress.

Silvatri pulled out and watched Heather lie there, unable to catch her breath. He hoisted up his pants and jerked his belt tight across his hips. He took a step back, sloped into the wall, brought his thumb up and dragged it across his lower lip. His eyes squinted, and he examined her, naked and arranged on his desk. Studied her as his breath continued to surge.

She could not move, could not get up, could not stop shaking. Silvatri pounded his fist into the wall and let out a grunt. He hobbled over and skimmed the bottom of his lip against hers. His tongue swept inside one final time. "I could fuck you all day, Heather."

He boosted her up, gathered her belongings and handed them to her. The pile of clothes, overwhelming. Unable to figure out which direction the thong went, her stockings hung low, one by the calf, the other by the knee, and buttoning her shirt was impossible with trembling hands.

As she dressed, he sat in his chair inspecting her, his feet back on the desk, hands clasped behind his head. A glint of arrogance in his guise. His blue eyes ogled her, making her feel prized.

She fastened her last button, glad she completed the ordeal. He lurched out of his chair and kneeled before her. Silvatri lifted her skirt, grabbed her thigh and dug his teeth in. He wrapped his arms around her legs and pulled her down on the rug with him.

He kissed her feverishly, and unbuttoned her shirt again.

Chapter 23

Catherine

Catherine completed meal rounds on her floor and then called the diet clerks with multiple food preferences. She knew it annoyed them and increased their workload but the patients came first. Obtaining long lists of food requests made her feel wanted and appreciated.

She hung up the phone and her heart fluttered. The charming and handsome Dr. Mangle entered the unit. Everyone else had vacated the nurse's station and the thought of being alone with him excited her. Would he finally acknowledge her? Would today be the day? But then claustrophobia consumed her. Please, someone drift in to alleviate the pressure. What would she talk about, her boring life compared to his glorious one? She loved hearing him speak about the wild parties at his home and vacations abroad.

He snatched a chart from the rack and Catherine thought his eyes penetrated hers. She wished they did, but he spent all his free time with prettier nurses, ones with more personality. What did she have to offer him?

All the doctors ignored Catherine.

Why couldn't someone like Dr. Mangle see her, was she that revolting? Sure three children changed the way she dressed, her hairstyle dull yet practical, but inside she wanted to be noticed. She wanted to be one of the women he spoke to, one he would sit next to and ask questions. She even had one of Colton's jokes ready for him, if he ever did.

"And how are you today?" He placed his hand on her shoulder.

Did he just touch her? Catherine absorbed Dr. Mangle's

warmth into her skin, arousing her. Feeling a man's touch on her body again caused her to melt into the chair. The last time she had sex was two years ago. It couldn't be the end of her sex life, could it?

Initially, Heather's infidelity angered Catherine. Her hero was a tramp, a sinner. The perfect wife and mother cheating on her husband.

But lately, Heather's sex stories made her jealous. Even with the infidelity, Heather still had the perfect life. She had it all. The detailed accounts of her sex with Silvatri reminded Catherine of all the things Peter asked her to do over the years. Things she refused because of her inhibited nature. Is that why he acted so cold to her lately?

She scurried to the bathroom, leaving Dr. Mangle, never speaking a word. What a loser. Was it so hard to say hello?

Her pathetic image in the mirror glared back. Her skirt practically grazed the tile floor, her blouse, buttoned all the way to the top revealed only her pale, dry neck. The thick, heavy lab coat concealed any shred of clothing anyway.

Catherine tucked the strands of hair back under her ponytail. Her pale lips craved some color, or, perhaps the taste of another's lips. What was she thinking!

She left the bathroom and found Dr. Mangle had left. She knew he wouldn't be interested in her. Heather nailed it on the head. Who was Catherine anyway? A fake.

"I thought I scared you away," Dr. Mangle asked.

Catherine jerked her head around. His hand rested on the back of her chair.

"No, I just needed to pop on over to the ladies room." She tried to act cool.

"I'm glad you returned." He grasped her hand, kissing the top. Lightheaded, Catherine looked away. She had seen him do that to others but only dreamed that one day it could be her.

"I'm not offending you, am I?"

"No, not at all." Offending her? Who would be offended? Heat rose up her thighs. She no longer knew what to say.

"You're very quiet, I'm not sure how to read you."

She smoothed down her white skirt and broke eye contact. She was blowing it. Her parched throat tightened. What was Colton's joke again? "I'm sorry, I suppose I was deep in thought."

"Oh? I'd like to hear those thoughts...Catherine."

He knew her name? What did he know about her? "I was

thinking about my patients."

Dr. Mangle let out a hoot. "Your patients? You're so innocent, aren't you now?"

"No, not at all. I mean, I'm not so innocent."

"Really? What do you do that's not so...innocent, Catherine?" He bent to the side, rested his elbow on the counter, thumb under his chin, and leered at her.

What was she doing? This was wrong. She looked away and shuffled the papers in front of her.

"I'm sorry," he said. "Let me start over. I believe the other day I heard you talking about your daughter, something about a dance recital coming up I believe?"

Catherine relaxed and spoke about Emily. The conversation moved effortlessly to her boys and he shared details about his two sons, both married now. Obviously, he had been joking, teasing her, and she took it personally. She needed to calm down and stop being so prudish.

"You're really amusing Catherine. When you're not too busy being shy." He threw a wink at her and then grazed her fingers with his. His touch, slow and reassuring, shot tiny waves up her hand and throughout her body.

She pretended to scratch the back of her neck and casually removed her beaded crystal hairpin from her hair, releasing her dirty blonde tresses.

"Beautiful. Simply beautiful, Catherine."

Catherine soared home. Disorientation, mixed with euphoria, whirled in a blender. He spoke to her. Actually had a conversation with her for over fifteen minutes. Was she dreaming? No. She played it over in her mind countless times today. He touched her too. Her shoulder, her fingers, even kissed her hand.

Her hand floated in front of the steering wheel and she could almost see his kiss on it. Why the sudden interest in her? Her fault, of course. Her shy nature, stiff and unapproachable. But he said she was amusing. Was she? What had she said? The conversation blurred and swelled repeatedly.

Wait. This was immoral. No, unethical. She should not be thinking this way about another man. What came over her? She would go to confession after work tomorrow, clear her conscience, purge this foolishness from her system.

Catherine said good-bye to her babysitter Arie, but as the door inched toward closure, Arie pushed back in. "I'm sorry, I forgot to tell you, Peter called." She giggled like the teenager she was. "He's eating dinner with, I think the guys from work. Said not to cook for him. Oh, and not to wait up either, he'd probably be late. Good-bye again."

Chapter 24

Victoria

Over the course of two weeks, Victoria spent a large part of her time speaking to Aiden on the phone. They never ran out of things to discuss and his intelligence sent a needed jolt to her brain, more than her work at the Cancer Foundation ever had.

She hung up the phone after another striking conversation and sauntered out of the doctor's dictation room into the hallway. She floated on air, right into Jean's path.

"Do you have a problem answering my page?" she demanded.

"I'm sorry, I didn't hear it."

"Obviously not. What were you doing in there anyway?" Jean yanked open the door to the deserted four-by-eight quarters and then reeled back to Victoria, perplexed.

There was no reason for Victoria to be in there and she froze, unable to formulate an answer.

"Well? Do I have to shake it out of you?"

A doctor approached and slid beside Victoria. "I'm sorry to interrupt, Victoria, but I just wanted to thank you for that advice you gave for Mrs. Randazzo. It worked like a charm. Her mouth sores from the radiation are remarkably better."

Jean flung her head back and smiled like an old withered actress whose fans had long forgotten her. The doctor squinted at her foolishness and marched away.

Victoria remembered everything Aiden taught her about Jean's insolence and felt his strength within her. She stood tall and folded her arms in front of her. "Is there something you wanted, Jean? You said you paged me several times, it must be rather important."

Jean scowled, not prepared to handle Victoria's direct nature. Victoria widened her eyes, pressuring Jean further.

Jean cleared her throat and glanced down at Victoria's tightly folded arms. "Never mind, I'll ask Catherine. She'll be more accommodating."

****

Victoria woke the following morning to an empty bed. She had posted flyers around the hospital advertising Ed as a handy man. It lured a few bites. A hot, leisurely shower in a deserted house relaxed her and set the tone for her peaceful Saturday. She read a few articles in the *New York Times* while eating her warm oatmeal with juicy, succulent raspberries, brilliantly crimson, dripping with their sweet flavor.

And stared at her phone, contemplating the call.

With Ed at work and her children on their way to the beach, the emptiness in the house persuaded her to dial his number. Would she wake him?

"Hello?" Aiden answered.

"Good morning."

"Now this is a pleasant surprise."

"I didn't wake you, did I?"

"Wake me? I've been in the office since seven."

"I'm sorry, I didn't mean to disturb you."

"You, Victoria, are the highlight of my day so far, and will probably continue to be.

Victoria closed her eyes and raised her fist to her forehead, biting down hard on her lip.

"Hello? Are you still there?" he asked.

"Yes, sorry, I...was just taking a sip of my tea."

"I'm having some tea myself. It'd be nice if we were drinking it together."

"If I was a scientist maybe we could be."

"Nonsense, you could come here. My staff is off and I'm just finishing up a project."

"No one else is in the lab?"

"There's a few around. Many experiments are conducted around the clock and it wouldn't be unheard of for someone to be here at 2 a.m. on a Saturday. It's never deserted."

"Too bad." Victoria snapped her mouth shut as soon as the words flew out. She paced back and forth in the kitchen and then ran out the back door. Silence overtook both ends of the phone. Idiot.

"Victoria," he paused. "Would you like a tour of the laboratory, personally led by me?"

"A tour? Well, yes, I'd love to see where you work, it sounds exciting." And completely wrong. What was she doing? She glanced back at Ed's seat cushion in the old couch. Cavernous and sunken from his never departing rear-end.

Victoria parked in the spot closest to the north end of the lab and strolled passed the gardens. The impatiens had grown significantly over the past month. She hiked up the sixteen stairs, counting as she climbed and when her foot reached the last one, an image blocked her way. Green eyes, matching the immaculate lawn surrounding the buildings, gazed down at her.

Aiden's silver-blue button down shirt hung out of his pants and several buttons avoided their holes. His dark blue jeans wrapped his legs perfectly. He held out his hand and helped her up the last step. His touch, warm and welcoming.

"Good morning, Miss Victoria. Welcome back to SandCrest Laboratories, may I begin your tour? I want to make sure you receive every penny's worth."

Aiden launched the tour by guiding Victoria around the various research rooms, laboratories and even the Genome center. He pointed to several areas of importance while Victoria absorbed his words.

"We try to determine the best methods to fight certain cancers based on its genomic profile," he began. "Even now it's altering cancer treatment."

He led her past the Double Helix Gift Shop, explained the history of the artwork covering the walls and provided a brief description on the statues gracing the hallways.

They turned the corner and landed in front of the auditorium where they first met. "Your presentation that day...woke me up," he said.

She dispensed a blank look and considered his words. Then he gave a wink, and her blood pumped hard through her veins. Victoria's focus skipped around the room pretending to observe the wood beams that encompassed the ceiling, but he noticed her unease.

"You know, nutrition truly is a vital part of genetics," Aiden said. "Environmental factors like nutrition imprint on our genes. This is important because it extends even prior to conception, back several generations." He stepped toward the back of the building. "Come, have you seen the grounds in the back of the lab?"

"No, I didn't realize there were any."

Aidan pushed open the wooden doors to reveal lush gardens and flourishing trees enveloped by the shimmering Long Island Sound. Sailboats floated by and birds soared overhead. The water sparkled and twinkled with its cobalt blue reflection but as she continued to stare, it changed to the color of gloom.

Victoria's spirit abandoned her each time she inched near happiness, as if forbidden to attain it. She looked away from the lake and toward an isolated bench.

Was her father wrong? Was it impossible to be that perfect, for everything to align and never have any flawed moments? She tried. Day after day. Made herself the best person she could be. Well rounded, intelligent, successful. Then what was missing? Why the despair? Where was the incentive and where was her reward?

"Are you okay, Victoria? You always look so sad when I see you. I feel it's me. Am I upsetting you in any way?"

"No, not at all, I'm sorry." *Don't let him see. Walk away.*

Even Heather had turned into a fiery ball of cheerfulness. A little too happy now. Giggling like a toddler, skipping down the hospital's hallways, dancing in the middle of cafeteria last week. Victoria even caught her hiding a smirk under a strand of hair during Jean's tirade in their meeting on Monday. Why couldn't she have that?

Victoria achieved more in her career than she did, yet Heather's optimism and downright exuberance far exceeded Victoria's. Still a kid at heart, perhaps. Maybe that's what was missing. Stop with the perfection and start having fun? Live a little, take some chances, abandon your fears?

Her eyes filled with tears but she staggered to her right to avoid Aiden. His hand locked on her shoulder and twirled her around. She kept her head down but he lifted her chin with his finger. A lone tear escaped and struck her cheek.

"I don't like to see you like this, Victoria. I wish I could take your sadness away. What is it? Please."

She could not speak, for the tears would only tumble faster. She could not show her weakness. A complete failure. What was wrong with her?

His gaze became one of concern and he drew her into his chest. His embrace, the closeness, feeling his hard chest upon hers plugged the flow of tears instantly. Her eyes fluttered as if fainting and she tipped her head the slightest degree. Aiden's lips glided onto hers and lay there, motionless, but she could feel their warmth.

Their lips blended and mixed, swirling and rolling. Aiden glided his finger over her eyelid and down her cheekbone as if to wipe the tear, and all her problems away. A breeze elevated wisps of hair onto her face, tickling her skin, arousing, encouraging, fueling. Invigorated, she was recharged.

Chapter 25

Heather

Gia decided to celebrate her birthday during the summer this year so she could invite her camp friends and because she was fed up with the cold weather that lingered on her April birthday. Leave it to Gia to change the date of her birthday.

This year, she opted for a giant mermaid festival in their backyard. Heather ran to the stores on her lunch hour, buying various materials to create a mermaid lagoon. She stayed up late creating games like mermaid races where guests covered their legs in plastic bags. She drew three mermaids on a large piece of plywood with the heads cut out for the guests to take pictures behind. Their goodie-bags displayed ocean themes they could color while waiting for other guests to arrive. She decorated a beach scene on the cake. The seashell invitations were hand written and she stuffed the mermaid piñata with an abundance of chocolates.

Heather stayed awake until 1 a.m. preparing food for the adults and children. She woke early to clean the house and decorate the backyard. By the time the guests arrived, Heather's eyes refused to focus and exhaustion roughened her words. The weather—a humid ninety-five degree day.

Children whizzed by her during the scavenger hunt and parents asked for everything from directions to the bathroom, to where they could change their baby's diaper, to if she had any more cups and some even attempted to have a conversation with her. She made more sherbet punch and overheard one small child tell their mother they were hungry.

Heather searched for Lance who had slinked into the garage

when the first doorbell rang. She made her way to the garage and found him with the four friends he invited, boasting about his recent promotion. "Can you help me with the food now?" A touch of sarcasm escaped her mouth as she pinned her sweat-drenched hair into a high ponytail.

She returned to the backyard in time to see a girl with long black hair knock a stack of napkins onto the grass. A stray breeze tossed them throughout the lawn, no one bothered to pick any of them up. Her parents perched themselves in the corner, chatting up a storm to their relatives. Victoria and Catherine were unable to attend due to work and a family wedding.

Heather reached down leaping from one airborne napkin to the next when Lance approached from behind. "What does everyone want to eat?"

"Hamburgers and hot dogs, that's all I bought, I'm exhausted." An orphaned napkin lifted and hovered in between them.

"Can you give me a list as to how many of each? How the hell am I supposed to know?" He bolted back to the garage as another mother approached. At least someone would help her.

"Hi," she began, "do you have any ibuprofen? I have a terrible headache." Her fake eyelashes blinked, her Coach bag hung from her wrist.

"Sure, come with me." Heather trekked into the house, found the bottle and dispensed two pills into her hand. Cold water from the refrigerator filled the glass a few inches and then she handed it to her. The woman lobbed it back like a shot of scotch and then dumped it on the counter without thanking Heather. Lance burst in behind the woman as she sauntered away.

"Where's my list? You ask me to cook and then don't even help me. There's gratitude for ya. Do you want me to cook or not?"

"Why don't *you* ask everyone what they want, I'm a little busy. "

"Doing what? Drinking a glass of cold water while I sweat? Get me the list or I'm not cooking." He strutted back to the garage again.

A toddler waddled into the kitchen with his pants around his ankles. "Can you help me wipe?"

"I don't do boys," she said.

Heather cleared the tables after lunch and tied the black lawn bag that overflowed on the deck. Gia tapped her mom on the shoulder and asked if they could do the piñata. "Let me just bring this bag to the curb, honey, give me a minute." She carried the heavy bag to the front without letting it to drag on the floor.

She scurried back up the driveway and tried to remember where she had left the piñata. Lance's friends gawked at her. The five of them watched her haul that freakin' bag down their extensive driveway and not one of them got off their asses to help. Low chuckles erupted behind her.

There was something seriously wrong with her. When did she become his bitch? She spent the past three hours busting her ass for their daughter's birthday. Why did she put up with this? Heather retained all her strength not to cause a scene, not in front of Gia, it was her day.

She snatched the stupid piñata, summoned the ungrateful guests to the front of the house, and then tossed the damn rope over the town's oak tree.

Heather gritted her teeth and yanked on the rope. The giant mermaid head shot up too quickly and smashed into a high branch. The children watched in horror as the mermaids smiling faced scraped and tore, knocking a small dead branch to the ground.

"Oops, a little too high," Heather said. A deranged, psychopathic cackle spewed from between her teeth.

She huffed out a growling breath, clenched her fists around the rope and then pivoted, greeting the children with a perfectly fake smile. Let the smashing begin.

****

"Want to go rock climbing with us?"

Heather turned towards the familiar voice. Silvatri and his partner Richard hovered like restless vultures. "I don't know how." Not to mention she was afraid of heights. The roller coaster rides her cousins forced her on when she was younger left their mark. She always dodged the portable rock climbing set-ups at carnivals and stuck to the games instead.

"It's easy, I'll show you." His eyebrows lowered mischievously.

That didn't help. Silvatri and Richard had climbed together for almost a year now.

But the limited summer days in New York would soon be over and she needed relief from her domestic prison.

Monday veered into Thursday before Heather had time to

think this through. She made sure the girls were in their pajamas before she left them with Lance, knowing he'd give them a brusque order to get in bed without so much as removing his ass from the couch.

The growl of the Jeep's engine caused her fluttering heart to pound into her ribcage and compress her lungs. Shallow breaths through her nose were all she could manage. Chest pain. Can't breathe. A heart attack for sure. No, no, ridiculous. She wanted to kill those cousins of hers. Giant roller coasters, ones that fell straight down thousands of feet, okay maybe not thousands but hundreds. Ones that went backward, upside down.

The Great Adventure trip that Nicolo had planned to take her on popped into her head. The one they never went on. She would do this for him.

Heather pulled into the parking lot facing the rock climbing facility and her jaw plunged. She beheld two transparent doors, at least fifteen feet high and twelve feet wide, which provided her with full view of the place. Grey pillars of manmade rock soared thirty feet into the air, with additional full-length walls surrounding them. The chunks of rock the climbers gripped came in a variety of colors. Fluorescent strips of tape hung underneath each piece creating a rainbow of fear.

Nine thousand square feet of climbing loomed before her. Too large for air conditioning, they warned her about the muggy, stifling conditions. She had raked through piles of gym clothes and hopefully what she chose sufficed.

Athletic, muscular, yet slim patrons, the majority of which were men, hugged the walls. They dressed alike, each in monochrome T-shirts, beige or grey cropped soft-shell pants with cargo pockets. They had what appeared to be fanny packs around their waists, all of them in little elf shoes. The outfit she chose surfaced in her head. Shit. What a moron. What was she thinking?

Silvatri and Richard greeted Heather when she entered the overwhelming playground, and directed her to the front desk where she rented a harness and shoes. She stalled removing her jacket as long as possible, but after ten minutes of harness fastening and shoe strapping, their patience cracked.

Heather reluctantly stripped off her jacket and revealed her hot-pink spaghetti-strap tank top and tiny purple shorts. Shorts that her butt would clearly fall out of.

The two of them flung back in unison. They glanced at each

other, then back at her. Their smiles twisted into wicked grins both trying to look elsewhere. Her eyes shot over to one of the only woman. She wore baggy black sweat pants and an army-green T-shirt. She slipped, fell a few feet and hung there swinging awkwardly from the rope. She squealed like a teenage girl and drew irritated glances her way. Definitely not a regular.

They ambled over to a center wall and then Heather watched Richard climb the towering structure with ease. Her knees quivered and she shifted her weight between both legs to hide it.

"There are different levels of difficulty," Silvatri began. "The numbers on the tape tell you the degree. Different grades, therefore different routes. 5.0 is the easiest, although they don't start that low here. The lowest I've seen I believe it 5.3, the highest about 5.15. The colors let you know which route to take, which holds to touch. You can only touch those colors."

Richard climbed to the top and then slapped the uppermost part of the wall. He climbed well, but struggled on a few holds. He was climbing a 5.8.

The two of them switched places and Silvatri climbed the same wall. He quickly reached the top and then pumped his fist in contentment, a pretentious smile burned on his face. Heather knew she was next and suddenly wanted to fake an illness. She glanced around at other climbers doing equal climbs, if not harder.

Clambering up a loser 5.3, everyone pointing and laughing at her, put her in full panic mode. The woman in the black sweat pants continued to wail like a child. That would be her. She couldn't make a fool of herself in front of Silvatri. If these rock-climbing excursions worked out, she could spend more time with him. Lately, that's all she wanted. He also promised a romp in her Jeep when the night was over.

When Silvatri fed the rope through her harness, her heart exploded. "Are you okay?" he asked.

"Just nervous," she peered into his eyes for reassurance.

"You must do the things you fear the most," Silvatri said. "Give up what's weighing you down."

The message stung her.

He gave a tug on the rope and said, "Climb on."

"Which one?" Heather scanned the array of colors.

"Don't worry about the colors for now, just go."

She grabbed the first hold with her right hand, glanced around, placed her foot on the largest foothold she could find and pulled herself up. She reached up with her left hand and continued to climb, careful not to slip like the sweatpants lady. One by one, disregarding the colors, the height, the ground, she focused on each grasp, and everything around her faded. The music and the conversations muted. Alone, free, strong, her muscles assisted her.

Heather reached the top and then peered down.

"Slap it," Silvatri said.

She slapped the top and relaxed. When she landed, Silvatri high-fived her and Richard stood behind him smiling.

"Alright," Silvatri said, "now let's do a real climb."

"Now?" she squealed like a mouse. "But I just went, it's his turn."

"Nope, you got here late. You're a climb behind us. Plus that wasn't really a climb." Silvatri grabbed the belay device from her waist and yanked her to the left. He pointed to an orange strip of tape. It was a 5.5.

"I can't do that." She stepped back but he tugged at her again.

"Sure you can. You're capable of much more than you think. Climb on."

She floundered over to the wall with the small orange pieces of tape. The first finger hold was as small as a quarter.

"It's still a beginner wall but on the high end," he continued. "5.6 starts the intermediate level."

She reached up with her right hand following the same routine that previously worked. She stepped onto a tilted foothold as her elf shoe slid off, then counted to three and hoisted herself up. She glimpsed back and forth at the available orange fragments and focused on the climb. Contemplations of her next move absorbed her thoughts. Halfway up, her palms filled with sweat and fingers slid off the slimy holds. She looked underneath her nails.

"That's a combination of dirt, sweat and chalk," Richard screamed up to her. "Gross, huh?"

"Don't worry about that," Silvatri cupped his hands over his mouth. "We'll give you chalk the next time you go up. For now, wipe your hands on your pants, I mean shorts, if you can find them," Silvatri snickered.

Both remarks brought fear back, her clear thinking gone. Silvatri was probably eyeing her ass and planning their late night activity. Her foot tumbled off another rock and sweat poured out. The higher she climbed the warmer it became and the lack of cool, clean air suffocated her.

Sweat drizzled down her face and neck, wet hair clung to it, mascara melted and smeared. Her forearms burned and she shook them wondering where all her strength went. Slimy chalk jammed under her nails and she covered her purple shorts in the muck, but a smile erupted when she stepped on that final foothold.

Heather reached the top, sensed the thumping from beneath her ribs. She whacked her slick hand over the dusty top ledge and then collapsed, threw her arms clumsily overhead, and moaned from the relief.

Silvatri loosened his grip and lowered her down, providing her with a little extra slack. She reached the ground and leaped into the air not allowing him to undo the rope from her harness.

"I did a 5.5!"

"The difference between fear and excitement is in your mind," Silvatri said.

A sudden iciness hit her core. It wasn't the first time someone had said that to her, but it had been so long since she heard it. She pushed it out of her head and waited impatiently for the rope to be untied. He freed her and she soared off as if still in the sky. She glanced back to the top of the climb in amazement. "It always looks impossible and then, you do it."

She spent the rest of the night learning techniques and completed 5.5's and even a 5.6. It fascinated her. She conquered one of her fears. But a greater one still loomed.

Chapter 26

Catherine

Catherine's block party brought anxiety instead of joy. She spent the morning preparing cranberry oatmeal cookies, a strawberry chiffon cake and homemade fruit ice pops. Her afternoon spent assembling tomato, mozzarella and basil skewers, black bean edamame burgers, shrimp spring rolls and prosciutto-wrapped mangos with gorgonzola cheese. Bentley and Colton played video games, Emily watched Lilo & Stitch for the hundredth time.

At 4:30, Peter took off to the beverage store to buy beer and ice. Her neighbors carried tables and chairs to the street and arranged them on the left side of the three gas grills.

Heather arrived with her girls and Emily ran over to her new playmates, hugging little Rori. Heather held out a platter of brownies and a bowl of quinoa salad. Lance, not in attendance.

"Don't ask," she said pushing the brownies at her. "Where should I put the quinoa salad?"

Catherine took the tinfoil off the bowl, the powerful scent of cumin and cilantro struck her. "Mmm, this smells delicious. It must have taken forever to prepare."

"Nah, just threw everything in the bowl and mixed it up."

Catherine's face tightened thinking of the amount of time it took her to cook today.

She placed the silken brownies next to her dry oatmeal cookies noticing how chewy and moist they looked. "Wow, so yummy." Catherine faked her enthusiasm. Jealousy brewed again.

"I had Laurel make those this afternoon."

"She cooks? You let her use the oven?"

"She's twelve." Heather twisted her face this time. "One Saturday when I worked, Lance left her home alone while he ran to the bank with Gia and Rori. She decided to cook scrambled eggs and toast. She was nine."

"Are you serious?" I would never allow Bentley or Colton to cook."

"We didn't allow her. She just took it upon herself to do it without asking." Heather shook her head at Laurel who hid her face. "You should teach the boys to cook, otherwise they'll make their wives do everything while they sit on the couch and watch the Giants game."

The boys could never cook. How ridiculous.

Catherine excused herself and brought the appetizers outside. She glanced around hoping someone would see her creations but the other mothers were too busy playing hopscotch and jumping rope with their children.

Bobby set up the water pistol game and aligned ping-pong balls on top of golf tees. Stephanie arranged two-liter soda bottles for the bowling game. Steve carried two tricycles and a pair of big wheels in his hands and grouped them with the other small bikes.

"It looks amazing Catherine," Heather appeared from behind, "but..."

"But what? What now?"

"It's just that it's a block party. This would be great for...a wedding."

Catherine compared her display with the others: Cole slaw, pasta salad, cheap frozen hors d'oeuvres and some cheese and cracker platters. The fathers operated the barbeques and tossed burgers and hot dogs on the grill. "I just wanted to make something special."

"How much time did you spend with your kids today?"

"Kids? Are you kidding? I woke up at six to start cooking. I just finished now."

"The whole point of block parties is to have fun and get to know your neighbors. Come, it's time to have fun." Heather seized Catherine's hand.

They proceeded down the block amongst children blowing bubbles, singing on the karaoke machine, and riding their bikes. Her neighbors piled their plates with food and the DJ orchestrated games with various props. Many of the games involved children against their parents. Heather grabbed Catherine's arm again and dragged her over to the center.

"No, I can't." Her skin tightened, suffocated her, then her muscles loosened as if transformed into a rag doll. Visions of her entire third grade class pelting her with dodge balls resurfaced.

"Why not?"

"I don't know how."

Heather laughed. "You'll learn."

Bentley and Colton put down their football and strolled over to the sidelines to watch their mother toss a grapefruit back and forth with Emily. Catherine tried hard not to drop it, for fear her neighbors would laugh.

On the last toss, Emily flung it too high. It missed Catherine completely and rolled under a red tricycle. Catherine did the walk of shame and hurried to the curb. Were they laughing at her? She bent to retrieve the grapefruit but a hand emerged, passing it to her. It was Bentley.

He smiled at his mom. Her dormant heart unearthed, not used to his kind gesture. She hesitated, not sure what to do, and he turned and walked away.

"You're next," she shouted, attempting to make up for her dillydallying.

Colton and Emily giggled when Bentley and Catherine raced their tricycles down the crowded street. Catherine's sandals with their little heels could not compete with the other parent's sneakers. Why had she worn these?

When Colton and Catherine ran through various obstacle courses, Bentley jumped up and down on the sidelines and cheered. Emily waved maracas and blew forcefully through a plastic whistle, piercing her ears. Heather tossed a subtle wink.

After almost two hours of games, the DJ switched to Top 40 dance tunes. Catherine appeared from within the crowd, drenched but smiling. "I hate you," Catherine smirked.

"No you don't. This is what life's about." Heather put her arm around Catherine's sweaty beige T-shirt. "Your kids will remember this, not your Gouda and brussels sprout finger sandwiches."

"They're not—"

"Eh, eh, don't ruin the moment." They wandered down the block stopping to get water. "Where's Peter? I haven't seen him all night. He should be here playing these games."

Catherine had not seen Peter since he left to buy ice. Unease filled her mind. Had he returned? Was the trip to buy ice another excuse to escape?

She cut through the tables of scattered food, passed the DJ, and jetted around the karaoke machine. Smoke from the barbecue obscured her vision and consumed her throat. She approached a group of parents lounging in a circle of folding chairs with enormous margarita glasses in their hands and asked if anyone spotted Peter, but no one had.

John and Terry sang, "You're the One that I Want" into the karaoke machine's microphone. Teenagers bopped to the DJ's tunes reminding Catherine of her senior year in college when Peter and her boogied at dorm parties. The spicy chicken she ate earlier found its way back into her throat.

On her final stroll to the end of the block, chatter and laughter erupted from her neighbor's backyard. She unlocked the gate and crept past the bursting marigolds. Several guests surrounded the inground pool.

Peter bounced off the diving board, tucked into a cannon ball and his splash drenched Catherine's peach Capri pants. She flicked her palms to release the spray.

"Peter, you got me wet!"

He propelled his arm deep into the water, legs pounded away until he reached the other side.

"Are you going to spend any time with me?" she demanded.

He spun back around, treaded water with slow calculated strokes, while disgust poured from his eyes.

Catherine scuttled away. She bit into her nail and ripped it down too far. Blood gushed from the corner.

What happened to them over the years? They used to enjoy each other's company. She couldn't wait for him to return home from work each day. Didn't he care about her anymore? What was wrong with her?

She joined the cluster of families and found Heather teaching their six children a lesson in hula hooping. Catherine stood a few feet away from Bentley.

Bentley chuckled at Heather's antics but then looked up at his mom. "You try."

"I haven't done that since I was your age."

He reached down and handed her a green hoop. Heather winked and nodded.

Catherine picked up the hula-hoop. "Only if you do it with me."

"No way, that's for girls."

Heather continued to twirl her blue hoop around her hips but her eyes caught Bentleys. "Uh oh, I don't think Bentley knows how."

"I do too!"

"Then let's see."

Catherine and Bentley picked up a hoop and both tried repeatedly to keep it up longer than five or six swirls. Colton twirled one too, but it liked the asphalt below him more than his waist. Emily used hers as a jump rope and soon the four of them fell to the ground exhausted.

At 9 o'clock, the orange ball dropped out of the sky. Steve cracked light sticks to weave through the children's bicycle spokes. Renee and Bobby joined in and suddenly a parade of glow in the dark bicycle wheels floated by.

With Catherine's three children riding away into the darkness, Heather gathered her children and plopped them into the car. Still no sign of Peter.

Was this it for their marriage? The end. No, she needed to survive.

Survive? Is that what she was doing? She didn't want to survive, she wanted to live, like she did today. It was the first time she laughed in years. Even the boys responded. No wonder they played video games all the time, no wonder why Emily hated all the shopping.

This wasn't a real family, it was a façade, like Heather said. Everyone going through the motions, separately. She wanted what everyone else wanted, a home, a husband, children, happiness. Where was the fun? Why didn't Peter love her anymore?

The block party broke up. Mothers put their young children to bed, fathers wheeled the grills away and disassembled the tables. A group of teenagers arranged themselves in the center of one of their lawns and continued to talk. Invited guests left, only a few chairs lay scattered across the street. A handful of neighbors sat around a fire pit with bottles of beer.

Catherine didn't understand. She gave him everything. The house, immaculate at all times, she cooked gourmet meals, took care of their kids' needs. She worked to bring in additional income and let Peter go out with his friend's, never questioning him. What more could she do? Maybe she did too much. She needed to give herself a break. Tonight proved it. Catherine needed to put herself first, knock off all the perfect mother attributes and start having some fun.

Chapter 27

Victoria

Three weeks passed since Victoria saw Aiden. Her attempts to avoid him were failing, unable to resist his uplifting conversations. The memory of his soft, wet kiss taunted her. His advances were tempting but she needed to contemplate the full magnitude of this.

Ed worked more steadily and she made sure she cooked enormous, mouthwatering dinners for him every night. She bought him his beers in a chilled glass, watched TV with him, and rubbed his tired feet on several occasions.

He came home Saturday evening dragging his arms beside him. He sunk into his couch, his eyes dull and apathetic.

Victoria made his favorite pot roast with mashed potatoes and poured an ice-cold beer into his Budweiser glass. The smell of onions and her red wine gravy flooded the kitchen. "Dinner's ready."

"Can you bring it to me? I'm beat. And bring me my tray table, I'll eat in front of the TV."

"But I set the table, with candles."

"Is it too much to ask you to just do what I say?"

Victoria smacked the tray table down in front of him, then brought in his plate and glass of beer. He stared at the screen and said nothing. Victoria sat at the kitchen table by herself, only the flickering of the coconut-scented candle kept her company.

The sound of loneliness crept in and she decided to join him. She put her plate on a tray table too and sat on the opposite side of the living room.

Ed's laughter sliced into her. Victoria took a bite of the cold pot roast, the gravy already hardening in her plate. A *Sanford and Son* rerun blasted from the surround sound. Her brain cells melted as each minute passed.

After dinner, Ed left his plate in the living room and occupied the bathroom for fifteen minutes. Victoria finished washing the numerous pots and pans, as well as their dishes and cups. The final knife clunked in the draining board when he sauntered into the kitchen.

Then the phone rang for him.

Victoria dried the dishes, stored them away and put the leftovers in the refrigerator. Ed returned wearing his bleach-stained Wrangler jeans and his *Up-Yours* T-shirt. "I'm going out."

"Out where? You said you were exhausted."

"I was, but now I'm not. Is that a problem?" He grabbed his chunky wallet from the counter and shoved it into the back pocket of his discolored jeans. "I'm meeting Ralph and Kenny at The Innkeeper's Inn, don't wait up."

Asinine name for a bar. Obviously the owner didn't have a wife, otherwise she would have explained to him how absurd the name was.

Don't wait up. Like she would. Actually, she would. Who was she kidding?

The telephone sat erect on the wall like an obedient soldier. No, that would not solve anything. But Victoria thought of Heather. Silvatri wasn't solving anything in her life but at least she was happy.

She descended the stairs, away from the phone, and switched on her computer. Another thrilling Saturday night by herself.

She waited for the computer to turn on and dragged her Word of the Day calendar closer. July 8th. Almost two weeks had passed since she used it. She ripped off hyperbole, rapier and euphonious. Then grabbed a chunk without reading them and tossed them in the trash.

She arrived at today's date: July 20th and rubbed the back of her neck. *Wanton* adj. Sexually lawless or unrestrained. Loose, lascivious, lewd. "Wanton behavior."

Victoria drove past manicured lawns twice the size of hers. She turned onto Hidden Autumn Acres and counted her way to number 244. Aiden's house, an English Tudor, had white stucco set above the exposed brick and was trimmed with brown decorative wood framing, beneath a trio of steeply pitched roofs. It reminded her of the buildings at SandCrest Laboratories. The prominent chimney, crowned with an ornamental venting cap helped her envision romantic nights in front of the fire. Her heart skipped.

She paused outside his front door and closed her eyes. What was she doing? She could leave. Run. It wasn't too late. It was too late. The click of the door jarred her eyes back open. Why did she call him?

After a second glass of red wine, Victoria lounged on his cozy loveseat overlooking the barren fireplace. The late-July temperatures and air conditioning squelched her fireplace fantasy, but her laughter so frequent, her cheeks burned. "Stop, stop," she begged.

Aiden chuckled too and rose to open another bottle of wine. He towered over her and dispensed the maroon liquid into her goblet. After an hour-long station on the sofa across from her, he lowered himself onto the cushion beside her.

She knew the wine removed her inhibitions but she also knew that she had too many. Too many unblemished qualities, her flawless way of living, practically perfect in every way. Ick, she was Mary Poppins.

Victoria laid her glass atop the dark-cherry coffee table, and then leaned her head onto the plush cushion. Aiden ran his smooth, uncalloused fingers down her cheek. His thumb reached up and explored her lips. His hand travelled to her neck, reassuring, calming.

Would he kiss her again? She wanted him to, she wanted him more than anything. Just a distraction as Heather said, that's all it would be. Temporary.

Aiden arched in and brushed his lips over hers. They moved rhythmically back and forth, pulsing and massaging. His thumb returned to her face and stroked her temple.

She hesitated at first, feeling like a fourteen-year-old girl experiencing her first kiss. Well, not her first. That was awkward. But maybe the first real one, with someone who knew how to kiss.

But soon Victoria's hand moved to his shoulder, then to that luscious hair of his. She opened her eyes to study it, but his dazzling eyes were studying her.

They kissed as song after song comforted them. The romantic jazz music floated through the room and cavorted in her veins. She imagined what making love to Aiden would be like but knew he would not try. The fruity flavors on his tongue and the softness of the cushion immersed her further into the dream.

Victoria placed her hand over his and then guided it up her shirt. He pulled his lips away and then his hand. She directed his head back to hers and let him know she wanted it. Her hand journeyed to his chest hairs and she swirled her fingers in figure eights, then unfastened his shirt buttons and extended her fingers down to his stomach.

Aiden's finger streamed along her shirt buttons as if contemplating, paused, then wrapped around her neck instead. She rested her head in his chest and he massaged her scalp. For the first time in her life, she wanted to break the rules. No longer the model for perfection, tired of being so proper, she wanted to be shameless.

Victoria twisted out of his embrace and then pushed him down on the couch until her chest rested on top of his, their chins aligned, green eyes mirrored each other's. Fifty-three years of living the 'good girl' life was about to disappear.

She inched herself up to reach his mouth and kissed him with more force this time. He returned the favor and weaved his fingers through her hair, embraced her face, pulled her close.

Victoria wrestled herself to a kneeling position. She grasped her shirt and liberated each button. He burrowed deeper into the cushions and watched her performance. The scarlet cloth cascaded to her hips and then glided to the floor. Her breasts overflowed from the cups in the navy blue lace bra, something she had purchased after their first kiss, something she hid in her sock drawer, something she planned to return.

Aiden slid his hands over her hips, thumbs touched her pale skin. They climbed to the dark blue material and Victoria closed her eyes and embraced the evening that was about to unfold.

He bolted up and removed his silky shirt. Then, in the midst of a kiss, swooped her in his arms and relocated to his bedroom.

The country French décor of his home continued into his bedroom. The wrought iron bed decorated with a red, gold and rust colored bedspread, luxurious yet inviting, called out her name. The sun setting outside the window made the foliage look black and seductive, while it cast orange light into the room echoing the orange clouds above the countryside.

He turned down the bedspread with one arm and then positioned Victoria on his crisp vanilla sheets, his lips still pressed onto hers. Aiden studied her. Would she disappoint him? How long had it been since she made love?

Aiden removed his khaki shorts, settled beside her and ran his fingers over her colorless body. Had time spoiled her appearance? His sturdy chest and trim stomach, his toned physique, all outshined her flabby layers despite their similar age.

His lips streamed down her neck into that cleavage, breasts bursting from their shelter. Aiden set them free and both his hands seized them. So long since anyone had touched them, neglected, they now responded, eager to entertain.

Her clothing peeled off piece by piece until the realization of her nakedness became apparent. The last of the sunlight peeked through the window. Grateful the dusk sky hid her imperfections, but in the darkness, she envisioned Ed. His beer belly, his bleach stained jeans, and his brusque cold manner. Victoria wrapped her arms around herself, the illusion progressed. The aroma of beer and his cigarette laced breath surfaced, along with his love for TV Land.

Aiden's fingers ran between her thighs. The rigidness of her body so tense, so obvious, he removed his hands.

"Are you all right, am I hurting you?"

The night also hid her embarrassment, her cheeks flaming hot. "No, I just..." Suddenly her flaws and blemishes seemed trivial compared to the images of Ed, and new courage emerged. "I want to see you. Can we have a little light?"

Aiden lurched off the bed, switched the bathroom light on, then lit the cranberry candle on his night table. The flickering light squelched her images and brought back the fantasy of making love to Aiden in front of his fireplace.

Victoria noticed his tight burgundy briefs remained in place. With one deep breath, she rose, guided her hands to his hips and slowly slid them down.

Aiden felt larger and firmer than Ed, part of her had hoped she would be disappointed, anything to end this folly, but instead it only solidified her yearning for Aiden.

They kneeled before one another, explored each other's bodies, hands clasped, kisses lingered, until they could wait no longer. He eased her onto the pillow and slid himself inside.

A hint of cranberry surrounded them. Their shadows bounced on the ceiling and flashed like teenagers dancing under a strobe light. Watching herself unbridled ignited her desires. Making love under candle light would one day become wild sex beside the fireplace.

This was better than any of the fantasies she had created in her head.

She rolled over and began to sob. Quietly at first, like always, but then her volume amplified.

Aiden rotated her onto her back and rubbed her forearm. "I didn't hurt you, did I?"

Victoria let out a chuckle, then a silly giggle, until a loud roar of laughter erupted.

"What's happening, what's wrong?" Aiden's bewildered face waved back and forth.

"Not a God damn thing." She grabbed the back of his neck and pulled him back down.

****

Victoria called Heather from the phone in the nurses' station and asked to meet her in the patient lounge. She hurried past a cluster of nursing students and flew around the corner. The closed door surprised her. It was normally wide open with various family members discussing their loved ones. At 10 a.m. though, visiting hours had yet to begin.

The knob rotated in her palm and she eased open the door a mere inch. A long lab coat obscured any definitive observation. She advanced the door further. A jolt ran through her. Dr. Mangle's mouth gyrated and rolled across a woman's face. His movements powerful, she appeared hypnotized. It was Megan, a new nurse on her floor.

Victoria closed the door and took a few steps back. Did everyone cheat? A bonfire ignited inside her. The rumors were true. That repulsive schmuck.

Instead of leaving, she pretended to stumble into the door and wrenched the knob in an exaggerated manner, looked back over her shoulder as if in the middle of a conversation and hollered, "thank you, I'll check on his tube feeding next."

Dr. Mangle and Megan stood on opposite sides of the room.

"Oh, so sorry," Victoria said.

"Not at all," Dr. Mangle began. "We were discussing the sad

case of Mrs. Neidman. So sad." He wagged his head back and forth like a dog. "Megan, we should give her the Roxanol at this point and discuss palliative care with the family."

Megan the dimwit stared at him, baffled. The skin around her lips, red and overcooked. He raised his eyebrows but it still eluded her.

"Very well then," he said. "Let's speak to the family, shall we?"

They skulked out together. Dr. Mangle patted Victoria on the shoulder like a small child and retreated down the hallway.

Victoria's shoes sunk into the plush carpeting of the lounge only seconds before Heather charged in and closed the door behind her. "What's up?"

"Well, I had one story to tell you but now it appears I have two."

Victoria described what she just encountered and Heather barred her teeth. "I can't stand that man, he makes me sick. Not sure why it bothers me so much, but it does. I wish I caught him, I wouldn't have been as nice as you. That door would have swung open, catching them in the act."

"I could imagine what you'd do. You're too much."

"He preys on these brainless low self-esteem women that fall for his crap because they're lonely or single or just pathetic. Ugh, why can't they see it?"

"Because they're lonely and single and pathetic."

The two of them laughed. "No wonder he never answers his calls," Heather said. "He's probably off having sex with them somewhere and doesn't want to interrupt his fun."

They shared equivalent judgments and means of torture until their stomachs hurt from laughter. At least they were able to joke about what bothered them.

Victoria glimpsed at the clock on the wall. "So, I have to tell you something. Do you remember that director of research from SandCrest Laboratories?"

"The one with the tight ass?"

Victoria giggled. "You would remember that part. Yes, him, Aiden. Well I'm sorry I didn't tell you sooner, really I am, please understand." She paused and played with the plain gold band on her hand. "We've been talking on the phone every day for two months."

"Get out!"

"No, seriously and it gets better. We met for lunch one day, about a week after the lecture, and talked for hours. Real conversation Heather, big words and thought provoking ideas, and it didn't involve any television characters."

Heather leaned back in the cheap torn sofa and her face beamed. "Go on, go on, you're killing me."

"About a month ago he gave me a personal tour of his laboratory, the meticulous grounds, the cloudless sky, abundant flowers, old fashioned buildings with wonderful architecture and magnificent sculptures. Magical to say the least. Ed worked that day, I woke to a quiet house, alone again. Because that's how my life's been Heather. Lonely and dark and depressing." She bowed her head.

Heather stroked her shoulder. "I'm sorry, I didn't realize."

"I've been depressed for a long time, longer than you I think. I fill my days with work and projects, but when I go home, it's all the same. I can't avoid what's there – or not there. Throwing myself into multiple jobs is a diversion but that doesn't fix anything."

"I completely understand, you're preaching to the choir."

"I tried, I really did. For years I pretended it was just a phase and we'd grow out of it. Thought once our children were older we'd be able to rekindle that flame, but I realized that the candle has burned down to the metal plate."

"Victoria, what did you do?" Heather released her arm, her face turned ashen.

"When we reached the lake, I started to cry. I don't know why, depressed of course but it was more than that. At that moment, I felt such internal happiness but wouldn't let myself be happy. I forced it down, deep down refusing to let it happen."

"Why?"

"It's wrong."

"To be happy? To feel good about yourself?"

"Yes. No. I mean I try to make Ed happy, I try to be there for my children, but the three of them don't want anything to do with me anymore. And Jean, well Jean she just…"

"Don't even mention her."

"No, but that's part of the problem, it adds to it. The miserable life I have. There's nowhere to turn, I go from work to home and it doesn't change. The insults, the lack of support."

"You deserve happiness, not just your family, we all do. Victoria, what happened, are you okay?"

"Yes, more than you know." She grabbed the lapel on her lab

coat and straightened it. "I started to cry. He's seen me upset before, senses it on the phone. I try to hide it, you know I'm not like that, one to show my feelings, but a tear fell and once it started, well..." She looked at Heather finally, refusing to let her eyes wander away. "He leaned in and kissed me! It was astounding. It had been so long. An extended kiss, lingering and just wonderful."

Heather turned away and shook her head in disapproval.

"Please, I know what you're thinking. I'm a big girl you know."

"I know, it's just...I feel that maybe I put the thought in your head and I– "

"No, no, I knew you would say that. It wasn't like that. It just happened it wasn't planned."

"But if I didn't cave with Silvatri maybe you would have thought twice, avoided him, stayed strong, maybe you– "

"I knew what I was doing, I wanted it. From the first time I met him, he had me walking into walls. I didn't have to go to the lab that day and I could have pushed him away. For once I wanted something for me. For *me*. Is that so horrible?"

Heather smiled. "How was it?"

"At first I was so guilt ridden, I avoided him for weeks. We spoke on the phone but I resisted offers to see him again. He understood. Felt bad that he did what he did but I assured him I wanted it to happen."

"Then this Saturday– "

"Wait, there's more?"

"Saturday night Ed was incredibly nasty, ignored me, then went out with his friends. I couldn't take it anymore. How much more can I do for him? I'm not his mother, we're supposed to be partners. We were at one point, you know." She waggled her head. "I called Aiden and agreed to meet him. The next thing I knew, his brick walkway appeared under my feet and then my shoes were off in his living room."

Heather's eyes expanded and she sucked her lips in to hide her smirk.

"Sure I could blame it on the wine, but I wanted him. Wine or no wine, I needed this." Heather remained silent but the smirk on her face, unmistakable. "Heather, I slept with him. And it was amazing. I cried, cried right there in front of him, only they were tears of joy this time. I felt like the happiest woman in the world."

Chapter 28

Heather

Heather cut through the kitchen to grab a few cans of Ensure for a patient. She selected a chocolate and a vanilla, and then raced out of the storeroom. She accelerated around the deserted tray line, the dietary workers all on their mid-morning break, and then bolted past the salad room. She would make it.

Jean took one enormous step out of the cook's area and into her path. Her bottom lip curled down and her left eye protruded like it was about to pop out. "Why do you refuse to wear a hairnet in my kitchen?" she asked.

"Just getting some Ensure for a patient. No one's in here, no food being prepared or served, nothing to contaminate." Her melodious tone echoed in the abandoned space. Silvatri's morning kiss, stolen in the back stairwell, lingered in her mind.

"You do realize your long, straggly horse-hair can fly off into various areas of my kitchen and make their way into my food?" Jean's short yellow hair, greased with some kind of lubricant, had no chance for escape. Throw in her tangerine muumuu dress, and her face appeared jaundiced.

Heather, in no mood to fight with the tyrant, stared back waiting for the punishment. Either way there would be fight, why waste her breath.

Tyrell entered the kitchen and upon seeing Heather, gripped his stomach, keeled over and pretended to laugh hysterically. She held her poker face and listened to Jean grumble on.

"Are you listening to me?"

"Yes."

Jean, hoping for a fight stared back, but Heather continued to fix her emotionless gaze on her. Tyrell broke into jumping jacks and then finished with a lame attempt at a cartwheel.

Jean dismissed her finally and Heather strode over to Tyrell who hid behind the wall in the main hallway.

"Think you're funny, don't you?"

"I know I am. You wanted to laugh, admit it. You're just good at holding in your true emotions." Tyrell flipped up the lapel on his cook's uniform and spun on his heels. "So...you going tonight?"

"Louisa's retirement party? I might make an appearance."

"Too good for it?"

"Nah, just need to make sure my mother can watch the girls. I'm hoping to drop all three off and not worry about returning at a reasonable hour."

"Planning on staying at the party all night then?"

"I'm planning on staying *out* all night, yes." She attempted to hide a smirk but failed.

"You dog! Whatta ya have planned?"

"Nothing for you to be worried about."

"You'll tell me by the end of the night. I have my ways." Tyrell flicked the strands of hair in front of her face and strutted back into the kitchen.

Heather and Victoria left the dance floor drenched, and searched for their waters. A scratchy paper napkin wiped the sweat from Heather's chest. She was glad she threw on that tank top and short skirt before leaving the house.

Victoria slung her pocket book over her shoulder and grinned at Heather. Heather's eyebrows dropped but then reality sunk in. "Where do you think you're going, missy?"

"You're not the only one using the party as an excuse to meet up with a fine gentleman. We have such limited time to see each other, have to make the most of it."

She continued to feel guilty about Victoria's decision. Heather didn't care what happened to her marriage, but Victoria's? Not many people celebrated thirty years with the same man. Heather suggested other resources but she would hear no part of it. Victoria made her decision and like everything else in her life, would stick with it until the end.

But what was the end? She hated to think of the consequences.

"Where are you meeting Aiden?"

"His home. And you?"

"Silvatri and I are meeting down the block in a parking lot. Car sex is just as good."

Heather said good night to her friend and then chugged the remainder of her water. Loud hoots emerged from behind. She swiveled on the barstool. Tyrell sauntered in wearing a black button down shirt, a loose black tie, black baggy dress pants and matching shoes. His skin color blended perfectly with his clothing. Such a different look from his white kitchen scrubs.

Heather asked the bartended for another water, drank it in four large gulps and then asked for one more. She fanned herself with a Stella Artois beer coaster and then combed her hair back into a high ponytail with her fingers. Before she could finish the last twist, a hand reached over and tugged the tail.

"Hey, hey Heather, what's happening?"

"Nice of you to join us Tyrell, I was just leaving."

"Leaving? You can't, the party's just starting."

"That's funny, it was going pretty strong the whole time I was here."

"Yeah, I heard, bat girl."

"Bat girl?"

He held two fingers up on each of his hands and made a V. Then he whisked each V over his eyes imitating a dance move. "Heard you were doing the bat girl dance, woo hoo!" He continued his bizarre undulating movements.

"No, I wasn't."

"Yes you were. Didn't know you could dance to hip-hop." His hips flexed, gyrated, then his legs kicked out side to side as the V shapes flew past his face. "You're a black girl in a white girl's body," he sang repeatedly.

Heather folded her arms in her chest and leaned back for the show.

"Bat girl, that's your new name. Come on, show Tyrell how you dance, show me what you got." Tyrell continued to sing and then turned around, bent forward, stuck his butt out and shook it back and forth like a food processor.

A snort erupted from the back of Heather's throat. She keeled over and grasped the bar stool in front of her.

"Yeah, yeah, you like it. Admit it, I got style. Oh, yeah." Tyrell threw his hands in the air, twirled once and proceeded to do the

Batman dance again.

"There *is* something wrong with you."

"Come on Heather, show me the Batman dance. Get up, let's go." Tyrell slinked over and slipped his hands over hers. He lifted her off the stool and then put the V shape's up to his eyes again, mocking her. "Show me. Show me how you dance, come on, don't be shy."

She stood there for a minute in disbelief. Then her hips shifted, shoulders rocked. Heather's hands flew up and the V's navigated past her eyes.

"There you go, there you go. I knew you had the Batman in you."

She swayed closer, fixing her eyes on his. Two could play this game. She journeyed in tighter, until her legs straddled his left leg, squeezed, then gyrated. He peeked down at her silver skirt as it lifted inch by inch, until the faint glimmer of pink lace fluttered before him.

Tyrell flashed his eyes up to hers. They glossed over. His knees weakened and he clutched the edge of the table behind him. He attempted to take a step back, lost his footing and tumbled into a chair. His eyes travelled along the length of her body, down to the three-inch stilettos.

Heather, not allowing him get off easy, sauntered in, arms raised high above her head as if ready to give him a lap dance.

Tyrell's lips parted, he rubbed the back of his neck, then lurched up. His chair flung back and crashed to the floor. He ran out of the bar area and straight into the men's bathroom.

Chapter 29

Catherine

Victoria called the second floor nurse's station and asked for Catherine. "Can I speak to you for a few minutes? Privately?"

"Okey-dokey-karaoke!" Catherine's cheery voice sang out. She hung up the phone but then plodded to the patient lounge at the end of the hall. Had she documented something incorrectly on one of her patients? Did she forget to counsel someone? She wouldn't want to disappoint anyone else.

Victoria arrived a minute later and immediately unloaded the past two months of escapades on Catherine. Her chest ached. "You're cheating too?"

"It's not a club, it just happened."

"I could see Heather, but you? You're planning your 30th wedding anniversary. How could you?"

Victoria recoiled at her accusation. Her harsh words criticized her integrity but Catherine didn't care.

Catherine clutched the box of tissues beside her and tore one out, then slammed the box back on the end table knocking over the table-tent of hospital phone numbers. The tissue ripped into shreds from her fingernails.

Victoria continued to explain, rationalize her behavior, but Catherine heard only babbles despite Victoria's clear speech. This could not be the answer.

She endured Heather's raunchy sex stories every week during their lunch hour discussions, now Victoria poured out hers. Details, too. Was everyone having sex but her? Did it have to be so tempting, seductive? Was that normal?

Catherine stormed out leaving Victoria behind, no longer wanting to hear happy tales of romance and all this God forsaken cheating, and sex and...how could they? Victoria was in her fifties! Did people that age run around and cheat and still have sex? At thirty-five, her sex life was over.

Visions of Victoria having sex nauseated her. Or was it anger, or jealousy? Could she really be jealous of Victoria? What was she feeling? Feel something, dammit!

Numb, she returned to the nurse's station and swept up her pen, but the drivel words marked in the chart only enraged her further. Her ribs squeezed and suffocated her. She deserved happiness as much as them. How dare they cheat the system.

****

2 a.m. Saturday morning, Peter's side of the bed remained cold. His late nights multiplied leaving her alone with the kids several times a week. She enjoyed the added time with her children but missed the intimacy with Peter. What a fool she was all these years.

She lay awake, face up, watching a thin band of moonlight travel inch by inch along the wall. Catherine needed her full eight hours of sleep for work in the morning or she would not perform up to potential. The weekends were brutal. Let's not mention the huge bags under her eyes.

The front door clicked, scraped open, then rubbed back into position. Shoes shuffled across the wood floor, awkward stumbling followed. Did he just trip? Tumble into the wall?

Her vision focused perfectly in the darkness, the full moon provided just enough light to see Peter hold onto the bedroom wall as he entered, one shoe in his hand. He removed the scraps of clothing left on him and tossed them onto the floor, pant legs inside out.

He attempted to crawl into bed, the smell of tequila over whelming. She should have chastised him but draped her arm around his waist and cuddled him instead. Heather and Victoria's stories filled her mind. She wanted to have sex again regardless of what her body looked like. She wanted her husband's touch, his warmth, his mouth on hers.

Peter swung his arm toward her but then jabbed her in the shoulder with his elbow. Then he took his leg and kicked her away. Twice. She rolled to her side and coiled into a fetal position.

****

Lunchtime arrived and Catherine needed the energy boost. Did she sleep at all last night? She dragged her feet down the long, desolate corridor to her office. Dim lighting, vacant rooms and closed doors saluted her. She unbuttoned her lab coat releasing the heat from beneath. Despite the air conditioning, the ninety-eight degree temperatures outside competed for their space in the building. She could remove the coat once safely in her office.

She inserted her key in the door but the silver piece of metal failed to penetrate the lock. She rotated it and tried again, her binder and papers ready to cartwheel onto the filthy linoleum.

"Need any help?" A voice echoed in the darkness.

Fear stole her voice. Had a psych patient escaped from his unit and followed her down here? Had a family member lost their way and cornered her in the abandoned passageway? The key dropped to the floor. She bent to sweep it up, but a man's hand extended to retrieve it.

"I didn't frighten you, did I?"

Catherine sighed. "Oh, it's only you."

"Well, excuse me, were you expecting someone else?" Dr. Mangle positioned his hand on the wall above her.

"No, so sorry, I just thought...sorry, I didn't mean– " How could she insult a man like him? The only man that spoke to her.

"Here, let me get that for you." He reached for the key, touching her hand with his and then trailed the sharp edge up her wrist eliciting a flood of goose bumps.

Dr. Mangle unlocked the door, pushed it open, secured a few steps in and mounted himself against the door to let her pass. She lowered her gaze, heard the door close behind her, and cringed. She set her binder on the desk knocking the picture of Peter and her down. He sprang towards her and helped upright it, never bothering to notice the image behind the glass.

He balled his hand into a fist and raised Catherine's chin until her eyes locked on to his. Dr. Mangle's gaze roamed from her sleepy face to her tight ponytail and then plunged down her neck into the cleavage exposed by her shirt. His brows shot up but his eyes remained on her huge breasts. Why had she unbuttoned her lab coat?

Her heart quickened.

His hand caressed her cheek and travelled to the back of her neck where he removed her hair tie in one sweep.

"You're simply beautiful, Catherine. You should wear your hair down more often. And your eyes, they hypnotize me, do you realize that?"

She shook her head, unable to speak.

"Every time I see you I cannot resist. You mesmerize me and I cannot escape. Do you understand that you have the power to do this to me?"

She shook her head again, quivering under his grip. How could someone as plain as her attract him? Were her eyes that amazing?

"Your blonde hair frames your face so perfectly, bringing out that warm hue you have that welcomes me. Do you realize what you do to me Catherine? Captivate me and lure me to you, drawing me in and I think of nothing else all day."

Lightheaded, a tingling swept up the back of her spine. His hand glided down her neck, paused and then bit-by-bit lowered. He reached her collarbone and his finger stroked calculatingly, back and forth in gentle waves. His eyes squinted, lips smirked. Dr. Mangle's self-assurance and control made the space between Catherine's thighs throb like a beating heart.

"I can't sleep at night because of you. I dream of you and my thirst cannot be quenched. It's torture being away from you. I look for you daily on your floors, do you know that?"

Catherine shook her head yet again, speechless, astonished that she could make him feel this way. Someone so charming, whom others adored, desired and sought-after, wanted dull, ordinary Catherine? Maybe all those girls that threw themselves at him turned him off. That's why he chose her. That must be it.

She had watched him kiss other women's hands wishing it would be hers. Observed how sweetly he spoke to the nurses, wanting him to whisper in her ear. Analyzed the way he touched their shoulders as he spoke to them in that smooth, captivating voice and yearned for him to touch her skin. She felt the pulsing between her legs quicken.

His hand made its way around to the back of her neck, the other hand joined in and he leaned in closer to her face. Both hands massaged the back of her neck in slow, soft gestures. "Catherine, you have not said a thing. Can it be that you do not feel the same way about me? That you don't find me attractive? Am I too old for you? Please speak to me, I need to know if my fantasy will be shattered right here before you."

Fantasy. She was his fantasy?

The throbbing intensified causing the heat to soar between her legs and the sensation of warmth flooded her causing her to orgasm right there in front of him. Her breath quickened. She panted out loud like a dog, pathetically. Her convulsing body must have aroused him, for he squeezed the hard object under his pants as if incensed and then lunged in and threw his lips onto hers.

Dr. Mangle kissed her hard and violently. Her muscles lost their tension and she relaxed her posture. She let him kiss her, firm and powerful. This is what it felt like to have passion for something, to be desired and coveted. Warm liquid from within, escaped and covered her underwear.

He nuzzled her neck, gnawing at it like a hungry grizzly bear. He grabbed her hand and crushed it into the hard object popping out from the top of his pants. "Do you feel this?" he asked. "You did this to me Catherine, no one else. No one else can do this to me but you. You make me hard."

She had never touched anyone else's. Well except for Herman Nowacki's. But her first year in college gave her the opportunity to finally experiment with boys, and well, it was so small she could barely grasp two fingers around it. That didn't count.

He pulled away, stroking his hard penis. "There is so much I'd love to show you Catherine, so much I'd like to do to you, experiences you've never dreamed of. I can take you there. I can make you feel things you never thought possible."

This wasn't happening. A crazy dream perhaps from lack of sleep. A man like him could never want her, but then again, maybe she had redeeming qualities. Qualities that Peter squashed and buried until even she no longer saw them.

She wanted to feel, feel something, anything. Living with this perpetual numbness was too much.

He lifted her up onto her desk, her binder smashed into the wall. He put his hands around her ankles and lifted her long tan skirt, caressing her calves. He resumed his journey up her left leg, and continued higher.

She froze. Fossilized and petrified. She felt like a patient at the OB/GYN's office with her legs in stir-ups. How much further he would go? Would he stop before he reached her knees, continue all the way up? She thought about the underwear she threw on, white briefs with red roses. Not very flattering but he would not see them today, not here in the middle of her office. Catherine suddenly thought of Heather and Silvatri having sex in here. Her heart raced. It was possible.

Dr. Mangle continued to move his persuasive hand up her leg and over her knee. He drifted toward her thigh, stopped, studied her and then looked back down.

"What?" she stammered, finally speaking. "What is it?"

He chuckled, removing his hand. "Are you wearing knee highs?"

"Yes, why?"

He burst out laughing. In the middle of everything. Humiliating her.

"What's so funny?" she whimpered. She *was* a loser. What had she done wrong?

"Knee highs, seriously?" He bent in, ran his tongue around her ear and then whispered, "We have to get you a pair of thigh highs with the garter to match."

****

Catherine stared at herself in the lingerie store's mirror. The sheer white thigh-highs with a back-seam and white lace trim had an attached garter belt whose wide lace straps caressed her butt, cuddling it and embracing the firm round skin. The straps hooked to the top of a matching four-inch band of material encircling her flat stomach. She chose a tiny white thong so as not to hide her sultry butt.

The white see-through bra, with its sheer material, did not come in her size since most bras that fit her had bulky, thick material. She chose one two sizes smaller and her huge breasts exploded out of them, nipples peeked over the edge.

She twirled around one last time, finger in her mouth rolling it on her tongue and ran her other hand up the back of her thigh to the bare skin above. She faced the mirror again and her hand travelled to the front of the thong, lingered and rubbed the area. Were there hidden cameras in the changing room?

She danced in the private fitting room and beamed at her twin in the mirror. Real, significant, desired, important. Catherine transformed. Resuscitated and revived.

Chapter 30

Victoria

On this unusual eighty-degree, non-humid August day in New York, Andrew and Sara drove to the South Shore beaches with friends and Ed completed construction of a storage shed. Victoria normally spent the Friday before she worked the weekend running errands, calculating bills and cooking meals to freeze for the coming days, but today Aiden took the day off to spend with her.

She pulled into his driveway. Aiden was already waiting and leaning on his sporty gunmetal grey Cadillac. The ideal man for a luxury vehicle commercial.

He held the door for to enter. His irresistible cologne permeated the interior, instantly seducing her. Victoria's fingers meandered over his maroon car seats, the color the same as the negligee she bought weeks ago for Ed, the one buried in the bottom of her pajama drawer.

"Are the windows too much?" he asked. "It's much too nice for air conditioning today."

Ed always insisted the air conditioner remain on inside the house even on gorgeous days like today. The silence from the locked windows prevented her from hearing birds and crickets, children playing tag, the distance sound of trains, and it dulled her as if she was in solitary confinement.

Her shoulder-length hair flicked and waved from the breeze off the seashore. The clear sea air became apparent as they neared the North Shore. Starfish Beach, a private beach one mile from Aiden's home, welcomed them.

The boardwalk bustled with lovers enjoying the weather.

Aiden obviously wasn't the only one playing hooky today. The lack of breeze made the air feel warmer as they strolled along the boardwalk. They approached a young couple holding hands and the pair knocked their hips into one another, laughed, then stopped to kiss.

Victoria's heart took a blow at the realization that Aiden and she could never do such a thing in public. They walked with three feet between them, casual, non-suggesting.

She envisioned him embracing her on the boardwalk, a fantasy for sure, but one that made her float like the seagulls above. Any time spent with him was a gift. It gave her reason to continue down her path in life, the path with the "Dead End" sign prominently displayed.

"I took my boys here when they were little." He leaned on the long piece of railing overlooking the bay. "The rocks hurt their feet but they never complained. We came later in the day, flew this bright orange box kite in the seaweed air. I brought a small charcoal grill and we'd cook up burgers and hot dogs, toast marshmallows. One was always sure to fall into the sand. Then we'd watch the sunset down past the rocks over there." He pointed to an enormous strip of boulders about a quarter of a mile down the beach.

"My wife loved the beach too. Before the kids were born, we snuck out to that last lifeguard stand and sat wrapped in a blanket and watched the sun set and the stars grow brighter. One night we watched for so long we fell asleep."

His story evoked a memory of her father and her gazing at the stars in a lounge chair on their back patio. She always thought they only shone in their backyard, no one else's. They were Victoria's stars. What did a seven-year-old know?

"Do you come to the beach often?" he asked.

"When Andrew and Sara were little I took them all the time. Ed hates the beach, the sun beating on his head. When they were older, I'd say eleven and fifteen, it wasn't fun anymore. Andrew was bored, wanted to be with his friends and Sara wanted to build sandcastle after sandcastle. It was stressful back then.

Ed withdrew from us. Midlife crisis perhaps. I was exhausted – between the kids, chores, work. I have to admit, by the time I made lunches, packed up the car, carried toys and towels, chairs and a radio, I just wanted to lie on the beach and read a book. They sensed it, I'm sure, and didn't want to go anymore.

Heather started working with me the following winter. Her

girls were seven and five at the time and she suggested we go together next summer. Andrew refused to hang out with three little girls but I brought Sara. Heather was amazing. The way she got down and built this whole sand house for Laurel's Polly Pocket dolls. She made rooms and furniture, a pool, all out of sand. Then she played with them, actually took a few dolls and named them. One was called Sarsaparilla I think. Oh, God." Victoria let out a laugh. "She had a whole story line going. The way the girls watched her. Heather knew how to have a good time, still does."

Victoria's smile curved down. She missed the fun, the spark in her life. Aiden rested his hand on her shoulder. Instead of helping, she looked around to see if anyone was watching.

This charade only blanketed her pain, like spreading icing over a broken crumbling cupcake, trying to hold the pieces together and make it look appealing on the outside.

Chapter 31

Heather

Heather, Victoria and Catherine sat in the cafeteria eating breakfast at their usual table in the back corner. Originally it was to hide from Jean since the alignment was perfect with the cash register and large fake palm, but now more to share their secrets without being overheard.

Heather finished her salad and snapped her double dark chocolate cookie in half. She bit off a piece and the richness of the soft cookie and melted chocolate chips cleared her mouth of the spinach and red pepper tang.

Catherine had been increasingly quiet since last week. Were they not giving her the opportunity to talk? Was she still angry with Victoria? But then this morning she spotted something. Catherine's short skirt. The woman must have been a nun in a former life because she always covered her legs with pants or long flowing skirts.

Heather flung another piece of cookie in her mouth and continued to stare while Victoria described her boardwalk experience to them. Catherine looked up from her strawberry yogurt parfait and locked eyes with Heather.

"So then this seagull swooped down right in front of us..."

Catherine tried to look away but Heather continued her gaze.

"Aiden tried to swat it away but his sandal caught on one of the wood planks of the boardwalk and..."

Catherine snuck a quick peek, then pretended she needed another napkin. Her other one untouched. Heather bit off a large chunk of cookie, refusing to remove her eyes. The two of them launched into a staring contest.

"...we didn't know what to do so Aiden grabbed my hand and dragged me over to the sand and stupid me tripped over a child's shovel and– "

Their staring match chopped Victoria's laughter in half. Catherine's nostrils flared, her veins in her neck strained against her skin. Heather on the other hand, plastered a huge smirk on her face and munched in an exaggerated manner.

"You're wearing eyeliner," Heather said, "and mascara."

"So."

Heather bent her head under the table. "Nice skirt."

"Thank you."

Victoria looked back and forth at them. "What's going on?"

"I don't know. Why don't you tell us, Catherine?"

"Nothing, can't I look nice?"

"Forgot to wear your hair clip today?"

"I had a headache. It was hurting my head."

"Who is it?" Heather snickered.

Victoria put her tea down. "Who is what? What did I miss?"

"Catherine's holding out on us. I can see it."

Victoria gazed at Catherine and detected it too. Victoria shot a glance at Heather and back at Catherine and then smiled. With Heather and Victoria staring at her, Catherine folded.

"All right, there is someone."

"I knew it!"

"Please. I'm still in shock.

"What...did...you do?" Victoria asked.

"I don't know how it happened. I would never...you know that."

"Yeah, you've thrown it in our faces enough times."

Catherine frowned at Heather. "I was taken by surprise. I guess I always had a crush on him but refused to admit it, plus I never thought he'd be interested in me." She took a sip of water. "Oh Lord, the thought of cheating, but it was only a kiss."

"You kissed someone?" Victoria knocked over her Styrophome cup. Tan liquid streamed across the table.

Heather quickly squashed it with a wad of napkins and silenced Victoria. "Someone from here?"

"Yes. A doctor."

"No fucking way! Who, Dr. Bishop?"

"Ew! No."

"Dr. Holben?"

"No. Why are you picking all these nerdy doctors?"

"Well..." Heather coughed.

Victoria chuckled. "Okay, how about Dr. Wachsman?"

"No, no, no. It's not anyone you would ever suspect. Someone totally out of my league. Attractive, charismatic, magnetic, desired by everyone in the hospital..."

"Okay, he's Prince Charming, we get it. Now who the hell is it?"

Catherine leaned in and they followed. Catherine screeched like Rori and closed her eyes. "I still can't believe he would want someone like me but it's..." Catherine blushed like the red pepper Heather just ate. "Dr. Mangle," she whispered.

A smile burst onto Catherine's face. Victoria gasped and Heather dropped the remainder of her cookie.

"I know, I know, can you believe it! Me. He likes me. I was entering our office last Saturday and he helped me with the key and the next thing I knew we were kissing."

"Catherine, no," Heather wailed.

"Yes! I can't believe it either. And you were right Heather, it was just what I needed, I feel like a new woman, he woke me up. I bought new clothes, underwear, makeup..."

"Oh God, no." Victoria looked at Heather who still had a piece of cookie resting on her back molar.

"Catherine wait, please. Stop," Heather said.

"What?"

"He's a pig. A filthy, disgusting parasite."

Catherine flinched at her remark. "No he's not. Just because he's not some young hot steroid head?"

"No, that's not what I mean."

"Then what is it? You're jealous that he didn't pick you all these years? That you got stuck with an arrogant conceited doctor that..."

"Whoa, whoa, whoa. Hold on there."

"That's what it is, you're jealous that he chose me. Or are you shocked that someone actually likes me?"

"No, Catherine. It's just he's– "

"What? That he's not someone you'd choose, so what? I like him. I'm not allowed to be happy, only you?"

"It's not that," Victoria piped in.

"Oh, so you're starting too?"

"Catherine, please, listen to us."

"I've had it with the two of you. I'll never fit in. I could work here for a million years and you'd still find something wrong with me."

"It's not you," Heather started. "Come on, these last few months have been great. It's just..." Heather cut off knowing she'd never listen to her. "Victoria, you tell her."

"Heather's right. I caught him a couple of weeks ago in the patient lounge on my floor. He didn't see me. He was with that new nurse, Megan, from my floor."

"Megan? The one that looks like she's on crack?"

"Yes. They were kissing, I saw them."

"And I've heard so many stories about him." Heather added. "He hits on all the new employees, I've seen him in action. He lays down the ground work, builds the foundation and then *bam*! Women come scurrying into his laboratory...of love." Heather sang out the last word in an operatic vibrato. "I watch everyone fall for it too."

"He's slick, has a way with them. He's perfected the performance."

"No, it's not true. He told me. Told me he thinks about me all the time, dreams about me. He even told me that he looks for me on my floors, gets upset when he can't find me. I acted like a complete idiot that afternoon, I couldn't speak. He kept complimenting me and I never returned the favor or thanked him."

"Thanked him?" Heather spewed.

"Yes, he treated me better than my own husband. He even bought me coffee yesterday. I'm happy for the first time in years. Why can't you be happy for me?"

"Of course we want you to be happy but..."

"But what, why are yours any different? Heather's off humping behind a row of bushes at the rock climbing place like a wild animal and you're having sex in Aiden's kitchen like two dogs."

Heather and Victoria both studied their spoons.

"Why is this any different?" Are you planning on marrying Silvatri?"

"No."

"Are you planning on marrying Aiden?"

"No!"

"Well I'm not planning on marrying him either. I'm looking for the same thing you are, a little escape, isn't that what you called it?"

Heather nodded. "I just don't want to see you get hurt."

"I won't."

"It was only a kiss." Victoria waved her hand.

"For now."

"What?" Heather's eyes widened.

"He promised me great things. I can't stop thinking about it." She leaned in and whispered, "I even bought this sexy outfit, hid it in my sweater drawer. I looked at it last night and almost threw up. But now I'm definitely going through with it."

"Catherine..."

"No. You're not the only ones that can be happy. He makes me feel good. The best I've felt in years, like a real sexy woman. And considering I haven't had sex in two years, that's a good thing"

Chapter 32

Catherine

Catherine left work and drove directly to Dr. Mangle's house. Her mother agreed to cook the chicken she left in the fridge for her children's dinner tonight, along with the salad she prepared this morning before work.

Her apprehension during the day changed to pure terror now. She pulled her car over to the side of the road a block from his house and tried to find a song on the radio. The music made her more anxious.

With her eyes closed, she reclined the seat back, felt the edge of the thigh high stockings through her pants and ran her fingers up and under the waistband, touching the lace. She let her mind drift, and pretended they were his fingers.

She opened her eyes and let her view roll to her shirt. She unfastened an additional button. "I'll show Heather. I can play this game too."

Catherine continued down the road, up his driveway and drove her car into the left side of the garage as he instructed. She pulled the garage door closed with her hands and then looked for something to wipe off the grime. A rag on the floor, no cleaner than her hands, would have to do.

She wobbled to the entrance that led into his house, knocked on the door, and waited. One of her nipples exposed itself and she tucked it back in. What on earth was she doing here? She buttoned her shirt to the top again. The tight collar prevented any air from reaching her lungs.

The door opened, Dr. Mangle placed his hand on the door jam

and an eager smile grew. His shirtless, hairy chest greeted her, only a pair of green bathing suit trunks remained.

Catherine stepped in and claustrophobia took over at the sight of his expansive den. Vaulted ceilings with skylights across the entire length suspended above her. Sunlight streamed in through the French doors that led to an inground pool surrounded by a thick green lawn.

"You're so formal, Catherine," he said, already pulling her shirt out of her pants.

"I came straight from work." Catherine stopped him and set her gaze on his bare feet.

"Are you having second thoughts? I thought you wanted to please me?"

"I do, I just thought we'd sit and talk for a while."

"Talk?" He mocked. "We did that all week at work."

"I know, but perhaps a drink?"

Dr. Mangle laughed. "Catherine, you surprise me. I thought you would be a professional at this, having had three children. You must love wild sex after producing all of them. Couldn't keep your hands off him could you?" He huffed. "Perhaps not with me, though?"

"No, no, not at all, of course I want to, it's just..."

"Just what? You were the one that said you couldn't stay long. Why waste what little time you're giving us. Maybe I misjudged you, chose unwisely."

Catherine cringed. Her legs trembled so violently it was obvious.

Her first girl-boy party, sadly at the age of thirteen, entered her mind. She could still hear the guests laughing when she refused to play spin the bottle.

"I'm just trying to give you what you asked for, what you desired. Yes?" He raised his eyebrows waiting for her to reply.

He would dismiss her for sure. Pick someone else. So many others waited in line for him. She needed to prove her worth, not disappoint him. Heather and Victoria had no problems pleasing their men.

"How can you stand there and say nothing? If you don't like me Catherine, then just say so. I don't need to be humiliated like this. I may be twenty years older but I assure you, I can perform. He whisked his hand over his erection that forced itself through his loose trunks.

"It's not that, I'm just nervous."

"Nervous? You have an amazing body. What's there to be nervous about?"

She stroked the bottom edge of her shirt. The feel of the garter reminded her why she came here.

"Catherine show me, show me all that beauty, all that you have to offer the men out there." He took a few steps back and sat upon the armrest of his couch. He crossed his left arm over his chest and rested his chin on his right hand, leering.

Catherine looked down but then shut her eyes while she unfastened the buttons. She released the final one, opened her eyes, and saw the bra was indeed too small. What an idiot. What was she thinking?

"Open it," he demanded.

She kept her head down and separated the two halves of the blouse. No time to tuck her overwhelming breasts back in their cups, it appeared she was not wearing a bra at all.

He sprang over to her, grabbed both breasts with his powerful hands, and his mouth secured the one on the right. The forceful pressure he applied with his left hand caused pain. She pinched her thigh to deflect it, but then he bit down hard on her nipple causing her eyes to unlock and see the sunlight flash on to the pool surface.

She stood like a statue in the middle of his living room unsure what she should be doing while he kneeled before her.

"Take it off. Take everything off," he grunted.

Wouldn't he undress her slowly like she envisioned? See the outfit she bought for him? She let her shirt fall to the carpeting and unhooked the tight bra.

He continued to suck forcefully. "Remove the rest, what are you waiting for?"

She unfastened her pants, dropped them to the floor and waited for him to notice.

"Why are you stalling?"

"I thought you would like to see the present I bought you."

He glanced down but then returned his sight to where his hands were. "Nice, remove them."

Catherine removed the white lace garments without Dr. Mangle detaching his mouth. She stood in his massive living room, naked. Bright light shone on her exposed body. The fear of someone appearing in the backyard and seeing what he was doing to her, caused her to hyperventilate.

"I'm so fucking hard Catherine. You do this to me, look at you."

He hoisted himself up, stepped back and examined her, licking his saturated mouth. Her body burst into flames and she repositioned both her arms to cover herself.

"Why do you do that, hide like that? Do you realize what you have?" He took her arm, led her to the French doors, slid them open and pulled her outside.

"No," she shook her head.

He seized both her shoulders. "You must not conceal such beauty." He steered her to the left, under the shade of a tree. He helped her down onto the soft grass and while she laid there, in one quick flick he dropped his bathing suit to the ground.

Catherine's stomach jumped into her chest cavity. A huge mistake. A doctor she had worked with for over a year stood above her naked, his penis surged out like a large infrared laser thermometer.

He buried his mouth between her legs and all Catherine could do was stare at the oblong leaves in the tree above her. She wanted to cry.

Peter and she only had sex in their bedroom. He suggested others rooms such as the kitchen but the awkwardness of it caused her to clam up. It angered Peter to the point he refused to touch her anymore.

She knew she had to overcome her phobias. She would allow Dr. Mangle to do whatever he wanted. She tried to relax and ran her fingers through the blades of grass beneath her.

"You are very silent again Catherine. Am I not pleasing you?"

"You are, very much."

"Then I want to hear it."

She searched the backyard left and right, then back toward the house.

"There's no one here, show me how I make you feel."

She closed her eyes and began to hum. Hum a song she sang to Emily last night.

He removed his mouth from her crotch. "Are you singing?"

"No. Sorry." She tried again but only a low groan emerged.

"You sound like you're dying, that's all I do for you?"

He plowed harder with his mouth. Catherine tried to moan but she never did with Peter, too embarrassed she would make weird sounds. This was more embarrassing.

He plunged his fingers inside, his tongue still hard at work. Her voice raised and snarled through the yard. Better, but still unconvincing.

He sat back, pulled her up and over to him, forcing her mouth between his legs. She only performed oral sex on Peter a handful of times, unsure if she even did it correctly. He never seemed fond of it, never requested it.

"Do you enjoy this?"

She nodded, but inside it made her feel dirty and obscene.

"Do you really?"

"Yes," she mumbled.

"I don't believe you. You seem to be faking it." Oh Lord, she was horrible at it. "Show me Catherine. Show me how much you love my cock." She moved her mouth up and down in awkward bursts. "Here, I will teach you."

He took her hand, wrapped it around the bottom of his shaft allowing only her mouth to touch the tip. "Use your tongue, don't leave it out of the fun." He placed his hand over hers. "Squeeze harder. Stroke it."

Catherine tried to perform his requests, learning as she went. Saliva poured from all sides of her mouth and she gagged and choked. Did she disappoint him? Would he return to work and tell everyone? He made her promise not to tell a soul, made her hide her car in the garage. He wouldn't tell, he had too much to lose. But still, how mortified would she be if she failed to satisfy him?

When she thought she could no longer breathe, he pushed her head away, rose, and yanked her up. He spun her around and shoved her up against the tree. Her nails dug into the crumbled pieces of bark on its trunk. Was she that bad? Would he leave her outside like this pressed against a tree? Thoughts of her father dumping her into the kitchen corner for punishment surfaced.

Catherine felt jabbing between her thighs, then he entered her, ramming it until it finally forced itself inside. He pounded so hard she had to support herself to prevent her face from smashing into the tree.

"This will not do," he said.

She was horrendous! No wonder Peter rejected her touch. If she was cheating on Peter, what was he doing when he went out at night? Finding other woman to fulfill his needs? All her fault. Everything.

Dr. Mangle dropped onto the grass again and hoisted her on top of him, reentering her.

She hated this position. Peter would lie there and make

Catherine ride him. After she had the boys, she preferred to lie on her back without him seeing her damaged body. Her large breasts no longer sprouted upward as they did in college. Their last few times together, she kept her T-shirt on, lights off, under the covers. It's remarkable they conceived Emily.

Bright sunlight poured from the skies, dapples of sun trickled though the leaves flickering on her breasts while she sat there fully exposed. She wanted to hide.

"That's more like it," he howled. "I could not see those huge tits of yours the other way." He reached up and grabbed her breasts, still sore from earlier. "Harder Catherine. Hammer away at me."

She tried to shift back and forth. Did she do this correctly at least? He released her breasts, clutched her butt and heaved her into him. Apparently not. When she figured out the rhythm, he let go of her cheeks, tugged both breasts back down and shoved one in his mouth.

Catherine glided back and forth as hard as she could. He felt good inside her. She let herself go. She moaned and let the noise sail through the vast backyard. He screamed too, loud enough for any passerby to hear.

"Yes, Catherine. That's it, louder."

She whimpered and squealed no longer afraid someone would hear. They both cried out, huffing and gasping for air. Her pain replaced with intense pleasure. She freed her mind, imagined the girl she saw in the mirror at the lingerie store, sat up, put her hands on her breasts and squeezed them for him. He let out a final roar, drove himself into her one last time, and convulsed.

Catherine reversed out of his driveway, still shaking. She drove a few blocks until she found a wooded area. She parked her car along the curb next to the tall pines and cut the ignition.

She peered down the road, hands trembled around the steering wheel, and gasped for air. Catherine rolled down the window, still sensing the intense throbbing between her legs. She unzipped her pants, placed her fingers inside her pulsing flesh like she had done in the dressing room and huffed in large gulps of air. Her mouth quivered and spun out saliva with each puff of air, then the tears began to fall. She was going to hell in a hand-basket for sure.

Chapter 33

Victoria

Jean called in sick. The first time since anyone could remember. At 10 o'clock in the morning, Victoria led the way to their corner table in the cafeteria. The silence in the vast room, eerie.

It took until the three of them finished their coffees to calm down enough to relax and not expect Jean to interrupt their conversation. The cool autumn air entered into their lives and Victoria was excited about her first fireplace rendezvous.

"Next weekend is the 10K race," Victoria began, "I can't believe how fast the summer flew by."

"I thought you and Aiden were going to train for it. What ever happened to that?" Heather dumped her napkin into the empty coffee cup.

"Please, I think we more than accomplish our exercise requirements for the week."

"I thought the point was to train and run the race together," Catherine said.

"Initially he suggested it, more as an excuse to see me, but once our relationship progressed, running was the last thing on our mind."

"Relationship?" Catherine's eyes squinted.

Victoria drank the last sip of her cold coffee to avoid her question.

"What do you mean by relationship? I thought this was just sex, an escape."

"Of course. I just meant we didn't need an excuse to get together anymore, we have our routine now. After the Board of

Directors meetings, on Saturdays when Ed works, my days off from here, and of course the occasional Jean-made-me-stay-late evenings."

"But what did you mean by relationship? I wouldn't consider what Mangle and I have a relationship."

Victoria didn't consider what Catherine and Mangle had a relationship either. Persuading her to come over when it was convenient for him, making her rearrange her plans and upset her schedule to satisfy his needs. "What *do* you call what the two of you have?" Victoria shifted the focus back to Catherine.

"It's an awakening. A discovery of who I am, releasing my inhibitions, experimenting, seeing what I'm capable of."

Catherine was capable all right. Capable of giving him blow jobs on her lunch hour in deserted parking lots. How low did you have to go to prove your worth to someone? Shouldn't it be equal?

"And what's he doing for you?" Heather piped in.

"Are you kidding? I had serious sex phobias. In one day, he set all my fears free. I wouldn't let my own husband see me naked. I spent the past month having sex in broad day light in the center of his wide-open living room, on his lounge chair on the pool deck, and not to mention skinny-dipping in his pool. He believed in me enough to stay by my side and guide me. I was pathetic."

"No you weren't," Victoria said. The way Catherine shifted his gluttonous perverted needs to some badge of honor, that he was helping her transform herself, *that* was pathetic.

"You are acting differently at work though," Heather said. "That much I have to say. You seem more alive."

"I am, thanks to you Heather. You opened my eyes and changed my world."

"Please stop saying that." Heather looked over at Susie wiping down the tables for the lunch crowd.

"Why not? You helped all of us. Last spring the three of us were miserable. Now we're euphoric and triumphant women!"

"Catherine, do you realize what you're doing, what we're all doing? This isn't right."

"What do you mean? You said you needed an outlet."

"Yeah, but where is this going, what are we really doing, what's the goal?"

Catherine laughed like a pretentious bitch that just found out that she won the PTA mom of the year award. Did they even have that? "Heather. There is no goal. I'm escaping my life as a neglected wife and mistreated employee and travelling to the land of hot sex and adultery."

Victoria gasped and fell back into her chair.

"I can't argue with that," Heather said. "I'm no better. I've been sleeping with Silvatri for almost four months now and I've yet to see his house. At least Mangle lets you into his home."

"You've never been invited?" Catherine asked.

"No. We usually fool around in my Jeep after rock climbing, or in his office on the weekends I work."

"Why haven't you been to his house, he's divorced isn't he?"

"Separated. His wife has an apartment a few blocks away. Maybe he's afraid she'll stop by."

"But they're separated, who cares? It was her choice to move out."

"He doesn't speak about it, not sure. I don't ask and he doesn't tell."

"Why did she leave him, why didn't she keep the house? They have a son don't they?" Victoria asked.

Heather huffed and pooched her lips out. "She chose to leave, I never asked. Didn't feel it was my place."

"Don't you think that's strange?"

"Honestly, if I wanted to get away from Lance and he refused to move, I'd take the girls and just go, too."

"I guess when the divorce is final maybe he'll feel more comfortable having you in his house," Victoria said. She couldn't help sense the same disappointment Heather felt in her current situation that she felt with hers. It seemed like they both wanted more. Still searching for that passionate romance.

"That would be nice. I'd like to see him more often." Heather smiled.

"Next week's your rock climbing trip upstate, right?"

"Yes, were going to New Paltz, the Gunks, with Richard and Jenny. He set it up. Meeting a guide up there."

"You must be excited."

"I'm excited but nervous. Nervous about climbing outside, real mountains, the height and all, but also nervous about leaving the girls with Lance for a full day. You'd think after almost thirteen years I'd be confident enough to leave them home alone with their father. Hopefully he'll feed them."

"He thinks you're going to a nutrition conference?" Victoria asked. "I'd love to spend a whole day with Aiden. And night. Fall asleep in front of his fireplace, wake up in his arms, have breakfast cooked by him in his kitchen."

Victoria faded off into fairytale land, envisioning Aiden running his soft finger up and down her body like he did. Beginning at her eyelashes, extending to ticklish crevices, then returning to her face once again. Lengthy massages on his bed with the curtain flowing in and out with the breezes. The way he kissed her, his soft pouty lips against hers. Too bad the cold weather was coming, they could've enjoyed breakfast on his back patio.

Our relationship. She thought about the word she used again. When she was with Aiden, it did feel like a relationship. They were a couple like any other. Loving and appreciating, concern for each other's wellbeing. Wasn't that a relationship?

No. Imaginative thoughts, like a child believing she was a fairy princess. It is what it is. They both knew that.

"Hello, earth to Victoria. Are you listening?" Heather said.

"Sorry, what did you say?"

"Nothing, never mind. The two of you are in la la land."

"It really is," Catherine said. "You forget you have your old boring life. Suddenly you're single, no kids, no job even. It's like I'm living two separate lives. This is magical. Why wasn't it like this before I had kids?"

"It was for me. Well not with Lance, but with Nicolo at least." Heather took both her hands and rubbed them up and down her face.

"Well, whatever this is, I'm glad we're going through it together." Victoria lifted her empty cup in the air and the other two toasted to their other lives.

Chapter 34

Heather

Heather rubbed her cheeks and laughed at herself in the mirror. Why the hell was she doing this? Laurel and Rori charged into the bathroom and cheered, followed by Gia whistling a high-pitched shrill of excitement.

"I'm on the goddamned phone," Lance screeched. "Every day is the same crap. Have you no respect?"

Asshole. "Come on girls, let's go before it gets crowded."

"Is daddy coming?" Rori asked.

Heather rolled her eyes. After almost five years, Rori still didn't get it. "No honey, he...has to work."

"On Saturday?"

"Yes, but we'll have fun, especially me." Laurel and Gia giggled but Heather did not find it funny.

The four of them pulled into Superstorm Adventure Park and jumped out of the Jeep. The girls ran to the ticket booth while Heather lagged behind.

"Come on, mom." Laurel tugged on her arm.

They purchased their four wrist bracelets enabling them to stay all day long. All day. Long. Heather strolled to the kiddie section holding Rori's hand, following her tiny steps.

Laurel leaped in front, preventing her from moving. "Where do you think you're going?"

"Rori's never been here before, I'm letting her go on her rides first, it's not fair otherwise."

"You're just stalling," Gia said.

"Before we leave today, it will happen."

Rori clanged the bell on the little blue tugboat, squealed with delight on the baby caterpillar rollercoaster and waved her hands in the air on the yellow number four helicopter. Gia snuck on the hot air balloon spinner with Rori, and then Laurel held her hand when they rode the Whale Swinger, the ride that made your stomach hurl out of your body. Ugh. Hurl was the wrong word to choose. With each ride, Heather faked a smile and tensed.

"Okay, no more stalling." Laurel tucked her arm under Heather's as if they were square dancing and dragged her to the roller coasters.

Heather cringed. "Can't we try something smaller first?" She twisted around and pointed to the ride behind her. "What about this one?"

"The Frisbee?" Gia shouted.

"Yeah, what's the Frisbee?"

"I went on that with my field trip last year."

"Was it...safe?"

"All the rides are safe, mom." Laurel sighed.

"Just pick one already. You said you wanted to ride a roller coaster and now you're chickening out." Rori clucked and waved her arms like poultry on crack.

"Rori! Who taught her that?" Laurel and Gia both giggled and ran away. "Okay, okay, I'll pick the Frisbee to start. It looks less frightening."

"I'll stay with Rori, you can go on with Gia. It's her favorite ride."

"Gia loves all the rides, that's not saying much."

The ride attendant unlocked the chain. The crowd took off and boarded the giant Frisbee. Gia gripped her mother's hand and guided her to two molded seats near each other. "I hate rides," Heather roared. "Hate them."

"You'll be fine."

The buzzer sounded and a large hydraulic lap bar appeared over her head and descended in front of her. "Oh, this cannot be good, the safety bar tells it all. This is a mistake. The roller coaster only had that thin silver bar across your lap!"

Heather watched the other kids kick their legs and wave their arms overhead. Shrieks of delight echoed within the silver Frisbee as the motor hummed to start the ride. She clutched the lap bar and closed her eyes.

The metal disk whisked them up to the right, then down and to the left. Up and down like the stupid whale ride Rori was on. Heather's stomach took a nosedive into her cervix and then retracted and flung up and out of her throat. "I'm gonna die," she screamed.

"It hasn't even started yet."

"What do you mean?"

"We're only going up and down. Remember mom, it's called the *Frisbee*."

Before she made the connection, the disc began to spin while rising higher and higher. "Oh my God, oh my God, oh my God." Her stomach no longer knew which way to go, it twirled in circles and then tumbled like Jack and Jill. Heather clenched her hands around the yellow bar and dug her nails into the padding, knuckles as white as the vanilla ice cream she just ate and now regretted.

"Gia, I'm going to die!"

"No you're not. This is coooool!"

"How much longer?"

"It hasn't really spun yet, it's just starting to get its speed up."

"What?!" Her eyes lids jerked open but couldn't tell if she was upside down or which side of the park they were on. She tried to turn her head toward Gia, but pressure prevented it, she could only manage to shift her eyes to the right. Gia's eyes were wide open and her hands loosely flying in the air.

With one last plummet, the Frisbee shot up and began spinning wildly, faster and faster, twirling and rotating. "Oh shit, oh my God, no, oh fuck!" The disc gyrated around the center axle every three seconds, tossing her out of control. Her heart began to race, ready to explode, her rock-hard stomach churned and bounced. With her jaw clenched, unable to scream anymore, she squeezed her eyes shut, unable to face the reality.

She had felt this way once before.

She wanted to get off, but impossible, she had to ride it out. She chose to get on, tried to prove a point, wanted to make everyone happy. Just silly fear, they said. Face it, control it and you'll be happy. Most of the things you worry about never happen they said. But it did. She knew it was a mistake. From day one. She felt it but went along for the ride anyway.

Peer pressure telling you what they think is right, not what's right for you, what's in your heart. She screamed but no one heard her. She cried but that only showed weakness. Be strong they said, stop being selfish, you're the luckiest girl in the world.

The panic attack did not subside. She walked down the aisle in her white gown, her straight jacket, and screamed from within. Her cries for help overlooked. She walked down the path to Hell. Wanted to run but fear prevented her. She was a coward for walking down the aisle that day. A coward for sticking around for so long and still there today. Coward for what she did to Nicolo.

What role model was she to her daughters by hiding and pretending everything was all right? A fake. Just like Catherine, just like Victoria.

She knew it was wrong way before he proposed. Where were her real friends? Princesses looking for their princes surrounded her. Heather, their guinea pig. She sobbed after she left the ceremony, unable to believe she went through with it, drank until inebriated, perfected the fake smile as usual.

The screaming resumed now, loud and deafening. Screaming for help. Once again, no one to help her.

The ride slowed, then came to a halt. Gia stood and took a step in front of her mom. She tapped her hand on Heather's shoulder, then bowed her head to look for a reaction. "Are you okay?"

Heather sighed. It was over. But was it really? She gave Gia her hand and smiled. "Yes, honey, I'm okay." Better than okay. She faced her fears again, but there was still a bigger obstacle to contend with.

****

Heather lounged on her bed reading *Oxygen* magazine. Laurel strolled past her door and then her footsteps came to a halt. An eyeball popped into the doorway.

"Yes?" Heather grinned.

"Can I talk to you?"

"Of course, what a silly question." Heather put her magazine down and propped the pillow on Lance's side of the bed.

Laurel jumped onto the bed and ignored the prepared pillow. "Mom, how do you know when you're in love." Heather's eyes bulged. Laurel was turning thirteen this month but she hoped her dating would hold off at least until she attended high school. "I mean, how did you know you were in love with daddy?"

Now the former question didn't seem that difficult. Nicolo, the only man she ever loved entered her mind. "Well, when you're in love you can't stop thinking about that person. Not simply because they're funny or popular, but for real reasons. They listen to you when you speak, really listen, while gazing into your eyes. They support you when you're upset but also push you to accomplish important things in your life. They think about you just as much, and you know this because they tell you how much they missed you, or surprise you with little gifts or plan a weekend away together. Phone calls at work just because, compliments because they notice something new about you and they make you laugh when they see you unhappy."

Her deranged marriage with Lance pushed through. "They walk around the house to see what needs to get done because it's our home, one we bought together and needs to be taken care of as a team. They play with their children because they realize what a special gift they are and want to spend every minute with them. Teaching them, experiencing new things, making memories. They tell you they love you every day because every day together is a blessing." Heather trailed off and looked outside the window. Her stomach still woozy from the Frisbee.

Yes. It was true. She knew now. Couldn't fake it any longer. She had fallen in love with Silvatri.

Laurel looked at her puzzled. "Mom, I was just asking 'cause Mallory Schipper told everyone at recess that she was in love and she's only been going out with Max Texeira for one day." Laurel hopped off her bed, shook her head and fled back down the hallway.

Chapter 35

Catherine

"**I** hoped you would've showed up this weekend my little Catherine," Dr. Mangle said.

"I told you it was my son's birthday."

"Guess you didn't want to see me. Couldn't even squeeze in an hour for me, eh?"

"It was just very busy. My cousins came in from out of town and between the set up and clean up..."

"Yes, yes, yes, but how are you going to make this up to me? It was so lonely at that big house of mine."

"I thought I made it up to you last time."

"That was nice but this is a new week. How 'bout another lunchtime blow job? They keep me going the rest of the day."

"I can't today. Jean scheduled a meeting to discuss the lecture I have to present to the Silver Sneakers group at a gym."

"I think you're avoiding me Catherine. Have you found someone else?"

"No of course not, I'm just so busy. School started up again, PTA meetings, homework, Colton's birthday, ballet will be starting soon, and– "

"You're doing that rambling thing again. I'm just interested in what you're going to do for me, Catherine. Haven't I done a lot for you? Haven't I brought happiness into your life? Fulfilled your wildest fantasies, taken you away from your hell? Isn't that worth anything to you?"

Catherine peered into his longing eyes. He *had* done so much for her. She owed him. Finding time now that the summer ended made it more difficult. "I'll see if I can leave work an hour early and come over, but only for an hour. I have to get home and cook dinner."

Catherine trudged down the hallway leading to Jean's office unable to shake her anxiety. Why couldn't she have Heather's fearless nature, always letting things roll off her shoulder? Jean's condescending manner erased everything Mangle helped instill in her. She faced her fears with him, why not Jean?

Catherine entered the decaying cavity.

Jean arched over her desk, hands clutched in front and around her huge torpedo breasts that sprawled across the desk like two rump roasts.

"I hope you can explain your lateness."

Catherine glanced at the clock. Two minutes after one. "I guess the clock in our office is a little slow."

"Is this some kind of joke? Do you think I have nothing better to do than wait around for you?"

Panic rose inside as the sound of her own heartbeat thundered in her ears.

A sharp grimace knocked Catherine back in her seat. "Why exactly did I hire you, to just sit there like a fuckin' mouse and squeak? You volunteered to give this lecture, but I have my doubts on your competence. If you failed to provide the necessary information or had stage fright, how do you think that would make me look?"

"I'm sorry, I can do this and I spent last night gathering information on nutrition for the elderly."

"The fuckin' elderly! Do you even realize what Silver Sneakers is? It's available to anyone eligible for Medicare. I'm eligible for Medicare, do I need a walker? Is that what you're saying?"

"No, that's not what I meant. I called the gym and they said the majority of the members are in their late seventies, a few even in their eighties– "

"You called the gym? You went over my head and called the gym?"

"I just wanted to gather the proper information so my material targeted the correct audience."

Jean lurched out of the chair and towered over Catherine. Her glasses slid to the tip of her nose and her blood shot eyes looked over the rims. "How dare you! They called me, not you. I gave you this job and I can take it away."

"You asked me to do this so I gathered information and I– "

"Did you graduate from an accredited college? Did you pay someone to make it through to the end? Did your husband marry you out of pity?" Are your children even safe being raised by a moron such as yourself, Catherine Bordeau?"

She shook under her gaze. The torment, merciless. "I did what I needed to do to get the job done," she managed to sputter.

"The job done? The job done? You're lucky if you can dress yourself every morning. Luckily for you, you wear a lab coat otherwise everyone would see that as well."

The choking fear reminded her of the day Mangle made her step out onto his diving board naked, while he observed her from his lounge chair clear across the other side of the pool. The pool, on a raised bed on his property, the diving board, two feet higher than the concrete deck, elevated her enough to see over the fence. So could the neighbor.

She panicked, went to step down. Mangle noticed her reaction and ordered her to stay put. The neighbor watched as Mangle instructed her to touch her breasts on the diving board. Each time she closed her eyes he commanded her to look at him. Her fear turned to excitement as it always did with him. She was a star on the diving board. Idolized by two men.

Her anguish over Jean needed to transform as well. A passage into a life filled with courage and resolution. Her pounding heart boiled her blood. She breathed in deep, visualized herself on the diving board. This was simpler. *You can do this.*

She bolted up, removed her lab coat and hung it over her arm. "By the way, the suit I'm wearing costs more than your entire wardrobe. I'm doing the lecture, I already spoke to the manager, we're on the same page, and she liked my ideas. Good day."

Catherine turned, strutted out of her office and down the hall. Her heart raced, as did her feet. She scuttled, progressed to a jog and then a full sprint, straight to Heather's floor.

Chapter 36

Victoria

"This chicken's dry," Ed shouted. "Did you get distracted while cooking?"

"Actually, yes, I did. I have somewhat of an important event in the morning, not that you noticed."

"What now? There's always something happening in your life. More important than...me." His pitiful expression inspected the defective piece of chicken, which he nudged with his knife. How utterly heartbreaking. A real tear-jerker.

"Here's an idea. How about cooking for me occasionally? Perhaps say, hey you have that huge race tomorrow that you've been talking about for six months, let's go out for dinner to celebrate all your hard work. You must be exhausted."

"Exhausted? You had the day off."

"To prepare for this event. And your meal."

"I don't need this shit. I'm going out."

"No! I'm going out, and this time don't wait up for *me*."

She snatched her jacket and dashed out the door. It would be the first time she visited Aiden unshowered and looking God-awful but all she wanted was to be in his arms.

Victoria's tires flew over the curb and into Aiden's driveway. There he stood on his porch in a white ribbed T-shirt with his silky navy-blue sweat pants.

She raced to him. His hands slipped under the threads of hair draped around her face. He kissed her forehead and then hugged her, his hold perpetual.

Aiden's fingers intertwined with Victoria's and he guided her to the kitchen, dispensing a glass of water. She gulped the cold liquid and then caught sight of herself in the microwave's mirrored glass-door. "I look horrible."

He clasped both her hands into his and kissed each finger. "You...can never look bad...my sweet...Victoria."

"I'm embarrassed by my appearance and I must smell vile."

Aiden giggled. "I love your scent. I can detect it on my pillow days after you've left."

"I'd feel better if I took a quick shower."

"Wait here." Aiden left the kitchen and entered the bathroom. The gush of the faucet echoed until he closed the door behind him.

Victoria wandered into the living room. A crystal vase filled with perhaps the last of the summer flowers from his garden, stood in the center of his end table. Marigolds and impatiens rotated around the black-eyed Susan's that burst from the middle. A silver frame treasured the memory of his sons on a sunset beach. The photograph of his wife lounging on a Cancun beach, no longer present.

She removed her shoes, collapsed into the velvety cushions and eased her head onto the pillow. What would it be like to sleep here tonight and never return home? Freshly chopped cherry-wood stacked to the left of the fireplace, caught her attention.

Aiden entered the living room and slipped his hand into hers. She shadowed his steps into the bathroom. Floating clouds of bubbles filled the vast square bathtub. The mosaic tile surrounding the tub reflected the twinkling candles set around the room.

"Take all the time you need, I'll wait in the living room until you're finished." He kissed her on the lips and retreated, closing the door behind him. Victoria melted into the warm foamy cocktail and closed her eyes. Daydreaming. Fantasizing.

When she left paradise, wrapped in Aiden's silver plush robe, Victoria entered the rapture of a roaring fire. *Her fire.* Its blaze flickered off two wine goblets.

She burrowed within his embrace, cuddled and nuzzled his chest. He stroked her damp hair as beads of water dripped onto her shoulder and rolled down the robe. They remained that way, their drinks untouched, and watched the fire smolder and burn out.

****

The gathering of 1,089 participants surrounded Victoria, almost double the size of last year. She greeted Ken from Gym Addiction and thanked Barbara from the Amorous Baroness Inn for their contributions. Cases of Robust Protein Bars stacked as tall as her, surrounded a booth on the far left. Runners chugged their CloverRidge water and children sprinted by with balloons and banners showing their support. White squares of numbers graced the colorful shirts on the racers.

Speakers blasted dance songs from local radio station WRLI, while runners stretched and jogged for their warm up. Porta-Potties decorated the sidelines with their powder blue and white stripes. Vendor tents and tables piled with sunshine-yellow bananas welcomed the participants. Warm light reflected off the shamrock-covered grass. Faces determined, nervous, focused, smiling.

Victoria glanced at the overhead digital clock. Only three minutes remained before the official start to the race. She watched the families gather to support their loved ones.

Heather promised to take her daughters to the fall festival celebration at Red Rooster Farms today. She couldn't wait to hear about their usual antics. She pictured Catherine beaming at herself in the bedroom mirror after yesterday's first victory with Jean.

"This is the worst managed race I've ever attended. Who's organizing this?" A voice emerged from behind.

Victoria spun to find a handsome, salt and pepper haired man standing less than a foot away, holding a bouquet of flowers. Her smile returned to its upward position.

"They're beautiful," she said.

"Unfortunately they're store bought. There isn't much left in my gardens to compliment your beauty."

She brought the flowers to her nose, breathing in their fresh scent. The mellow-harvest bouquet with its scented geraniums and rustic autumn colors warmed her heart like a bonfire celebration. Amongst a crowd of thousands, she could not thank him as she wished, could not embrace him for his gift. It stung like a yellow jacket, the burn excruciating.

Boom! Shrieks and applause bellowed from behind as the athletes fired across the start line. She turned to watch throngs of contenders leave their mark – their families cheering them on.

Aiden twisted her back towards him and stole a kiss from her thirsty lips. The hollering continued as spectators ran passed them in hurried leaps. She didn't care who saw anymore. Didn't care one bit.

Chapter 37

Heather

Heather and Silvatri travelled up the winding road that led to the rock climbing facility in New Paltz. The two and a half hour drive provided them with various conversations ranging from hospital gossip, his son's seventh birthday party, Rori losing another tooth and the plan of finding a secluded area with a perfectly shaped rock to throw her against.

They met Jason their guide, hiked for a quarter of a mile on a narrow mountain trail to a flat base and waited while Jason secured the first hold. Heather and Silvatri ate the clementines she brought and then he climbed upon a pile of rocks nearby. Heather took pictures of him posing like the God he was.

The late September weather released the humidity, blessing them with seventy-degree temperatures. At 9:30 in the morning though, under the shade from the tall trees, Heather shivered in the cool air.

"Are you cold?" Silvatri asked.

She smiled, remembering the first time he asked her that six months ago. So much had happened since then. Their sexual trysts blossomed into strong feelings of passion and love.

"Yes, it was warmer when we were hiking in the sun carrying all the equipment."

He sat behind her, straddled his legs around, then took his fleece-covered arms and insulated her. They rocked back and forth on the granular earth.

"Are you upset Richard and Jenny couldn't make it?" she asked.

"Not at all."

Heather's body warmed from his answer. Every week spent together, she felt closer to him. She thought of Victoria's romantic relationship and Catherine's sadistic one and wondered where she fit in.

Jason secured the last of the ropes and looked up. "Who's first?"

"I'll go," Silvatri said.

Silvatri began his climb and made it appear effortless. Halfway up though, he slipped. Jason coached him as to where he should place his left foot. Although strong, his massive frame meant more weight to lift and swing around.

He made it to the top, let out a gorilla wail and hopped down at a fast pace.

Heather held up her hand to high-five him, but wobbled, her locked knees noticeable.

Silvatri hugged her tight. "You'll be fine, relax." Then kissed her on the lips.

She smiled at the massive rock. Good fear she thought. Except this wall was real, no cute-shaped holds to dangle from. She completed 5.9 climbs right alongside him at the facility, but this presented all new challenges.

She began her ascent carefully gliding her feet from ledge to crack to crevice. Heather leaped to reach the next hold, fell and swung wide. Her heartbeat quickened and despite the cool temperatures, the sweat mounted on her palms. Large sprays of chalk floated down on the men below.

"It's only September Heather. There's no snow yet," Silvatri hollered.

She quivered at the height she scaled. Seventy feet higher than the indoor place and she only clambered half way up so far. She panicked, rested her foot on a tiny ledge and heaved out breaths.

"You okay?" Jason asked.

"Yes," she lied. This would be her one and only climb. Just one to say she did it. She would be more than happy to watch Silvatri scramble up the various crags the rest of the day.

Heather reached up to the next hold and saw the flat, smooth surface before her. No fissures, no jagged edges to touch with the tips of her fingers, no slits or openings anywhere.

"You have to lean your entire body into the mountain. Face, hands, arms, against the rock. Use your feet to step up. Once you get your foot where your hand is now, you can push yourself up a few feet and then reach the next level which has a tiny hand hold on the left."

Was he insane?

"Heather, remember that exercise Richard taught you where you do an entire climb with your hands behind your back? Do that."

"This is totally different."

"No, it's not," he shouted back.

She rested her chest, hips and face against the cold rock, then extended her arms up the mirror-like surface, spread eagle.

"Oh yeah," Silvatri said.

"Knock it off." How could he think of sex at a time like this? She slowly lifted her right foot to where her hand was and stepped up as if skipping an entire wrung on a ladder. With the new height, she searched for the handhold. "Where is it?"

"It was right there."

"Your arm reach is longer than mine."

"Excuses."

Heather brought her other foot up still unable to grasp hold of anything with her hands.

"You're going to have to jump," Jason said.

"Never again," she mumbled. The top ledge an additional twenty-five feet at least. "I hate this, I hate you."

"What?"

"Nothing." She peered above and noticed the ridge on her left. The rope pulled her toward the right though. If she missed, her entire body would swing to the right, with no way to get back.

Heather counted to three, pushed off with her left leg and propelled herself up, catching on to the sharp gravelly hold.

"All right!" Jason shouted.

Holy Shit. She did it. Relax, breathe, catch your breath. Heather finished the elevation as quickly as possible, reached the top and smacked it.

"Keep going," Jason said.

"But I'm done."

"Climb up and over the ledge."

"For what?"

"The view."

"The view? No way, uh uh."

"No regrets, remember?" Silvatri said.

Heather kicked her foot skyward, rested her heel over the top, and pulled herself higher as if doing a pull-up. She rolled over flat on her back, gasping and looking at the sky. Only one small cloud that looked like Mr. Snuffleupagus floated by. She heard their shouts, disappointed with her stalling.

She rolled onto her stomach, crawled an inch at a time to the edge, peered down at them and felt ill.

Then she looked to her right and beheld nothing but aqua sky and treetops with speckles of orange, red, and yellow feathery-spikes resembling rows of Celosia dispersed throughout the green trees.

Mountaintops surrounded her and the full understanding of how high they were, struck. The road that encircled the area, the quarter mile hike, the one hundred foot climb, brought her to the height of the clouds.

She stood. The sun shone upon her, a breeze fluttered the leaves on the scraggly tree where Jason tied their ropes. She was free. No Lance, no Jean, nobody to restrain or suffocate her. She imagined her daughters standing beside her and breathing in the fresh air.

Heather conquered this, another fear dismantled. Victoria's 10k success last week had empowered her, and Catherine had laid into Jean. They were strong women and still growing.

Heather took in one final crisp breath and knew she could defeat all her demons.

"Are you okay?" Silvatri's voice echoed.

"Yes." Heather beamed, then hitched herself back over the ledge to make her descent.

She touched the earth where her backpack relaxed on its side and then reevaluated the climb she completed. "What's next?" She pretended to yawn.

After lunch, the three of them gathered their gear and tracked to the next climbing spot. "I meant to tell you," Silvatri dumped their belongings beside a tree, "that new rock climbing facility they're constructing near the hospital is supposed to open next month. I drove by yesterday on the way home."

"How does it look?"

"Huge."

"We have to check it out." Heather raised her eyebrows up and down.

The suggestion jolted Silvatri who spun toward Jason. "Where's the bathrooms?"

"If you go down this trail to the bottom of this section you'll see a path. Follow it to the right, down about one fifty yards and there's a Porta-Potty. Otherwise you have to walk back to where you parked."

"We'll go back to the parking lot." Silvatri grabbed Heather's hand and helped her up and over the boulders spread around them. They strolled down the path until he stopped at the Porta-Potty.

"I thought you said we'd go to the parking lot bathrooms."

"Nah, that was to give us extra time. He'll be busy setting up the next climb for at least twenty minutes if not longer. Now's our chance." He pecked her lips then dove into the portable facility.

They both used the bathroom and then Silvatri led her off the path into a wooded area. He searched the isolated terrain and then hoisted Heather up on a low boulder. He stood before her, his hands on her shoulders and paused. He peered into her eyes as if never noticing the hazel coloring before. Silvatri's fingers touched the tendrils of hair and tucked them behind her ears. His eyes continued to stare.

He shifted a few inches forward, hesitated, and examined her lips like a tourist. For the first time, he brushed against her lips with slow silent movements. Lips caressed, grazing and tasting. Gentle and comforting.

He had never kissed her this softly before. Why now? Heather leaned in forcefully and moaned but he pushed her back, and then resumed his unobtrusive movements. His gentle style calmed her. She eased up and let him take control.

The slow discreet manner in which he removed her pants sent tingles up her spine. He entered Heather, gradual nudges, until she felt all of him in her. He slid back and forth unhurried. For once she could feel the full length of him and every inch of her that he rubbed.

This new side of him sparked curiosity. She found herself enjoying it, delighted by his tenderness. She let him operate and maneuver himself while he continued to kiss her in delicate wisps. His blue eyes, wide and inquisitive. Why were they open now? He always kept them closed in the past.

A shiver crawled through her veins and she allowed the love she felt for him to fully emerge. She had fallen in love with Silvatri, and now it was clear he felt the same. The way he studied her, his tender kiss, the gentle lovemaking. Yes, that's what it was. He was making love to her for the first time. She had felt it and now, so did he.

Months of spending time together, rock climbing every week, deep conversations and stolen kisses in abandoned hallways of the hospital, had cultivated and here, alone in a corner of nature, his love for her had sprung. No longer in a cramped car, struggling to have her. No grunting, no sharp thrusts, no firm pressure of his lips onto hers. At this summit, surrounded by earth's wild primitive state, he expressed his true feelings to her. Alone, with no one to rush home to, he could reveal it. Should she say *I love you* here, or wait until their drive home tonight?

She experienced freedom on the mountaintop, but now understood which direction her life would go. She would leave Lance, leave him for Silvatri. He would be divorced soon and she would follow. Her daughters would finally have a father that adored them, would take them on trips and play with them in the park. They would have a real role model to look up to when they chose their husbands.

He slid into her one final time, vibrating when he finished. He did not howl, did not move, pressed his eyes tight and squeezed her shoulders in his chest. The powerful way he hugged her confirmed their destined future. She watched his expression and knew it was true. They had fallen in love in this magical scenery. Things were different now, the start of something real and endearing. The first time she loved another man in over fifteen years.

Chapter 38

Catherine

"Bentley, thank you for helping Emily with her homework. I know she looks up to you."

Bentley ducked his head but the cherry-colored skin shone bright enough for Catherine to catch. Since she attended several of his soccer games, he seemed eager to help Catherine more. She gave him additional responsibilities which lessened her stress but he responded by taking over as the man of the house.

He picked up the lawn mower last month and took pride in carving diagonal strips in the lawn. Of course he held his head high whenever a car drove by, but as long as the arguments decreased and the four of them enjoyed each other's company, who cared.

Colton entered the kitchen and Catherine glared at him. "What?" he asked. She nodded toward his jacket on the floor, her arms pressed against her chest and waited. "Oh, sorry." Colton picked up his jacket and hung it over the kitchen chair. "Are we going to that haunted house thing?"

"Yeah. You're going with us, right mom?" Bentley chimed in.

"Me? In a haunted house?"

"Yes, please mom, it'll be fun. Come on, you'll love it." Colton folded his hands as if praying.

"Yeah, especially when that zombie with the tarantula coming out of his eye attacks her."

"Ew, ew, no way." Catherine made a gagging face and turned away. They continued to beg when she twisted abruptly and came at them with hands shaped into claws and a wrinkled face with her tongue hanging out. She snarled and lunged at Bentley. He tripped over Emily's Dora the Explorer backpack and fell backward on his butt.

Colton snorted as Emily entered the room in her pink ballet outfit and spied her brother on the floor. Emily giggled. Bentley, embarrassed at first, began to laugh as well.

"The zombies will be more afraid of me I think," Catherine said.

"Especially with that shirt," Bentley said, standing up.

Catherine viewed the olive green blouse she still wore from work. It *was* ugly. She glanced at the clock. "Emily grab your ballet bag and meet me in the car. I'm going to change my clothes quickly."

"Why?" Emily asked.

"I feel like looking like cool-mommy today."

"Yay!" She hopped up and down and then hugged Catherine around her hips.

Catherine removed her work clothes and rummaged through her drawers for a polo shirt. Instead, she found the T-shirt Heather bought her for her birthday last year and pulled it out. Originally, she thought it as a joke but looking at it today, she knew. She yanked out a pair of jeans and raced to get dressed.

Emily tiptoed into dance class and Catherine caught sight of Odessa at the window. She groaned. A summer away from her did not feel long enough. She greeted other moms along the way and then took one final stride in front of the window. A smirk couldn't help but emerge in the corner of her cheek.

Odessa flicked her long black nest of hair over her shoulder. She sensed Catherine's presence and jerked her head around like an actress exiting a limousine for the red carpet. "Oh, Catherine I didn't notice you."

Catherine ignored her and waved when Emily stretched her leg upon the ballet barre. Emily winked, but Catherine noticed Madison more. Madison stopped stretching and watched the exchange between the mother and daughter. Catherine's heart ached for her.

"What are you wearing?" Odessa barked at Catherine.

Catherine continued to ignore her and gave Emily the thumbs up when class began. She remained calm, kept her composure. She stood with an erect posture and then turned toward Odessa as if the first time spotting her. "Oh, hello Odessa," she said in a clear loud voice, "I didn't see you there. I'm so excited about Emily starting this new year."

"I asked you what you were wearing."

Catherine glanced down at her tight *Pink Panther* T-shirt and hid her smile. Then she brushed off a piece of lint from her jeans. "These jeans? I bought them over the summer, clearance rack, Marshalls, ten bucks, size four. Can you imagine?" She ran her hand down her butt caressing it in a seductive manner.

"I meant the shirt."

"Pink Panther? You mean to tell me you don't know who he is? Odessa I'm shocked at your ignorance, everyone knows who he is." Catherine cackled, then waved her hand brushing her off.

"I know who he is. Why are you wearing it?" Odessa's face contorted.

"To support breast cancer awareness this month. Are you saying you forgot? They're selling bracelets at the school. I'm surprised at you. Are you feeling all right this evening?"

Odessa stood silent. Her body tensed, nostrils flared. She was muted like the Little Mermaid.

"Emily's having a great year in school so far and she just couldn't wait for ballet to start. How's Madison's fifth day in a row? She looks positively exhausted, Odessa."

Odessa glanced into the window at Madison. Madison lagged behind the rest of the class, each move off by a second or two. "She's fine."

"How's she doing in school? Third grade can be so hard with all those tests this year."

"Why are you asking, what did you hear? Did Roslyn tell you?" Her face shrunk as if left out in the sun for days.

Catherine, no longer having fun, returned to the window. Odessa meant nothing to her. She didn't care anymore. She needed to stop worrying about what other people thought of her.

The haunted house tour entered her mind instead. This time with images of Odessa shrieking in the middle of one of the rooms because she missed the latest sale at Aldo's. A chuckle escaped her lips.

Chapter 39

Victoria

"**M**om, why haven't you made plans for your anniversary party yet?" Sara asked. "Isn't it like a month away?" Sara filled her bottle with icy water from the refrigerator and then gulped down a quarter of it.

"Yeah," Andrew piped in, "usually you've got these things hooked up months in advance. Losing your skills there?"

Victoria normally craved their attention and to have them both home this weekend with no plans should have overjoyed her. Instead, their questioning of a topic she avoided made her want to flee. "I thought of a few places to have it."

"Thought of? I'm surprised you haven't stayed up late to make party favors at this point." Andrew chortled.

"Party favors? I have to do that?" Victoria lurched from her chair and paced to the other side of the room. The last thing on her mind was throwing a party for someone she barely spoke to anymore. She'd rather spend the money on Aiden at a bed and breakfast in Montauk. What was she thinking? Completely unrealistic.

"Do you need help mom?" Sara asked.

"Yes, I think I do. That would be great. Would you Sara?"

Victoria spent the weekend visiting restaurants able to accommodate at least fifty guests. She perused her guest list not wanting to burden anyone to come to a party honoring two hosts that were not in love anymore. What a deceptive preparation.

Misleading people, faking an evening, for what? To show off her prize, her honor, thirty years of lies? She should never have told anyone.

Her cheeks burned, a blank look overtook her face, hunched shoulders met each catering manager at the restaurants. She wanted to fade into the background and let Sara take over.

Unable to stomach it any longer, she chose the fourth restaurant they surveyed. Victoria found herself choosing food items Aiden would enjoy and imagined him feeding her.

"I don't think dad likes salmon," Sara interjected.

"I do. I like salmon. Is that all right with everyone? It's my party too isn't it? Can't I order what I like? I'm paying for the entire thing myself."

The catering manager winced, asked if they needed a minute alone and then retreated.

"Mom, are you ok?" Sara patted her mother's shoulders and Victoria let her daughter see her cry for the first time. "Mom, there is something wrong, what is it?"

Victoria convulsed as if trying to hide the sobs within her, shook her head and let the menus, and her tears, crash to the floor.

Release it, that's it, let it all out. Get rid of it, enough's enough. Years of hiding her pain exploded in front of her daughter. She held nothing back, and it felt good.

After another minute, she clenched her eyes tight and slowed her breathing, deep and slow, deep and slow through her mouth.

"Is this too much pressure, mom? You don't have to do this you know."

"I have to, he earned it. We achieved something many people will never do. It's only right to do this, it's a huge accomplishment." She retrieved the menus refusing to let Sara see another drop from her eyes. "Now where were we? Salmon. Yes, I like that, and the beef tenderloin. Any fingerling potatoes? And what about dessert, any blueberry tarts?"

Chapter 40

Heather

Heather and Silvatri left the new rock climbing facility and strolled toward their cars. "Want to come back to my place?" he asked.

Heather's heart flipped. Did he say his house? What she felt a few weeks ago was real. Things were different, and now an invite back to his home. "Yes, sure, of course."

"Follow me with your car."

He led her to a bedroom decorated in lush fabrics. Curtains to comforters adorned with red and aqua flowers accented by similar color pillows, candles and a throw rug. The scent of apples lingered in the air. He tossed the decorative pillows from the bed onto the floor beside the dresser.

Her initial uncomfortable feelings about being in his home were diffused by his welcoming gestures during a passionate round of sex. Finally seeing him completely naked, his muscular shoulders, tight little butt, rippling abs. Watching him lounge across his bed like a Playgirl model, the light from the ceiling fan reflecting off his skin. He tickled her ribs and squeezed her nose like a bunch of neighborhood kids goofing off in the summer grass.

The bright light and increased space to roll around and experiment in comfort provided them with enhanced intimacy. The affection and tenderness between them reached new heights. He rolled his finger over her thighs and she dreamed of this being their bedroom one day.

Silvatri rested his head on her chest and wrapped his arm

around her naked body. She stroked his hair, twirling her fingers behind his ear and watched their chests rise and fall with each relaxing breath. "This is your bedroom?" she asked.

"This?" He sprang up. "No way, this is the guest room, our bedroom's upstairs. You can't go in there."

Our bedroom? "Why not?"

"That's mine and my wife's bedroom." He shook his head like she was a moron.

"But you're separated, and I thought..." She pulled the blanket up to cover her bare body, suddenly feeling like a whore.

"Thought what?"

"You invited me back to your home tonight, you never did that before."

"The new rock climbing facility is only a half mile away from here. What did you want, to squeeze into your truck again?"

"But you never invited me here before."

"The other facility is all the way in Northdale Springs. Besides, it's getting too cold for the car." He twisted his body to face her. She looked toward the door not speaking. "Heather, what are you saying? You thought because I invited you back here it meant something?"

"But last month, at the Gunks, on that rock, it was different, slower. The way you kissed me, touched me."

"We were only yards away from the trail." He laughed. "I was trying to be quiet. I also kept an ear open in case anyone was coming. Kept my eyes open too. Why are you turning this into something it's not?"

"I just thought..." She slid down under the covers, only her face visible. "We've been together for five months. The slow kiss, the soft touches, the lovemaking on the rock."

"Lovemaking? When was it ever love making? Heather, it was always sex. We agreed from the very first day this would only be sex."

"We've spent every week together rock climbing, talking."

"And having sex in your truck. I don't believe this." Silvatri stood and grabbed his shorts. "I chose you because I thought you'd be safe."

"Chose me? Thought I'd be safe?"

"I mean, you're married, not single. We agreed no feelings involved."

"But it progressed, we became close."

"You're married."

"I told you I was unhappy."

"And what were you expecting?" He held his palms out, waiting for an answer.

"I thought possibly when you got divorced, maybe it could work with us and then I'd get divorced too."

"Heather, I'm not getting divorced. I love my wife, I miss my son."

"But you're separated."

"And going to marriage counseling. I'll do whatever it takes, I don't care how long it takes."

"But she just renewed her lease for another year."

He swung around, deep frowns formed in his forehead. He seized the edge of the comforter and yanked it toward him, leaving her naked body exposed. "Look, I made a mistake, I got caught. I went to marriage counseling, I let her get her own apartment, gave her space, let her think it through. I'm doing whatever it takes to get her back."

"Then why are you with me?"

"I did it all, everything she asked, I did it. But after a year of jerking off, it wears on you. I have needs too. While she's figuring out her life, I have needs."

"What?" Heather reached for her bra and T-shirt. "I don't understand any of this."

"Look who's talking, what are you doing? You're no different. You spend your life with someone who treats you like crap, and then you cheat on him to get what you're missing. "

She took his cargo pants, heaved them onto the floor and far away from her. She pivoted to the edge of the bed and plucked her thong from the floor.

He sat next to her and touched her knee. She recoiled. "Heather, I fucked up. I love my wife, she's amazing, I can't complain at all. She was good to me, we had fun together, we enjoyed playing with Robbie. I can't even say the sex was bad because it was great."

"Then what the fuck?"

"In my office, there was an NP. She worked evenings with me. I won't lie, she was hot. Tight ass, wore these low cut scrub tops. Young, cute, flirty. I avoided her at first, but it became more difficult. When everyone left for the night, she stayed and helped me finish up. After several weeks, we started sitting in my office at the end of every night, talking."

"One morning I woke and realized I had this vivid dream about her. I went to work that evening and couldn't stop looking at her ass when she bent over. Then at one point, she bent toward me and she had this purple and black striped bra on. It reminded me of those can-can girl outfits and how they lift up their skirts when they dance and kick their legs in the air. The whole evening I walked around with a hard-on.

After everyone left, we sat in my office flirting. Bad. I started and I kept it going. After an hour, I mentioned that I saw a glimpse of her bra earlier. She asked if I got a good look. The next thing I know, she lifted her scrub top over her head, threw it to the floor and sauntered over to me. Put her bra right in my face."

Heather pulled her T-shirt up over her breasts wishing she had the rest of her clothes so she could run. Talking about his wife was one thing, but now, another woman. She felt cheap and used.

"God, I can't believe I'm telling you this." He rubbed his right eyebrow as if to scrub it off. "The next thing I knew, she was sitting in my lap and we were having sex on my chair. I went home, saw Robbie, felt instantly guilty. The next time I saw her I said we couldn't do it again. It was a mistake."

Heather moved her eyes down to the bottom of the bed where her feet were. "So what happened?"

"It was too late, our friendship had grown, the chemistry was already there. The yearning didn't go away, it only intensified because I knew I couldn't have that body in my hands again.

We started again, only it progressed, to use your own word. I enjoyed her company, she was a lot of fun." Silvatri twisted on the bed a few inches and caught his expression in the mirror. "Then I crossed the line. I bought her gifts, took her out to romantic dinners, we even went away one weekend. I lied to my beautiful wife and told her I had a medical conference to attend. The girl told me she loved me, I fell in love with her too."

Silvatri glanced away from the mirror and down at his hands in his lap. "This went on for a year. We called each other daily, texted, emailed.

One night I was reading an email from her. She sent me a long note saying she couldn't live this way anymore, hopelessly in love and she wanted to be together permanently. No more long distance, strained relationship. I sat in front of the computer for fifteen minutes trying to think what to write. I loved them both, but my wife, my son..."

My service called. A very dear, long time patient of mine just found out she had stage IV cancer. I spoke to her on the phone but she became hysterical. I was so distraught myself that I finally stood and paced around the kitchen while talking, trying to console her.

I must have been gone for at least a half hour, maybe longer. When I returned to my desk, my wife was sitting at the computer. I don't know how long but long enough to have read the girl's email and several others. A weeks' worth perhaps.

My wife exploded. I begged her, told her I'd never leave her." Silvatri punched his fist into the mattress. "She took Robbie the next morning and left. She moved in with her mother initially. I pleaded with her to come back, offered her the house. She refused to be near me or anything representing me."

He placed his hand on Heather's leg again. She let him this time. "Heather, I hurt my wife and son. He was only five, he didn't understand. But the worst was the girl, I hurt her. I made her fall in love with me. I had to stop seeing her immediately. She had to quit her job in my office, I ruined her life, ruined four lives. I promised I would never do that again.

I understand I broke my wife's heart and I deserved everything I got but after a year I couldn't take it anymore. I know it's selfish but I wanted to touch a woman again...know what it felt like to be wanted and touched. I'm sorry, I only wanted this to be sex between us. You're married, you said you were unhappy and wanted an escape. I thought you wanted the same thing I wanted while you worked on your marriage. I didn't know you were leaning toward divorce because you were having feelings for me.

The girl in my office was single, it was never fair to her what I did. Falling in love with her was wrong. I never meant to hurt her or you, Heather. I thought we were on the same page." He smiled at her and patted her thigh.

"What is this then?" She motioned to the bed they sat on.

"This isn't the same. I let my feelings grow with her, fell in love with her. That was wrong. This is nothing like that."

"Nothing like that? You have absolutely no feelings for me?" She jumped out of bed, grabbed her clothes into one big pile, and thrust them back onto her body, not sure if they were even on correctly, then jerked her yoga pants over her left leg.

"No, that's not what I meant, I'm sorry." He grabbed her and pulled her next to him, one leg still without a pant. "It was wrong to cheat on my wife for any reason, but allowing it to go as far as I did was worse. Sex is one thing but the dinners, the gifts and cards, the long sentimental emails. Christ, we even snuck off for that long weekend together. I hurt my wife but I hurt her more. I had to stop speaking to her, completely. She lost her job. Do you know what that did to her?"

Was he still babbling about the girl? Heather was done. She tied the lace on her sneaker and refused to look at him. How could he sit there, go on about two other women, and not see the hurt she was feeling. Was she invisible? Did he really think that little of her? How could he sit there and think by explaining all of this it would all be okay?

"Heather, if your relationship's not working, fix it or get out."

Now he was giving her advice? She shook her head, she needed to run. Run away from him and everything, but where would she go? Not home, not now in this state. She grabbed her keys and looked over at him. Tears streamed down her face.

"Oh shit," he said, finally noticing the effect on her. "I'm sorry Heather, I thought we were having fun. I only wanted sex from you."

What an arrogant dick. How dare him. Catherine was right. Heather pushed the hair out of her face so he could have a good look at her anguish. "Goodbye," she answered.

"No Heather, wait, please." He locked onto her arm and stopped her. Tears rolled freely now, no need to hold back any longer. She was done, with everyone, and everything.

She unlocked his grip, pulled away and stepped back into the dresser. Silvatri's own eyes welled up but she was unsure why. Was it because he hurt her too? Because he did have feelings for her but refused to admit it, even now? She took a long look at him and thought. No. Heather thought not. He had no feelings at all. Cold, egotistical ass. It was because he just realized he'd have to make friends with his right hand once again.

****

The itchy bedspread rubbed against Heather's arms. Sprawled face down in front of her, he gazed out the window. She shifted on the bed and kicked off her sneakers. She reached forward to touch him and chills darted across her arms. She waved them off discreetly and leaned in to caress his back. Her finger twirled in naïve movements, feigning self-confidence. One finger ran down his spine, to the bottom of his sweatshirt and lifted it to reveal his black T-shirt underneath. She inhaled deep, her ribs tightened, eyes closed, while he continued to watch the car lights pass on the boulevard.

Heather attempted to raise the fabric and reveal his spiced flesh but the shirt did not budge. The clothing she tried to remove was his skin, the color of hot fudge. Alarmed, she leaned back, shuddered, unable to continue with this aberrant behavior. He sensed the break in her touch. Her mouth, wide-open, slammed shut as he rolled over to face her. Breaths quickened, she smiled to mask it, then he pulled her to him and she found herself side by side with Tyrell.

His hand outlined her face, as if touching it would make this real. It glided to her lower lip and her tongue welcomed a single finger. Drenched, it sailed past her neck, to her sweatshirt, unzipping the obstacle. Heather's hand drifted to his heart, its vigorous pulsing soothed her, if only for a moment.

He tilted in and kissed her, his trembling identical to hers. He wrestled with his sweatshirt and removed it to reveal all that was foreign and puzzling. She gazed at him in awe, curiosity beckoned her and she aligned her hands over his chest. Her skin appeared flavorless next to his rich hue but he grabbed her shoulders and drew her in, tasting her pale skin with his insatiable mouth.

Any apprehension, replaced with confidence, he tore the yoga pants and T-shirt from her, making the contrast of their skin more pronounced. He unzipped his pants and her eyelids closed again. She bit down on his shoulder, terrified to look.

He entered her. Any quivering was camouflaged by his quick jabbing movements.

Heather's eyes squeezed tight like on the roller coasters, afraid to experience the full enjoyment of it. To see the danger, knowing it could be wild, and that having the crap scared out of you might actually satisfy your deep hunger to feel. Feel something, anything.

She opened her eyes.

What the hell was she doing?

Chapter 41

Catherine

Catherine sat upon Mangle's granite countertop. Naked. He clunked chunks of ice cubes into two tall glasses and dispensed water from the tap clear to the top.

"Why do you get to wear clothes while I sit here nude?" she asked.

"Are you questioning me, Catherine?"

"No I just—"

"I think you are. I don't like when you question me."

"Sorry, I'm just curious."

"Curious?" he snorted. "I think you lack trust."

"I trust you, but why can't we both be nude?"

"You only grace me with your presence once a week. Make me wait and wait. I even beg you at times. I don't like to beg. I don't need to beg anyone, do you understand what I mean?"

She nodded understanding completely.

"If I'm lucky, you allow me a blowjob once a week in my car, which you complain about and make seem like a big ordeal after all I've done for you."

"No, I—"

"Then when you do finally come over the first words out of your mouth are always 'I have to leave in an hour' or 'I have to leave by nine.'" You make me feel rushed, like you can't wait to leave."

"No, I love being here."

"Now, if I stood before you naked, there would be no barrier between us. I'd be more inclined to take you again." He set the two glasses next to her. "But, you have to leave. You always have to leave, so I'm doing you a favor by placing a barrier of clothes between us, otherwise you'd be late arriving home and I'd have to hear it again."

"But why can't we both wear clothes then, and why must I always sit upon here like a sculpture?" As the words escaped her mouth, she flushed with dread.

His jaw clenched, he grasped the back of his neck, kneading it. He raised his chin high drew in a long breath and then released it before speaking. "Your first visit here, when you stepped into my garage to leave, do you remember what you said?"

She nodded.

"You said you hoped that you did not disappoint me, that you would be better next time, that you only wanted to please me. Do you remember that?"

Catherine nodded again.

"Well this pleases me. Seeing you naked on my counter top, legs spread apart, tits begging for more. I love the marks I leave all over your tits Catherine. I leave my mark on you so no one else can have you. Are you letting anyone else touch you?"

"No." Her eyes widened. "Never, only you."

"Good."

"It's just...cold in here."

"I know. I intentionally turn off the heat."

"What?"

"I enjoy seeing your dark nipples harden and stay that way the entire time you sit before me. Is that a problem?"

She shook her head.

"Good."

"It's just that I'm dripping all over your nice kitchen counter top. My thighs are all wet and sticky." Hopefully he'd want her off his expensive granite now.

He shook his head. "You shouldn't have told me that Catherine." He extended his hand between her legs and scooped up the creamy puddle. He let his fingers linger on his tongue.

He fetched an ice cube from one of the glasses and coasted it down her neck, pausing for a moment on both her nipples until it stung, then dragged it down between her legs. He grinned as he inserted it inside her. Catherine joggled.

"Don't move," he instructed.

"It's too cold."

He grabbed a second and inserted it. "Complain again and I'll make it three."

She shivered from the frosty air and the frigid temperature within her. Her trembling intensified as she tried desperately to sit still.

"I like the way your tits jiggle like that. Like you're belly dancing." He stuck his finger in her and whirled the cubes around. "Gyrate for me, like it's my cock that's inside you."

Catherine arched her back, positioning both her hands behind her and thrust her hips up and down.

"I love how your tits fall to both sides of you when you lean all the way back. Can you do a backbend? We may need to experiment with a new position next time. Practice for me at home."

She bit her lip from the frozen sensation, praying for the cubes to melt. The icy puddle beneath her bottom caused her to shudder violently, uncontrollably.

"That's it," he screamed. "Shake those tits, shake them hard for me. Harder. Whiplash!" He cackled. The maddening shrill made her nervous. He grabbed a third ice cube anyway and inserted it forcefully.

"Catherine I would take off my jeans right now and fuck you but you're probably so numb you wouldn't even feel me. And what fun would that be?"

"Take me," she begged. She yearned for his warm penis to remove the agony.

"Oh, now you want me?' I thought you had to leave?"

"Please."

"No. You will know what it feels like to be so horny and crave something, yet be denied. You will not refuse me again, do you hear? You will be at my beck and call from now on.

"Yes, I promise, please."

"Are you sure Catherine? I can find someone else."

"No, please no."

"You told me you were jealous when I spoke to that nurse Megan, perhaps she will please me more."

"No, not her. Anybody but her."

He stared right through her, as if contemplating. "You'll give me a blow job on the vacant wing on Six East first thing in the morning? Let me squirt it in your face, ruin your precious makeup."

"Yes."

"Ha! You lie."

"No I promise, I promise. Please."

"Will you let me fuck you in the back of my car during your lunch hour?"

"Yes."

He inserted a fourth one. "Let me suck on those tits on the top of the back stairwell by the roof entrance?"

"Yes, yes! No more, please."

"Then why have you refused these requests in the past? Why now? I don't believe you!"

"I was scared, but I can't lose you, I want you. I'll do whatever you ask. Don't find someone else, I can be whatever you want. Your sex slave."

He sneered at her, removed his finger, the melted liquid oozed out. He pinched her nipple to pull her up to a sitting position. "Tell me when you have ever felt so much Catherine." He crushed harder, twisting it. "I make you feel, feel for days. Sore, unable to walk straight, unable to wear your bra without aching, unable to sit from the rawness of me smacking your ass. But you're alive. You're alive now, all because of me. And the throbbing makes you think of me, doesn't it?"

She nodded.

"You think of me when you walk, as you dress, as you sit. I did that to you. I woke you up, but perhaps not enough. When the aching wears off so does the longing. For now on when I want you, you will drop what you're doing and please me, Catherine."

"Yes I promise, whatever you want, whenever you want. I want you, no one else. I'm here for you, take me now, I need this so bad. Please."

"No." He stepped back and licked his fingers. "You will leave now, but you will come when I want you." He paced out of the room, entered his bedroom and slammed the door.

Chapter 42

Victoria

The crackling of the fireplace resounded over the soft lulls of music playing in the background. Aiden's new pear and apple-scented candle ushered Victoria back to the days when her grandmother gathered fruit from the trees in her backyard and baked fresh pies during the idle summer days.

Aiden slipped the white cable knit sweater off Victoria's shoulder and ran his finger over her lustrous skin. He leaned in and kissed her shoulder with his wine drenched lips. The scent of the wine mixed with pears and apples, and the heat from the fire, the comfort of his velvety cream-colored rug and her head resting against the lavish pillows that leaned alongside the brick fireplace ledge, sent Victoria's thoughts to the bed and breakfast she found online one night when loneliness threatened to close in.

"We should go away," he said.

"Away? Where?" Did he read her mind?

Aiden chuckled. "I didn't get that far. I just meant it would be nice to spend a weekend away. A night even. Going to sleep, knowing you'll be there in the morning, not having to worry if you've arrived home safely. Wake up with you in my arms, warm French toast breakfast with blueberries."

Victoria sat up, knees pressed against her chest, and arms clasped around them. Aiden shifted his body and tilted onto his right shoulder to face her. His finger twirled over her knuckles and up under her sleeve.

"Did I say something wrong?" he asked.

"No not at all. I'm sorry, I was just thinking."

"Of what?"

"Did you ever hear of the Light from the Lighthouse Inn?"

"No, what is it?"

"It's this little bed and breakfast, in Montauk. Quaint yellow Victorian house, overlooks the water. Tall grasses, Adirondack chairs surrounded by giant coral-colored lilies. A large porch with tiny bistro tables to enjoy breakfast on, a dock several yards away leading to the peaceful water."

Victoria paused, sensed his never shifting gaze from her. He did not interrupt, waited for her to finish, but what was she thinking? Why did she tell him this silly vision? She shared his longing but it was an impossibility, hopeless romanticism. She giggled, shook her head and sloped back into the pillow.

"What is it? Tell me."

"Never mind, just babbling."

"It didn't seem like babbling to me, sounded more like an aspiration."

"Well, there's many things I want, but you can't always get what you want."

"Why not?" Aiden sat up and spun, his toes touching hers. "Let's do it."

"I can't."

"Next weekend, after Halloween."

Victoria's heart sank into a cavernous pit. It twisted and wrenched until the brie and raspberries churned in her stomach. Her face lost its rosy color, lost its spirit and intensity. She curled forward into a ball and closed her eyes.

"That sadness is back, I never know what to say. After all this time, I feel as if I speak from my heart, I say what's on my mind, but it's always wrong."

"No Aiden, please. Your idea is wonderful. I want the same as..." She clenched her fist to avoid the tears. "I would like nothing more than to go away with you. That place I described is real. I often...I often dream of going there with you– "

"So let's go." He placed both his hands on her knees. When she did not look up, he lifted her chin.

Victoria opened her lids and his green eyes pulled her to him as they always did. She dug her nails into her calves to fight the tears. "Next weekend– "

"Yes, next weekend, let's do it," he interrupted.

"Next weekend...is mine and Ed's 30th anniversary."

Aiden released her chin, bent back and waited for her to finish.

"We have a party planned to celebrate the occasion. Forty-two people are attending. Green and orange balloons. Orange chrysanthemums will adorn the tables. A beef, a fish, and a poultry will be elegantly served."

He blinked, but nothing more. His silence ripped through her like a frozen New York evening. She waited for his tender words, perfect words he always held, something pleasant and encouraging and something that would take the pain away. The pain of her dissolved marriage, the pain of throwing a charade of a party and feigning happiness, the pain of hurting Aiden like this. What did she have to offer him? A visit once or twice a week, brief and strained.

"I think that's wonderful," he finally spoke.

"Stop, don't validate me."

"I'm not.

"How can you be happy for me after what I'm doing to you?"

"Doing to me? What are you talking about?"

Victoria huffed. "What kind of relationship is this? It's bad enough my marriage is a sham but how is this fair to you? Seeing and talking to me only when I can break away, then you sit there and you're happy for me?"

"I am happy when you are happy."

"I'm not happy, I'm a fake."

Aiden swiveled around to sit next to her. "Victoria you don't understand how happy you've made me. After my wife died, I thought I could never love anyone again like I loved her. I dated much to the urgings of my sons, but they were utter disappointments. Senseless, witless, lifeless beings. They thought objects made them happy. Their idea of fun was to drag me shopping with them when I wanted to show them the world.

I overlooked many of their faults thinking it was me being irrational, picky. I promised them excursions and adventures that we could share together and build into a life, but they couldn't carry on a conversation with me, couldn't keep up. There were no heated discussions on politics or religion as you and I have, no conversations on diseases and cures. I couldn't even discuss stories of my youth growing up in my parent's home upstate because they obviously lived in another world. One filled with wants and greed and possessions.

I gave up you know. Accepted this new position at the lab, threw myself into my work. I love it, of course but each night when I crawled into bed, alone, the ache didn't dissipate."

A sad countenance overtook him. A look she had never seen until now. She removed the tight grip around her legs and ran her fingers through his hair.

"Victoria, the day you walked into our auditorium you gave me hope."

"Hope of what? Living half a life, having me only periodically? Don't you think that kills me?"

"Stop, stop this right now. You're not hearing me. I would rather have you sporadically than not at all. I'll live this life forever as long as I know I can hear your sweet voice every day. As long as I know I can hold you in my arms again and again. Knowing you will call, you will be here in my home, seeing your face before me. You incredible laugh and feeling your hands upon me. I have never been happier. I love you, I love you, Vicki." He fell back onto the couch, his head smacked the cushion.

She shuddered at the sound of her name. The way he spoke it. Then the realization of what he professed struck her. She felt the same, she always did, but refused to admit it to her co-workers. Or him.

In the past four months they never spoke these words. How did she let this ripen into such a mess?

"Tell me you feel the same, please say something, tell me I'm not dreaming." Aiden begged.

She continued to wander off. How could she admit her love for Aiden with her anniversary quickly approaching? How was this fair to him, to anyone? This would only hurt Aiden more, give him false hopes. Cheating on Ed may have brought joy to her desolate life but it would surely end in misery, for all. Mostly for Aiden. He may say he enjoyed their current relationship but his words only trickled out to make her feel better.

She would not say it, she needed to think clearly, figure out what she wanted to do. Unable to look at his dejected face any longer, she rose, slipped on her shoes and strode to her coat hanging by the front door.

"Vicki, please, what did I do? I'm sorry, I shouldn't have said that, I was being selfish."

She turned, coat half on, and shook her head. He was being selfish? Him? Punishment for her behavior clobbered her now. This make-believe fantasy was only an act on stage, a role-playing diversion and her leading man just got crushed.

"I'm sorry Aiden, I need time to think. Please give me some time, I beg of you." With that, she retreated out the door and slammed it behind her. She dashed to her car, the harsh October gale ripped through her.

Chapter 43

Heather

Heather looked at Victoria's miserable face. How did such happiness disintegrate? What a weekend.

"Heather, I'm really sorry." Victoria said. "I thought for sure it was moving in that direction, there was every indication."

"Maybe in *my* head but not his. Why do we take these misconceptions and turn them into something they're not? He never wanted me. Well only for sex. I fell in love with him, what a fool."

"You're not a fool, you really felt love. It happens." Victoria trailed off and searched the utensil display in the cafeteria. A doctor in a hurry, grabbed a fork, spilled several to the floor and left them there.

"At least he explained himself to you," Catherine said. "That was nice." Heather glared at her. As if her comment would make her feel better. "I just meant that he could have dumped you with no explanation and then you would be left wondering what went wrong, what you did."

"I didn't do anything," Heather shouted.

"I didn't say you did. I just meant that we tend to think it's always us. There was no way to know he was still in love with his wife and trying to win her back. He should have told you from the beginning."

"Yeah, well I'd like to see where that goes. It's been a year and a half and she just renewed her lease for another year."

"Maybe she's doing it on purpose to punish him. Perhaps she has no intention of ever taking him back."

Heather noticed Victoria still searching the room. "Are you okay, Victoria? Anything we can do?"

"No, I just need to think what I want to do about Aiden, and this big party in five days is not helping. Sara is so excited for some reason and now she's bothering me about what shoes I'm wearing."

"Do you love him?" Catherine asked.

Victoria's gaze snapped shut, unsure which man she was referring to. But it didn't matter. She twisted back toward Catherine. "I don't think that's relevant. It's not about what I feel, it's about what's right. Right for both Ed and Aiden."

Heather finished the last of her salad and shoved her plate away. "You've always put yourself last. Maybe you should try putting yourself first for a change."

Victoria did not look up. Just pushed her stuffed filet of sole around.

"Well to make matters worse, I think I messed up with Mangle this morning before our meeting with Jean."

Heather scowled. Was she serious? Catherine's deranged relationship did not compare with the two of their broken hearts. Heather could feel the shattering of her heart once again. She thought of Nicolo and the memories they made, like snap shots thrown across a marble floor.

Maybe she didn't love Silvatri, maybe it was just the feeling of being wanted and not ignored, someone paying attention to her, a man's touch. Silvatri did resemble Nicolo in ways. Maybe she planted her love for Nicolo onto Silvatri. Wanted him to *be* Nicolo.

It would be strange not talking to him ever again but still seeing him in the hospital. Would he still sit next to her or avoid her and write his notes inside the patient rooms instead? Heather gulped the last of her water and then coughed, choking up the liquid. Then she started to laugh.

"What's wrong?" Victoria asked.

"I just realized I can never go rock climbing again." She bent forward knocking her head onto the table. "Shit."

"Why not?" Catherine asked.

This time both Heather and Victoria stared her down. "How can I go anymore? I can't even look at him. It's so unfair. I love it and I was good at it." She rested her head in her hands.

"Isn't Dr. Bettman going to wonder why you stopped going?" Victoria asked.

"Probably. He didn't know. Silvatri made me keep it completely sports related when I went. I was just a curious participant."

"How could he not know? He must, how obvious could you be?"

"Silvatri hid it well. Tried not to talk to me too much when we climbed, waited until Richard drove away before we took off to the abandoned parking lot to have sex."

"Are you serious?" Catherine wiped her lips on the napkin and threw it on top of her plate.

Heather tittered. "Now that I think about it, he was right. There was no romance, nothing progressed. We climbed together and he basically ignored me. Come to think of it, I spent more time talking to Richard at the place than him. After sex in my Jeep, he took off immediately, never let me inside his truck either. The conversations at work were less frequent. I thought he was being cautious, but he really just used me for sex. What an idiot."

"What are you going to do now?" Victoria asked.

"Not climb anymore."

"No I mean about—"

"Lance?" Heather pondered for a minute then looked at the two of them. "I have no idea, Silvatri was my out. Now I'm right back to where I started. There is no escape." She nodded to Victoria, "What about you? Will you call Aiden?"

"No. I need to get through this week. I need to get through that God-awful event and then I can think clearly."

"Has he tried to call?"

"No, I asked him not to and he has respected my wishes. What's strange is that I keep looking at my phone to see if he called. I may have destroyed him. He must be devastated."

"We need time to heal. All of us." Heather included Catherine although she wanted to whip some sense into her. Did she need Mangle's approval that much? It was sickening and he slowly brainwashed her, manipulating her with his passive-aggressive ways.

Heather thought about how he changed her though. Standing up for herself with Jean and even Odessa, dressing more her age, her boys behaved better, there were less fights, more cooperation and she enjoyed having fun with her children like never before.

"Are you going to the Spooky House at Allenger Farms Halloween night?" Heather asked.

"The boys were telling me about it, I'd like to. There are separate areas, one for older kids and one for younger."

"That's why I thought it would be great for Rori."

"Let's do it."

"How about you Victoria, are you in for a little scaring?" Heather asked.

"No, thank you. Next weekend will be scary enough."

****

A devil, a pirate and a ladybug stood before Heather. She donned an Edward Scissorhands costume and waved her scissors in the air wildly as if cutting off all her daughter's hair.

"You look cute mommy," Rori said.

"Thank you my little ladybug." Heather kissed her on the nose and then pretended to cut her wings off. Rori chuckled and scuttled behind Pirate Gia.

"Ahoy there mateys," Gia wailed. "Are we ready to set sail?

"Just waiting for your dad. I was hoping he would be here by now."

"Is he really coming, mommy? Really, really," Rori asked.

"He said he would."

"Yay!" the girls screamed in unison.

Heather thought of the long talk she had with Lance yesterday. Her sarcastic tone over the past few years did not help the situation. She apologized and asked him to go tonight despite his lack of interest in the whole silly ordeal. She promised to be more understanding of his career and he promised to spend more time with his daughters.

Fix it or get out. Maybe they needed marriage counseling as well. Their marriage may not be perfect but she made the decision to marry him. They would find a way to work it out and hold it all together. For their daughters at least.

They were meeting Catherine at 7 o'clock and it was 6:30 now. A chill ran up her spine as a cold thought passed through her. She put the camera down, the hope of Lance taking a group shot of them before leaving the house vanished. "Why don't you guys find your coats and I'll warm up the car."

"But what about daddy?" Rori asked.

"I'll give him a call to see how close he is to arriving home. Go get your coats."

"What's the point of having a costume if you have to wear a coat?" Gia asked.

"I'll hold it for you once you get in. Moms were made with extra-large arms to hold multiple things." Heather walked into the bedroom, removed her scissor hand and dialed Lance's cell. He picked up on the fourth ring. Loud music blared in the background, while a clatter of voices weaved in and out. "Hello?" Heather shouted.

"Hello? Who is this?" Lance mumbled.

"Your wife."

"Sorry I can't hear you. What is it? Make it fast."

Heather sat on the edge of the bed and pictured stabbing him with one of her fake foam scissors, wishing they were real. "Where are you?"

"At the Neon Pistol, can't this wait 'til later?"

"When, Christmas? It's Halloween. The girls are dressed and waiting for you. You promised."

"What? I can't hear you, can you hear me? I'm with Doug having a drink. It's crazy in here, you wouldn't believe it. Sick costumes. Holy crap! Look at that girl."

"Your daughters have great costumes too."

"Costumes? Yes everyone here is in costume. There's a guy dressed like a soccer mom." Laughter erupted.

Heather closed her bedroom door and then walked into the master bathroom. "Your daughters are waiting for you. When are you coming home?" she shouted.

"Waiting for what?"

Heather clicked off the phone. He ruined yet another evening. But it would be the last.

Chapter 44

Catherine

"**I** think the two of you will be scarier than the people working the haunted house." Catherine inspected Colton and Bentley. "Enough blood dripping from your body parts? What is this thing?" She touched a rubbery item hanging off Bentley's neck.

"Flesh," he said. "Hacked off and half-eaten flesh."

"Lovely."

Emily skipped around the corner and spun in the center of the kitchen. "Wonder Woman," she roared.

"Perfect costume, Emily."

"Are we going or what?" Peter entered from the garage and left the door open. Glacial winds streamed into the warmth that surrounded them.

"Let's get in the car guys," Catherine said.

They parked a few blocks away and then Peter led the boys into the warmth of the converted barn. Emily held Catherine's hand and she analyzed her mother.

"What are you dressed as again mom?"

"A French maid." Catherine sauntered up the stairs in high heels and the outfit she had worn for Mangle last week, the night he scolded her in his kitchen. She felt uncomfortable in it now with her children around, even more so with Peter. She questioned why she avoided her husband's requests all these years. The costume should be for him, not another man, but he did not deserve her, did not deserve all she could offer him. Mangle alone savored her talents and skills.

She had not seen Mangle all week, he deliberately avoided her. She would search for him tomorrow, apologize for what she did Monday morning and make it up to him.

Heather charged up the stairs behind her to catch up. The girls, without coats, ran into the building past them. "It's freezing," Heather said.

Peter greeted Heather then took the four older children into the Mayhem of Doom section of the barn. Catherine and Heather took hold of Emily and Rori's hands and strolled into Spooky World.

An hour and a half of lines, earsplitting noises, mostly from the children themselves and watching the kids stuff their faces with caramel apples, black-cat cookies covered with sprinkles, cupcakes drenched with marshmallow fluff and orange Rice Krispies balls, Catherine had enough.

Heather and the girls departed and Catherine squeezed through the crowd to find Peter. An additional twenty minutes leaked from her life before she found Peter outside with a cluster of his friends.

"Peter, we've been looking for you. It's almost 9 and the kids have school tomorrow."

"Take them home in my truck. I'm going out for some witches brew with these characters. I'll get a ride home."

Catherine's mouth dropped open, her children stood beside her.

"Problem?" he said.

Catherine flew home narrowly avoiding the trick-or-treaters on the roads. She helped Colton remove his make-up while Emily dressed in her pajamas. Bentley jumped in the shower, unable to remove his glue and make-up in the sink.

With her children in bed, the last of the Halloween candy left on the front porch for late night visitors, Catherine went to bed.

At 11:30, the phone rang. Catherine sprang up and fumbled for the phone.

"Cath? It's me, I need a ride home. Not sure where everyone went."

"Are you serious? I have to work tomorrow."

"I'm stranded, are you picking me up or not?"

Catherine grinded her teeth until her jaw ached. She threw the phone and flung the covers off her.

She pulled up to The Copper Roof Pub and Peter stumbled into the bright porch lights. Neither of them looked at each other nor spoke. Fierce words approached her lips but the midnight hour fell upon her.

Peter dumped his hooded sweatshirt on the couch. Catherine stood in silence in the unlit room wanting to address the issue. Her new self-assured manner with Jean and Odessa improved her confidence, but she had yet to direct her strength toward her husband.

Peter staggered, then came face to face with her. "What now? I don't want to hear it."

"What happened, where were your rides?" Catherine bit the inside of her lip and pushed the hair out of her face.

"Why do you care? Go to bed, get your beauty sleep." He tossed his sneakers on the rug.

"No." Only one word, but she discharged it. Her eyes adjusted to the lack of moonlight.

Peter's head cocked, he leaned forward as if he didn't hear correctly. "No? Did I hear right?" Explosive laughter erupted from him.

"No," she repeated. "I'm not going to bed until you tell me what happened."

Unsure if her defiance shocked him or the alcohol impeded him, but he remained motionless. "Who do you think you're talking to?"

"I asked you a question." Darkness fueled her strength, like sunglasses hiding the emotion her eyes would reveal.

"You stand there and order me?" His voice climbed and resounded through the tranquil house. "I'm sick of this, sick of your shit."

He pounced, arms outstretched. Catherine stepped back but tripped over Colton's beanbag chair and stumbled. Peter lunged with both hands, seized her shoulders and forced her into the recliner. The chair and both of them flew back and over. His weight on her and the stench of beer released from his lungs, immobilized her.

She gasped for air, but then blinding light flooded the room. She closed her eyes to shield the irritant. Peter rolled sideways off her.

Bentley's expression was more frightening than any of the

zombies they saw tonight.

****

Catherine finally breathed easier. Mangle had avoided her all week and his normal pleads vanished. She even caught him speaking to Megan near the OR yesterday. But today, after searching all morning, she located him and explained to him what happened on Monday.

Three days after the kitchen counter incident, Catherine had rushed down the hallway to Jean's intolerable Monday morning meeting. She neared the conference room, already five minutes late, and spotted Mangle at the end of the hall. He grabbed his crotch and motioned to his mouth.

Jean appeared from around the corner and glared at her. Before entering the conference room, she asked Catherine if she planned to join them or would she "continue to stand there like a fuckin' lost mime."

She pretended to search for something in her lab coat and assured her she would be right in. Jean refused to budge.

Catherine nonchalantly shook her head at Mangle. He clenched his fist then released it, pointing a finger at the ground, requesting her presence. Now.

She glanced at Jean who had her hands on what should have been her waist. Catherine looked at Mangle one last time and then slowly stepped into the conference room. That was the last time she saw him.

Out of desperation, she approached him today and begged to give him a blowjob. He refused. She offered to have sex with him in his car, something she denied him from day one. He refused that as well.

She reached out and grasped his shoulder, a tightness formed in her chest, her dry mouth spat out emotion-choked words. He shook his head.

She pulled him into the lounge, unbuttoned her shirt and released her breasts for him to see. She played with them, rolling them in her hands, even put one in her mouth.

"Catherine, you seem so desperate to please me," he said. "Where were you on Monday when I needed you?"

Her pained-gaze threatened to fill with tears. She fought back in earnest.

"Are you sure you want to please me still?"

She swallowed hard, her desiccated throat struggled to speak. "Oh yes, you know that. I'll do anything for you." She ignored her frantic words, only wanting his touch on her. She could not live without him, only he made her feel alive. Not even Jean would stand between them, even if it meant losing her job.

"Megan seems so eager to do what I ask though. In fact, I might ask her to come over this Sunday. She likes my ideas."

Catherine grasped his hand, placed it on her breast and clenched it tight. "Not as much as me, this time will be different."

"You said that last time." He snickered and wrenched her nipple. She let out a yelp. "That doesn't seem too convincing, you should enjoy what I do to you, not whimper."

"I do, I love it. I won't complain or refuse. You can do whatever you want to me and I will welcome it."

He squinted, stepped back and inspected her. She stood before him, her desperate breasts exposed, her palms reaching for him while she sobbed. Pitiful.

"Come over on Sunday. Noon. No excuses this time. You will only leave when I say it's time, you will do whatever I ask of you and not complain or refuse, do you hear me?"

She exhaled knowing that she could not disappoint him. She had to work Sunday but would not mention that to him. She'd fake an illness, leave early, find an excuse.

After three months, he obviously grew tired of her constant denials and complaints. His past women probably more granting, fulfilling his needs without any reservation. She would concede to him, grant him the rights to her body. The thought of him touching Megan crushed her.

Whatever he asked of her she would do, she could not lose him. Catherine needed him to rescue her from Peter and then she would be his, always.

Chapter 45

Victoria

Victoria sat in Jean's office and waited for her to acknowledge her. Jean pounded on the computer keyboard with her fist, ignoring Victoria. She had three patients to counsel before she went home and the clock ticked like a slow thud on a door. The three cases of diet coke stacked in the corner and the empty plastic bottles overflowing in the garbage pail, confirmed the amount of caffeine Jean consumed each day.

Jean swiveled in her hefty chair and glared at Victoria as if she had no conception why she sat before her. Jean leaned over and folded her hands into tight knots, inhaling one massive gulp of air. And held it. As Jean's face reddened, Victoria's patience ran out.

"Is there a reason you summoned me to your office?"

"Yes," Jean expelled. The smell of French fry grease zoomed up Victoria's nose. She winced and held her breath until clean air replaced the odor. "I need you to pick up equipment from my house tomorrow morning. My chefs and salad room staff need it for a last minute catering event but I have a conference to attend tomorrow and you live the closest to me."

Victoria stiffened, her mouth unable to form any conceivable words. Jean's residence churned repulsive images through her head. Filth, yard sale debris, dog hair, foul odors.

"Well?"

"I don't know your address."

"I'll give it to you obviously, you dimwit. Did you think you'd just drive around blindly? Sometimes I wonder about you, Victoria. You portray this air of intelligence but it may just be a smokescreen like those lavish suits of yours."

Victoria struggled upward with the slip of paper in her hand. A wet, brown stain curled the edge of the paper. She swallowed hard, her throat burned with blistering pain. She drifted out her door and into the hallway like an aimless ghost.

At least the conference would keep Jean out of work tomorrow. The week progressively deteriorated and a Friday conflict with Jean would put her over the edge. The three of them, at one point so euphoric, now funneled toward an ever-expanding hole of hell. When did it all go so horribly wrong?

****

Victoria drove to Jean's house at seven o'clock the following morning. She parked along the street and contemplated whether to hike up the gravel driveway or the crumbling cobblestone walkway intertwined with weeds. The crabgrass lawn guaranteed a few hidden surprises for her.

Her heel wedged into one of the cracks but the eeriness remained in front of her. Shrubs donned with badly tossed fake spider webs, which appeared more like blobs of cotton on a string. Clumps of the polyester fiberfill garnished only the top of one bush and lay low across the bottom of a distant one. A small gravestone made from cardboard, smack dab in the middle of a burnt dirt lawn, had the word *Died* illegibly handwritten across it. One hospital latex glove, inflated and hung from a tree branch, blew in the wind. She neared the door and grimaced. To her left stood a rusted propane tank propped next to the stairs with a rotted pumpkin on top of it and a weathered picture of a lobster attached to it.

She rang the splintered doorbell and waited. The doors bond held tight, then released with a swoosh of air. A man in his late sixties wearing a faded grey sweat suit stood before her.

"Good morning. I'm Victoria, I came to pick up equipment for Jean."

"Yes, yes. Come in. Please do."

Victoria stepped in and the musty odor surrounded her instantly. She tried not to gawk but the yard sale décor jarred her memory of every decorating blunder she read about in her magazines.

"Nice of you to come, I'm Stewart."

"Nice to meet you." She extended her arm to meet his.

"Jean insisted I show you around, especially her plantings.

She's very proud of them."

Victoria wanted to grab the needed items and run but his kind gestures tugged on her empathy. She followed behind him, passing oddities such as a wrought iron starburst clock from the sixties, orange and yellow striped kitchen wallpaper, and her owl figurine collection. They strolled by the Danish walnut credenza which matched the dark wood paneling lining the hallway.

He led her toward the enclosed mudroom; the whistling of polar air through the broken screen window chilled her exposed legs.

Jean was the recycling ambassador. Every scrap of garbage that could retain soil, transformed into a container to nurture weeds. No, she meant flowers. Of course she did. There must have been flowers growing at one point. Somewhere. Hopefully Stewart would point a few out.

Three-liter soda bottles decapitated, soup cans with the labels still adhered to them, a potato chip bag sliced in half and dog food cans, all contained soil and some form of greenery. There were a few clay pots strewn around but they were cracked and neglected.

He struggled to open the once sliding glass door and then entered the backyard. Victoria tried desperately to hide her stunned appearance from poor Stewart. She must have looked as if she witnessed the ruins or a hurricane but composed herself before he turned around to meet her gaze.

Stewart led her through more crabgrass to the grounds beyond the disintegrating cement patio near the row of untrimmed bushes. The only color appeared to be the remains from a few green weeds that survived the cold night temperatures. Where were the luxurious gardens?

"She really does a lot with the plantings," Stewart said. "It's a hobby and I know she really enjoys it." His shoulders drooped like a flower in the rain. "I wish I had her strength, her health."

Victoria scanned his expression but did not know how to respond. She offered a grin instead.

"My health's been ailing. My diabetes catching up on me after all these years. Doc says I might need dialysis pretty soon."

"I'm so sorry," Victoria finally responded, "I had no idea."

"Yeah, well Jean keeps her home life pretty private I figure. But she truly is my nightingale. She's my nurse, my cook, my chauffer." He bent to pick up a branch from the ground and tossed it into a pile of leaves, undoubtedly there from last fall. "Might need surgery

224

on my foot now, toes aren't looking so good."

Victoria tried to picture Jean caring for him. Her brusque nature at work left any visions of compassion for the imagination. Stewart's fingers formed a steeple then folded together under his chin. His distant, unfocused smile revealed the deep affection he had for his wife.

"You're very lucky to have her," Victoria found herself saying.

"I am. She's my best friend and I worship that woman. I only wish I could do as much for her as she's done for me." His voice cracked as he laid his hand over his heart. He peered down to Victoria's left hand noticing her simple gold wedding band. "You married long?" he asked.

"It'll be thirty years tomorrow."

"Lucky man. I hope he appreciates you as much as I appreciate Jean. Treats you like a princess."

Victoria swallowed hard, dropped her chin to her chest and managed to raise her lips enough to imitate a smile.

"Sorry, I've been talking your ear off. You have to get yourself to work. Come on, let me help you with the items."

Victoria walked a few paces behind Stewart, lagging behind as her heels sunk into the moist grass. When a squish penetrated her ears and glued her shoe to the ground, she glanced down and noticed the pile of dog poop she stepped in. She padded the rest of the way, dragging her shoe in the crabgrass, releasing as much of the wet mess as she could.

Stewart helped her lug the four kitchen bowls, seven platters and an array of utensils into Victoria's back seat. When they carted the last of it from the house, he grabbed hold of the roof of her car in obvious discomfort.

"Are you all right?" she asked.

"Yeah sure, just gotta elevate my feet the rest of the day."

"Thank you for showing me around and for helping me load everything into my car."

"No problem, glad for the company. We don't get many guests here."

She smiled, knowing why.

Chapter 46

Heather

Heather pulled her car into the driveway thankful it was Friday. Jean took the day off and Heather took advantage by leaving work at 3 o'clock. She trudged into the house toward her bedroom to remove her clothes.

Heather opened the bedroom door and Laurel, near her jewelry box, slammed the drawer shut.

"Borrowing my jewelry? I don't mind if you do but please ask first." Heather plopped onto the edge of her bed and removed her shoes.

Laurel did not budge. Her mouth slackened and she turned away.

"What's wrong?" Heather asked. Laurel's widened eyes worried her. "Did you lose an earring? Break a necklace?" Laurel glanced back at the jewelry box. "Laurel, I won't be mad. It's all costume jewelry I bought for myself, nothing of real value. Please tell me."

Laurel opened the drawer and pulled something out. Heather strained to see and then lumbered over to her. Laurel held a picture in her hand. It was Silvatri and her on the top of a large boulder when they were in the Gunks. Hugging. Her favorite picture. She forgot she hid it there. When she first saw the picture, she thought love and adoration filled Silvatri's expression. Seeing it now, he looked more like he had a hard-on.

Laurel threw Heather a scorching glare. Heather jolted out of her memory and into the awareness of what Laurel presumed. "Who is this?" she demanded.

Heather's body locked, her clammy hand took hold of the picture. She fumbled for words, her cheeks now burning. "He's one of the guys I went climbing with that Saturday. I told you a whole group of us went."

"Let me see the other pictures," Laurel said.

She had deleted them all, only printing this one. "I didn't bring my camera, I forgot. One of the women took this and gave it to me."

"Why would she only give you this picture of you hugging some guy?"

Shit.

"And why is it buried under your bracelets?"

"I forgot it was even there."

"That doesn't answer the question mom. Who is he?"

Heather had never lied to any of her daughters, never had reason to. The two of them also shared a special bond that only a mother and her first-born daughter could.

She rubbed her sweaty hand down her skirt. She gave Laurel a quick scan then back at the picture. Her posture stooped, she fidgeted, then her gaze darted around the room. "He's the main guy that got us all started."

"Why are you hugging him? Mom, are you dating him?" Laurel crossed her arms.

Heather stood solidly, adjusted her chin and laughed. "Dating?" She flung the picture onto her dresser. Absolutely not. He's an arrogant, conceited butthead. "Sheryl..." she made up a name "...gave me this as a joke. We don't get along and she made him hug me because he picked on me all day. That's why we look like we're smiling. We're actually laughing at the awkwardness of it all."

Laurel crinkled her eyebrows and tilted her head to the side. Heather continued to smile. Laurel picked the picture up and looked at it again. Heather hoped his hard-on facial expression stood out more than the one of love. "He does look like a jerk." Laurel said.

"Yup, totally." Heather's eyes rolled up toward the ceiling. "Did you want to borrow some jewelry?"

"Nah, your stuff is lame." Laurel strolled out of the room and back into her bedroom.

"Lame?" Heather shouted down the hall at her. She picked up the picture again and surveyed it one last time. Silvatri appeared different again, as if the image kept transforming. Not horny like she first rationalized. Now he looked genuinely euphoric, like

Heather made him the luckiest man in the world.

Did he secretly have feelings for Heather but hid them, lied to protect her? Had he realized he did it again, fell in love with another and repeated his pathetic history? Had he tried to spare her the misery the other women faced? She'd never know for sure, but believed strongly in karma.

She hid the picture at the bottom of her cedar chest and changed into sweat pants with a long sleeve Giants T-shirt. She threw on her purple Converse high tops and decided to lift weights in the den while the girls watched TV.

She finished off a set of squats when she heard rattling in the garage.

Lance rifled through a milk crate and tossed rags across the floor along with car wash soap and a chamois.

"What are you looking for?" Heather asked.

"I'm looking for the Armor All for my Corvettes tires."

"Your Corvette?"

He stood and looked on the shelf. "This is my house and it's overrun by girls."

"We live here too, it's our home."

Lance faced her, the scowl on his face dropped and his eyes squinted. "What are you wearing? Can't you be normal?"

"Normal?" Heather's eyes ate him with hate.

"Why can't you be like the other wives that cater to their husbands and act like real mothers? Can't you understand your place is at home and volunteering at the school and trying to make me happy? That's your job. When did you become this deviant non-conformal wife?"

"That's the problem, I was always this person! You just tried to transform me. I'm not a soccer mom or a PTA mom, and I'm not going to pretend to like the wives of your lawyer friends. I don't huddle at the bus stop gossiping or feel the need to be involved with every school activity to show off how wonderful I am and pretending I'm doing it for my kids when my poor kid's wandering around the gym by herself."

"You're nuts," Lance said. "Absolutely crazy."

"I love who I am and in case you still haven't figured out who that is…I'm different. I love Converse high tops, my *Felix the Cat* T-Shirt and my Jeep. I love rock climbing and weight lifting and how strong and powerful they make me feel, like I can conquer anything. I don't follow stupid rules and I hate conforming. I love exploring museums and zoos with my girls, playing silly board games, and venturing off to an amusement park or beach with them. But most of all I love talking to them. *That* they'll remember twenty years from now, and all I can hope is that they know how much I love them."

Lance struggled up and shoved the car products back in the milk crate. The car wash slammed against the crate. "I don't need this, you're sick."

"I've always been this girl, and I always will be and I'm tired of trying to be who you want me to be or make you love who I really am."

Lance kicked the milk crate against the garage wall. A nervous laugh escaped his lips. "There's something seriously wrong with you, Heather."

"Yes, there is. I married the wrong man. And don't bother coming with us tomorrow either. It's a party for my friend, not you. I wouldn't want to see you cry because no one was paying attention to you." "

"My mother was right about you all along. She said you would never take care of me like her and she was right."

"Your mother? Take care of you? I'm not your mother! I'm your wife and you're a grown man." Heather shifted to her right. "Your mother's the one that's sick, she's a fuckin' nut case."

He reeled around, his molten eyes devoured her face with rage. He grabbed his hair with his white knuckled fists and tugged on it repeatedly. "How dare you. Don't you ever speak about my mother that way, do you hear me?" He took a badminton racquet, flung it across the room into a row of clay pots and knocked one to the floor. It smashed into useless shards.

Heather's face glazed with horror and she stepped back. All a big lie, her life was a lie.

Laurel finding the picture of her and Silvatri suddenly emerged. The vision of the Frisbee ride flashed before her. The peak of the highest climb in New Paltz resurfaced, then the view from the top and the freedom she felt at that moment. There could be no fear now, no more silent screams, no more fake smiles and pretending, no more sarcasm. She needed to stop running, she needed to be a role model for her daughters. Her daughters gave her strength. This would be the day she turned from the altar.

She stood her ground refusing to acknowledge Lance's request. Enraged, he lunged at her, she spun and he missed her shirt by inches. Heather stopped at the head of the driveway and glared back at him again. He snatched Gia's bicycle and flung it into the wall to the left. He twisted back, his chest heaved, fists clenched into tight balls.

He let out an animalistic growl, spewing spit, teeth clenched and seething. He grabbed a screwdriver and that was all she needed to see. She vaulted out of the garage and into her Jeep. She turned the ignition and he banged on the hood while she careened out of the driveway.

Lance threw the screwdriver at her windshield, leaving a depression that resembled a crushed spider. A jumbo piece of pink chalk followed and she floored it down the street and steered towards the elementary school.

Heather sped into the parking lot and ended her ride positioned sideways over three separate spots. She leaped out of the car and jogged past the swing set, veering toward the rear of the school.

Her body tackled the side of the building, and with her back against the beige bricks, she squatted down. Heather sucked down desperate gulps of air, collapsed and crumbled into a ball. The sandy dirt brought up billows of dust. She coughed from the dirt and the tears that invaded her throat. Her nails dug into her skin.

Unable to catch her breath, she thought of her oxygen-dependent patients. Faces blistered from the masks melted on to their faces. Gasping, holding the mask tighter as if to help the oxygen move into their lungs more effectively...lungs that no longer worked.

Heather opened her eyes and inhaled deeply. She needed to get home to her daughters. How could she have left them home alone with that psychopath? She struggled upward, legs numb from the lack of blood flow. She whisked the dirt off her pants and turned toward the brick. The graffiti on the school wall provided its sharp retort: *Why do you stay in prison when the door is so wide open?*

Chapter 47

Catherine

Catherine hurried to finish her work at the hospital so she could return home, dress and reapply her make-up for Victoria and Ed's 30th wedding anniversary celebration at 6 o'clock this evening.

Peter refused to go. She didn't mind after their fight three nights ago. She was done with him and no longer cared. Her only thoughts involved pleasing Mangle tomorrow at his home. She would pretend she was sick, leave work a little before noon, and have the entire afternoon to spend with him.

Silvatri had used Heather, never wanting anything more than what it always was, ending their five-month affair. Victoria gave up on her romance and deserted Aiden after he acknowledged his love and offered his heart to her. That would not happen with her. She would prove to Mangle she was worthy of him. No other woman would do. He would fall in love with her and take her away from her madness.

She entered the ICU less an hour before her shift ended and sat on one side of the egg-shaped nurses' station. Patty, an older nurse, sat across from her filling out a clipboard. Catherine rushed through another chart but thoughts of her afternoon with Mangle tomorrow filled her mind. She wondered what he planned, ready to fulfill his fantasies.

Dr. Feldman entered the unit from the rear stairwell. Catherine cringed. Hadn't he retired? He sat across from her, next to Patty, and grinned. His stained crooked teeth nauseated her. His dyed black hair, slicked over his bald head, reminded her of her father's boss at Crayola Crayon Company. She looked away and concentrated on her chart.

She felt his relentless gaze. A hazy memory returned, one that took years to forget. The time Catherine's father brought her to his office as a present for her 10th birthday. Only her older brothers had accompanied him to his office. This would be her first time. Instead of excited, she feared she would disappoint him. Again.

She tried hard to act grown-up and responsible. Maybe he would love her as much as them. Today would be her big chance.

He gave Catherine a tour and then they strolled into his office. A picture of him fishing with her two brothers sat in the corner of his desk. None of her.

His boss appeared at the door. Oily black hair combed over his scalp to hide the bald roof, his eyes were tiny, of a much younger child, but his hands large and hairy. His white business shirt carried mustard colored stains beneath the armpits, the buttons parted to reveal a similar wooly chest.

He bent down to see her. His yellow teeth jeered from inside his mouth, his breath foul. He asked if she wanted the enormous crayon kit her father had promised. The most her father ever brought home was a 64-count box of crayons. Now he promised an activity set complete with watercolors, pastels, and sheets of drawing paper.

The boss hid it behind his back, asked for a kiss, but she refused. Her father frowned, but she continued to shake her head. Catherine took a step back, then another. The man's face contorted and he refused to give it to her. Her father called her rude and his brow sprouted with sweat. How dare she deny him when he was giving her what she wanted. She whimpered until tears fell.

Her father left to get a tissue, a ploy to avoid the humiliating situation and hopefully give her time to make the right decision.

His boss stepped closer and clutched her shoulder with his hairy hand. "One little kiss and it's all yours, princess."

She held her hand up as a shield. This time he tossed the activity kit on the desk, seized both shoulders and crushed them in his palms until the pain froze her. He leaned in and kissed her on the lips, the taste of tuna fish transferred to her. She withdrew, licked the filth on her mouth and then wiped it off with her hand. She felt dirty, filthy, impure.

He withdrew his hairy palms, but a few fingers reached forward and tugged the collar of her shirt down. "No boobies yet?" He peeked in.

Catherine's hand slapped on to her chest, her other hand pushed his face away. Her jaw shuddered, heart pounded so furiously, she knew the Devil was coming for her now. Her heart would implode, she would die and punishment would ensue for allowing a man to look at her privates.

Her father returned to find his boss grinning. "Did you do it?" He handed his daughter a tissue. The elderly boss relinquished the kit along with a glare. "That's my girl." He lifted Catherine into his arms and hugged her for the first time in years, her father's touch suddenly repulsive. She was sure to go to Hell. Kissing before she married, men touching her, ogling.

Soiled. Defiled. She needed to scrub the disgrace from herself.

Catherine chucked the patient's chart back in the rack and shuddered. She reached for her last chart and Dr. Feldman leered at her. He had not opened a chart or visited a patient yet. What was he doing? Taking a break, resting his tired bones? Had the walk up the back stairs proved too arduous for him?

"Nurse, nurse." A voice called out from Room 3. Patty jumped to her feet and darted to the room, closing the curtain behind her.

Catherine resumed her charting. Dr. Feldman's presence suffocated her. She leaned in and discreetly pulled her lab coat over her white sweater. He gulped down breaths, as if he had run a race. Was he having a heart attack? His panting increased, became rapid, until he finally stood and walked toward the front door.

Catherine sighed, thankful for his departure. Let him have a heart attack outside in the other unit, away from her. The vision of her father's boss crept back into her head. She squeezed the pen in her hand and tried to bury the image back where it came from, but then sensed someone to her right.

"Catherine you look lovely today," Dr. Feldman said. The smell of his putrid breath pierced her.

Her eyes bulged. He had never spoken to her before, glad for his disregard.

"Mangle tells me we're in for quite the party tomorrow." He took his hand and eased back her lab coat revealing her thin transparent V-neck sweater. "I look forward to having these enormous breasts in my mouth." He smiled exposing the dark stains between his teeth. "I jerked off for hours last night with the image of having them in my face while he fucked you in the ass. Maybe I can be inside you too while he's in there. Do you like having two dicks inside you at the same time Catherine?"

He extended his finger down her lapel and over her breast touching her prominent nipple with his untrimmed, yellowing fingernail. "I see I'm arousing you already. You must like getting fucked in the ass. Do you like pain?" He flicked her nipple and licked his lips. "I look forward to biting it off. I can't promise you I'll be as gentle as Mangle, I enjoy giving pain to my woman. You'll appreciate my toys from what he told me about you."

The curtain rings slid across the steel rod, opening the patient's room to their view. Patty guided the tray table closer to the bed and then turned to leave. Dr. Feldman backed away, winked at Catherine and fled through the main door. Her pen rolled onto the floor.

Peter was right, Jean was right, everyone was right. She was a complete moron, a loser. Heather and Victoria had told the truth about Mangle from day one. How could she be so blind? How low *did* she need to go to prove her worth?

Chapter 48

Victoria

Victoria paced the marble entranceway, hoping either Heather or Catherine would arrive first. Her stomach grumbled from lack of food, too nervous to eat. The butterflies in her stomach starved as well.

She fidgeted, checked that her earrings still hung from beneath her hair and that her dress draped squarely. Ed entertained the female bartender with Andrew, and Sara lingered in the bathroom with her friend.

The first guests to arrive were Ed's friends. His drinking buddies piled in and headed straight to the bar. An Uncle, a cousin and a neighbor soon followed. Her brother, his wife and their children next. Her co-workers absent.

With her post at the door no longer acceptable, Victoria joined her guests and managed to toss an Asian chicken meatball into her mouth. Andrew handed her a glass of white wine and music from the era in which Ed and she met, strummed through the speakers.

Loud conversations developed, drowning out the music. Chatter and laughter surrounded her, but not her friends. Victoria searched for Ed whom she had not seen in over an hour. The door to the restaurant opened and Ed trickled in with three of his friends after an apparent cigarette break. Behind him, Heather and her girls hurried to the door.

"Victoria, your dress is gorgeous," her aunt said. "It's simply gorgeous, what material is this?"

"It's taffeta, Sara picked it out." Victoria waved at Heather hoping she would rescue her.

"And the color is divine, the burgundy works well with your coloring."

Catherine jogged in with her children a minute later and the eight of them handed their coats to the attendant. Where were Lance and Peter?

Before Victoria made it to the coat check, a swarm of people enveloped her.

"Mom, you remember that time Katie and I fell off the swing in the backyard and it was all muddy and..."

"Victoria, where is the restroom?"

"Mrs. Ehling, we will be serving the salad course soon if you'd like me to start seating your guests."

Victoria's head spun. She was in no mood for a party or questions or the loud banter. Her stiff dress tugged at her shoulders. The duck sauce from the meatball churned together with her wine in an explosion of syrupy fizz. She searched the room for Ed's help, but his shot glass held high, announced their oncoming toast.

The guests took their seats and Stephan the banquet manager, snapped his fingers at the waiters to proceed with the salads. Victoria watched her co-workers help their children find a seat. She strolled over to them, a smile sparkled on her face for the first time all night.

"Mrs. Ehling," Stephan blocked her from reaching their table, "we usually have the couple do their toast to each other before the main course otherwise it becomes too late and some guests start to leave. My staff will be pouring the champagne into the glasses now."

"Yes, that would be fine." Victoria groaned. Last night before bed, she prepared a quick speech. She had mentioned the customary toast to Ed and wondered what he had prepared. Maybe this evening would be a blessing after all. They could express their feelings for each other while surrounded by their loved ones. Sentiments he expressed to her when they first met would resurface. Perhaps his spoken feelings for her tonight would erase the past year of doubts and loneliness, and rekindle their love. Her time with Aiden would fade into a memory, a clear mistake.

Victoria sat at their private table for two. Alone. Isolated once again. The waiters placed the champagne on the tables and she motioned to Stephan to find Ed.

"Victoria!" Heather and Catherine charged toward her. The three embraced and they complimented her on her expensive dress.

"You've been so busy, we couldn't find a minute to say hello."

"I know and you've been pretty busy yourselves, I remember when Andrew and Sara were that little."

Stephan strolled over with Ed beside him.

"This is the first I've seen Ed all night," Heather said.

"Me too. He's been reminiscing with his friends I suppose."

Ed took his seat and grinned at Heather and Catherine without welcoming them.

"Ed, you remember Heather, and this is Catherine, our newest co-worker."

"Hello." He smiled, tipped his beer at them and glanced at Victoria. "Why'd they make me sit? I was in the middle of one of Ralph's hilarious stories."

Ralph worked in the same supermarket since high school. Same people, same jokes, which he told repeatedly. She knew them so well she could relay them herself.

Stephan pointed to Victoria, clinked on his glass with a knife and then announced the couple's toast. Heather and Catherine retreated to their tables. The room hushed with an immediate blanket of silence.

Victoria stared at Ed. If he spoke first, she could change her speech last minute, but he continued to stare. After a minute of uncomfortable silence, she stood and raised her champagne glass.

"I would like to thank all of you for attending our huge celebration. Thirty years I've spent with Ed and we've survived longer than most marriages." This already sounded horrible. She needed to shift gears.

"Most of you may know, Ed and I met in high school and married after he patiently waited for me to finish college, the internship and land my first job. We bought a humble house and Ed renovated it to the grand home we have now." Why was she speaking about the house? This was supposed to be about them.

"We raised two beautiful children whom I couldn't be more proud of." Now she was talking about her kids. This was awful.

"Ed and I have crisscrossed through many obstacles but have come through it smiling and content." Great, now she reverted to lying. "There are so many wonderful memories." None that she can remember. "From working on the house together..." That was fun? "...to raising our children..." Which she mostly did. "...to all the glorious vacations..." The ones where he sat at the bar talking to the bartenders instead of spending time with her or their children.

Victoria's stomach constricted. If it wasn't for the wine, words would elude her. She rubbed the back of her neck and glanced down at the champagne. She took a gulp and surveyed the room with its guests.

A man in a chef's uniform pointed to a server and then turned back to face Victoria. He leaned against the wall, hands clasped in front of him. His salt and pepper hair twinkled from the chandelier above, like icy frost on morning dew. He smiled at her and it melted her heart.

"Marriage is mutual understanding, teamwork, and communication. It's about supporting each other, even when you're down. Encouraging each other to be the best you can be, even if life's not going so great for you. Long conversations on the sofa, laughing at the silliest of things, little tokens of love, surprises just because, and sentiments whispered in your ear. Wrapping an arm around you when you sleep, calling to say I love you, telling you how wonderful you are, all because you want to. You can't help not to. You never want to be apart and can see it will be this way forever." An enormous lump formed in Victoria's throat. She wished she could blame the meatball.

Heather stood, then held her glass up high. Eyes focused on Heather, directing away from Victoria and her certain collapse.

She sacked the rest of her speech, downed the champagne and took her seat beside Ed before she said too much. The chair legs scraped the wood floor beneath her, she adjusted her dress and smiled at Ed. Hopefully he would salvage her abrupt conclusion.

"Cheers," he said. His beer mug banged her delicate glass, threatening to shatter it. "When's dinner coming? We've been here almost two hours. I can't eat those tiny quiche things."

Victoria squeezed her champagne glass so hard she expected to see blood coating her fingers. Her ears pounded as boiling liquid pulsed through them.

Ed wiped his mouth on his sleeve. "Can I remove this tie now? It's killing me."

Their meals arrived and she ate her beef tenderloin remembering the last occasion she had it. The company far better then, the conversation, existent.

Ed scarfed down his meal, rose and sat in a vacant seat next to Kenny and Ralph. Victoria finished her meal alone, in front of forty guests that examined her like an animal behind a cage.

Rori strutted over to her wearing a black and hot pink sweater dress. She donned a black sequin cap and a pair of pink Converse high tops. Rori handed her a card and Victoria bent down and kissed her on the forehead. "You're so much like your mommy, you know that?"

Rori tilted her head, eyes squinted. "Nope. I'm Rori. I'm gonna be five in December."

"I know, I remember when you were born. You're mommy was so happy. You were a blessing."

"No, I was a girl." Rori skipped off back to her table.

The guests bolted for the door after the cake. Victoria gave her hugs and kisses and handed the departing children goodie bags filled with toys. Heather, Catherine and their six, stayed behind.

She thanked Stephan for the remarkable job, then congratulated the chef and waiters on the fabulous food and service. She snatched the last of the goodie-bags and headed toward her co-worker's table.

A harsh tapping struck her shoulder. "Hey, I'm splitting," Ed said. "Gonna hit the bar up the road with Ralph and the boys and have a few beers. Andrew said he would take you home."

For the first time all night, all week, all month, Victoria heaved a sigh of relief. A slow smile emerged, a giggle and then she smacked Ed on the shoulder. "Don't worry. Not at all. Go out with your friends, have fun, tell Andrew I'll catch a ride with Heather."

"All right, see you back at home." He hiked his denim jacket over the dress shirt, the tie scrunched into a ball in his hand, and strolled out with the boys. No kiss, no gift, no card, and not even a thank you.

Victoria froze amid a room of empty tables. The music switched off. Silent, but for the first time, not alone. After thanking Andrew and Sara for all their help and support, she joined her friends at the table.

"Hey guys, I have goodie-bags for all of you. Age appropriate." She winked at Laurel and Bentley. The six of them ran off with their entertainment and Victoria sat with her friends for the first time all night.

"How are you?" Catherine asked.

"I think I'm really quite well. Going to be alright." Victoria's hands trembled around the cloth napkin she clutched. "I don't want to spoil the evening though, we'll talk next week. Plus I'm sure the kids want to leave."

"Don't be silly. Those activities will keep them busy for at least a half hour." Heather waved her away. "I'm sorry, I hope you didn't have to pay for Lance. We had a huge fight yesterday and I told him not to come." Heather filled her in on the past twenty-four hours.

"Now I'm the one that's sorry. What will you do?"

"I've been a coward for too long, always with an excuse why the time isn't right. There's never going to be a good time."

Catherine placed a hand on Heather's shoulder. "You're the bravest person I know, you don't even falter when Jean flips out."

"Jean's easy, this isn't"

"Why?"

"I'm a different person now. Jean came into my life after raising three daughters, nothing frightens me anymore. Lance entered my life when I was seventeen. Too many demons holding me back."

"But you're sarcastic and stand up to him."

"Making rude remarks is not the same as dealing with a situation. Plus the two of you were in love with your husbands when you walked down that aisle. I knew it was wrong the day he proposed."

Emily and Rori held hands and danced in a circle. The two girls blew their fake bugles and dragged themselves around the room in clumsy figure eights.

"What happened with Peter? Still not talking since Halloween?" Victoria asked.

"No, I refuse to speak to him. He tried to talk to me today when I got home from work but I ignored him. He said he didn't want to go to the party if I wouldn't speak to him."

"What are you going to do? Victoria asked.

Catherine turned toward Heather with a crumpled smile and rubbed her forehead.

"Tell her," Heather said.

Catherine told Victoria the full story of the night in Mangle's kitchen, the morning before Jean's Monday meeting, how Mangle avoided her for over a week and the finale with Dr. Feldman.

Victoria wrinkled her nose and recoiled as if she just ate another Asian meatball. "Mangle makes me sick, but Feldman? That man's been there since before I started and he wasn't much to look at fifteen years ago. He's a dinosaur. Luckily he's half retired and doesn't come to the hospital that often."

"I actually believed Mangle would be better for me than Peter. So brainwashed. You guys were right, I should have listened, I'm so sorry. Not sure how I even got into this mess."

"That would be my fault." Heather raised her hand.

Catherine chuckled. "I'm a big girl, Heather. I made a mistake, you even warned me so please don't blame yourself. I'm actually grateful that Feldman approached me. If he didn't I hate to think what nightmare would have occurred tomorrow."

"Too bad you can't get revenge," Heather said.

"Oh, I will." The other two tilted their heads to try to understand. "It's called karma. Tomorrow at noon, when the two of them sit there staring at each other in Mangle's home, with their toys and strategies and hard-ons, I won't be there. Mangle will look like a fool, Feldman will go back home to jerk off, and in the end, I'll win. I'm even going to say I planned the whole thing. Tell him he didn't deserve me."

Victoria laughed. "Can't you report him?"

"And say what? I cheated on my husband, fulfilled a high prestige doctor's fantasies for three months and then when he wanted to invite a friend and some toys, I got upset? Please they'll laugh at me and then find a way to fire me." She took a sip of water and then choked on it. "Imagine if human resources told Jean, oh Lord, what would she do to me?"

The three of them burst into hysterics.

"Ugh," Heather gagged. "I just pictured Jean having a threesome with Mangle and Feldman. There's something seriously wrong with me."

"Yes, there is," Victoria said. "You're imaginative, fun, creative and the best friend anyone could ever have." She held up a glass of water. "Here's to a great group of gals, a better coming year, and one filled with more laughs than tears. An auspicious one."

"Word of the day?" Heather grinned.

"Yup."

Chapter 49

Heather

Heather spent her Friday off opening a new bank account at a nearby bank. She removed half their savings and placed it into the new account. She would have her direct deposit check forwarded there as well.

She obtained a free consultation from a lawyer and used a dozen or more tissues while disclosing her story. "It wasn't supposed to be like this," she said. "You're told you'll meet the perfect man, buy that beautiful home, raise your children together and then retire out east in a tiny home with a huge front porch."

Her lawyer grinned but evidentially heard this same pathetic story a thousand times. He exhaled, a thoughtful expression filled his face. He nodded throughout her story, leaned in and listened intently.

"Heather, this will be difficult, perhaps the most taxing decision in your life. It will test your strength and be demanding on your resolve. The only way to get through this is to become mechanical, robotic. If you still have feelings then maybe this is not the right decision."

"But I'm a compassionate person, of course I have feelings."

"If you let yourself." He fell back into his chair and folded his arms in his chest. "Are you only staying with him because you feel bad? And bad for whom? Yourself? Him? The children? You need to decide if you'll come out a better person in the end. Have you only kept the marriage together to benefit him? Are you afraid to be classified as divorced? Are the children suffering in any way from the two of you staying together? There are many questions you need to ask yourself."

Hollowness filled her chest. Her pulse slowed as did the spinning world around her. "I can't picture my future anymore, only escaping fills my thoughts. I cringe when he's home, happy when he works late. I used to be upset when he didn't spend the weekend with the girls and me, but now I enjoy it. I'm nasty to others at times, negative, wanting only the pain to end."

"Then what makes you so upset?"

"I think only that..." she paused. Her unfocused gaze relaxed her body. She lowered her voice. "That, for the first time in my life I'm facing it. I'm finally speaking up and doing something about it. I'm fearful but at least the pain will go away. It won't be like the eternal Hell I'm in now, only temporary pain, right?"

He chuckled. "That, Heather, will be entirely up to you. Figure out what you want, picture your future with and without him, what will make you happy and what will be best for your girls. I can't answer that, I can only guide you."

Heather spent her last few hours before the kids arrived home from school at the gym. She took her favorite turbo kick-boxing class, tuned out the techno music and the high-energy chants of the instructor, and concentrated on her future.

The bass beat pumped heavy on her chest, blood pulsed. Sweat dripped down her brow and covered her chest. She swiped the coating of moisture from her abs and flung it behind her. She pictured the girls and her on a Disney vacation, splashing in the pool, the bright sun above them.

She sucked in air through her gaping mouth and huffed as sweat trickled onto her lips. With each overhead strike, she clawed at her Hell. Freedom. She wanted out. Her knees kicked high, higher. With each kick, she toppled the walls in front of her. Sweat covered her arms and dispersed with each grasp for the ceiling.

Visions of Lance cooking and doing his own laundry fueled her. Images of his mother doing the laundry at her house incensed her to the point her grunts resounded throughout the room. Louder she roared. A man in his thirties, his grey tank top now dark with perspiration, studied her. She smiled at him while pounding her feet on the hardwood floor.

Heather's hair escaped her ponytail, beads of water on the tips sprayed and misted sweaty-guy. Heather panted, then chuckled.

Thoughts of Lance trying to pick up the girls for the weekend in his Corvette caused her to miss the beat, punch instead of kick, and she had to stop. She bounced over to her water bottle on the far corner and sweaty-guy watched her in the mirror. Didn't he realize she could see him? Heather smiled again, held up her water bottle to him and then chugged the contents.

****

Heather showered while the girls finished their homework and once in a fresh pair of sweats, she emerged from the bathroom and strolled into her bedroom. Lance stood there with his back to her. Her eyes veiled themselves with doubt, but there comes a time when diversions and avoidance are no longer options. Face what life deals you.

A drop of water fell from her bangs and landed on her cheek. The image of sweaty-guy saying "great class" to her as they departed reinstated her confidence. There were plenty of guys out there for her.

Heather tiptoed back to the bedroom door and shut it. Lance whirled around, his scan ping-ponged from her and then to the door. He tilted his head up and a booming laugh erupted. "If you're going to apologize, save it. I'm sure after several days of not speaking to you, you've withered, but I assure you, I am not that forgiving. It will take a lot more than an apology for me to exonerate you."

A sneer touched the corner of her lips, she made a vague sound in her throat. "I want a divorce," slithered out in a low murmur, too low for him to hear.

"And another thing, I intend to have a grand Christmas party here with my colleagues from the firm, and you will insure that my making partner is mentioned– "

"I want a divorce," she hollered.

Lance stiffened. 'What?"

"I...Want...A...Divorce."

Lance winced, shook his head and then snickered. "Divorce? Are you mad? Divorce Lance Milanesi? Do you know how many other women would kill to have me?"

"Just one. Your mother."

"How dare you." He jerked his head back and squeezed his eyes shut. "I forbid it."

"Too bad." Heather sneered.

"How can you do this to me? Ruin my image. What will the firm think?" Giddiness overtook him. He spread his fingers out in a fan against his chest. "I'll ruin you. You'll get nothing."

"I'm not afraid, I have a good job. I don't want your alimony, you will have to pay child support though and since you spend zero time with your daughters, visitation will not be a problem."

"You're serious?" His voice now shaky, soft, halting.

"Never more. I'm not walking down this aisle again. I opened an account in a separate bank and secured my own lawyer. You'll be hearing from him."

"You can't do this to me." Lance backed away, his shoulders hunched, eyes became vacant. He looked at her, mouth open but no more words surfaced.

"You're blind, self-absorbed, and a terrible husband and father. You don't deserve us. You want the world to revolve around you? Well, now it will. It will be all about you. You no longer have to worry about the four of us embarrassing you and forcing you to do childish things."

Lance collapsed on the side of the bed and placed his head in his hands.

"I've closed my eyes on this ride for too long. It's time for me to open them, throw my hands into the air and enjoy *my* ride for a change."

"What the hell are you babbling about? What ride?"

Heather retreated and walked out the door. Lance followed her into the kitchen where Laurel and Gia ate brownies. "You listen here– " he began.

She shot him a glare. "Don't you dare bring this up in here."

Chapter 50

Catherine

Catherine sat in the church pew alone. Peter was on the other side with heir children. Almost two weeks had passed without speaking to him. The hurt was too great.

She could see him looking at her from the corner of her eye as the priest began his Sunday homily.

"With Thanksgiving less than two weeks away, I would like to speak about family and for us to be thankful for that alone. Not possessions or goods..."

Catherine glanced at her Michael Kors bag. Thoughts of Odessa and things Heather had mentioned entered her mind. She shoved it aside, then flung it onto the floor.

"...as you sit around your Thanksgiving table, whether it be a family of two, or a grand affair, be thankful for the people in your life and what they bring to the table. And I don't mean the food." The priest chuckled along with half the congregation.

In no mood to laugh, Catherine played with the loose thread on her skirt.

"...it is the people that shape our lives and make us who we are today, each one bringing their special gift..."

She was tired of giving. She did everything for Peter and the boys, all the cooking and cleaning, raising their children while he worked long hours, practically ignoring her. Sure they had nice things, but what did that prove, and to whom?

The conversation with Heather last night about her divorce proceedings sounded ideal.

Catherine bent forward. Bentley played rock, paper, scissors with Emily keeping her occupied. The increased time she spent with Bentley improved their relationship. She initially thought Peter should be a big part of the boy's lives, but when she shut Bentley and Colton out, it only damaged her relationship with them. They wanted a mother as much as a father. Bentley would be twelve soon, but he still needed time to play and have fun and she needed to have fun with all of them.

Colton leaned in and showed Emily the Steeple People hand trick. She giggled. Perhaps Catherine behaved the same way with Peter. She had so many responsibilities she forgot to have fun. No wonder Peter ventured out with his friends so often. In college, they had the times of their lives. Heather even ridiculed her for being an uptight bitch.

Catherine laughed. She disliked Heather so much when she met her. Looking back, Heather only tried to get her to loosen up, live, experience life and enjoy it to the fullest. The activities Heather did with her girls had made Catherine jealous, but now she held on tight to the rest of her children's carefree days and made the most of them.

She experienced life with Mangle. He helped her in a twisted, perverted way but everyone comes into your life for a reason. Maybe she needed someone like Mangle to bring it out of her. Lord knows Heather tried. Peter too.

"Which leads us to the start of the family," the priest continued. "Husband and wife, for surely they are the start of every family. For a marriage to succeed it requires effort, a couple growing together. The relationship should always move forward, if not, then it may move in reverse until they've gone back too far..."

When did life become so busy that you lose sight of each other? Passing each other as you run from one life event to another. It's a team effort and everything should be shared, chores, children, fun times, too.

"...those who kept fidelity proved that they can survive and grow..."

Catherine curled her toes. She had pushed these feelings of guilt away but now in church, with her family so close, they rose again. Who was she to chastise Peter when she cheated on him? Perhaps he did the same, but none of this had solved anything. What a mess.

"...faithfulness is not just about avoiding another with whom you have relations with. Faithfulness is staying together and working out your differences to come up with solutions. The day you walked down the aisle, you chose one another. Then let that day be a reminder of your promise. For as Jesus had once said, whoever divorces and marries another, commits adultery."

The five of them returned home from church and changed their clothes. They grabbed garbage bags and rakes, then collected the remainder of the leaves from the front lawn. Peter assembled a pile of leaves near the driveway, then laughed when the three of them jumped in and out and spread the leaf pile further and further away. Reds, yellows, oranges, like a fruit basket, flew into the air and floated into remote corners.

A tear trickled down her face and mixed with leaf dust and dirt. The rake handle, no longer in her grip, plunged and smashed the crumpled leaves beneath it. She stared at her family. Then turned, and ran.

She sprinted down the street past her neighbor's house.

"Mom, where you going?" Bentley shouted.

Catherine yanked the hood from her sweatshirt over her head. She rounded the corner and continued up the street, her feet pounded the sidewalk. She sucked in air, water vapor filtered out of her mouth, and she worked through the pain in her side.

She crossed the street and headed west to the next neighborhood. Cold air pierced through her lungs. Clean, brisk air. Fog released from beneath her nose in short quick gasps, her blood circulated, but fingers numbed from the frosty air.

Time alone. Far away from where she was, who she was. Her body thawed. The warm light sprinkled through the remaining maple leaves. The roads were still, she was just a lone runner treading along. No one disturbed her, her mind cleared. Free and vibrant.

Autumn colors paved her way down the roads. Branches snapped under her feet. She slowed her pace to let her breath catch up but then jogged again once more. She hiked uphill, her shins stung, but Catherine surged through the pain. She detected sweat stream down her shirt although the cold air turned her nose cardinal red. Her mind wandered.

With each slap of her feet, stress released. She entered the next neighborhood unsure how she would make it home, but for the first time she was doing something for herself. She could think, far away from everyone and everything. Maybe not forget, but purge herself. Inner demons flew off into the leafless trees.

She glanced down at her expensive sneakers realizing why they cost so much. They hugged her feet and propelled her farther. This was a healthier way to work out her emotions. She never knew how amazing something as simple as a run could make you feel. It was magical. She dreamed of something greater. She could be great you know, prized as much as a stupid handbag. Cherished and respected, loved for the person she was.

Running saved her life that day.

Catherine leaped over a Sunday newspaper and sucked in another deep mouthful of air. "Yeah!" She waved her fist in the air pretending she was Rocky. "Yeah!" She skipped to the following neighborhood, then did a cartwheel down the center of the road, narrowly missing a Mercedes. The driver rolled down her window and gawked at Catherine. It was Odessa.

****

Catherine trudged up the street, her home in view, family no longer outside. Her runner's high, paired with fiery emotions, made her cringe at the sight of the five leaf bags lining the street.

She entered through the garage and found Peter on the couch. Emily put the last piece into her Hello Kitty puzzle.

"Where were you? Where did you go now?" Peter demanded.

"I went for a run."

"Since when?"

"Since today." She removed her damp sweatshirt and threw it on the rug.

"What the hell is that supposed to mean?"

Bentley strolled in with his hands in his pockets. "Come on Emily, I have this cool game to show you." He lifted her up and wandered out.

Peter dipped his chin, hid his gaze. A loud swallow followed. He fell back into the couch and wrapped his arms around himself. "I don't even know you anymore Catherine. When we met you were so quiet. I remember when you entered that party with those girls, you stood out. They donned that stupid mile-high permed hair, giant hoop earrings, chewing gum like repulsive cows, all with their mini-skirts and belly shirts – no jackets of course, despite the cold temps."

"What...what are you talking about?" Catherine collapsed onto the couch.

"But you. You walked in with that giant green winter coat. It came down to your ankles." Peter laughed. "You took it off, hung it in the closet neatly and then turned. You had this light purple sweater on with a pair of jeans, white Keds. I wasn't sure where you came from or how you got in."

"You remember what I wore?"

"I watched you for an hour. You had the same beer in your hand. Maybe you took a sip or two, faked it at best. You never noticed me, but I kept an eye on you. When the group started dancing I approached you."

"I remember, I thought it was a joke."

"A joke?"

"I couldn't understand why someone like you wanted to talk to me."

Peter scratched his forehead. "Tired of the same old, same old. Just broke up with another melodramatic twit. Curious, I guess. I asked you to dance but you refused to look me in the eye."

"I was nervous. No, petrified."

"You were cute, though. Very sweet."

Catherine shifted on the couch. "Peter, what's the point of this? I'm really not– "

"I thought about you all night after you left. Soon this quirky fun side came out of you. I like to think I brought it out. I fell in love with that girl. I loved my college years but that last year, with you, made me see things through your eyes, things I never noticed before were suddenly visible."

Catherine quivered, unsure if it was from the jog or his words.

"When we graduated I was devastated that we wouldn't see each other every day, I couldn't wait to move in with you. Our first apartment, that was really something. We had so much fun and all I thought about was marrying you."

"I thought it was all a dream, kept thinking I was going to wake up," Catherine said.

"I thought we brought out the best in each other. I even offered for you to stay home, raise the kids, not have to work. I thought you enjoyed it. But then...you became this miserable person. I gave you more money to do things with, but you just shopped and shopped, bringing home more objects, but it never made you happy."

Catherine sniffled, wiped her nose.

"I thought maybe it was because we had boys but when Emily

was born, you pulled away from me more. The boys, too. I tried to take them out and away from you, but you just yelled and nagged all the time." He ran his hands through his hair. "For years you only seemed to find joy in cleaning the house, I don't get it."

"Well the house needed to be cleaned– "

"No, I've seen their closets, Cath. I went into Emily's closet to get a jacket. What's with that? Color-coded, lined up? The boys showed me their closets, too. Then the sex stopped. You never really seemed into it, faking it I thought. But after Emily was born, you told me I needed to take a shower first, brush my teeth, the lights had to be off. Do I repulse you?"

"No! No, of course not."

"Then you wanted to go back to work. It was like you were avoiding me. I thought maybe you were overwhelmed so I took the boys to their games, bought them some video games, tried to give you time alone with Emily."

"I didn't want to be alone with her, I wanted us to be a family."

"When? Where did that fun Catherine go? I couldn't take it anymore and I started to go out with people from work. I had fun for a while, I really did. It was like the old days when we used to all party together."

"You went out a lot Peter. All the time."

"You ignored me, went back to work, shouted at the boys and me constantly. And all that obsessive cleaning."

Her wet, dull eyes burst. She attempted to speak but stammering sobs leaked out instead.

"But, then I started to see the old Catherine again this summer. You changed. Playing with the boys, having fun, laughing. I figured maybe you did need to go back to work. Maybe you needed an outlet, so I stepped back, thought in time you'd come back to me."

"I tried."

"No. Not with me, Catherine. What did I do to you, I don't get what changed?" Peter tapped his fist against his lips waiting for an answer. "Then the past few months you started working late, going out alone on the weekends, coming home late. Where'd you go? Who were you with? Then the weird thing is, you just stopped cleaning all together. I didn't mind, but what were you doing on your days off then? Look, I'm happy your relationship is better with the kids, but where does that leave us?"

She tried to speak, but couldn't.

Peter shook his head, annoyed with her lack of answers. "I've done everything to make you happy but I can't do it anymore. My job is stressful and I hate it. I tried to tell you countless times but you attack me as soon as I walk in the door and don't give me a chance to speak. I thought about switching to financial planning but then you wanted to go back to work. I let you go and I stayed thinking I could stick it out another year.

Instead of sharing my grief with my wife, you ignored me. I admit I messed up, going out a lot, and the other day...I'm sorry, I got caught up with these guys and they party hard. But I'm sick of all that, I'm not twenty-three anymore, I can't live like this." He glanced around looking for answers. "Maybe I should move out."

She remained silent despite his repeated request for answers. How foolish she was not noticing the needs of her family, becoming a self-absorbed troll, no different than her boss. A vision of Dr. Mangle lying naked on his diving board, surfaced. Gastric acid crept up her esophagus and a nasty sour gush coated her mouth. Speak, say something.

"Who are you Catherine? Answer me. What's going on with you?"

She inhaled steadily, clamped her eyes, then released them to find Peter leaning forward, his eyes locked on her. "I've learned a lot about myself these past few months, and I'm sorry I shut you out. You did wake up this shy little girl and showed her how fun life could be. My church upbringing and a disturbing event of my past haunted me. I *was* different with you. We did have fun.

But your long hours at work and the monotonous droning on of my day made me feel worthless. I appreciate that you gave me the opportunity to stay home but I needed to prove I was someone. I love my job and I'm great at it, despite what my boss might say. My patients come first and I feel for every one of them. I have compassion, understanding and I'm a great person."

"You are," Peter said.

Catherine held her hand up to finish. "I love working in Emily's school because it makes me feel important. Maybe that's the wrong reason for doing it but when people around you make you feel less than who you are, then you take whatever you can get, wherever you can get it. The fact that I had no friends, well, I hoped I would make some at the school but that didn't work out as planned either.

I'm sorry if I changed into a miserable person, sorry for what I did to the boys. I didn't mean to yell or become a bore. I should have talked to you but I wanted everything to be perfect and held it all in.

I thought your partying reflected some sort of mid-life crisis but now I see that I wasn't much joy to be around." Her nose continued to run, she suddenly felt fatigued.

"I realized this summer that I forgot about the good times, got so caught up with being a good wife and mom that I forgot how to have fun, and that's why I finally let loose around the children and started having fun with them. And I just realized today that I love running. Running until I'm emptied of all my misery. Sweat pours out instead of tears." She shoved the drenched hair out of her face. "And I love my kids more than anything. I feel terrible for how I treated them." She wiped her face on the sleeve of her sweatshirt, both just as wet.

"And what about me?" Peter asked. "Do you still love me?" He pressed his lips together, his hands kneading each other.

Irrepressible sobs consumed her. She sucked in and then slowly released deep breaths, but any shred of composure escaped her.

Peter threw himself out of his seat. He bolted around the coffee table and towards the left, straight to Catherine. He kneeled in front of her and grasped her knees. "Tell me. Tell me you still love me. Tell me you want this to work, Catherine."

Tears soaked her face, she no longer bothered to wipe them. Catherine lifted her head, blinked and gazed into his brown eyes for the first time in years. Breathless, she reached up and touched his face. Tingles ran through her fingertips.

"I love you more than anything, Peter. I loved us, I wanted nothing more than for us to work and I tried so hard but I was so unhappy. I failed us."

"You didn't. We just lost sight of everything. Like Father Frank said this morning, we get caught up with work and possessions, failing to see what's truly important."

"I want to work on us Peter, can we? Is there still enough there?"

"Like he said, we can only work forward." Peter placed his hands around Catherine's moist face, arched in and kissed her gently on the lips, as if it was the very first time.

Chapter 51

Victoria

Victoria parked near Aiden's house, hidden behind a row of hedges. Her phone shuffled in her hands. She planned to call right after the party but wanted to make sure her thoughts were clear. But now, two weeks since their last meeting, she convinced herself that Aiden had moved on after her insensitive rejection. She abandoned him at the height of their relationship, never bothering to contact him again.

Ed continued in his altered state of reality. Zoned out in front of the television today, viewing a Sunday marathon of *Ice Road Truckers*. She voiced her need to go to the mall but he looked right through her.

She dialed Aiden's number and concealed her vision with her hand.

"Hello," His brusque tone revealed.

"Aiden, it's Victoria."

"I can see that."

"I wondered if I could come over and speak to you."

"I'm not home. Very busy with work this week."

"Aiden, please, I'm parked right next door. Your car's in the driveway."

A hush devoured her frigid car. She tucked her hand into her coat pocket and her head inside the collar. She waited for an answer. Had he hung up? She glanced at the phone to see if the call dropped and then returned it back to her ear.

"You may come in but I was on my way to the lab. Nonetheless, I don't want you sitting in the cold."

She hurried up his cobblestones, the usual rainbow of colors replaced with desiccated soil. Leaves infested the lawn. The door groaned and he stood there with a look of pure aggravation on his face. She never saw him angry before, his cheery smile gone forever. She drifted in, headed to the couch but Aiden remained at the door. "Oh," she said. "Sorry, I'll make this quick."

Her planned speech vanished due to his brusque behavior. Thoughts of him running to her with a hearty welcome evaporated. With no clue how to begin, she collapsed onto the wooden bench.

"Did you want something Victoria?" Aiden folded his arms into a tight lump around his chest.

She knew she delayed this too long. She played with his heart, then destroyed it. He loved her from day one and she used him like a gluttonous cheater. She was no better than Silvatri or Mangle. She used him for her personal needs, crushing his soul. With his wife, he had no choice, but to suffer through the anguish of losing someone again? This he did not deserve.

"I have only to say I'm sorry." She forced herself to look him in the eye. "I hurt you and for that I was wrong. I left you waiting without a word, left you to wonder, speculate, hope, and then despair. I didn't want to speak to you though, until I knew for certain what I wanted. "

His impassive glare answered her. Static. Frozen. Detached.

"I just wanted you to know that," she stammered. He continued his unsympathetic pose. Unaffected, her words meaningless to him. She struggled up from the bench. He didn't care to hear her decision, he had already made it for her. There was no point in continuing. "Thank you for letting me in." She struggled over to the door and he released it. Releasing her.

Victoria lumbered down the driveway towards the neighbor's house to retrieve her car. She shut the door behind her and crumpled into a ball, thankful the hedges shielded her from Aiden's house.

Worried the neighbor would see her and call the police on an apparent trespassing drug dealer, she toppled to her side and cried silently. Whimpered and sniffled like Andrew used to do when punished to sit in the corner.

Victoria had ruined Aiden's life. And hers. The only thing she had to look forward to now involved cooking dinner while Ed viewed his Sunday TV marathon. Nothing had changed since the summer. Her pathetic life continued, her escape indeed only temporary.

When they first hired Jean, she counted the days until her vacations, only to find when she returned, her problems still existed. This was no different. She needed to find a permanent solution to her worn-out marriage. A vacation alone with just the two of them? Finding a hobby they both enjoyed? Marriage counseling? Ed would never go.

She laid there for five minutes, wiping her nose on a Subway napkin. The calories and protein content of the food was saturated with her tears. When she advanced to a yellow Wendy's napkin, she knew it was time to leave.

She leaned forward and gathered the rumpled napkins on the floor-mat when a thump on the window jolted her. Hoping the neighbor didn't call the police, she lurched up and turned to her right. No one appeared. She must have banged her foot on the door.

She tossed the napkins into her plastic garbage bag and the thump came again. She peered into her rear view mirror looking for the police car, then whirled to her left and there he mounted himself. Hands in the pockets of his black leather jacket.

She turned the ignition and rolled down her window. "Yes?" she mumbled.

"What are you doing here?"

Victoria bowed her head. She must look like an idiot. "Crying," was the only answer she could offer.

The door swung open. "Step out of the car, please."

Victoria did as he said. She removed her car keys and gazed up to find green eyes locked with hers. Aiden clutched her upper arms and drew her into him. He pounded her lips with his kiss, fierce and powerful. His hands clamped around her head, massaged and tangled her hair in his fingers.

She pulled away, caught her breath. "Aiden, I love you, I always did. I just didn't want to hurt you but I did anyway and– "

He pressed his finger on her lips, then searched her face. He guided her back into his home, and then onto his bed.

Aiden sat beside her, his finger traced her face. He laughed.

"What's so funny?"

"I never asked you what your decision was."

"I think curled up in a ball and crying was a pretty good synopsis."

"Maybe you looked forward to crushing my spirit. Watch me languish before you as you broke my heart."

Victoria's stomach twisted and she averted his gaze. She shifted on the bed. He nudged her head back to him. "Tell me," he urged.

Her perfect speech, long gone, Victoria searched for the only words left. "I planned on telling you that our anniversary was a fiasco, our marriage a tragedy. That I was in love with you. I always was, I knew the first time I met you, but I felt guilt-ridden. Afraid to tell Ed, afraid..." She turned back toward the draped window.

"Afraid of what? That it wouldn't work with us, that it would be a disaster, a mistake?"

"No." She gripped his hands tightly. "Afraid I would be happy and have everything I always wanted."

"Hmm, that is a possibility. What would you ever do?" He beamed.

Victoria grinned too, then flopped back onto his pillow and stared at the ceiling. "What went wrong, why did it fail? We were so in love, what did I do wrong?"

"Why does it have to be something you did? You married young, perhaps you weren't emotionally mature at the time. Most spend so much energy planning their wedding day, they forget to plan the marriage."

"No, I was ready, I understood. I think in our twenties we wanted what most want. Marriage, home, kids, but we forgot to look at what we wanted individually and if it corresponded with each other. Hobbies, careers, friends."

Aiden whisked the hair away from her face and combed his fingers through it while she spoke.

"In high school we only knew we were in love and enjoying ourselves, we never thought that would change."

"But people do," Aiden said. "They change and grow and that's normal and expected, but they need to grow together. It seems as if you have grown tremendously but Ed is still that boy you met in high school."

"Part of that is my fault, I coddled him too much. But we have nothing in common, nothing. His friends are a bore, some never married. He only enjoys watching TV and a night out for him is having a few beers at the local bar. I can't have any intellectual conversations with him, he doesn't understand what I do at work or at the Cancer Foundation. There's no support either."

"Then why did you stay for so long?"

"I think I felt bad. Where would he go, who would take care of him?"

"Take care of him? Victoria, he's a grown man, in his fifties. That's part of the problem, he needs to grow up, take care of himself. If he can't take care of himself how can he possibly be there for you?"

She buried her head in the pillow. With her neck fully exposed, he ran his tongue up the ivory surface. She wriggled under his control. Aiden kissed the skin behind her ear while his fingers found their way under her shirt. The supple flesh of her abdomen heaved at his touch.

He removed her blouse, not allowing her to help. He guided her onto her stomach where he massaged her tense muscles. The kneading released her thoughts and he rubbed away her nightmares.

She melted into a puddle of drool, tranquil and sedated. Two weeks away from him, two weeks had dragged and crawled, leaving her strangled with loneliness and guilt. In a mere instant, he wrapped and protected her from her unease.

The sun ignited the room with a warm glow. The welcoming rays, like the start of a new day, gave her hope. Her future lay before her, filled with optimism and courage. Aiden and her friends would see her through. She tried not to think of Ed now.

Aiden eased her over and then up, grabbed hold of her face. "I love you Vicki. From that first day you climbed up those stairs to my heart."

Chapter 52

Heather

Heather needed a break. The stress Lance put on her in the evenings gnawed at her strength. Patients asking to see a dietitian because they wanted a cheeseburger when she had malnourished patients with multiple pressure ulcers chewed on her patience. Jean hollering at them in their Monday meeting because cantaloupes didn't come in for her catering event, devoured the remainder of her self-control.

She fled to the employee lounge in the basement with her *Clean Eating Magazine*. She charged in and found Tyrell in the corner with his hand over his eyes.

She flicked her finger at his skull. He jumped and lurched out of his chair. "Oh, it's only you," he laughed.

"Only? Gee, a couple of weeks ago I was more than just an only you." She plunked herself down in the chair beside him and rested her chin on her palm.

"Sorry." He knocked her elbow off the back of the chair and she fell to her side.

Heather caught herself before her hand hit the ground and then vaulted. "You think you're funny huh?" She said putting her fists up. "Wanna fight, do ya? Come on, let's see what you got."

Tyrell chuckled. "Nah, been fighting with Jean all morning. Don't need more of that shit. Plus, remember, I'm a lover not a fighter." He winked.

"I remember quite well." She smirked. "What did Jean do to you today?"

"The same thing she does every day, yell at me in front of

everyone, embarrass me, insult me. It's okay."

"We've spoken about this before, you have to go to human resources."

"Yeah, me against the world."

"I'm sure there are so many others that would back you, especially if she does it in front of witnesses."

"Witnesses? Those punks wouldn't help me, all in it for themselves. Why would they believe a bunch of kitchen workers anyway?"

Tyrell and Heather spent the next fifteen minutes teasing and mocking each other. Their moods lifted enough to forget Jean for the time being.

"I had fun that night, you know," Heather said.

"Me too. Break-up sex is some of the best sex. Women all riled up, pissed off, releasing all that tension and anger."

"Oh, so you're a professional at this then I guess?"

"Women just know I have a kind heart and listen well."

"That you do. I must have chewed your ear off that night." She coughed a few times, then winked.

"The talking was kinda nice too." He fidgeted in his chair.

Heather tapped the tip of his nose and smirked. "Thank you," she said. "You saved me that night."

"Just trying to be a good friend. The benefits part was a bonus."

"For me and for you. I really just needed someone to talk to, I'm sorry I attacked you."

"Sorry, why?"

"I felt bad afterward," she said.

"Are you serious? I felt bad for allowing it to happen in the condition you were in. I should have stopped it I suppose."

"Well I'm glad you didn't. Hope you don't think I'm a slut."

"You? Are you kidding? You're far from that from what you told me."

"So, you're not mad?"

"Heather, we're friends. You've helped me out so many times, I'm just glad I was there for you for a change."

"Friends?" she said, holding out her hand.

"Friends." He held out his hand, gave hers a nice squeeze, and then tossed her a wink.

Chapter 53

Catherine

Catherine tried to hide her revengeful intentions under a guise of collaboration. Jean thundered on, her lack of deodorant today and her pungent aroma in the cramped area of the kitchen where they stood, burned Catherine's nose.

Jean led her to the salad room and lifted up four commercial size bags of purple grapes. "I need every grape removed from its stem, washed and then put into these bowls." Jean plopped the bags on the counter and lifted a bowl close to Catherine's face as if she was a nursery school teacher during show and tell.

"I have a patient I need to counsel. He has new onset diabetes and it takes a considerable amount of time."

Jean slammed the stainless steel bowl down and rammed her palms onto hips that begged for release under her unyielding green smock. "I sent Louise home. I don't need pathetic workers sniffling over raw salad items."

"I told him I would do it before lunch."

"I don't care. Do it after lunch," Jean scoffed.

Catherine gritted her teeth. "Patients come first, without patients we wouldn't have a hospital to work in."

Jean poked her finger into Catherine's chest. "Without administration, we wouldn't have anyone to run this hospital, they come first. Always. Now get to work, we're already behind."

She was clueless, so illogical that it defied explanation.

Jean waddled into the adjacent cook's area and her wrath continued. "Why aren't you using the fuckin' number-six scoop? Are you that inept?"

Catherine cut open the first bag of grapes and popped one in her mouth. It crunched and squirted its sweet liquid. She stretched a pair of gloves over each hand and then reached for the bowl.

The absence of any noise next door made her pause. Had Jean walked away? But the eerie silence continued. The normal banter from the cooks, nonexistent.

She propped the bag of grapes against the others and crept toward the wall that separated the rooms. Less than a foot away, she edged close to the wall.

"And what the hell do you think you're doing?"

"Putting this away in the fridge," Tyrell whispered.

"Collard greens?" Jean cackled and snorted. "Sure you're not stealing them for yourself? I know how much your kind likes collard greens. Too bad we don't have fried chicken on the menu or you'd be stealing that too, right?"

"Stealing?"

"Don't play dumb with me, I know you must have a half-dozen illegitimate rugrats running around town that you have to feed. Not sure how you're doing it on this salary but it's evident you're not college material."

Catherine peered around the bend. Jean parked herself in the middle of the kitchen, surrounded by three other cowering chefs. They chopped and stirred, pretending not to hear the slander. Tyrell held a silver container covered with saran wrap in his hands. His head bowed.

"Well don't just stand there, I don't need my slave standing around. Work for your money."

Catherine whisked back behind the wall and covered her mouth. Her chest heaved, her face pale, her brain unable to muster a word. Heather spoke of Jean's abuse toward Tyrell, but she thought she exaggerated.

Catherine glided back to her grapes and plopped one into the bowl. It pinged and sat still. The tiny sphere stood alone in the massive basin.

Then they multiplied.

She tugged on the grapes and plunked them into the bowl with a hurried toss. The globes bounced and careened over the sides. She chucked them in, two at a time, then seized a huge clump and threw them in too, harder and faster.

The counter and floor, covered with grapes. Grapes making a stand, taking a position, coming together. A determined effort.

Chapter 54

Victoria

Victoria lied awake all night. Her four hours of sleep would have to do. 6:30 flashed on her digital clock and Ed rose to start his coffee. The conversation that played in her mind all week needed to occur before he left for work. Another week passed without the discussion. Fear seized her, but love nudged her forward.

She searched for Ed, found him in the backyard smoking a cigarette and waited for him to return.

Ed entered the living room, saw Victoria waiting for him and his head flew back. The first light of day streamed above the trees tops. She said nothing at first, horrified. The word divorce too unpleasant to cross her lips.

"What is it? I gotta jump in the shower."

Every bone locked. She looked at the blue socks on her feet unable to face him. Annoyed, he strutted past her. "I think...I think we..." Victoria developed a thickness in the back of her throat. A repugnant taste built until queasiness threatened to overtake her. "I want a...separation," she mumbled.

He paused by the coffee pot and gawked at her. "Preparation? For what, another damn lecture?"

"I said," she straightened, "I want a separation. I can't do this anymore, I'll move out after Sara and Andrew's Christmas break. I need time to think, to be alone." For the first time, the word alone didn't seem so scary.

"Separation? What the hell you talking about?" He leaned into the counter and rubbed his bald head.

"We've grown apart Ed. Far apart. I've tried, God knows I have, but with Sara and Andrew both out of the house now, I…"

"You're saying you want a divorce?"

The word was out. Glad she didn't say it, but it was still painful. The ultimate failure. "I'm not your mother Ed, I feel I've been your mother from day one. Protecting you, helping you, paying the bills when you don't work, cleaning, cooking, even buying your underwear and socks."

"And I've done nothing for you? What about the house?"

"You've done a wonderful job on the house but I'm talking about me. You only watch TV and drink beer. We don't communicate, I try to talk to you and everything goes over your head."

"I'm sorry I'm not as intelligent as you."

"I'm not asking you to be, but you could listen, look me in the eye when I speak, ask questions and try to remember the things I talk to you about."

"I'm not going to sit here and defend myself."

Victoria's perplexed look was all she could rally. "Thirty years and that's your answer? You're not going to fight for me?"

"I have to fight for you? No, you obviously made your decision already." Ed trekked out of the kitchen, avoided her like a child dodging their mother when being punished. The spray of the shower resonated.

Chapter 55

Heather

Heather rubbed her temples repeatedly, hoping if she did it hard enough her skull would crack open for her to remove the part of the brain responsible for thoughts, emotions, and anything that had to do with reasoning.

Jean's meeting would not begin for another half hour, but she sat in the conference room alone in the dark, trying to clear her head. The past weekend with Lance proved to be the most challenging. As expected, he called his mother to rescue him and the woman spent her Saturday spewing rude remarks and sarcastic comments. The immaturity of both of them generated concern in the girls. Heather took them to her mother's Sunday and sat Laurel and Gia in her old bedroom to tell them the news.

Although not shocked, it still sparked an intense crying jag from the both of them. Laurel surprisingly asked if it had anything to do with that photograph she found of Silvatri and her. Gia only worried if she would have to change schools. Heather made them promise not to tell Rori. She would wait until right before it all went down.

Heather folded her arms on the conference room table, leaned forward and laid her head on them. Her red shirtsleeve soon darkened to maroon.

A nurse on her floor told her this morning that the pain and destruction her husband caused throughout their divorce did so much damage to her self-esteem that she elected to stay with him rather than continue with what would surely be perpetual torment. That was a solution?

How long would the divorce proceedings last? How long would she have to pass Lance in the hallway, listen to his agonizing retorts, the childish whining? Oddly, she pictured Silvatri's wife picking up and leaving. She understood now. When you want away from someone so bad, nothing else matters.

The dark room and its stillness lulled her mentally exhausted body to sleep.

The door crashed open, the sound like an explosion. Heather sprang up and fluorescent lights burned her bloodshot eyes.

"What the hell are you doing?" Jean slammed the door behind her.

Disoriented, Heather searched the clock. Ten minutes until their meeting. Early, but why? She wiped her eyes and sat back. "I was waiting for you."

"The meeting is not for another ten minutes and you're in here sleeping? I'm docking fifteen minutes from your pay."

"I'm salaried."

Jean scowled. "I've had just about enough of your insolence, Mrs. Milanesi. I'm in charge and I will not tolerate your insubordination." She banged her papers on the table, raised them and then continued to slam them four, five, six times. With each smack, Heather flinched.

"Obviously you don't have enough work to do. My staff in the kitchen is overworked while you take a fuckin' siesta. If you have no work to do first thing on a Monday morning after being off all weekend, then your job description will change." Spit sprayed across the table and the sunlight illuminated it like boils on skin.

"Starting tomorrow, you'll report to me first thing in the morning, before you see your precious patients. You will redo the patient menus, create new food items and calculate their nutritional value. You can help Cliff purchase and order the food as well. You can also go to that annoying Infection Control meeting I attend monthly. I hate that meeting." She rubbed her fingers over her hairy chin.

Heather stared past Jean to the podium behind her. This was it. A total collapse of her mental stability. Gravity compressed her, there was nowhere left to escape. Jean would torture her for eight hours a day only for her to endure harassment from Lance in the evening.

"...oh the schedule, you can do the scheduling for the staff." She paused. "Are you even listening to me?"

Heather snapped awake. "The schedule? There's more than seventy-five employees in the kitchen, when will I see my patients?"

"I guess you'll have to stay late. You're salaried, remember?" Jean's sneer looked like melted putty on her bulging face.

The door opened and Victoria entered. She saw Heather in her usual seat, but then noticed Jean slumped over the table, red faced and huffing. Victoria hesitated for a second, then took a seat, but this time selected the chair right next to Heather.

Jean glared at Victoria and Heather, both on the far end of the table, but said nothing. Jean gathered her papers that had made their way across the table, the top ones covered with spit.

"Where is that Bordeau? She's another one. The three of you comprise some of the worst dietitians I have ever worked with. Irresponsible, unintelligent, lazy, argumentative, selfish. And without any passion."

Heather tilted her head and massaged her eye with her hand. Victoria gazed out the window.

"The three of you are clueless and have no idea what you want. You wander in and out of here like you're high on something. If it wasn't for me giving one hundred and twenty percent to catering events, administration would think this department was a joke. A fuckin' joke you three are."

Loud hammering pounded inside Heather's head. Victoria remained silent. Her days and nights were as dismal as Heather's. Life could not be worse than now. At least Victoria had Aiden to run to. Maybe Heather should have continued with Silvatri. Life was pretty good over the summer. So she'd be his sex slave, was that so bad?

"I have no idea where that worthless crumb is. I'm starting the meeting and she'll be reprimanded later." Jean piled her papers under her armpit and trudged over to the podium.

Before she could start, Catherine hurried in, steered toward her chair, then noticed the two of them in the back, understanding completely. She retreated to the far end of the room and grabbed a seat on the other side of Heather.

Jean wrinkled her nose until the flesh from her cheeks rolled up. She gritted her teeth and stacked the papers into a neat square. Catherine looked at the other two for answers, but they stared off emotionless and drained.

"Now, to begin– "

The phone in the conference room rang. "Now what?" Jean scanned the three of them but they refused to get up. She tramped over to the phone herself.

"Hello? Oh, what do you want? Don't you know I'm busy?" Her hand parked itself on her enormous ass, the ass that was encased in a brown muumuu like a sausage. "They do? Why? Well, what good are you then? Isn't that part of your secretarial duties, to take proper messages? Secretaries are a dime a dozen you realize that, right? Hello, are you still there?" Jean slammed the phone into its cradle snapping off the right side. The phone plunged to the floor and cracked.

"Get that fixed," she said. "I have to go. People that are more important than you want to speak to me. We'll have to resume this later this afternoon." She scooped up her papers and left.

****

Heather sat in her nurse's station staring at the computer screen. She had been unable to write a word in the chart for almost an hour now.

"Heather, 612a wants to speak to you," a nurse's aide said.

"Did you ask him what he wanted?"

"No, he just said he wanted a dietitian now."

"I'm sure it's about a bedtime snack of cookies and cake, or extra packets of salt on his tray, or that he didn't get enough bacon this morning."

The poor nurse's aide froze.

"Sorry Jenna, just having a bad day. Ignore me."

Heather stared at the patient as he droned on about how his roommate received two blueberry muffins at breakfast and he only received one. She tried to explain how he was on a calculated carbohydrate menu for his diabetes but he threatened to report her to administration if he didn't receive it. A freakin' muffin. This was the last straw.

Heather headed to her office at one o'clock for lunch, her appetite absent as it had been for days. Catherine and Victoria walked in together and observed Heather's miserable expression.

"What's wrong?" Victoria asked.

"I'm done."

"With all your work?" Catherine said with an uncertain tone.

"No, with this place."

"You're leaving early? How are you going to pull that off?" Victoria asked.

Heather leaned forward until her elbows rested on her thighs. "Guys, I'm done with this place. I typed up my letter of resignation just now."

"You can't," Victoria shouted

"Oh Lord, no, please don't leave." Catherine's fingers flew to her parted lips.

"I can't do this anymore. The divorce is bad enough but I didn't go to school for seven years to be bullied by my *superior* and by obnoxious patients who think I'm their personal waitress. I'll find something else. Maybe in a gym or a school."

"Please don't, please think about it."

"I have, for weeks now. Today was the sign I was waiting for." Heather stood up and reached for the doorknob. "I'm not sitting through her degrading meeting this afternoon or starting my day tomorrow with her abusing me. Please understand." Her eyes glistened from the overhead lighting. She staggered through the door and down the hall.

Victoria and Catherine followed and begged her to reconsider. What was there to reconsider? Stay and continue working for an oppressive brute. No. The crisp sheet of paper flapped with her swinging arms.

She turned the corner and Victoria grabbed her arm before she could knock. "Please, Heather I'm begging you. We need you, we'll work through this. We'll figure something out together."

"Yes," Catherine said. "We have more power together."

Jean's door swung open. This time, they all cringed. Heather steadied herself, the other two stepped back. Now or never. No more putting things off.

Tyrell exited the office. A triumphant smile covered his face.

"What did you do?" Heather squinted. "You didn't kill her did you?"

"Didn't have to." Tyrell stepped back, opened her door and served his palm toward Jean's desk. Heather, Victoria, and Catherine stepped in.

The office was bare. No pencil cup with that ham-shank pencil topper. The display of empty Styrofoam cups, Post-its, used hairnets and latex gloves, all missing. Her cases of diet coke gone.

Staggering towers of papers threatening to topple, absent.

The smell of musty body odor and discarded food still lingered.

Heather narrowed her eyes. "What happened?"

Tyrell examined Catherine. "You didn't tell them?"

"No, I didn't know which way it would go and well, we've all been so stressed."

"What are you talking about?" Victoria leaned against the back wall.

Tyrell's arm swung around Catherine's shoulders. He arched over and tapped his head onto hers. "Last week Catherine went to human resources, for me. She told them everything and even got the other cooks down there to support me. They called me down on Thursday, called a few people from the line down on Friday."

"I wasn't sure how they would take it, what they would think. Initially they seemed concerned but..." Catherine looked away.

"Today was strange, right?" Tyrell said.

"They called us back in this morning. Me, Tyrell and Cliff. That's why I was late to Jean's meeting."

"They acted like they didn't believe us, like we were a bunch of liars."

"Yes, as if they were questioning our integrity. I left there thinking I made a terrible mistake, that there'd be repercussions, that our lives would be worse off."

"I was scared all morning, messed up the Chicken Marsala."

"When Jean received that phone call during the meeting I thought I was going to be sick. I didn't see any patients all morning and I thought our evening meeting would be sure death."

"But then what happened?" Victoria asked.

"I went into the storeroom around 11 to get more corn and Roger told me there was a security guard outside her office. Lots of boxes. He joked that maybe she got in trouble for it being a fire hazard in there." Tyrell chuckled. "Then the lunch line started. I was so nervous that I overcooked the chicken, forgot to bring out the corn...but then people started coming in saying she was fired. That she was cleaning out her desk and then they escorted her out. As soon as the line ended I ran in here."

Heather drifted to the other side of Jean's desk. Her custom-made chair was gone. She sat on the back counter and looked down at the paper in her hand. It had crinkled from her grip. She held it up to her face, skimmed it and then grinned. She crumpled it into a tight ball and threw it at Tyrell's face.

Heather smiled at Catherine and Victoria and then raked her hair back with her nails. "Peaz and Chaoz?" she said.

"Peaz and Chaoz," Victoria agreed.

"I'll buy the drinks," Catherine added.

"What time do you get off of work, Tyrell?"

"Half hour."

"Good," Heather laughed. "Meet us there when you're through. We're taking an extended lunch today."

Epilogue

Victoria
One Year Post the Beast

Victoria unwrapped the Christmas present their new food service director Jacqueline, bought her. A glass vase with a fun frosted swirl design. "Thank you," she said.

"I thought you could use it in your apartment with all the flowers Aiden always sends you."

Victoria chuckled. "In the summer he brings me flowers from his garden. In the winter he apologizes that the florists' are not as fresh as his." Victoria placed it next to her in the booth.

"Toast?" Heather said. The four of them held their water glasses high and toasted to the new year. Peaz and Chaoz had streamed the inside with dozens of colorful lights. "We should have the waiter take a picture of us by the Christmas tree before we leave."

"It's much more festive this year. The ornaments are extra trendy," Catherine said.

"I just wanted to thank the three of you for making my first few months here less stressful. This is more demanding than my chief clinical position," Jacqueline said.

"Jean did away with our chief clinical when they first hired her. She thought it was a wasted position. Of course she divided her responsibilities amongst us." Heather made a choking noise.

"I can't believe the stories everyone has been telling me. It really is a shame."

"You've increased the morale in our department tremendously, and the healthier cafeteria fare has everyone buzzing upstairs," Victoria said.

"I mainly changed it because I couldn't stomach the meatloaf and chicken wings every day. I felt like I was back in my high school cafeteria."

"Jean would pile on four or five pieces of the meatloaf in one plate and then had them pile mashed potatoes on a separate plate because it wouldn't fit." Heather laughed.

Jacqueline grimaced. "Well, it's been tough, but you've made it fun for me. Let's hope next year is even better."

****

Victoria left Andrew's apartment surprised at how immaculate he kept it. She remembered his old bedroom piled with clothes, unable to tell which ones were dirty and which ones were straight out of the dryer. Stacks of plates and cups, filthy sheets.

Now he scolded his mother for draping her coat over his kitchen chair and instructed her to hang it in the hallway closet. If she knew this years ago, she could have conserved her energy. Sara's dorm room was another story. How two girls could destroy a tiny room baffled her.

Victoria strolled into her apartment passageway with the bag of Christmas presents from her co-workers. Before she inserted her key, the site of a fresh wreath on her door, adorned with cranberries and a green velvet bow, greeted her. The nutmeg and clove-scented pinecones, welcoming.

She entered and placed the bag on the end table. Garlic mixed with cinnamon made the apartment feel like home. She sauntered into the kitchen to find Aiden with a silly chef's hat on his head. "Hungry?" he asked.

"Very." Victoria kissed him on the lips while he stirred the pan of garlic and butter. The cinnamon candle on the table made her wish she picked up an apple pie.

Aiden turned off the burner and slid the pan back. "You don't mind that I snuck in here early to cook do you?"

"Not at all. It's actually a wonderful surprise. You should do it more often."

He brushed his fingers over her lips and then gazed up at her eyes. He had not seen sadness in them for quite a while.

They ate his salmon and asparagus meal and then ended their evening on her couch with a glass of white wine. "I want to give you

273

one of your Christmas presents early," he said.

"Now? Why?"

"You'll see." Aiden reached behind the couch and removed a flat two by two square, wrapped in brown paper. Victoria ripped the thick layers off to reveal an 8 x 11 gold-framed photograph of his fireplace, blazing with an inferno.

"Are you trying to convince me to move in with you?"

"No, not at all. I know you need your space and time alone. I just wanted you to think of me whenever you see this, and also, I thought it would be nice to look at while we sat on your couch."

"Like a yule log?"

"Exactly." He winked.

"Thank you." Victoria kissed him. "It's perfect. I love it and I love you."

"I love you too Vicki." He eased her back on the couch and slipped her sweater off her shoulder, tasting her skin.

Catherine
Two and a Half Years Post the Troll

Catherine bounced down to the cafeteria excited for this year's National Nutrition Month celebration. Due to their delay of hiring a Food Service Director, they decided to forgo the event the past two years. With fresh eyes and new blood, this year's celebration even excited Heather.

Catherine developed a nutrition quiz to hand out to the employees with prizes ranging from nutrition magnets to free meals. Heather obtained Cardiac Rehab's body fat analyzer and couldn't wait to tell everyone their body fat percentage.

Victoria and Jacqueline decided to construct a quarterly nutrition newsletter. Their premier issue would appear in the cafeteria today. The four of them wrote one article each and then asked Cliff and Tyrell to add in their favorite healthy recipes. Jacqueline invited Victoria to write up and design the layout. It came out gorgeous.

The crowds arrived and the four of them answered questions and explained the ingredients in the lunch items. The line for the body fat analyzer blocked guests from using the microwave. By 1 o'clock they only had a few copies of the newsletter left.

Catherine helped herself to some fruit salad and the CEO of the hospital strutted in. After five minutes of surveying the cafeteria, he ordered his meal and sank into one of the booths with a copy of the newsletter. He called Jacqueline over and she eased into the seat in front of him. After fifteen minutes, they both stood and she guided him toward their booth.

Heather proceeded over to them for support and the three stood with raised eyebrows.

"Hello. I'm Guy Copher, CEO of the hospital." He reached out to shake Catherine's hand.

Victoria smiled when he shook her hand, but winced at Catherine as he turned towards Heather. It was the first time he had spoken to any of them in the five years he worked here.

"Jacqueline just told me about all the hard work you placed into this year's function. The food was so colorful, so flavorful."

"The salmon with Caribbean salsa was Tyrell's idea. The recipe's in the newsletter." Heather said.

"Yes it was delicious, and the newsletter was informative. I didn't realize how healthy eggs were. I've always ordered those tasteless egg whites, but I look forward to having a real omelet tomorrow." He peered back over his shoulder. "Now who's operating that body fat tester? I failed your nutrition quiz and I need to see how much of this I need to lose." He grabbed his belly and walked away with Heather.

****

Catherine's wails pierced everyone's ears on Splash Mountain. Bentley took water from below his feet and dripped it down his mother's back. "I'm going to kill you Bentley!"

Peter laughed and nudged Colton. Catherine shook her head. "Just wait. Emily and I will find a way to get you all back this afternoon."

"And worse," Emily said.

They exited the ride and Catherine tried to look angry but burst out with laughter instead. "I hate you all."

"No you don't, you love us." Emily threw her arms around her mother.

Peter ogled her and motioned toward her T-shirt. Wet and practically see-through. Catherine sauntered over to him and wrapped her arms around his neck. "Don't be getting ideas now, this is a family park you know."

"We can dump them in the arcade and run off behind some bushes." The memory of Heather and Silvatri having sex in the bushes always grossed Catherine out, but now in the center of Disney, it seemed magical.

They stopped by the Plaza Ice Cream Parlor and Catherine ordered a hot fudge sundae in a waffle cone bowl.

"Some dietitian." Bentley wrinkled his nose.

"I'm on vacation, and having fun." She stuck her tongue out at him.

Peter dug into the sundae and fed her a spoonful. "Just wait until tonight," he whispered. "Once the kids are asleep." His eyebrows raised and dropped.

They'll be up later than us, who are you kidding?"

"Then we'll ship them off on some kid centered activity in the hotel."

Catherine choked on a glob of hot fudge. A drizzle of it streamed down her chin.

"Slob," Colton said.

Catherine put a dollop of ice cream on her spoon and flicked it at him.

"Hey, you'll get us kicked out for sure," he muttered.

"Look who's talking, the king of getting kicked out of class."

"It was only one time, mom, and it was Craig's fault."

"Yeah, yeah, yeah, I've heard it all before."

"I'm good, right mommy?" Emily asked.

"Of course. You're good and pure and sweet just like this ice cream."

"Oh that's a load. You and Kelsey covered Bingo in mud over the summer and then ran off without cleaning him," Bentley said.

"When did this happen?" Peter asked.

"Beginning of the summer. I had to hose him down."

"He was just a puppy," Catherine said. She eyed Emily who pursed her lips and looked away.

They returned to the hotel and their children jumped into the pool. Peter watched them while Catherine changed into her bathing suit. She glanced around the adjoining rooms at the chaos and toys, opened suitcases and towels, Mickey Mouse ears and Cinderella crowns. She wouldn't want it any other way.

Grateful for the year Peter and her went to marriage counseling, Catherine thanked their therapist Kellie repeatedly for saving them. She attended privately counseling for herself as well.

Peter had quit his job and switched to financial planning. His job as a stockbroker was all about generating commissions and nothing to do with taking care of the clients. Now he focused on helping his clients reach their goals.

With Emily in middle school, Catherine quit the PTA and any volunteering for school activities. She enjoyed spending the time with her family instead. Their friends and neighbors looked forward to the lively Christmas party they hosted in their home every year.

Catherine threw on her indigo bikini and headed out the door. Their vacation together only beginning.

Heather
Four Years Post the Tyrant

Heather and Rori finished off the rest of the zeppoles while Laurel and Gia chatted with a group of friends. This year's spring festival in Glasspond Park packed in thousands of participants due to the weather. Sixty-five degrees dragged everyone out of their winter blues. Heather hoped it would be this warm next Sunday for Easter. The downfall to Easter falling in March was always the weather. It's no fun wearing flowery dresses when it was only fifty degrees.

"You have powdered sugar all over your face," Heather said.

Rori giggled. "That's the best part. If you don't have powdered sugar all over your face, then you really didn't eat a zeppole."

"And you would know. What's that, your seventh one?"

"They're sooooo good."

"Where do you put it all? What nine-year-old weighs only forty-nine pounds?" Rori licked her lips from one corner to the other and back again. "You're licking the paint off your face." Rori chose an orange and black cheetah this year. The sparkly paint mixed with the powdered sugar. "Gross."

Gia jogged over and landed with a thump beside Heather. "Ugh, if I have to hear her talk about the prom one more time I'm gonna barf."

"In two years you'll be doing the same thing."

"No way. My friends and I are blowing it off and hitting the beach."

"Oh really? This coming from a former cheerleader."

"Oh please, that was over five years ago. We're all gonna wear black and drive by the prom as they're walking in and spray silly string at them."

Heather laughed out loud almost falling out of the picnic table. "Oh, this ought to be good, I can't wait."

Laurel gazed up at a tall blonde boy. Was that Laurel's boyfriend of the month? Heather's own dating experiences were far from what she expected. After a year of divorce proceedings, she decided she wanted nothing to do with men. By the following summer, the warm glow of the sun beckoned her to venture out again.

The thrill of spontaneous sex, like she had with Silvatri, vanished and the real life of dating began. Getting to know people and thinking they were perfect only to find they were lying, just another large child, or horrible in bed, made her give it all up.

With Laurel and Gia out every weekend at high school parties and activities, she spent her weekends with Rori. But even Rori went out occasionally leaving Heather home alone on a Friday night.

Laurel strolled over chewing a giant wad of gum. Heather rolled her eyes and glanced away. "Mom, I'm going to the mall with Erin and a bunch of people, okay?"

"Just be careful driving. Will you be home by dinner?"

"I don't know." Laurel marched away with four others including the tall boy.

"When am I going to get a car?" Gia asked.

"When you're old enough to drive."

"That's only another year or two."

"Well, save your babysitting money and then when you're old enough to get a real job, you can buy one."

"No fair. Laurel got yours."

"The Jeep was nine years old. Save all your money and you can put a pretty nice down payment on a new car."

Gia snorted. "I'm going out with Hannah tonight. Gotta take a shower when I get home. All this dirt and dust all over me."

"It hasn't rained in a while."

"I thought it rains a lot in the spring." Gia stood up and brushed the dirt off her.

Heather and Rori snapped up and headed to the parking lot. "It does," Rori said." April showers bring May flowers."

"It's not April though." Gia stuck her tongue out at Rori.

"Hey, don't start. Geez, I knew you'd be the one to be the pain in the ass teenager."

"I am not." Gia crossed her arms and stomped away.

"Teenagers." Rori shook her head.

"Come on. Let's go before she has a tantrum." Heather giggled.

Heather neared their home and Rori rolled down her window. "Hey Becca, I'm coming over, don't leave."

"Can you wait until I pull into the garage at least?" Heather drove up the driveway and before she could come to a full stop, the back door unlocked and Rori sprinted down the block. Gia ran out too and then jumped directly into the shower.

Heather checked the mailbox and threw her bills on the table. There were two messages on the phone that she played while opening a letter from Rori's school.

Beep. "Heather! It's me, Victoria, I tried calling your cell. We just got back from our honeymoon. It was glorious. You have to travel to St Lucia. I thought ten days would be too much but you were right, it flew by. You had to see our room, the back door opened into our own private pool. We had sex in it. Oh my God, I hope your children aren't listening. Oh Heather, I'm so sorry. Erase this! Erase this immediately. It was delightful though. I'll tell you all about it at work Monday. Hope you didn't miss me too much. I didn't miss you guys at all. Just kidding. Love you, bye."

Heather played the message one more time to hear the excitement in Victoria's voice then erased it for good.

Beep. "Hey, it's Catherine. I just finished. My best time ever! Twenty-six fifteen. Twenty-six fifteen. I can't believe it. It was a little warm to run but luckily I wore that tank top and I stayed cool. Oh and the best part was Peter was there at the finish line. He surprised me. He lied and said he had to meet a client but showed up. Alone, without the kids and we came home and well, you know, *cough* *cough*. Post-race high and then that. Wow! It was thrilling. Call me, I'll tell you all about it. I thought you'd be home."

Her friends were having more sex then her, and with their husbands no less. Catherine assumed she would be home? What was that supposed to mean? Single, home, alone. Catherine was right. All she needed now was a bunch of cats.

Heather threw her dusty clothes in the hamper, changed into sweats and traveled downstairs to her computer. She checked her emails and then went on Facebook. One new message and one friend request. Heather hated the new friend requests she got. It was always someone she didn't know or some friend of a friend that saw a funny comment she wrote on someone else's wall. That entitled you to be her friend?

She liked her measly 125 friends and enjoyed deleting people even more. She never understood the ones that had 800 friends and how they read their home page every day.

Heather popped an Oreo in her mouth and clicked on the new friend request. *Nicolo Trevisani.*

Hey Heather. Hope you are good. I just joined Facebook and I'm not even sure if I'm doing this right. I only have three friends so far. My brother forced me to join. I got divorced six months ago and he told me to get on here to find old friends. The only old friend I want to talk to is you. You look beautiful in your picture. And your girls are the spitting image of you. Four beautiful girls. Hope you get this message. Love to the moon.

THE END OF BOOK ONE

Author's Notes

Dear Reader,

Thank you for reading *Cheating to Survive.* I hope you enjoyed it. If you did, I would love it if you would write a review at your favorite book review site. Reviews are the best way for readers to discover great new books. I look forward to seeing your review on Amazon or Goodreads.

I also invite you to visit my Website at:
Christine-Ardigo-Author.com/,

or on FaceBook at:
Christine.Ardigo.Author, to stay in touch with me and follow my next book project.

Thank you for spending a few hours with my story and its characters. I hope you had fun living in their world as much as I did, and will join me as we go back to when it all began, in *Every Five Years,* Heather and Nicolo's love story.

Christine

About the Author

I'm a registered dietitian/personal trainer who writes contemporary romance novels in my spare time. When weight lifting, rock climbing, white water rafting and jumping out of airplanes wasn't enough, I decided to fulfill a dream I had as a child: to write a book.

I've lived in New York my entire life and can't imagine living anywhere else. I have the beaches, the bay and the city, all a half hour away. I've built memories here with my husband, two silly daughters and a bunch of crazy friends, all whom I love very much.

Available Now

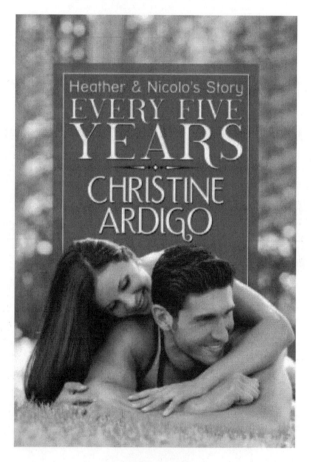

Every Five Years

Chapter 1

Heather

Heather Di Pietro sat across from Brooke Kempler in Zeke's Pizza and watched her rip the entire slab of cheese off her slice and dump it into her plate. Too bad you couldn't do that with the crap in your life. One quick tear and into the garbage.

Spring air floated into Sterling Ridge Long Island, and reminded Heather that only a few months remained before she graduated from high school. The past four years, jammed with adventures and escapades, pushed the limit on her teenage restrictions, and made her the zany non-conformist.

The pizza parlor, located across the street from their high school, proved far cooler than the cafeteria. Each day after a slice and a small Coke, Heather attempted to beat her score in Centipede, the only video game in their hangout. She was currently in second place, trumped by someone with the initials GMW.

Three freshmen boys appeared through the rear door, chuckling. They kicked and shoved each other until one boy careened into a garbage pail and knocked the lid onto the floor. Its *thud* onto the glazed tile turned heads. Their rowdiness caused the cashier with the blue-spiked hair to slam her drawer shut and throw a rag across the counter. Heather giggled. Neil, the shortest of the three boys, waved at her.

A fresh pepperoni pie emerged from the oven and filled the room with its spicy scent. Heather closed her eyes, inhaled and leaned back in her booth. She would miss this place. She reopened her eyes and found Brooke adjusting her gold-hoop earring.

Something stirred to her left. She glanced out the window and watched two boys in black Converse high tops and leather jackets make their way up the snaky path to the high school. It was Matt.

She redirected her attention to Brooke who was scrunching up her blonde hair like a giant haystack. Bigger the better. "Matt likes me," Heather said.

"Matt who?"

"Matt Balderas."

"Ugh, gag me."

"What do you mean? He's nice."

"You're dating Lance Milanesi, please."

Heather fiddled with the neon-pink shoelace on her purple Converses. She had doodled all over them with a Tri-color pen. "We pass notes between classes. He leaves them in my locker vent."

"Are you serious? How old is he? Isn't he like, a sophomore?"

Heather didn't answer.

"Fuckin-A Heather. Lance is eighteen, how can you be interested in a sophomore?" Brooke pushed her half-eaten slice away and took a sip of her diet coke. "Does he even have a job?"

"He's getting his working papers next month."

"And working where, McDonalds? You're actually considering dating a sixteen-year-old with no job and no car. Are you totally ill?"

"We talk for hours on the phone. He's interested in what I do."

"Of course he is, remember? No job, no car."

"I don't have a car." Heather gulped the last of her soda.

"That's what Lance is for. Do you know how many people would kill to date him? You got yourself a preppy little boy-toy." Brooke examined her teeth in her pocket mirror.

"Matt's getting tickets to see Depeche Mode at Jones Beach this summer and he made me a few tapes of his Ramones records."

"You're gonna make me ralph, you know that? Put your punk rock days behind you. You're lucky Lance even chose you, do you understand? He saved you."

"Saved me?"

"Fer sure. You were buying your clothes in the village at consignment shops. Fluorescent jewelry, purple lipstick, and oh, that ridiculous Boy George hat you used to wear. Still not sure what he saw in you." Brooke shook her head. "Stick with your Guess jeans Heather. You'll be much happier in the end."

Was she happy? Her classmates certainly looked at her differently. They watched with amazement when they drove out of the parking lot together, and her friends loved the invites to the popular kids' parties.

Brooke dug into her bag and pulled out her gold shimmering lip-gloss. "Heather, think about it, what could a space cadet like Matt possibly offer you?"

"It's just nice to hear someone ask about my day. And he's funny."

"Funny? Funny doesn't pay the rent. You wanna go back to the days of walking everywhere on foot? Begging your dad for rides? You'd be in deep shit. Besides, the prom's just around the corner."

"The old days were awesome. Remember when we went to—"

Neil strolled toward his table holding a tray overflowing with two slices of pepperoni pizza and a large cup. One of his friends locked his foot around Neil's ankle. He stumbled and his tray tipped to the right. The cup of orange Crush soda toppled and splattered over the white tile like a mutilated pumpkin.

Brooke, splashed with three whole droplets, sprang from her chair. "You stupid freshman. My suede boots!"

Heather lurched from her seat and dashed to the counter. She snatched a pile of napkins and hurried back to the mess.

"Oh, thank God." Brooke held out her hand. Heather spread the napkins on the floor instead, covering the spill.

"Thanks," Neil said. His face flushed.

An employee arrived with a cotton-string mop, dispersing the mess and the scene.

Heather plopped back into the booth, took a huge bite of her slice and gazed out the window.

Brooke scowled. "Look Heather, this is exactly what I mean. Enough of this nonsense. We're graduating and have to look sophisticated next year."

"You're going away, I'm not. Sweatpants, hair in a ponytail, then off to work."

"Well that's one smart choice you made."

"What?"

"If you went away, you'd lose Lance for sure."

"I'm not staying on Long Island for him. I'm just not into all that sorority, rah rah garbage. Besides, I have a good job...getting my dad's old car this summer."

"You won't need to work once Lance gets his degree."

"I like working."

"What are you majoring in again, cooking?"

"Nutrition, we don't cook."

Brooke's head jerked toward the window. A gold metallic 300zx pulled into the pizzeria parking lot. The passengers climbed out and Brooke stuck her finger in her mouth. "Oh barf me out, look who's with your Lance."

Lance emerged from the car with Robin Levine and her posse, all from the Crystal Lake section of town. Their gold jewelry shone in the sunlight - large earrings, thick chains and matching bracelets. Lance donned his aqua Ralph Lauren shirt, collar up, and a pink sweater tied around his neck. His khaki pants cuffed to show off his brown leather loafers and argyle socks. Heather's eyes narrowed.

"Told you he's a wanted man. Robin will steal him right from you."

"As if. She won't put out."

"You barely did."

Heather glared at Brooke.

"Take a chill pill, just stating the obvious. You don't make guys like Lance wait."

"I had to be sure he was the right one."

"Trust me, he's totally rad."

Lance had laughed when she told him she was still a virgin at seventeen. Afraid of losing him and terrified of her classmates finding out, she consented one night when his parents went out to dinner.

Under his covers, her B-52's T-shirt still on, he rammed her repeatedly despite the pain. When he finished, he vaulted off the bed, pranced around as if he just finished a marathon, then stared at himself in the mirror and stretched. She found the condom inside her two days later, the pain lasted three.

Brooke lost her virginity at the end of ninth grade. So desperate to fit in, she begged her brother to take her to one of his senior parties. A senior named Victor supplied her with a steady stream of kamikaze shots and Bacardi and cokes, until she couldn't see, then led her to a vacant bedroom. The next day, Victor walked past her as if he had amnesia.

Brooke never told her. She only graced Heather with good news, leaving all the horror stories tucked under her mattress. News of her casual sex with a senior spread around the school though, leaving only hormone-crazed boys to ask her out. One by one they used and dumped her.

Lance strode in with Robin and her sidekicks, and their phony laughter echoed through the pizzeria. The cashier glanced up from her register and then made a face as if she was forcefully vomiting. The employee with the mop snickered.

Robin spotted Heather at the corner table and her face lost its color. She recovered, adjusted her posture, nose upturned, and then jabbed her fingers into Lance's ribs tickling him. He keeled forward holding his side and snorted. Robin cackled loud and obvious like a hyena on crack. She motioned to her friends, alerting them to Heather's presence. The three girls circled Lance and took turns jabbing him.

"You're not going to just sit there are you?" Brooke asked. "Fight for your man."

Lance wriggled in a fit of hilarity and then made eye contact with Heather. His laughing ceased. Heather smiled, but her throat tightened corking the glob of pizza in her stomach. She quickly hid her red-leather, spiked bracelet under her sleeve. Lance sauntered over and she stood to greet him.

"Why are you here, shouldn't you be in math?" he asked.

"Mr. Roesler's out, we had the period off." Heather gripped her wrist and covered the spikes that forced their way through the cotton material.

Lance crooked his neck toward Brooke and leered at her. "Hey Brooke."

"Hey Lance, looking good."

He put his arm over Heather's shoulder then noticed her sneakers. He frowned. "You said you wouldn't wear those anymore."

"I had gym today."

"Can't you buy yourself a normal pair of white Reeboks?"

"I don't do aerobics."

Lance huffed. "You know nothing about style. You should hang around girls like Robin more, then you'll fit in."

The soda she had gulped returned in her mouth. She re-swallowed it and glanced at Robin who stared her down. She had the same stupid pair of Guess jeans on as Heather. The ones that cost her two days salary.

Heather grabbed the sweater from Lance's neck, drew him in and kissed him. Mouth wide and exploring, fervent, she rubbed her pelvic bone between his legs. Lance didn't retreat, instead he welcomed her unusual aggressiveness.

She pulled away and smirked. "Still care about my sneakers?"

"What?" His voice hitched.

"I'm going to play Centipede, get yourself some lunch." She strode over to the machine and ignored glares from Robin. Heather inserted a quarter, her three middle fingers positioned on the trackball, and began her battle. The centipede made its way back and forth across the screen, spiraling down, further, faster. The spider appeared and sprung at her, she twirled the ball to avoid it. She swooped up and to the left and then back down before ambushed. She rolled back to the right and then they surrounded her.

"You think you're so smart Heather, don't you?" Robin snarled. She leaned on the arcade game and her two friends shadowed her blocking the sunlight. Lance ordered his calzone unaware of their threat. "Listen, you may have Lance now, but not for long. Not sure what he sees in you but soon he'll realize he should be dating someone of my caliber."

Giggles erupted beside her. She continued to spin the globe.

"Mark my words, Heather Di Pietro, I'll be going to the prom with him, and we'll be prom king and queen. Not prom king and quack." Robin thrust her hand over the track ball, then walloped Heather in the shoulder as she departed. Her cohorts followed. Heather's gnome player piece knocked dead.

She grumbled, cracked her knuckles, and then reached into her pocket and found another quarter.

HDP, the new initials to take first place.

17259211R00173

Printed in Great Britain
by Amazon